ONLY

THE

GOOD

BY

CHRISTINE ROI

Contents

Dedication

For my hopelessly romantic heart.

And for the girls who grew up incredibly sheltered and socially anxious... How's that obsession with fictional men going?

Trigger Warnings

This story contains graphic content that might be troubling to some readers, including, but not limited to, depictions of and references to:

Mentions of Alcoholism

Child Abuse - Neglect

Murder/Assassinations

Hypercritical Parenting

Narcissistic Abuse

Passive Suicidal Ideation

Your mental health is important to me. Please be mindful of these triggers before reading this book. Seek assistance if needed.

One

Sierra

Chicago makes a liar out of everyone in the spring. The warmth of daylight had melted away like the last of yesterday's snow, only to yield itself to the sharp sting of a cold night. It was supposed to be an early spring. Our days had been bright and sunny. A whip of icy wind stung at my exposed arms, causing the fabric of my dress to peel away from my legs at the high slit and quickly disabused me of that notion. The evening dress was made of black silk. Appropriate for the event, but not the weather. My mother arched a meticulously groomed eyebrow at me, the only sign of her disapproval she'd wear in public.

"They're waiting for us inside," I muttered through my smile.

Catarina Volpe stood on the step-and-repeat, beaming at the small gathering of photographers documenting tonight's event. She would never ask if I was alright. If I was shivering from the cold or the momentous events that lay before me. I was here because I was doing as I was meant to. Being sold off to another powerful family wasn't just normal for a woman in my position. It was what I'd been preparing for my entire life.

A lot of girls in my situation aren't allowed to attend college. Or get jobs. I'd done both of those things, once I managed to convince my parents that getting an Ivy League education would only make me more valuable for my marital prospects. My job at the art museum was allowed so long as I was always available for family affairs and events like tonight.

Walking the red carpet at a charity for the city opera, I wasn't Sierra Volpe, the daughter of the city's most powerful mafia boss. I was the daughter of Enzo Volpe, founder and CEO of Chicago's largest real estate development company. A socialite. My brother was groomed to take control. My mother worked to keep our family in good standing with high society by throwing benefits for local causes. My job was to stand here, make good headlines, and look pretty while doing it. No, not pretty. Perfect. Tonight's benefit was no exception.

"Mrs. Volpe, over here!"

"Sierra!"

"Catarina!"

A few cameras flashed. With my father and brother having already disappeared inside, my mother and I were left to show our faces to the world, along with all of the other socialites. Sweet smiles. Matching dark brown hair. Matching green eyes. Flawless pictures of charitable perfection to help the city forget how my ultra-wealthy family got our money in the first place. As I wondered if they could see the blisters these heels were giving me, I shifted my weight and turned to go inside.

"Thank you, gentlemen. We're going to miss the curtain," I smiled.

A flicker of irritation shadowed my mother's eyes. Small enough for only me to see. With an indulgent smile, she took my elbow to follow me up the stairs as she tossed a careful wave over her shoulder. The deep hunter-green velvet of her long sleeve made me envious of her dress choice, but I'd only ever been allowed simplicity. Where her hair was down in cascading waves, mine was up. Even if it was too thick for a chignon. Even if the weight of my hair was starting to make my eyes hurt from an oncoming migraine.

"Your presence here is an investment, Sierra," my mother said as she smoothed a loose strand of hair away from my face.

My mother said this to me often. It was her way of scolding me into perfection because invest they did. Much like the pearls at the end of the delicate drop earrings I wore, they worked tirelessly to create the person I was today. Every detail of my life decided for me with a litany of rules. Every aspect of my appearance meticulously curated in order to fetch an offer from the highest bidder.

Dazzling Harry Winston emerald-cut studs glinted in the chandelier's light. These earrings were her favorites because they matched her ring. The four-carat diamond winked at me as we entered the main hall. I wondered if the ring I would be getting would look as nice. I hadn't even seen one yet, which felt odd.

"I'm sorry," I mumbled. "This dress doesn't leave much to the imagination if I'm cold."

It wasn't a complaint. I wouldn't dare complain. Not to her. My mother let out a gentle laugh. The kind that warned me of her inevitable criticism.

"I can't argue with that. They were starting to grate on me, anyway," she sighed as she pulled her phone out of her clutch. "The Serpas are waiting at the bar upstairs. Your father and brother are with them."

I stifled the urge to groan as we climbed the stairs to the marble hall.

"Stand up straight, Sierra."

With a terse smile, I straightened my shoulders and continued climbing silently. My mother examined my dress out of the corner of her eye. Her lips pressed together disapprovingly.

"I told you to wear the white Ralph Lauren. This is?"

"Saint Laurent, Mother."

"It's too revealing. If I'd known you were wearing this, I would have put you on a fast."

Blowing a breath out through my nose, I ignored the sting of irritation at my mother's disapproval. I'd known when I put it on that she would disapprove. The dress she'd picked out for me was pretty. But I'd felt trapped by the high collar. In a fit of panic, I'd torn a button loop trying to get it off.

This dress had been a backup. Something I'd purchased without my mother's supervision. Simple spaghetti thin straps held up the silk gown. Its plunging neckline showed off my cleavage, which was barely hidden by the fabric. The slit showed off my legs, which had been honed with hours of workouts. The back dipped down to highlight the curve of the ass my mother repeatedly criticized for being too large. She undoubtedly looked at me in it and saw a meal I could have skipped. Despite all that, I felt powerful in it. Like I was going to meet my destiny.

Large iron chandeliers hung from the ceiling, illuminating the space with their gentle light. High tables were scattered throughout, covered in white tablecloths and dotted with low floral arrangements my mother and I had argued over for weeks. She wanted to do something ornate to pay homage to the opera house, while I wanted to keep it simple. When her eyes landed on the low silver vases filled with crimson roses, her face fell. I'd placed the final order.

"Sierra!"

Relief slackened my shoulders at the sound of Enzo's voice. My brother lifted his arm to wave us over to their table as elegantly clad partygoers looked at him in carefully disguised horror. He tossed a wink at the nearest, an elderly lady in purple sequins. Enzo had the luxury of being the only boy in the family, so he never had to worry about what people thought. I quickly walked away from what was about to be a very polite tongue lashing from our mother to sidle up to my brother and three other men gathered around a high table. Each of them had a hand around a tumbler with brown liquor in it, probably something rare and expensive. Two champagne glasses sat there untouched.

"She's mad about the dress, isn't she?" Enzo said through his smile as he tilted his glass toward me in salute.

"Yeah," I sighed. "She said it was too revealing."

"Relax," Enzo muttered. "In a week, you'll be in charge of your own house. No more tiptoeing around Mom and Dad."

"Sure. Just tiptoeing around my new husband."

He pushed one of the two glasses of champagne in my direction. I wasn't allowed to drink anything except for one glass of wine or champagne. I frowned, wishing for something stronger to get through this night as Enzo gave me an apologetic look.

While sipping the fizzy beverage, I took a quick look around. Other socialites kept a casual distance as they observed us. Well, observed my brother. Except for being six inches taller, he was the male version of me in every way. Women in this town loved him. From the way he was being stared at in the flawless Armani tuxedo he was wearing, I had no doubt he wouldn't be coming home tonight.

"To the future- Mr. Antoni-Serpa."

My father lifted his glass to me as he wrapped his other arm around my mother. She took her glass in hand and sipped delicately. He kissed her temple and said something unintelligible into her ear. They'd gotten engaged under similar circumstances, but my parents were very affectionate with each other. Even if they were never that way with us. A small part of me always wished I'd gotten my father's blue eyes instead of her green ones. Those cold blues watched me carefully as an unfamiliar hand rested on my shoulder.

"You look lovely tonight, Ms. Volpe," Bruno Serpa said as he squeezed my shoulder. "I can't wait to welcome you to the family."

With a polite smile, I thanked him. But his hand didn't move. Instead, he pulled me closer. In time my father and this man had been working out their deal, I'd only met him once. In my father's study. For about five minutes one week ago. That afternoon, he'd been wearing an oxblood polo shirt and charcoal slacks. His stringy black hair had been combed over a rapidly expanding bald spot. He'd taken in my figure then as he did now. Only now he was close enough to give my ass a proprietary squeeze. I hid my cringe at the contact.

"Bruno," my father snapped. "Shall we go to our seats?"

Under normal circumstances, a man touching me would have resulted in him losing that hand. My father suffered no fools. Even fewer when it came to his daughter. But that afternoon one week ago, he'd told me the Serpas had us over a barrel.

My father ran real estate deals in the city. He had the local government in his pocket, and he had all of the unions at his beck and call. Until recently. Then the Serpas replaced the mayor with one of their own. City council quickly followed.

With little to offer the Serpas that they didn't already have, I was offered as a show of good faith. It wasn't up for debate. At least, that was what my father said as he left me crying on the floor of his study.

"Tony," Bruno huffed. "Come on. The show is about to begin."

My mother gave me an admonishing glance as if Bruno's misdeed was my doing somehow. I clenched my jaw, lifting the champagne to my lips to finish it off.

Antoni buttoned his tuxedo jacket as he straightened from the table. Then he extended an arm to me. Where his father was short and round, he was not. Antoni's face was cruel and dark. Sharp at every angle. It would have been handsome if it had any kindness in it. I took his arm and gave him a soft smile. His mouth flattened in an attempt at a smile that didn't reach his brown eyes. Eyes that were so dark, they made my stomach tighten.

Run.

"Let's go," he groused as he tugged me along.

The feeling tightened every muscle in my body. I shook off the instinct. This was just nerves. That's all. We were strangers to each other. This man, who I was about to marry, was a stranger. On the way up to my family's box, I watched him. Black straight hair that showed no signs of falling out like his father's. Matching thick eyebrows. Muscles that seemed hard and lean, tense under the fine fabric of his suit.

"So," I started, trying for pleasant. "I guess it's official after tonight."

He spared me a glance. I tried again.

"You and me, I mean. Then we have the wedding in a week. We might make a good team. Like my parents," I continued nervously. "They've always been good partners."

Antoni halted. With everyone having taken their seats for the show, I watched my family filter into our box through the curtain until it was just the two of us in the middle of the stairwell. He turned sharply, backing me against the wall as he snarled at me. If I'd thought his face was hard before, I'd been wrong. Now there was only pure hatred in it as he took my jaw in his cold hand and squeezed.

"You're just a spoiled bitch who needs to be housebroken. You mean nothing to me," he spat. "Once you're my wife, you will mean even less."

TWO
Sierra

r. and Mrs. Enzo Volpe and their son Enzo Volpe Jr. were found dead inside the City Opera House last night. The family was hosting a benefit for the opera. Though the three Volpe family members appear to have been shot, no witnesses have confirmed. Their daughter, Sierra Volpe, was also in attendance. Her whereabouts are currently unknown.

I wasn't sure they were dead until I heard it on the radio. The radio in my father's car that I'd taken just to get away. After my uncomfortable conversation with Antoni, I'd made an excuse to go to the ladies' room and hide until I could steady my nerves. I'd been gone ten minutes. Maybe fewer. The show had begun. Loud triumphant music covered the sound of my footsteps up the stairs. What caused me to linger outside of the curtain instead of entering my parent's box, I would never know.

"When she comes back, get the little princess out of here. We'll deal with the trust later."

Fear caused my steps to retreat at Bruno Serpa's crass command. As fast as my feet could carry me, I ran for every exit I knew. Every side door I'd snuck out of. The valet box my brother had shown me how to bust into for the keys to our town car. It was enough.

Twenty-two hours. That was how much time had passed between the last time I saw my family alive and now.

My eyes burned as I stared out at the road, listening to a woman on the radio. I'd only stopped for gas. Filled up as much as I could on what little cash I had in my little clutch. The glove box didn't hold much either. I wasn't dumb enough to use my credit cards and I'd thrown my phone into the trash on my way out of the concert hall. They'd be looking for that. Anything to pin down my position. I'd seen the things my father's men would do to find their targets. I couldn't imagine the Serpas were any different. As far as they were concerned, I was a spoiled little princess. A stupid little girl with nowhere to go.

They would only be half right.

Enzo Volpe, owner and CEO of Volpe Development, has been under recent pressure from city officials following a zoning dispute for their planned housing project set to break ground next year. Enzo Volpe Jr. recently overtook project management for new home construction, promising in recent interviews to bring the cost down for entry-level homes. Catarina Volpe was a well-known philanthropist in the city, most notably working with the children's hospital. We will have more as the story develops.

A light jazz interlude piped in through the speakers. Though the report had only confirmed what I suspected, I bit down on the ache in my gut. Somewhere, the slaughter of my family was just news to someone. The same people who gobbled up headlines about my father would now read about his death with the same zeal. My father, whose last words to me were a half-hearted farewell as he left for the opera. The car still smelled like his expensive cologne. I was lucky he'd driven himself.

As my hands flexed on the steering wheel, I felt their ache. I hadn't noticed my white-knuckle grip. I'd left them. My mother and father. My brother. Everything the Volpes were would burn to the ground now that the Serpas' real intentions for the arranged marriage had been revealed. They weren't burying the hatchet. They were cutting us off at the knees.

Large forest-covered mountains rose on the horizon and the sun dipped below them. Black peaks were dusted with snow. The sky was filled with orange and pink whisps of clouds from the setting sun. I wondered if I'd ever see my home again. I hadn't seen a town for a while now. Other cars were few and far between. Just open plains dotted with patches of snow and barns. And cows. Lots of cows.

My only instinct had been to run. Run and get as far away as I possibly could. I couldn't go home. Couldn't call anyone for help. If they'd taken out my father, who knows who else the Serpas may have had on their side? So I ran. Even if I'd driven myself right into the middle of, what, Nebraska?

Maybe they'd find me. Maybe I'd end up on the other side of the world using a completely different name. How I'd get there, I had no idea. My bachelor's degree from an Ivy League school seemed hardly worth it now. The sour taste of regret was still fresh on my tongue when metallic knocking and ticking interrupted the soft jazz music of the public news station. Switching off the radio, I listened.

Ping. Knock. Rumble.

"No, no, no. Please," I sputtered.

The engine sputtered in reply.

Empty. I pulled the car off of the road, still begging the car to not be out of gas when it so clearly was drained. Tears stung my eyes. I'd not showered. Not slept. I was still wearing the increasingly uncomfortable silk frock that felt more and more like a shroud than an evening dress. The sheet of hair I'd taken down helped to conceal my face as I let it rest on the steering wheel and began weeping.

"Fuck!"

My scream grated over my throat. I couldn't tell if it hurt from screaming or crying. If my mother were here, she'd tell me to stop my blubbering. Yell at me for swearing. Tell me to pull myself up and find a solution to the problem. My father. He would ignore me. But Enzo. He'd just try to make me laugh. They were gone. They were all gone, and I was completely screwed in the middle of nowhere. I had no solution. Nothing left. I just cried. And cried. And cried.

A knock on the glass scared me half to death. Jeans, dark brown leather chaps, a shearling-lined brown jacket, and a white tee shirt were on the other side of the window. The owner's big hand knocked on the window again. I rolled it down.

"Everything alright here?"

The voice was a deep drawl. I looked up, way up, to see a pair of hazel eyes looking down at me. Not quite green, not quite brown eyes that were nearly hidden by the brim of a dark brown cowboy hat. Thick chestnut brown brows pulled together with concern as he rubbed at the matching short brown beard that was just a little too long to be considered stubble. He braced a thick arm on the roof of the car and gave me an expectant look. This guy looked like he just rode out of a Stetson commercial. Had he asked me something?

"What?" I sniffled.

"Car trouble?"

I nodded absently, unsure of how to explain my situation. He tapped the roof of the car and walked toward the front as he spoke over his shoulder.

"Pop the hood. I can take a look."

Opening the door, I hopped out and immediately kicked myself for taking my shoes off as tiny rocks dug into my bare feet. The cowboy stuffed his hands into his pockets, waiting for me to do as he'd asked. As I cursed the ground, I finally noticed the horse. A brown and white piebald mare with a beautiful brown saddle strapped on her back. She just stood there, staring at me. I remembered myself and approached the front of the car.

"No, it's not anything like that. I'm just out of gas."

The cowboy blew out a breath and looked over my shoulder, back in the direction I'd come. He turned toward his horse as if having a conversation with it. I knew exactly what he was thinking.

Just a stupid city girl lost in the middle of nowhere.

"Look, I'm fine," I explained. "I'll figure it out. Thank you."

He took a step toward me. The striking cowboy couldn't be more than thirty and up this close, I realized just how large this guy was. If Enzo was six feet, this guy had at least five inches on him. Making him a whole foot taller than me. Then I realized how stupid I'd been to get out of the car in the first place because this was possibly the biggest man I'd ever seen up close. And I was on the side of the road with him. In the middle of nowhere.

As if sensing my discomfort, he pulled his hands out of his pockets and faced his palms toward me in a placating gesture. With a step backward, he pushed his hat up with a finger and smiled gently. Those hazel eyes softened.

"I'm not going to hurt you," he murmured like he was speaking to a frightened animal, which wasn't far off.

I wrapped my arms around myself to block out the cold and considered. What in the hell was I supposed to do now? Every fiber of my being insisted I get back in the car. I picked my way back to the driver's side door. Gravel crunched behind me. He was following me. I plopped down into the seat and huffed. Cold sliced down my face as a tear rolled down my cheek. Apparently, I hadn't stopped crying.

The cowboy let his arm rest on the roof as he looked down at me. I wondered how pathetic I must have looked when he made his offer.

"I can go get gas for you in the morning. But Mary closes up the station at seven o'clock and I won't be able to ride back to the house for my gas can and drive there in enough time to get it."

I blinked.

"That's the only gas station nearby?" I asked, trying not to sound ungrateful. "Great."

With a look around, I wondered if anyone would bother me out here. Besides the square-jawed cowboy with kind eyes and his judgmental horse. I picked a rock out of the sole of my foot and slumped against the backrest of the chair with a sigh. The cowboy squatted down, coming eye to eye with me. I was grateful for the way his broad frame blocked the icy wind. At least there was that.

"Is there anyone I can call for you?"

Three

Alden

Tears rolled out of upswept almond-shaped green eyes. I was tempted to ask her if I could call anyone again, but she was curling into herself like a cornered animal. I took the opportunity to look around the car. No bags, though maybe they were in the trunk. With a car as nice as this and her fancy-looking dress, she didn't seem like the type to travel without luggage.

"I don't have anyone."

The statement sounded so hollow that I wasn't sure if she was actually talking to me. Her eyes were fixed on her hands, which were clutching her knees to her chest. The dress covered her well enough except for her ample cleavage, but it didn't seem to be doing much against the cold as she shivered. With the sun going down, it wasn't going to get any warmer out here. I shrugged off my jacket and held it out to offer it to her. She gave me a wary look.

"It won't bite ya," I smiled.

She extended a shaking hand to take it from me. Polished nails, but no rings. However, that didn't necessarily mean anything anymore. If she didn't have anyone, what was she running away from? Because as frightened as she seemed, she definitely was running away from something. She was dressed for a party, which meant she was probably driving all night.

"Thank you for your offer," she sniffed, then she draped the jacket around her shoulders. "I'll be fine."

It was luck that had me out here in the first place. I was no knight in shining armor, but the way this woman was curled in on herself made me want to protect her. Shield her from the world. Especially when she looked so frightened putting on such a brave face.

"I'm not leaving you out here. You can come back to my house for the night. This isn't a good spot to be alone. Especially for someone like you."

The woman gave me a hard look. Annoyance seeped into her voice as she brought a hand out from her jacket, my jacket, and pressed it to her chest.

"I'm really grateful for your help, but I'm not going anywhere with you. You're a complete stranger. Not to mention like three hundred pounds," she said, muttering that last part to herself.

"Two fifty. And you're not going to stay out here all night. You'll freeze. Besides, there are coyotes. Bison. Elk. Moose. Bears."

"Bears?"

"Yup," I quipped as I offered another easy smile. "Bears. I don't expect you've got any bear spray in that little bag of yours, so you can come with me and Annabel. Spend the night at my house. Then we'll get you sorted out in the morning."

Those hypnotizing eyes narrowed. A small line appeared between two thick, perfect eyebrows.

"I won't try anything funny, I promise."

For a minute, I thought she'd turn me down. A strange man inviting a stranded woman to his home. Lots of bad stories started that way. But she wiped her eyes and nodded, weakly agreeing with a hiccup. The woman looked around her car, grabbing the little bag off of the passenger seat.

"You got any shoes in there?" I nodded toward the car as she stepped out. "Any bags in the trunk?"

"No bags. Shoes..." the woman trailed off.

She bit a lush pink lip and examined the vehicle. I took the opportunity to get a better look at her. The silky-long black dress hugged her curves, dipping down in the back to show off her hourglass frame. This woman looked like she'd been designed to tempt men. With the plates I'd noticed on the car, I wondered where in Illinois she'd come from. Someone as beautiful as her didn't just fall out of the sky.

Long, dark brown hair that fell straight to her chest blew in the evening air. Shit, she smelled good. The woman turned and crawled over the seat to grab something from the floor. I tried not to notice her shapely legs that led up to a plush ass. Or think about sinking my teeth into it while she retrieved whatever it was. Right, shoes.

Focus, Boone.

"Here they are," she sighed. "They're not great for walking, though."

Black straps of leather attached to a pair of gold spikes. No. Not good for walking. I shrugged and took the jacket from her shoulders. She angled her head in confusion. I held it up for her to put on properly.

"We're not walking anywhere. Put this on and we can get going."

She looked in Annabel's direction. My girl had been waiting patiently for me to wrap this up. After spending the afternoon walking this stretch of fence, she was ready to eat and sleep off the day. As if she'd had enough of the city girl, Annabel huffed. I huffed back at her.

"Ok," the woman warbled, juggling the shoes as she slipped her arms into the jacket. I could have sworn something like amusement crossed her features. "Let me just put these on."

I snorted.

"Allow me," I grunted, scooping her into my arms. She let out a yelp of surprise, then looped an arm around my neck. Her hair blew into my face as I lifted her to the saddle. Fuck, she really did smell really good.

"Can you get a leg over in that?" I asked as I set her down.

"Um," she looked down at her dress. "Yeah."

The woman lifted her skirt to slide a leg over to the other side of the saddle.

My jacket was doing a better job of where her legs were parted than the dress could do now. Ignoring that thought, I grabbed the pommel in front of her and swung my leg up.

"We're gonna take this nice and slow. She can carry us, but she's going to need a little time with the extra weight."

I took up the reins and looped an arm around the woman's waist. She stiffened in my hold.

"You don't want to fall off."

The ride back to the house was nearly silent. Annabel's hooves thudded in the dirt. Wind whistled through the trees. I wondered how clean I'd left the house, hopeful that there wasn't a stack of dirty dishes in the sink or a pile of laundry on the floor.

Every now and then, I heard a sniffle. She was still crying. Between that and her shivers, it was enough to take my mind off of the way her body felt pressed against mine. Or the way her hair smelled. Her ass shifted into me with every bump. Nope. Don't think about that. As we made our final ascent to the house, I tightened my hold on her.

Light filled the windows from within the little house, looking out over the little valley. The woman turned to look up at me with concern as we approached the front porch.

"Is your wife going to be alright with you bringing me home?"

"I don't have a wife," I laughed. "That light's on a timer. It's just me and sometimes this one out here. Alright, now stay put. I'll help you down."

I leaped down as my horse grunted. I'd need to give her an extra apple or two for forgiveness because Annabel wasn't going to let me live this one down. She didn't like sharing attention with me. Hell, she hated the last girl I dated. She was giving me that wary look again as she watched me.

"Put your hands on my shoulders," I ordered. "I'll need to grab your waist to get you off."

She watched me as she obeyed my command. I took her waist in my hands, feeling her weight shift toward me as I helped her down onto the steps. The woman tugged the jacket around herself and watched me. I unhooked my keys from my belt and handed them to her.

"Go ahead and let yourself in. I have to get this one fed and ready for the night," I nodded toward the small stable a few yards away. The woman eyed my house for a moment. Fuck, why did that make me nervous? "Help yourself to whatever's in the kitchen. I'll find something for you to sleep in when I get inside."

She looked up at the sky. Stars had started to wink into view. I glanced up in time to see a falling star streak overhead. I heard her take a breath, interrupting a foolish thought, and looked back in her direction. She'd climbed the steps, but she still watched me. All I wanted to do was settle her. This woman's discomfort was making me uncomfortable. I gave her another easy smile.

"You know, you're a stranger. I'm a stranger. We might not be strangers if we knew each other's names."

She cocked her head to one side, weighing my obviously flawless logic. Arching a perfect eyebrow at me, her eyes narrowed.

"I'm Alden. Alden Boone," I offered with a hand over my heart and a smile.

Her tired eyes finally softened. This woman looked so small in my jacket. So breakable. Watching her glance around to take in my home was definitely doing strange things to my insides. I found myself hoping it didn't disappoint her as she held her two sleeve-covered hands over her chest.

"Sierra. My name is Sierra."

Four

Sierra

Alden Boone's little house was surprisingly tidy. The whole thing could have fit in my bedroom, but it was clean. While the cowboy was outside tending to his horse, I busied myself with finding where he kept his guns. He must have had several. There was the Winchester rifle he'd had strapped into a holster on his saddle. Though I noted it as we rode up to the house, I probably couldn't get my hands on it.

Then there were the guns in the lockbox under his bed. I couldn't get it open, but I'd seen the type before. It was almost the same type of lockbox my brother had in his room. At that size, it could hold a couple of pistols. Probably the shotgun, too, along with any valuables he might have.

I didn't care about any of that. I just didn't want him to pull a gun on me. Even if my gut had told me I could trust this man, that didn't mean I had to be stupid about it.

His bedroom wasn't what I was expecting. There was nothing aesthetic about it. Everything was mismatched like it had been cobbled together from hand-me-downs, maybe thrift stores, and bargain shopping just like everything else. Normal and much cleaner than some dorms I'd been in.

There were no stupid movie posters on the walls. No weird collections of anything. The bed was large, taking up most of the small bedroom. Probably a California King, which made sense for someone his size. His feet would dangle off of any other bed, for sure. The bedding was faded but soft as if it had lost any roughness from its thousands of washes. I was grateful the green plaid material was free of any stains and it smelled like fabric softener. The pale blue sheets were the same. Clean.

Two nightstands flanked the bed, only one of them had a small black banker's lamp on the far side. I assumed that was the side Alden favored because there was a book on that side of the bed. I picked up the tome. Walden by Thoreau. A little on the nose for someone living in the wilderness, but alright. I set it back down, thinking better of going through his nightstand.

"Let's not go there, Sierra."

Large windows looked out over the small valley. Facing away from the mountains. If he was up early enough, the sunrise coming through the windows probably wouldn't bother him. Just outside the bedroom, there was a locked door. Maybe a coat closet. Then there was the kitchen and living room, both of which made up one open space. A laundry closet next to the kitchen. It felt relatively large for as small as this little red house had looked from the outside.

The appliances were all from different decades. The gas stove was yellow and looked old enough that I thought it might have been original to the house, putting the construction of this place at about the 1970s. It was a very faded mustard yellow that wasn't exactly pleasing to the eye, though I did like the little atomic design details. Nothing like the giant steel French range back home that my mother never touched.

The refrigerator, thank heaven, looked to be made in this century. Black, shiny, with no magnets or personal things stuck to the outside of it. I opened it, finding little. Some meat. A few vegetables. Eggs. A loaf of bread. Some condiments. Even though I was practically starving, I made a slice of toast with butter and jam. As I ate and sipped from a jar of water, he didn't seem to have any actual glasses, I propped a hip against the butcher-block kitchen counter and took in my surroundings.

Faded avocado green cabinets lined one side of the kitchen with a small peninsula that separated the kitchen and breakfast book from the living room. It had butcher-block countertops that were old but in good shape. Someone regularly oiled the top, probably the cowboy, since I didn't see any evidence of anyone else around here. No woman lived here, that was for sure. A small white Formica table and three vinyl-covered chairs were where the giant man probably had his meals.

Imagining his gigantic body maxing out the weight capacity of one of those chairs made me chuckle a little as I poked through his cabinets. Everything was relatively orderly, except for pantry things. I said a small prayer of thanks to whoever was watching out for me that this man was a coffee drinker. And not one of those black coffee people. He had cream and sugar.

All of this furniture is secondhand, isn't it? Mismatched plates and glasses. Everything in here is about thirty years old or cheap, cheap, cheap. Sierra, this is no way to live.

My mother's voice popped into my head as I looked around. Catarina Volpe would absolutely hate this house. She was such a snob. Shaking the image of my mother's disgusted face out of my head, I continued to look around. This place may not have been from out of a magazine, but it was comfortable. Cozy, even.

Alden Boone's living room comprised a rocking chair, a black wood-burning stove whose pipe went up through the brick wall it sat in front of along with a small pile of wood, a faded kelly green sofa that looked wide enough for him to sleep on and beaten up enough to suggest that he had. There was a lamp that seemed to be on a timer and a small table with a reading lamp beside the sofa.

This guy didn't have a TV. Odd for someone who apparently lived alone. Only a bookshelf stacked with lots of tattered paperbacks. I tried to picture the very tall, very brawny cowboy lounging on his sofa with a book in hand after a long day. He didn't seem like the literary type on his first impression, but I'd been wrong about people before. I was examining the titles by the floor lamp's light when he came inside.

"Find anything you like?" He huffed as he took off his hat and placed it on a shelf beside the door.

After sliding off his boots, he walked over to me on socked feet. He'd taken off the chaps. Hands in the pockets of his jeans. It was almost like he was silently promising to keep them to himself. With his hat off, I could see locks of wavy chestnut brown hair flicking out around his head. It fell over his forehead and dusted his ears, but was only long enough to hit the middle of his neck. My fingers curled with the strangest urge to touch it. Shaking the thought from my head, I spoke.

"You have a lot of poetry here," I pointed out.

"Are you surprised I can read?" He squinted one eye at me. For a second, I worried I'd offended him until I saw the corner of his mouth tip up. He was joking. I huffed the nearest approximation of a laugh I could muster. God, I was tired.

"No, I just don't know that many men who collect Whitman, Keats, or Byron."

He shrugged. No more explanation. That was it.

"I expect you located the bathroom."

I nodded. Of course, I had. It was the first thing I did. Then I went through his medicine cabinet to look for any anti-psychotic medication he may or may not have been taking. He gestured toward the bedroom and the bathroom within.

"The water heater doesn't work too well, so you can shower first while I find you something to sleep in. I'll wash off the day after you're tucked in."

He waited for me to answer. To thank him. I was really going to do this. Sleep in some random stranger's house. I ran through my options again, trying to think of something, anything, to make myself more comfortable. No one was coming to save me. My father's money couldn't help me. My name, which used to open doors for me, was now the one weapon that could be used against me. So I said nothing. Like the spoiled little princess, he probably thought I was.

Alden backed away a step, giving me space to get up and go to the bedroom. Then a hand came out of his pocket. To help me up. Everything he'd done in the last hour had been to help me. I gave him a grim approximation of a smile and took his hand. It was probably nothing, but it still felt like too much. Hard calluses met with my soft skin in a strange slide that sent goosebumps up my arms. Strong, large fingers nearly swallowed my fingers as they curled to pull me up.

"I'll, uh, sleep on the couch here. You can lock me out once I'm done in the bathroom," he huffed as we came eye to eye. Well, as close as we could for as short as I was compared to him.

I gave him another weak smile as I slipped my hand from his. My mind still racing, I tried to focus. To be here. Except it wouldn't stop. I was stuck in a tiny house with a gigantic stranger. Albeit, a seemingly nice stranger. Before I could berate myself for completely abandoning my manners, I forced myself to say something nice. Anything.

"Thank you." Okay. Not a bad start. "Good night."

He gave me a small nod. A polite smile.

"Good night, Sierra."

Though I'd done a quick once-over of the bathroom when I'd gotten here, desperately needing to pee made me less observant than I was now. Even though the guys I'd dated in college usually paid someone to keep their bathrooms clean, there was always an element of horror when men were left to their own devices. Not this guy, though. Even though the combination shower tub was from the 1990s, the frosted glass doors were free of mildew. The bar of Irish Spring was in the caddy beside a bottle of 2-in-1 shampoo and conditioner that smelled like cedar.

When I emerged from the shower, I saw a white tee shirt and a clean pair of boxers laid out on the dresser. After pulling the shirt over my towel-dried hair and leaving the boxers where they were because they kept falling off of me, I climbed into bed. His incredibly soft, incredibly comfortable bed.

My eyes popped open at the sound of the shower handle squeaking as the water shut off. I'd drifted off. The bedroom door was open. So was the bathroom door, though that one was barely cracked. Warm light filtered in from the small opening. I was watching the very sturdy-looking cowboy dry himself. He turned the light off and opened the door.

A towel was wrapped around his wide hips, barely containing the very thick lower half of his body. Water still clung to miles of hard-earned muscle as his hair dripped onto shoulders packed with muscle. I wondered how physical being a rancher could be since I didn't see any gym equipment around except for an old pair of dumbbells. The golden tone of his skin suggested he spent a lot of time in the sun. With lounge pants in one hand, he turned to find me staring at him. Like a weirdo.

"Sorry to wake you," he whispered hoarsely.

"It's ok," I said, trying to sound pleasant. "It's your room."

With a nod more to himself than to me, he made to exit without putting his pants on. Except he paused beside the bed. I watched him carefully.

"Don't worry," he said evenly like he was trying not to spook me. "I'm just grabbing a pillow."

He did. Alden shuffled to the bed and took the pillow I wasn't using. Pillow in hand, he exited the room and shut the door behind him. I watched the door, even though my rational mind screamed that if he was going to do something untoward, he would have done it when he found me passed out in his bed. That thought didn't stop me from getting up and locking the door, hurrying back to the soft, welcoming bed.

I hadn't slept in two days. It had been two days since the morning of the opera. The morning I got up from my equally large bed. An upholstered bed that was covered in shades of soft pink and ivory with fuzzy blankets for reading and Egyptian cotton sheets with a thread count higher than I even know. A bed that sat on a plush ivory rug adorned with pale brocade designs. An ivory box for me to live in until I was moved to another box.

Except there was no other box. I was freefalling.

My body wanted me to fall asleep again. To let the weight of everything crash into me and carry me to the depths of slumber that my anxiety hadn't yet let me succumb to. Instead, my mind raced like my eyes opening had wound it up again.

A smart girl would be afraid of the colossal cowboy sleeping eight feet away from her. A girl who got into a prestigious Ivy League university would be figuring out what to do next. A girl who was a junior member of several boards and raised millions for non-profits would be mourning the life she'd built.

Instead, I wondered what my mother's last thoughts were. If my father tried to protect her. If my brother had died before he felt any pain.

Last night I was with my family. My mother and father had looked at each other with love in their eyes. My brother was there to support me. I could almost feel the weight of his arm resting on my shoulders as he tried to calm me down. Smell my mother's French perfume as she looked at me with that relentlessly critical eye. Hear my father's voice as he commanded the room.

Staring up at the wood-paneled ceiling, tears rolled out of my eyes onto the pillow beneath my head. I'd lost them all in ten minutes. Ten minutes of feeling sorry for myself in the blue velvet box that was the ladies' room. I lay there wondering what would have happened if I'd let Antoni's iron grip pull me in behind him.

He could have made my father watch while they murdered me. Or worse. I squeezed my eyes shut to push away the memory of Bruno's unwelcome touch. Nothing good had waited for me on the other side of that curtain. As I tried to force myself to fall asleep, I kept thinking that at least I would have gotten to say goodbye to the people I loved.

Five

Alden

She was still sleeping.

I couldn't remember the last time I'd slept past seven in the morning. Even if I'd spent the better part of the night thinking about the girl in my bed. Wondering about her. The old man had been kind enough to let me take the morning off, but he was curious when I called him last night. While I almost told him about Sierra, I couldn't get the words out of my mouth. I thought about the white lie I'd told him as I relieved myself outside and fed Annabel.

Hoping the smell of bacon would get her out of bed, I started breakfast. Nothing. Not even a peep. She'd cried all the way to the house. Between that and the vacant look on her face, I couldn't stop wondering about what she'd gone through and why it left her with no one. What was that girl running from?

Coffee sputtering in the pot was what finally did it. The door cracked open at quarter to nine. I kicked myself for not grabbing a shirt to sleep in as her eyes trailed over me. Her dark brown hair was a mess, much wavier than it had been yesterday. Those green eyes looked tired. Puffy like she'd been crying all night. But her cheeks had more color than before. They were a lovely olive tone in this light.

"Mornin'," I said, taking a sip from my coffee.

"I'm sorry I slept so late," she apologized as she tugged the hem of my shirt down. "Normally, I have an alarm or something."

I averted my eyes after noting the motion, realizing she was wearing a little slip of black underwear beneath that shirt, not my boxers. Which meant the most beautiful woman I'd ever seen in real life was basically half-naked in my kitchen.

Do not think about the half-naked woman. Do not think about those legs.

"Didn't want to wear the boxers?" I asked with a cough, trying for a casualness I didn't feel.

Just curious. Definitely not thinking about the glimpse of that round ass I'd just gotten. Or the fact that I could sort of see her breasts through the white cotton in this light.

Stop it, Boone.

"They didn't fit."

She pulled up a chair at my table, tugging the shirt down to keep herself covered. This wasn't the first time I'd had a lady's company for breakfast, but it was the first time I hadn't already seen them naked. When was the last time I had a girl here? I was able to count back about a month and a half as I filled a cup of coffee from the pot and fixed it up the way I thought she might like. Then I fixed her a plate. They clacked together as I set it down in front of her, forcing my eyes to remain on her heart-shaped face.

"We can get you down to the gas station and on your way after breakfast," I offered.

Sierra didn't say anything. Scooping eggs into her mouth, she just nodded. Having eaten my breakfast almost an hour ago, I just watched her. Something about this woman made my mind flood with questions. First and foremost, why was she crying? Was it a man she was running from? Did he hurt her?

I expected her to get up when she was finished, but she just sat there staring down at her plate.

"That's nice of you, but," she finally responded, mouth half full, still looking at her plate. Sierra took a sip of coffee and swallowed. "I don't have any money for gas. Well, I do. It's all in my bank account. But I can't touch it. It's complicated."

She released a defeated sigh. I fought the urge to reach out and take her hand. Something made me want to comfort this woman. What she said last night resurfaced in my mind.

"I don't have anyone."

Of course, that was why she was crying. Because she had no one left. She was alone. That feeling wasn't an easy one to live with. I knew that much. She didn't have any bags with her. It was obvious that she'd been running away. I'd checked her bag for ID while she was sleeping. I knew she'd been honest about her name. I also found out that she was from Chicago, and that she was twenty-five years old.

"I can give you some money if you need to get somewhere."

I didn't know where the hell that offer came from. I had maybe fifty dollars in cash, but I'd give it all to her if it helped. She finally looked at me. That pained expression had returned to her face. Shit. What did I say?

"Thank you. That's not necessary, I just need to figure it out," she paused, sniffed, and cleared her throat. "I don't have anywhere to go."

The statement was tossed away with a laugh of disbelief. Sierra tugged her coffee mug toward herself and stared down into the liquid. She didn't want to look at me.

"I see," I said.

I did not see. I didn't understand at all. She was driving a damn Bentley. She had a few credit cards in her wallet, but no cash. I didn't know anything about her clothes, except that they looked expensive. Everything in me wanted to ask what happened. But I didn't push. Instead, I just said, "You can stay here."

What in the actual fuck did you just say?

Her head snapped up as she gave me a look that said my offer sounded as insane as it had felt coming out of my mouth. Alright, time to figure out how to fix this situation.

"No. I've imposed enough already. This isn't your problem. I'll figure something out. I just need a minute to get my head on straight. You don't even know me," she said, finally sipping her coffee. An appreciative little moan followed.

"I'd like to."

Idiot. Idiot. Such an idiot.

"I mean," I cleared my throat, shifting in my seat. "Tell me about yourself."

Her perfectly manicured nails tapped the mug. Dark brown eyebrows furrowed as she began examining her coffee again. After a deep breath, she finally looked me in the eye. I was either going to have to get a whole lot tougher or just give in because every time she looked at me, I was ready to get on my knees for her. Damn, I really needed to get out more.

"Look," she sighed. "You seem really nice. And I appreciate all of your help. But I can't ask you to take care of me. I have nothing to offer you."

I opened my mouth to respond as a knock sounded at the front door. Sierra's eyes went wide as her head swiveled toward the noise. She wasn't just running from something. She was running from someone.

"Boone! Boone, you in there?"

Eddie. Shit.

I forgot he was coming over. The guy has been my best friend since second grade but took on a nomadic lifestyle as soon as he graduated from high school. Since then, his parents moved to Vegas and my place became his hub in our county, especially when he was helping out at the ranch.

Sierra watched me as I shot up from the table to answer the door. I didn't miss the way her hands had started to shake. Before I could get to the damn door, it shot open. I forgot he had a key. A situation I was going to remedy right now. Eddie pushed a hand through his blonde mullet and immediately clocked the woman sitting at my table.

"Whoa, sorry man," he huffed out with a surprised laugh. "Who's this?"

My absolute knockout of a houseguest looked him over with surprise in her eyes. Acid-washed jeans, beat-up black boots, and a Coors tee that had seen better days. He'd at least taken off the damn straw hat at the door.

"I'm uh," she stammered.

"This is my wife."

What.

It just fell out of my mouth. She shot me a flash of a look that seemed halfway between shocked and angry. But she got out of her seat, plastered a sweet smile on her face, and covered her breasts with one arm. Right. No clothes.

"Nice to meet you," she crooned as she extended her other hand in greeting. "I'm Sierra."

"Wow, you're too pretty for him."

Her cheeks flushed at the compliment. It was true. With a face like that and a mouthwatering body, Sierra belonged on the cover of a magazine, not in my kitchen. He shook her hand looked over her bare legs, and finally smiled as he met her eye. I ignored the rotten feeling that look stirred in me.

"Would you like some coffee?" Sierra offered, already playing the part of a dutiful wife.

"No, thanks. The old man called me in. Told me you had personal business today, Boone. I was just loading up the trailer outside and wanted to make sure you didn't need anything. I didn't realize it was this kind of personal business. Sorry, I'll get out of your hair."

I scratched at my jaw. This needed to end. Now.

"Why don't you give us a minute, gorgeous?"

"Of course," Sierra nodded and stood on her toes to plant a kiss on my cheek that sent a jolt through me before heading to the bedroom. She ran a hand through her dark mane and bit her lip as she smiled back at me. Man, I'd give anything for that look to be real.

"It was nice to meet you," she paused, waiting for my intrusive friend to offer his name.

"Eddie."

"It was nice to meet you, Eddie. Don't be long, baby," Sierra winked at me as she walked into my bedroom, swishing her hips as the curves of her perfect ass peeked from under my shirt.

Damn.

For the briefest moment, I let myself imagine what I'd be doing to my wife in that room. Why did I have to say that? Why, of all the things I could have said to my best friend, did I choose to go with that? This was already such a bad idea. Eddie watched her leave and close the door behind her. I slapped him upside the head.

"When did you get married?" Eddie whisper-shouted.

"It just kind of happened."

"Tell me everything. I mean everything! Where did you meet her? Does she have a sister?"

I laughed. Then realized I didn't actually know anything about her. This was such an unbelievably bad idea. Great. Time to lie to my ass off about having a wife. Eddie had known me since we were kids. He could read me like a book. I straightened and cleared my throat, ready to do my best to cover her tracks.

"She had some car trouble, and I helped her out. She spent the night and we haven't been separated since."

Eddie nodded, blue eyes alight with excitement like I'd just told him the most interesting story of his life.

"Love at first sight, huh? That's some romance novel bullshit right there."

"She's the one," I shrugged. "When you know, you know."

"I bet that little hot rod handles great," he grinned with a wink and a suggestive pump of his eyebrows.

I slapped him upside the head again. He flinched.

"Don't talk about my wife like that, man."

Eddie rubbed the back of his head.

"Sorry. I'm still kind of stunned. Listen, I came by to see if you were alright. You're clearly fine. More than fine. Probably exhausted, right?" He laughed, slapping me on the stomach. "Anyway, I've got to get back to the ranch. I already loaded Annabel up since she's on the farrier's list for shoes."

Propping his hat back on his head, he gave me a wink.

"Thanks. See you later, buddy," he slapped my stomach again, this time hard enough for me to let out a grunt. Asshole. "Nice to meet you, Sierra!"

"Bye, Eddie!" She shouted from behind the door.

I waited for Eddie to let himself out. As soon as the door closed, I made for the bedroom door. I opened it to find Sierra perched on my bed, legs tucked to one side as she leaned on her hand. So much smooth skin on those legs. I kicked myself for the long look I gave them as she let out a little sigh.

"Your wife?"

She arched a brow at me as she pushed her hair off of a shoulder, waiting for my explanation. The most stunning thing I'd ever seen was in my clothes, on my bed, and I'd just made myself look like a complete idiot in front of her.

"Sorry. I didn't know how else to explain you being here," I offered.

"That's quite a leap in logic, Alden."

"Look, I don't know your business, but it seems like you don't want anyone to know where you are."

Sierra squeezed her eyes shut and let out a big breath as she tucked her legs under herself. Thick, dark lashes blinked away tears. Shit. I sat down beside her on the bed, putting a hand on hers as I fought the urge to take her into my arms.

"I'm sorry," I offered.

"No, I'm sorry. You don't have anything to be sorry for. I just. You're right. I don't have anywhere to go because I can't let anyone find me. My credit cards are useless. I can't access the money in my bank account. God, someone has probably called in the car by now."

"Did you steal it?"

"Of course not. It was my father's. He's gone. They all are."

That detail hung between us as she went quiet. I rubbed a thumb over her hand. Damn, her skin was so soft. Too close. I was sitting too close to her.

"But I can't stay here."

"Why?"

"I don't have any clothes, for starters," she said with a wet laugh and looked around the room. "I also don't have anything else I need. I can't give you any money. I can't ask you to take care of me like some gold-digging freeloader. I'm a total stranger."

Sierra's eyes were fixed on one of the bedside tables. A pink lip wobbled. I don't know why I did it. But the tear that rolled out of her eye met with the edge of my thumb as I brushed it away.

"You're not a stranger. You're my wife," I joked. "Don't worry about the stuff. I can take care of it. I'll go into town to get you some clothes. You can stay here as long as you need. We can take care of the other things as they come."

She leaned into my shoulder with a soft laugh. Green eyes, rimmed with red, gazed up at me.

"I don't think I've ever met anyone like you."

It didn't sound like a compliment, the way she said it. Just an observation. I couldn't help myself as the question fell out of my mouth.

"Like me?"

"You're," she paused, gaze softening as her eyes bounced between mine. "You're kind."

I hummed something like an agreement as I threw an arm around her and gave her shoulder a squeeze. Kind. It was not the worst thing she could have said. Uneducated. Big. Poor. All of those things would have been true. Kind? I'd take that.

Six

Sierra

I examined the summer dress Alden bought for me. My cowboy husband had good taste. Though it was still a bit too cold for summer dresses, I liked it well enough. Periwinkle. Polyester, but it felt nice even if it did sort of make me look like a milkmaid with the gathered bust and tiny buttons.

You look absolutely ridiculous. That dress is too fussy. It shows far too much leg. And cleavage. Look at all those little buttons. He's dressed you up like a little doll.

I shook my mother's voice out of my head.

This was nice. Really. He'd apparently grabbed several others like it in various colors. Pink. Yellow. Lilac. He'd gotten me a couple of pairs of jeans and some tee shirts, socks, and even some toiletries. I'd told him my size so he wouldn't have to guess. On top of everything, he was a good listener. The cotton panties and bras left something to be desired, but designer lingerie probably wasn't available at the big box store. Since we hadn't exactly discussed how long I'd be staying here, I didn't want to act like an ungrateful cow.

He even bought me pajamas.

They were periwinkle blue. Same as the dress I had on. Covered in little daisies with a little white bow on the shorts that definitely wouldn't cover my ass. Since he was sleeping on the couch for the foreseeable future, that wasn't an issue.

The straps on the dress were too thin, so I skipped the bra, which was fine. At least now I had underwear on. Meeting a complete stranger in someone else's threadbare t-shirt and a thong made me want to crawl out of my skin. I finished buttoning the tiny buttons and exited the bedroom.

"Well," I said as I did a little spin. "What do you think?"

Alden was leaning against the back of the sofa, one leg crossed over the other. Arms folded over his broad chest. God, he was big. His eyes raked over me and he smiled. I felt my cheeks go hot with color under his assessment.

"Gorgeous," he winked.

"Thank you. For this. I feel normal again. Sort of."

Between the way his jeans clung to his thick thighs and the stretch of his white tee shirt over his broad chest, my fake husband was built like a brick wall. At least he was nice to look at. The beard, made of short and scruffy stubble, was actually kind of nice. Somewhere, a cowboy influencer was trying hard to replicate the look that this guy had effortlessly mastered.

"It's nothing." Alden cleared his throat and stood up. "If you get cold, I've got some hoodies in the closet you can throw on. Look, I have to get to work now. It's not far, but the road winds out because of the ridge. Are you alright on your own here?"

I nodded. No one could find me out here. Probably. It wasn't like anyone would be looking for a mafia socialite in some cowboy's house. I must have looked uncertain because Alden approached me. At this distance, I could see his eyes were more sepia than green. The shaggy chestnut hair on his head had a few natural curls in it. When he was clean, he smelled like pine and Irish Spring.

"Come on," he ordered and walked into the bedroom.

Alden got on his knees beside the bed and threw the faded green plaid comforter up to reveal the safe I'd discovered yesterday. I tried to look surprised as I sat on the bed and watched him. His hat hid his face as he spoke.

"There are two guns in here," he started, punching in the code to the safe as the keypad beeped. "I'll write down the code. Memorize it. The guns aren't loaded, but the revolver is easy to load. The bullets are in the box next to it. Load it up. Point. Shoot."

The drawer opened. I'd been right. Two guns. A revolver that looked pretty old and a 9mm pistol. The ammunition for his rifle was also in the safe. I wondered how much he kept for that rifle in his saddlebag. Alden braced an arm on his knee and looked up at me. I gave him a weak smile.

"Do you know how to use a gun?"

"No."

Yes.

Hours spent in a firing range floated through my mind as I eyed the weapons. I hadn't yet decided how much to reveal to him. For all I knew, he'd turn me over to the police because he thought he was doing the right thing. Some people don't understand the world I come from. It wouldn't be his fault if he didn't. But I knew I'd be a fool to trust him this soon.

Alden's eyes skated over my crossed legs. It was the second time he'd done that. He stood, adjusting his belt as he cleared his throat. There was no reason for that motion to make me feel lightheaded.

None.

"Alright, well. I can show you how to shoot it when I get home. I don't have a television, but I can get one."

"No, please. I don't need one. I don't want to put you out any more than I already have," I rushed out. "Have a nice day at work, honey."

He smirked. His hand flexed by his side as he gazed down at me. Hazel eyes flicked to my mouth, quickly moving away again. The hand moved to the back of his neck, brushing through the ends of those curls as he turned and left the room. I stood up and followed him to the door, anxiety bubbling up in me at the thought of being alone with no way to call for help. It's not like I could ask this guy for a phone.

"What time will you be back?"

Alden laughed.

"Married only one day, and you're already keeping tabs on me."

"Do we really have to tell people I'm your wife?"

Alden lifted his hat, pushing a hand through his brown strands before setting it back on his head with a sigh. He grabbed his jacket off of the hook, shrugging it on as he looked down at me.

"Nope. We don't have to tell anyone because I guarantee Eddie will tell everyone he knows, which is everyone I know. He's probably told the whole ranch by now. Whether you like it or not, you're my wife to everyone in this county."

Great.

"It's not so bad so far, right?"

Alden drawled as he tugged the hem of my skirt, fingers barely dusting across my thigh with the gesture. The touch was barely anything, but I blushed at the contact. A nervous laugh bubbled out of me.

"No, it's not so bad."

He opened the front door and plodded down the steps. I followed him and stood on the porch as he approached the brown and cream-colored Chevy I'd noticed the night before.

"You're not taking your horse?" I asked.

"She's already at the ranch. Eddie was here to take her out in the trailer for me since they were shoeing some horses this morning. She needed a new set."

"Oh. So you drive to work, then?"

I was educated at some of the finest schools. Rubbed elbows with some of the most powerful men in the country. So why on earth did I feel like a foolish idiot when I was talking to this man?

Alden propped a foot into the truck's open door and braced a hand on the frame, looking up at me with a smile. Some girls would go weak in the knees at the sight of a rough, muscle-bound cowboy smiling at them like that. Some girls. Not me. Definitely not.

"Yes, I drive to work. Annabel lives on the ranch since she technically belongs to Mr. Weaver, the owner, and my boss. She only stays here when I have things to do on this side of the ranch. Now you have a nice day, and I'll make dinner when I get back, darlin'."

"Okay, cowboy."

Alden chuckled as he climbed into his truck. It roared to life as he backed the Chevy out of the little niche he'd parked in. I watched him drive away. Leaving me alone. Again.

While he'd been at the store, I was able to figure out where exactly I had ended up by looking at his mail. After looking at his Thomas Guide, something I was amazed Alden even owned in this century, I determined I was in the mountains somewhere south of Jackson and closer to Hoback. I assumed we were closer to Hoback because I would have noticed passing through Jackson. Far enough away from everyone I'd ever known and with no way to contact anyone, I was as hidden as I could possibly be. It was a small comfort.

Distraction. That was what I needed. Because thinking about my family was too painful. Thinking about the years I spent trying to become a perfect trophy wife for someone powerful, the woman behind the man, only to be left with nothing, made my skin ache. No. Distraction was absolutely necessary.

"Never forget that you exist by the grace of me."

There was no Pilates reformer. No laptop. No phone. No appointments. Anxiety rippled through me at the missed emails and classes. The lack of it made me itch as if I'd later be punished for shirking my responsibilities. But who would do that? My bosses at the art museum didn't know I was still alive. And the person who ruled over my life with an iron fist, well. She was gone.

Maybe there were plenty of things around here I could distract myself with? A fleeting thought of the cowboy's chest hair entered my mind. That perfect smile with canines that were a little sharper than average, gave him a wilder look than I was used to. Falling into bed with the guy offering me shelter felt a little too transactional. No matter how good-looking he was.

I wandered over to the bookshelf to pick through the paperbacks and worn-out leather-bound books. Everything looked about twenty years old, which meant he probably inherited the collection, or he had a thing for used books. I pulled one from the shelf and flipped it open. His name was scrawled into the inside in pencil. Alden R. Boone.

I set it down and wondered what the middle initial was for as I picked up another book. Alden R. Boone. Then another until they were all on the ground. Every book had his name written inside. No one else's. Surrounded by books, I started arranging them in stacks. Then I went through the names. With every book I picked up, I thought about what the middle initial might stand for.

Ryan.

Richard.

Roman.

Sierra, you did not get an Ivy League education just to sit around and do nothing in some shack in the middle of nowhere. Find a way to be productive.

It wasn't until I started stacking them on the shelf again that I realized what I'd been doing. A lifetime of guilt from my mother had so thoroughly left its mark that I was able to predict what she'd say to me at any given moment. And if my mother wasn't complaining, she probably wasn't talking.

Halfway through alphabetizing Alden's books, I decided this would do for now. This house. This plan. The task was mindless enough to leave me spending the entire day trying to come up with a solution to my problems, only to come up empty. I'd not been involved in my father's business. I didn't know who I could trust outside of the man I'd only met yesterday.

I could do this. Pretend to be his wife. For now. It wasn't that bad. After all, I was getting the better part of the deal here. Staying with Alden Boone until I figured out what to do next was the safest option I had. I kept telling myself that no one around here knew me. They didn't know the Serpas. The

Serpas wouldn't look for me in some random guy's house in the middle of the mountains. Even if they could trace the location of my father's car, all they would know is that I broke down and kept going.

So, fine. I could stay here. Just for now.

After finishing my organization task, I picked up his copy of The Hobbit and started reading. They were entering the dark forest when Alden R. Boone walked through the front door to find me sitting on his floor with the book in my lap. He was covered in dirt and looked like he'd spent the better part of the day sweating. With a little tip of his hat, he removed it and tucked it onto the shelf beside the door. I ignored the way that little gesture made my stomach tighten.

"Let me grab a shower and I can make dinner."

He shrugged off his jacket and hung it on the hook.

"Hey, what's your middle name?" I asked, closing the book in my lap.

I set the old paperback on the table as I got up to follow him. Alden paused at the bedroom door. He untucked his tee shirt and pulled it overhead. Wiping his face with the fabric, he braced an arm on the doorframe and looked down at me.

"Your name is written in all your books. Alden R. Boone. I feel like I should know my husband's middle name," I laughed awkwardly.

He was still staring down at me with an exhausted but amused expression.

"I'll tell you mine if you tell me yours."

I took a step backward and bumped into the other side of the doorframe, realizing how close we were standing next to each other. He was a very large, very close stranger. A very shirtless stranger who was completely fine with pretending to be my husband. He blinked at me expectantly. Right. My middle name.

"It's Briar," I stammered. "Sierra Briar. Like Briar Rose. My mom is really into fairy tales."

Making myself busy with the bookshelf had been a welcome reprieve from thinking about everything I had lost. But I couldn't help but correct myself as the brutal reminder of my loss crashed into me.

"Was. She. She was into fairy tales."

Because she was gone. They were all gone. My father. Enzo. Even if I hadn't died beside them, life as I knew it was over. My breath started coming in smaller and smaller sips of air.

"Hey, it's alright," Alden said, wrapping a long arm around me as he pulled me into his bare chest.

When did I start shaking? He stroked a hand over my head and murmured soothing words to me. Telling me everything would be alright. That I was safe. I closed my eyes, attempting to settle myself. His warm skin smelled terrible and wonderful at the same time. I found myself taking deeper and deeper breaths.

I didn't know how long he held me. The sound of his breath soothed me. The consistent boom of his beating heart. The heat of his bare chest against my cheek. But after I stopped trembling, Alden slid a hand under my jaw to turn my face up toward his.

"You're alright. You're safe," he soothed, hazel eyes soft with sympathy as his lips curled with a sympathetic smile. He made soothing strokes over my skin. "It's Russell. My middle name is Russell."

"Alden Russell Boone is a nice name," I warbled with a watery smile of my own as he wiped the tears away from my face.

His thumb brushed my bottom lip, drawing his eyes to my mouth. The mouth that was mere inches from his own. The warmth from his body melted the icy grip of grief from my extremities. Had I moved closer, or did he?

"Well, your name is almost as pretty as you are."

Then his eyes flared wide as his eyebrows shot up his forehead. Alden straightened quickly and pushed both hands through his shaggy waves. His mouth tightened into an apologetic smile as he backed away slowly. Then he bumped into his bed. He let out a little yelp.

"Um," he stammered. "Anyway, I'm going to shower real quick. I'll be out in a bit, and I can make dinner."

"You said that already."

Alden let out an uncomfortable laugh and shut the bathroom door. Water sputtered on. I left the room and went to the kitchen, smiling a little to myself. The big, strong cowboy was kind of cute when he was flustered.

Seven

Alden

"**Y**ou are such an asshole!"

If there was a prize for the world's biggest idiot, I would win it. I'd set the record for it, probably. The room was filled with steam and the bathroom mirror was completely fogged over by the time I finished berating myself. The girl was in tears and I dropped a stupid line like that on her? I mean, shit, I almost kissed her! She didn't need some sweaty giant to paw her and tell her how pretty she was. For heaven's sake, she was shaking like a leaf and I was too busy noticing how soft her lip was under my thumb. Looking into those big green eyes made my brain fall right out of my head.

And what she said about her mother.

Something bad had happened to this woman. Something bad enough for her to believe she had no one to turn to but me. I washed from head to toe, trying to imagine what happened to her. Nothing. I couldn't think of anything. I was still trying to put together exactly how to ask her about it when I noticed the scent in the air. Something smelled good. I pulled a fresh shirt over my head and my sweatpants on as I hustled out of the room, nose in the air as I tracked the source of the smell. My ears were met with sizzling and Dolly Parton. At least she'd found the radio.

My wife was shaking her ass to "Randy" in the kitchen. Just a little. She used a kitchen towel to pull the cast iron skillet off the range and plated a steak next to what looked like broccoli. Then she dropped the skillet back on the range and picked up the mismatched plates. She spotted me as she put them on the table.

"I was going to do that," I drawled as I entered.

"It's the least I can do," Sierra shrugged as she looked over her work. "Being your little housewife and all. I'm used to work, work, work. Doing almost nothing all day might make my brain short circuit."

"You rearranged my books," I noted.

She flipped her hair over a shoulder and gave me a little smile. Sierra was good at putting on a brave face. I wondered what she would look like when the smile was genuine. Every one I'd seen so far was small. Pained. I walked past her toward the fridge and pulled it open to hunt for something to drink, pulling out two bottles of Coke.

Sierra grabbed some cutlery and set it on the table. Before she could hunt for napkins, I grabbed a couple of paper towels off the roll.

"I don't entertain much," I explained.

There was that little smile again. Sierra took up the same seat as this morning, facing the window, back to the door. I sat down on the other side. Having someone else at my table, someone other than Eddie was sort of nice. Having someone who looked like Sierra was better than nice. I cut into my steak. Medium rare. Perfect.

"Is that alright? I didn't know how you like it done."

I cut off a piece and stuffed it in my mouth, giving her a nod as I chewed. "Well done."

"Oh, you like it cooked more than that? I'm sorry."

I laughed and took a sip of pop.

"No," I explained. "You did a good job. This is how I like it."

Sierra nodded and picked up her cutlery. She cut a small bite for herself and pushed it onto the back of her fork. It was a delicate act. Like she'd been trained to eat beautifully. Nothing like breakfast this morning. I wondered how hungry she must have been to drop all pretenses and just scoop food into her mouth like a wild animal. Except now she made a kind of yum sound that went right to my dick.

Easy, Boone. You're not a caveman.

"I think we need to talk about this wife thing," she started as she dabbed at her lips with the paper towel.

"What about it?"

I stuffed another bite of steak into my mouth and smiled. I wasn't sure what she did to the thing, but it was better than any steak I'd ever made.

"I appreciate your help. I do need to hide out for a while, but I don't need to be your wife to do that. You probably have a girlfriend or a long line of women to get back to."

I snorted at the idea. Natalie came to mind at Sierra's statement. If she had shown up two months ago, there would have been someone to worry about. But I wasn't worried about that girl and Sierra shouldn't be either. I took a pull from the bottle of Coke and set it down.

"Sierra, I don't want to pry into your business, but I'm not blind. You're running away from something or someone. My guess is you left in a hurry since you didn't have anything with you. You want to hide out? This is a small town and people talk. Around here, a girl on her own brings questions. A cowboy bringing home a new wife, people will understand."

She picked up her pop and looked at me thoughtfully. After taking a sip, she set it down again.

"No one will think anything of a cowboy just sweeping a city girl off her feet?"

"Happens all the time," I winked.

She rightfully rolled her eyes and sipped her pop with a smirk. Then she picked up her fork and knife to resume the eating ballet. I decided not to mention the fact that the only part people wouldn't believe is that I managed to land someone like her. Even out of the expensive clothes and fancy car,

down before she said anything. "No nudity in common areas."

"Fair enough. Third rule." I offered, trying to move on from what she must look like naked. "We have to be honest with each other. Husbands and wives don't keep secrets." From the nervous look that crossed her features, I was willing to bet she was already hiding things from me. I amended the rule. "We don't have to be honest one hundred percent of the time."

Sierra's shoulders sagged with relief. She scooped some broccoli into her mouth and chewed delicately.

"But," I picked up my fork and knife and cut away another piece of meat. "If I say *sassafras*, you have to tell me the honest-to-goodness truth."

"Sassafras? That's the word you want to go with?"

I nodded.

Sierra let out a little laugh and took another bite. Then a sip of her pop. Another dab at her mouth with the paper towel. Another movement in her elegant eating dance. Then she just stared at her plate. I could see the gears turning behind those mesmerizing eyes. She was weighing her options. With a breath that seemed decisive, she peered at me with narrowed eyes. Her expression became serious.

"Alden, if I'm going to stay here, I think you should know something," she said, hesitating as her gaze searched mine for something. Evaluating me. "The reason I need to hide is that there are people who are looking for me. Really dangerous people. People who want to hurt me."

My fist tightened around the steak knife. People. Not a partner. Not a husband or boyfriend. People. The idea of anyone, let alone multiple parties, wanting to hurt this creature made absolutely no sense to me. Sierra continued.

"Where I come from, people know me. My picture has been taken more times than I can count. I can't move on until I know the people who are looking for me aren't a problem anymore. Or until I figure out what to do. That might be a long time. That could be weeks. Months, even."

"I could use the company," I shrugged as I tucked into the broccoli, thinking about what she said. Having her around for a while didn't feel so bad, especially when she could make food that tasted like this. Damn, how did this broccoli taste better than I ever made it?

"What did you do to this?" I asked, unable to keep the question from tumbling out as I chewed.

"Roasted it with some seasoning and olive oil. I know steamed is technically healthier, but I figure that doesn't matter as long as you're eating vegetables. I think it tastes better."

I nodded. It really did.

"Where'd you learn to cook?"

A shy smile crossed her lips.

"Our housekeeper taught me before I left for college. She insisted I learn to feed myself since I was going to be living on my own for the first time. I could have eaten in the dining hall like everyone else, but I liked being able to do something for myself. My roommates were well-fed all four years," she laughed. "Did you go to college?"

Housekeeper. She said it so casually that if she hadn't shown up in a six-figure car, it would have hinted at her wealth. It was my turn to laugh.

"No. No, I barely graduated from high school."

Her eyebrows drew together.

"Oh. How come?"

There was nothing judgmental in her tone. No spoiled rich girl. Just curiosity. Talking to her made me feel both at ease and on edge. I found myself really wanting my wife to like me.

"Well," I grunted as I stuffed another floret into my mouth. "I've been living and working on Evergreen Springs, this ranch since I was sixteen. I only finished school because the old man insisted. But college isn't very useful for someone like me. I got my education from experience."

Dark hair shifted over a shoulder as she angled her head, considering what I was saying. Talking about myself always made me uncomfortable. Especially on dates. The minute people heard everything, they started feeling sorry for me and that was worse than anything. Eating dinner with an absolute stunner felt like a date. Anxious to change the subject, I turned things back to her.

"What did you study in college?"

She sighed and looked down at her plate.

"Art history."

Sierra sort of muttered it like it was a confession. Something to be ashamed of. Her eyes dropped away from me as she pushed her food around her plate. I didn't let myself think about why that might be, instead pressing her for more.

"You like art?"

She finally looked at me again.

"Art. And music. Books," she explained, eyes lighting up as her words came out faster than they had before. This excited her. "They're these things humans make because our souls need a space to announce their existence to the world. You can look back thousands of years and see art. Art is the first thing we did as a species to say I am here."

I smiled at her.

"You like art."

"It's not very useful. Not technically. My mom wanted me to study something more functional, so I enrolled as a business major, but I changed to art history once I got to school. It's the only thing I could ever choose for myself."

As I thought about what she could possibly mean by that, the radio filled the room with the warbling of Willie Nelson. This family she came from seemed pretty buttoned-up. I was starting to get a mental picture of the kind of life she came from. It wasn't even close to this. But she looked comfortable in my kitchen. Even after I finished my meal, I stayed at the table, having gobbled down everything in front of me, and waited for her to finish her food. I couldn't keep my eyes off of her.

Sierra Briar was a beautiful woman. Standing on the side of the road with all that makeup and wearing a fancy dress, she'd been a sight to behold. But now, her hair wavy, and a dusting of freckles across her nose. That little blue dress showed off miles of olive skin. Green eyes that looked like sunshine passing through a rushing river that were even prettier when she was excited. This woman was drop-dead gorgeous.

"I guess that doesn't matter now," she muttered, more to herself than to me.

As she finished her food, one thought floated back up to the surface. The bad people. Her family. I couldn't help myself as the question came flying out of my mouth.

"Did the people looking for you hurt your family?"

Sierra's face fell in a way that made my stomach tighten. She stood, collecting my empty plate along with her own, and paused before walking them to the sink.

"They hurt everyone, Alden."

Eight

Sierra

Somewhere a woodpecker was pecking. Birds chirped outside. The cold morning seeped into my skin as I exited the bedroom to find Alden gone. Out of one of the large living room windows, I could see a light dusting of snow that was melting under the bright morning sun.

I stood there, taking in my new surroundings. Yesterday, I'd been too busy feeling sorry for myself to pay much attention to the outdoors. When we'd arrived on horseback, the sun had already set behind the mountains. Everything was hidden in darkness and shadows. The only available light came from the windows I was looking out of now.

Trees surrounded the house. Pine. Oak. Aspens. Their leaves varied in color and density. Bright chartreuse. Whiskey brown. Deep green. All of them freshly unfurled in the early spring sunlight. There was no front yard covered in a tidy lawn. No manicured bushes. Everything was wild. Natural. Grass grew beneath the trees in long, inconsistent patterns. Flowers pushed through here and there. Wind rushed through the trees, bringing the peaceful pastoral image into real life.

Padding back into the bedroom, I threw open Alden's tiny closet to pull one of the hoodies he'd mentioned down from the top shelf. I pulled the dense green fabric over my head as I headed into the kitchen, sniffing the collar that definitely still smelled like him. Something like grass and Old Spice. A torn-out notebook page was on the countertop with a hastily scrawled message.

I'll be back by supper. Don't get into trouble.

Right. Work. He'd told me he had to be up bright and early to get to the ranch. Had I really slept through that thunderous truck engine firing up? It had announced itself pretty loudly yesterday. Deciding I'd slept harder than I thought, I realized he hadn't even woken me when he got dressed this morning. Leaving him locked out of his room felt pretty selfish when I was already sleeping in his bed.

Staying busy felt like the only way to keep myself from falling apart. With nothing else to do, I got to work on organizing the kitchen. Moving things out onto the counter until it was full of Alden's food. Canned vegetables. Cans of beans. Canned meat. Jam. Peanut Butter. Cereal. So many packages of spaghetti. Macaroni. Rice. Not much in the way of ingredients. Spices, but only six or seven.

All I could do was keep moving. Keep moving so I could forget that I had no one to call. No one to talk to all day. There was no charity event for me to plan. No fitness class for me to go to. No argument to have with my mother that I would have ruined my day only for her to act like nothing had happened the next morning.

My friends, if you could call social climbing gold-diggers all angling for a shot at my brother "friends," probably all assumed I was dead. Extended family members never bothered with me in the first place. Our family wasn't really a family. Except for us. The core four. Outside of my father's household, it was a business. There were no cousins who'd come looking for me. No concerned grandparents. No one who loved me was still breathing. To the rest, I was as good as gone.

All of the spices, what few there were, were now in one place. Along with the oils. The grains and cereals were all in a cabinet I designated as the official pantry since it was as tall as the refrigerator and right next to it. In the middle of the day, I started to get hungry. Alden had come home with a lot more food when he brought me new clothes, which I was grateful for. Especially because he'd only had enough food for one.

With the same cast-iron skillet I'd used to make dinner last night, I made myself a late breakfast of an egg on toast. Something our housekeeper used to make for me whenever my mother wasn't around to force egg whites and spinach down my throat. That is, if I wasn't on one of her juice cleanses. I cut the hole into the bread, dropped in the egg, and listened to it sizzle as I poured the coffee Alden had made hours ago over ice into a jar. Not a mason jar. A washed and repurposed jar. Probably a jam jar. After inspecting everywhere else again, I realized I'd been right the first time. He didn't have any actual glasses. Just jars.

For a second, I missed sneaking over to the coffee shop next door for a lavender honey latte and croissant after Pilates. After enjoying the food my mother would never let me eat in her presence, I'd go home to my gigantic marble shower, only to dress myself from a closet full of designer things. I did. I missed it.

Just for a second.

With my iced coffee all prepared and wilderness brunch ready, I sat down and ate. No one was there to tell me there was too much butter on my bread and I should have boiled my egg instead of frying it. Or that there was too much cream in my coffee. My mother's relentless criticism felt like a phantom limb.

"Calories in, calories out, Sierra. You're going to have to work that off. You look like you've gained a few pounds. I'm putting you on a fast."

Each bite of food taken without my mother's permission felt like a small rebellion. After I finished eating, I picked up the Hobbit and continued reading. At some point between enjoying my coffee and Bilbo finding the ring, I realized with no small amount of horror that I needed to ask Alden for one more favor. But I couldn't live without this.

The small lamp on the end table made the sofa a perfect spot to read. I'd moved back to the sofa to read after bathing and dressing myself and curled up under the blanket. Halfway through a chapter, I heard Alden's truck rumbling down the dirt road up to the house. My stomach did a little flip. The idea that I was excited to see a man who was practically a stranger to me was jarring, but I'd been alone all day. I probably would have felt the same way about seeing that blonde guy with the mullet. Right?

Boots clopped up the stairs and the door swung open. Hazel eyes peered at me from under that dark brown cowboy hat. He tipped the hat in greeting as he took it off and set it on the little shelf. Alden shed his jacket and hung it on the hook. Today he was wearing a black tee shirt that stretched over his thick muscles with his worn-in pale Wranglers that barely contained the powerful tree trunks that were his legs.

He looked filthy and tired like he'd been sweating for a better part of the day. Suddenly asking him for anything on top of everything he was already giving me felt like a terrible thing to do.

Just ask, Sierra.

"Hey, how was your day?" Alden asked, grinning at me like he was happy to see me.

I blinked at the question, trying to remember when anyone had asked me that. Even Enzo didn't ask. He always knew. This man asked after spending twelve hours doing something that made him come home covered in sweat and dirt. He was just so friendly. A walking green flag. It was easy to see. It was why I'd left the door unlocked for him. So he could get dressed and use the bathroom when he needed to, but also because I knew I wasn't in danger when I was in his company. He was going to make a great husband for some girl in this small town.

"It was fine," I said as I closed the book with a random business card I'd found to use as a bookmark and set it on the end table. "It's nice to have some time to read, but it still feels strange. I don't think I've existed without a packed schedule in, well, ever."

Alden raised a thick chestnut eyebrow as he ran a hand through that shaggy brown hair, his solid bicep flexed with the movement. Noting the direction of my gaze, he smiled a little. I started picking at my nails just to give myself something else to look at.

Stop drooling like a schoolgirl and ask him for what you need like a grownup.

"But?"

Was I really that transparent?

"Uh," I swallowed. "Look, I really appreciate everything you've done for me. I feel bad asking for anything else."

"But," Alden smirked, folding his arms over his chest with an amused light in his hazel eyes.

I chewed on my lip. Did he flex a little? I squeezed my eyes shut and tried to focus on my question rather than wonder if every cowboy looked as good as he did.

"Do you think we could maybe find me some shoes? I just feel kind of cooped up in here and it would be nice if I could go outside. Not far. I'd just like to be able to go for a walk or something. To get some air."

Stop babbling, Sierra.

My mother's bored voice popped into my head. During event meetings. During family dinners. Sometimes my mother would just look at me in that way that told me I was disappointing her with every passing second and I stopped talking. I was a nervous talker. I was definitely nervous now. The tight feeling in my belly I got from the way he watched me confirmed that this guy made me nervous. Caring what he thought wasn't a new feeling. I cared what most people thought of me. I didn't want him to think I was some spoiled little girl, but what was so bad about asking for one pair of shoes? Why did it make me feel like an ungrateful brat to even mention it?

Ungrateful.

I'd heard that word a lot. Thought it as I remembered the card in my wallet and all the money in a bank account I couldn't touch. I could picture all the pairs of shoes I'd bought with that money lined up in my perfectly organized closet. Stilettos that made my feet ache. Boots crafted by master ateliers to be beautiful instead of practical. Pristine sneakers I'd refused to get dirty. I'd thought about it all day, finally understanding how it felt to be a goldfish.

"Yup," Alden nodded as he unfolded his arms, grabbed his keys, and walked out the front door.

"Wait! I didn't mean right now," I called as I stood up to catch him. I threw the door open and ran out onto the front porch. I'd been home alone all day. The last thing I wanted was to be alone again. "You don't have to go anywhere. I just meant if you had time someday soon."

The door to the old cream and brown Chevy was open and the little cabin light was on, illuminating the big man who'd gotten into his truck. Alden wasn't listening to me, instead, he seemed to be digging around for something. He picked up the shoes I'd brought with me the first night.

Great.

He thought I was asking for the shoes I'd come in. I couldn't walk around in those. As pretty as black stiletto sandals are, they're not so practical for this terrain. Or, like, ever.

Then Alden sat up and slid off of the seat and out of the truck, shutting the door behind him. My stilettos dangled from one large hand. The other hand was holding what looked like a pair of old brown cowboy boots.

"I had to steal your shoes to make sure the size was right. I apologize if you missed them," Alden drawled. "These should hold you over until we can get you your own."

I took the stilettos from him and examined the boots he held up for my inspection. Little toffee leather boots with minimal decorative stitching. They had practical, low heels and a blocked off toe. The boots were a little beat up from wear but they were still in good shape. I almost cried with relief. Alden's face fell.

"I'm sorry they're a little worn in," he huffed, rubbing the back of his neck.

"We can get you a new pair tomorrow."

Oh god. How materialistic did he think I was? I shook my head as I took the boots from him and smiled.

"No, no. I love them. I've never had a pair of cowboy boots before. Where did you get them?"

Alden's face split into a broad grin like he couldn't help himself. Something about his smile warmed me from the inside. No one ever smiled at me like that. My father's smile was always terse. Hard-won. My mother's smile was irritated. As if I made her smile despite herself. My brother's was filled with laughter, especially when we were sharing a joke. I missed them all. But this one. This smile was broad and open, like sunlight pouring in through an open window. I was still appreciating it when the cowboy forced a more serious expression to his face.

"First of all, these are not like the fashion cowboy boots you get in the city. These are waterproof and durable. They're made for work. Second, they used to belong to my boss's wife. Mrs. Weaver. She passed a few years ago, but he still has a few of her things around. They're a half size bigger, but he said you could keep these for as long as you need 'em."

I wasn't sure what possessed me to do it. Maybe it was being alone all day. Maybe it was because I didn't have anyone left in the world. Or it could be because this guy was doing everything he could to make me feel safe and comfortable. No one in my life had done that for me. No one except for my brother. Even that had its limits. There was safety in that I had people watching me all the time. There was comfort in the luxuries I was afforded with my father's money.

None of it compared to how I felt now. So I dropped both pairs of shoes on the porch and threw my arms around his neck to hug Alden Boone. He went still, as if not sure what to do with himself. Then he chuckled and wrapped his thick arms around my waist. His face nestled into my neck, where I could swear he took a deep breath.

"I'm sorry I smell bad," he mumbled into my hair.

He did. Like sweat, sweet grass, and wood chips. I breathed him in. It was a weirdly enticing scent that made me want to keep smelling it. I sniffed him.

"I like the way you stink," I admitted.

"You do, huh?" Alden pulled back to look down at me, still smiling, my arms still circled around his neck.

"Yeah," I hesitated, then released him to put a little distance between us. "It's. It's nice."

He chuckled again. Even a step below me, he was still looking down at me a little. We stood there awkwardly for a second. I moved aside so he could actually walk into his own house.

"You still smell fancy," he noted as he stepped past me and toward the front door, holding it open for me to pass. "Is that your natural scent?"

"If you call Tom Ford natural, sure," I snorted, thinking of the little pink bottle I still had with me. "I have some perfume in my bag. It goes everywhere with me."

Alden let out a thoughtful grunt as he slid his boots off beside the door. Then he pulled his shirt off and made his way to the bedroom. I tried not to stare at the sweaty chestnut locks that curled at his ears or the way the hair on his chest made a dark trail down his stomach that disappeared below his belt. Even if it felt impossible.

He turned in the door, his hand on the knob as he got ready to shut it, and tossed me another easy smile.

"Then tell whoever Tom Ford is that you stink nice, too."

Nine

Alden

I rolled over, trying to get comfortable on the sofa. Though it was pretty old and very lumpy, I couldn't blame the furniture for how I was feeling. Nope. That tornado in a teapot, skin three sizes too tight feeling had everything to do with the woman sleeping only a few feet away from me on the other side of a closed door.

"I like the way you stink."

Hugging her had been a mistake. All I could think about was her body pressed up against mine. Smelling her was even worse. And her hair...

I'd assumed that my attraction to her would go away. That time away from her would dull the blade. Nope. I just felt its sharp edge with every passing second. It wasn't just that Sierra was beautiful. She was. She was the kind of beautiful that made me feel like I should find a new word for it. Sitting across from her at dinner, all I could think about was running my fingers through the undulating waves of her dark chocolate hair. Wondering what it would feel like to bury my face in it. Those silky strands would feel so good wrapped around my fist.

No, Boone.

She'd told me more about her education. She went to a prestigious school in Connecticut for her degree after going to an all girl's school in Chicago. Sierra explained that she'd been kept so busy with private tutors and family obligations that she didn't date anyone until college.

"I got to college knowing absolutely nothing about men. I still don't," she chuckled. "By that time, everything I knew about guys had come from social media or, well, some of my brother's friends."

"You didn't spend time with maybe friends or brothers of your friends?"

"I didn't have any friends. I wasn't really allowed to."

We had moved our conversation to the sofa. I watched her carefully. The more she spoke about her life, the more sheltered I realized she'd been. Locked away in some tower with lots of money but no freedom. Sierra played with her toes, not really looking at me. Like she was embarrassed. Of what, I had no idea.

"A lot of people don't date until they're older," I offered.

"Oh really?" Sierra laughed incredulously, looking up from her toes. "Do a lot of them have their first kiss at nineteen?"

Surprise must have shown on my face because she winced. Shit. I schooled my features into neutrality before trying to move the conversation forward.

"No one kissed you before you turned nineteen?"

Sierra shook her head.

"It was my first date, too."

Her admission sparked memories of my first date. Clary Woodbridge. I took her to the movies. She held my hand. We kissed at the end of the night. I was seventeen. Now she was a pharmacist over in Hoback. Thoughts of Clary were quickly pushed out of my head with a nagging curiosity about the woman beside me.

"So, who was the lucky guy?"

Sierra gave a soft laugh, tucking her legs under herself as she tried to pull the skirt of her dress over them. I offered her my blanket, which she accepted and draped around herself.

"Graham Johnson. He was a trust fund baby everyone knew. We dated for a little while, actually. He, um," she paused, going pink in the cheeks as she smirked down at her lap. She was so pretty when she blushed. With a small shake of her head, she stopped herself. "Never mind."

"Oh no, you can't leave me hangin' like that. You have to tell me now."

Sierra gave me a playful look of reproach and sighed at the ceiling, taking her hair out of that long ponytail. She shook it out with her fingers, biting back a smile.

"Fine. Fine. He was my, uh. First. You know?"

I nodded, unable to speak past the surge of jealousy I felt over a total stranger and the itch in my palms seeing her hair down created. Rubbing my hands down my thighs, I waited for her to fill the silence with more information before I said something stupid.

"We dated for six months. He wanted to do that sooner and I put it off until I was comfortable with him. I tried keeping him happy in other ways. I just didn't." She paused as she knotted her hands together, mirroring the tight knot that had formed between her brows. "I wanted it to be my choice."

"Why wouldn't it be your choice?"

Sierra shook her head and put on that pleasant smile that didn't reach her eyes, avoiding my question as she changed the subject. That question had clearly been out of bounds. Strange.

"Anyway, Graham took me to this fancy hotel in Manhattan, and we spent the weekend there. It was nice."

Nice. If it had been me, it would have been more than nice.

I blinked that thought away, regretting it as soon as it popped into my mind. Saying I didn't know where it came from would be a lie. I was attracted to this woman, there was no denying that now. Not being attracted to her was impossible. She was magnetic. She was charming. She was staring at me because I hadn't said anything.

"Uh," I started. "A fancy hotel sounds a lot better than the back of a pickup truck. I took my high school girlfriend to a lookout when I was seventeen. We put some sleeping bags in the back of my truck and went at it."

Sierra snorted, covering her mouth with a quick apology. Fuck, she was cute when she laughed. It was an addictive sound. Throaty with just a hint of melodic lightness to it. I thought about trying to make her laugh again. Then I thought about just reaching out and tucking that hair behind her ear. Kissing the sensitive skin beneath that ear, licking and sucking it until she was purring for me.

Quit it, Boone.

"At least you were under the stars," she argued. "That sounds really romantic."

I laughed. The cold, wet memory was filled with the kind of embarrassment that only teenage memories could provide.

"It wasn't, actually. No stars. Clouds. It rained on us halfway through and I took her home. It didn't occur to either of us to check the weather."

Sierra laughed again, this time a loud giggle as she shook her head in disbelief. It was one of the prettiest things I'd ever heard. A small surge of victory washed over me at the sound.

"Well, it wasn't exactly perfect with Graham, either. It was pretty awkward for me. I didn't know what I was doing at all. But the hotel was nice. I guess that's what I meant. Nice sheets. Candles. Flowers. Very romantic. We broke up right after that, though."

Disgust snagged at my gut as I imagined how that happened. Some guys just run until they hit the goal and then abandon a girl. Plenty of guys were like that. I knew that well enough, but how anyone could do that to this woman was beyond me. When it came to Sierra, I got the sense that one taste would have me crawling over broken glass for her. My hips shifted in my seat at the direction of my thoughts. Show her she was worth more than one night in a hotel room. I should kiss her. No, no, no. I should definitely *not* kiss her.

Sierra was playing with the ends of her hair, looking up at me through her lashes as she chewed on her lip. My instinct was to reach out and bring her into my lap. If this were a date, that's what I would do. If she were flirting with me, I would. But she might not be flirting. No, she was definitely not flirting. She was acting friendly, and I was just being stupid.

"Sierra, I," I hesitated, unsure of what was going to come out of my mouth because my head had become a tempest of testosterone and bad ideas. "I should get to sleep."

"Okay," she sighed sleepily as she got up from the sofa, handing me back my blanket. I stood up and started making up the sofa for bed.

"Good night, then," she said quietly, giving me a brief smile over her shoulder before shutting the bedroom door behind her. "Thanks again for the boots."

Now the blanket felt like cement. Bags of cement. Or sand. Hundreds of pounds crushed down on me as my mind drifted to the woman in the next room. A nice hotel. Nice sheets. Candles. Flowers. Long, dark hair spilled across a soft duvet like molten chocolate. That brown sugar and rose scent in my nose like it had been when my arms were around her waist, lush body pressing into mine.

Rule one was scratching at my brain like a hangnail. No sex. This wouldn't count. It couldn't or I wouldn't survive.

Shoving down the blanket, the one that smelled like her now, I glanced at the door. Closed. Closed but not locked. The light was off. She should be sleeping by now. In fact, she had to be asleep by now. Had to be. I prayed she was as I palmed my aching cock through my sweatpants.

Please. Please be asleep.

Stifling a groan, I shifted the fabric down to stroke myself as I imagined her coming out here. Those haunting eyes watched me as she slid a hand up her thigh. I'd stand up, shedding my clothes as I approach her. Kiss her as soft curious hands run over my body, exploring me.

Let myself unbutton that dress until it fell down around her ankles. Kiss every bit of that olive skin. Lift her into my arms to take her into my bed, languishing in the feel of her full pink lips on mine. Pull those panties down to taste and lick every inch of her until she was shaking with need. Push inside of her and watch as her eyes go wide at the feel of me.

"Shit."

Biting down hard on my lower lip, I cursed as I panted through my orgasm as quietly as I could. Evidence of my lust for this woman splashed across my stomach. This was not good. She didn't have anywhere else to go. She needed me. I couldn't let her know I wanted her like this. Not when she might feel obligated or something. She didn't owe me anything for being here. I shouldn't even be thinking about this!

No.

I got up, walking softly on the balls of my feet into the kitchen to grab paper towels and clean myself up, hoping a squeaking floorboard wouldn't give me away. Two fucking days. It had only been two days and I was already crawling out of my skin thinking about her. Fantasizing about her. There was no telling how long Sierra would be here, but I couldn't let myself think about her that way. That's why she was in there. And I was going to keep my ass out here.

Ten
Sierra

Only a few weeks ago, I attended a board meeting with my mother. I could remember how nervous I felt as I got ready. Putting on my perfectly pressed little grey blazer dress. Applying my "no makeup" makeup look because I was never allowed to look like I was wearing it during the day, but always had to look like I had flawless skin which meant I was using several different products. Taming flyaway hairs into a ponytail that my mother would later tell me was "too casual" even though it was tight enough to make my scalp ache.

Wearing a black skirt suit, she waited for me in the backseat of her Mercedes town car, claiming to be too busy to drive herself. She tapped the face of her Tiffany watch with a red polished nail and arched a brow at me as I got in.

"You're late. Show me the presentation."

Before standing in a boardroom full of the city's wealthiest and most important benefactors to present a proposal for the adaptive reuse of a historic building, I had to present the information to my mother for her approval. Not a single person in that room would make me nervous. No one but her. Catarina Volpe's impassive expression as I showed her my slides on my laptop set my teeth on edge more than anyone else.

"Fine."

Her single-syllable response was enough to keep my heart thundering like a hummingbird's. Still, I lived with it as I got through the presentation and did well enough to earn funding for the project. Just like I lived with it every day. That overwhelming anxiety became the beat I lived my life to. Thoughts that turned into weights dragging me down to the depths of the ocean of their expectations.

I better not fail. I better not let myself gain weight. I better not associate with anyone who might sully my reputation. I better not do anything that might reflect poorly on my family.

Each morning I woke up in this little red house in the middle of the mountains, surrounded by trees, with nothing to do. Each morning, the beat of that drum was a little harder to hear. No one was here to tell me my hair was too wild. Until now, my life was filled with rules and barked orders. I could still feel them pulling me down like a phantom limb.

Don't swear.

Sit like a lady.

Are you sure you want to eat that?

Don't ogle the cowboy.

The cowboy who made me dinner for the third night in a row even though he had worked another long day. He was very nice to look at and the food wasn't bad either. Pork chops. Rice. Broccoli. It all tasted lovely. Even if the voice in my head, the one that sounded exactly like my mother, was telling me the caloric value of everything he was heaping onto a plate for me.

Are you sure you want to eat that?

Yes, yes, I did.

Even if I was already thinking about the Pilates I'd do in the morning, every bite of that dinner felt like a personal victory over my mother. Followed immediately by crushing guilt that I'd need to feel any sense of victory over a dead woman. For a while, I tried to think about only the good memories.

Things about my family that made me happy, except those memories were so few. So thin. They disintegrated in my mind like so many layers of tissue paper to reveal the painful truth underneath.

The relentless, painful, forever-dissatisfied truth.

Brushing my teeth, I got lost in a long mental apology to my deceased family. That I was sorry they were gone. I was sorry that I was here, and they weren't because I ran away. I must have looked as lost as I felt because I'd forgotten Alden was in the room with me until he came into my eyeline.

"You alright?"

The question was asked through a mouthful of toothpaste, mouth cocked to one side to keep it in as he arched a brow at me.

"Oh," I blinked, spitting into the sink. "Yeah, I was just thinking about my parents. Well, my mom."

Alden followed my movement, then folded his arms over his broad chest, that was now covered with a clean white tee. It was damp at the shoulders from where his hair had dripped onto it.

"Do you miss her?"

"No. I mean, yes. I do. But that wasn't what I was thinking about."

He propped a sweatpants-covered hip on the bathroom's small vanity. With the tub and toilet, there wasn't much room in here for the both of us. It felt even smaller sharing it with someone who was looking at me the way he was. Alden watched me, waiting for me to continue.

"My parents had a lot of rules for me. I wasn't allowed to do a lot. I was just thinking that it feels strange."

"What does?"

I felt embarrassed. Expressing myself didn't come naturally. I was taught that I wasn't allowed to complain. To share my feelings. The only person in the world I'd tell my secrets to was gone. I wanted to tell Alden about him. My brother. That I was struggling with the fact that I missed my brother, but not my parents. And that the pain I felt from their loss wasn't from their being gone. This pain I felt. I couldn't explain it. So, I did my best.

"The lack of them. The lack of like, someone telling me what to do. At home, I was always watched. Always on a schedule I couldn't deviate from. Even when I was at college in New Haven, I wasn't really on my own. When I wasn't flying home for some responsibility, I had to check in all the time. My mother used to text and call me constantly," I sighed, rinsing my toothbrush out in the sink. "I swear I can still hear my phone ringing from a trash can a thousand miles away. I don't know. I feel relieved. But also, guilty that I feel that way because I know that makes me a horrible person."

Alden started brushing his teeth again. I worried I'd horrified him with my confession so much that he decided the conversation was over, but then he rinsed off his toothbrush. Placing the blue toothbrush on the edge of the sink beside my pink one, he let his hand rest on the counter next to my hand.

"My parents are gone, too. Died a long time ago. They weren't what you would call good people. Sometimes I miss them. But not who they were. More like who I wanted them to be," he paused, staring down at the sink as he seemed to search for the words to describe some intangible thing.

Pain rippled through his features, darkening his eyes in a flash of anguish that was there and gone in a second. My fingers twitched like they wanted to move to touch him. To ease the pain. The urge to soothe it stayed with me as he spoke. My eyes locked on his, looking for another hint of that agony.

"Sometimes we're not mourning the people they were. We're mourning the people we wish they'd been for us."

Both of us stood there in that tiny bathroom, letting the truth of Alden's words sink in. His hand moved away from mine as he stood up. Then he rubbed the back of his neck before stuffing it into the pocket of his sweatpants.

"Anyway, I'm just saying I understand. That kind of pain leaves a mark. It doesn't make you a horrible person," he said, watching my face. A curious look narrowed his brows as he gazed at me, as if he was trying to solve a puzzle I couldn't see. "What if you just did nothing?"

"Nothing?"

"Yeah. You said you aren't used to not having obligations. A schedule. So what if you just," he shrugged. "Did nothing."

I shook my head. No. Nope. I could not do nothing. I could not sit around like some freeloading spoiled brat and just do nothing. Alden smirked at me as if he knew exactly what I was thinking.

"Do nothing," he repeated it as if it was a command.

Do nothing. An hour later, my thoughts still circled me like hungry dogs as I lay in Alden's bed, staring up at the ceiling. On a near-moonless night, there wasn't enough light to see a thing. The bare truth of Alden's words still pealed in my ears. Again and again.

I didn't miss them. It was a bitter truth I'd been ignoring up to now. My parents. They never told me they loved me. They never told me how proud they were of me when I got into an Ivy League school. They pampered Enzo. Let him do whatever he wanted. I wasn't pampered. I was tended to. They were constant gardeners, pruning away the parts of my life they deemed unnecessary.

I had never been allowed to explore myself. To discover my own taste. Find my own joys. It was difficult for me to comprehend how anyone could love their child with any depth without truly knowing them as an individual. The truth was that I was just an extension of them. The ugly part was I'd known that longer than I wanted to admit.

"Enough," I huffed to myself, rolling over and tugging the pillow into a bear hug.

If I kept thinking about that, I wouldn't get any sleep. Instead, I forced myself to think about something a little bigger. A little sweeter. It was safe enough to think about. He was sleeping in the next room, and it wasn't like I was actually going to do anything. But I could fantasize about him. Right?

I wasn't blind. Stolen glances. A fleeting, hungry look in his eye. The moments of interest were fast, always followed by some regret-filled expression. It made the fact that he slept on the sofa, giving me his bed every night, so much sweeter. He gave me space.

That night on the sofa, I thought about it. Just for a second. The table lamp lit his golden skin as he clenched his stubble-covered jaw. All muscle, even from the neck up. That large, rough hand squeezed the cushion he was sitting on like he was holding himself back.

I'd never seen any man like him in my whole life.

Falling asleep that night had been an effort, too. Our conversation replayed in my head as I wondered what Alden was like with women. If he was as caring and gentle with them as he was with me. If maybe he was more wild in the bedroom than the polite cowboy he was everywhere else. Not that I had much basis for comparison.

Graham had been so, well, selfish. So had the others. Selfish in a way I had a feeling Alden wouldn't be. Selfish didn't seem to be in his nature. As I handed him his blanket and our fingers touched, skin grazing mine, I felt the urge to find out. As I revisited that night in the darkness, I drifted off as I imagined what could have happened if I'd invited him into this bed. With me. That would have been the opposite of doing nothing.

What a crazy, reckless idea it would have been.

Eleven

Alden

They say idle hands are the devil's plaything, but it could be that an idle mind was Sierra's worst enemy. I wasn't sure of exactly what she'd been through, but it was clear that she didn't want to spend much time thinking about it. I didn't know the details. Just that she'd lost everything. After I had burned up one day, I didn't want to spend my time dwelling on it, either. She still hadn't told me much, but it seemed like that's what it was. An indescribable disaster.

Avoiding the topic was just another part of our routine. It felt like Sierra and I fell into something of a pattern after about a week. I'd get up and sneak around my room to get dressed, roll the truck down the road in neutral until I was far enough away not to wake her, and get over to the ranch. She would do whatever it was she did all day and I would spend my day trying not to think about her.

Don't think about those lips.

Don't think about those legs.

Don't think about those eyes.

And I failed. Every time.

The first day, I tried not to gawk at her as she showed me how she rearranged all the food in my kitchen. The next day, she'd organized my closet. I wasn't sure how that entertained her since most of my clothes were tee shirts, jeans, and a few pearl snap shirts for going out. But she did it. The way she smiled at me, so proud of herself.

I was still thinking about it.

"I just want to contribute," she'd said.

Annabel huffed beneath me, sensing my mind wandering again. We were trailing the herd of mares through the rocky outcropping by the creek. Not a great place to be daydreaming about the girl who was making me dinner every night. The baked potato she'd whipped up for me last night was something else. I could smell them when I walked through the door. Something with cheese and broccoli. She even got some bacon in there. I didn't know you could improve on a baked potato, but she managed it. I even ate her leftovers.

Annabel shuffled her feet and huffed. Strange enough behavior that it snapped me back to reality.

"You alright?"

The old man called from up ahead, turning to look at me over his shoulder.

"Yeah," I said. "She's just giving me a hard time."

My girl snorted again and started taking backward steps. Before I could register the sound of a rattle, she reacted. A snake. Annabel's biggest fear. And she let me know it. Bouncing on her front hooves, desperately whinnying. I gripped her with my legs, trying to stay on. Then she bucked. Hard.

"Whoa, girl. Hey, girl. Hey!"

I shouted as she reared back faster than I could get a hold of her. Annabel, who I'd been riding for over twelve years, threw me. If I hadn't blacked out when I hit the ground, I would have been pissed. Instead, air rushed out of me. I saw black and red.

And a pair of green eyes.

When I came to, I realized I was on my back. Breathing made my chest feel like it was on fire. Tight through my ribcage, I tried to push past it and wheezed. The old man stood over me with concern etched into his weathered face as he smoothed his bushy, grey mustache with his hand, blue eyes were filled with worry.

"You alright, Boone? I took care of the rattler before it could get you," he gestured to the headless snake to my side.

I could barely hear him through the ringing in my ears. Pushing my hands to the ground, I tried to sit up. Stabbing pain shot through my side. Hard air rushed out of me with a grunt, even if it still felt like I could barely breathe. It was aching something fierce now. Moving didn't help.

"I think I broke a rib or something," I seethed through clenched teeth.

"Can you breathe?"

"Yeah, it hurts, but I can breathe. My head is all fuzzy."

The old man puffed a sigh of relief as he helped me up. We both groaned with the movement. I heard the four-wheeler coming before I saw it. He must have called Sam Jr. to come and get me. His son charged up on the Polaris, a vehicle we normally used to move equipment or survey the property, and hopped off to help the old man support me as we walked over.

"Boone! You alright?" He squeaked.

Junior was a sweet kid. He and I weren't in school together since I was ten years older than him, but we'd known each other for so long that he was like a little brother to me. He'd just graduated from high school last year and was doing everything he could to help his father around the ranch while he was getting his degree online. With bright red hair and freckles, the boy took after his mother more than his father.

It took a lot of convincing to get the old man to let me go home instead of to the hospital an hour away. Mr. Weaver flat-out refused to let me drive myself and asked Sam to follow him in their truck. Both of them rattled up the drive loud enough to alert Sierra to my arrival.

Instead of watching out for me from the window, she came outside. Dressed in one of those little dresses I was coming to love, this one a soft yellow color, and wearing the old boots. Her hair was in a loose, thick braid that didn't contain all of it. Even with my head spinning and my ribs bleating in pain, it was hard not to appreciate the sight of her.

"What happened?" She exclaimed as she saw the old man hop out of my truck and Sam help me out on the passenger side.

"Who's this?" Junior asked.

"You must be Boone's wife," the old man interjected. "Nice to meet you, sweetheart. Your husband took a tumble. He's going to have to stay off his feet for a few days while his ribs heal. Also, he might have a small concussion, so keep an eye on him."

"I told you I'm fine," I gritted out.

"Proud as an ox, this one," the old man chuckled. "Don't listen to him. I already spoke with the doctor and he said that with some rest, you should be back on your feet by Monday."

Sierra opened the front door to let us by. Forgetting about my pillow and blanket folded on the sofa, I winced as the old man clocked it and gave me a knowing look.

"Did y'all have a fight already?"

"Yup," Sierra answered without missing a beat. "A big one."

"Me and Mrs. Weaver never met a problem that couldn't be solved with a little whiskey and," he leaned in to whisper to her conspiratorially. "A little whiskey and a lot of hanky-panky. But none of that while he's hurt."

"Yes, sir," she smirked. "None of that."

"Dad!" Junior scolded. "She doesn't need to hear that. None of us do."

I tried to give Sierra an apologetic look as they helped me into the bedroom. She followed with my pillow, tossing it onto my side before I could lie down. I toed off my boots and let them thud to the ground as I reclined on the bed, my back against the wicker headboard.

"Dinner's not ready yet, but I'll bring it in here when it's done," Sierra said as she exited the room.

The old man nodded as he hooked his thumbs into his pockets, watching me as she left. As soon as she was out of the room, he tossed me a wry grin.

"You did well for yourself, Boone. She's a looker," his voice was low as he rushed out his compliment. "Get him out of those clothes, Junior."

"Yeah," Junior laughed. "She's too pretty for you."

Shifting my hips as the young man helped me undress, I grunted in pain. Then I attempted to put on my lounge pants alone. The old man headed to my bathroom, where I heard him open the medicine cabinet. Pills rattled in their bottle as he carried them to my nightstand.

"People keep saying that," I said, rolling my eyes and smiled at the girl as she reentered the room with a glass of water in her hand.

"People keep saying what?" Sierra asked as she set the glass on my bedside table.

"You're too pretty for me," I groaned as I shifted to grab the water. "They're right."

Sierra snorted, shaking her head. The old man elbowed his son in the ribs. Time to go. She crossed her arms and eyed me with a smirk as she shifted to let the Sams pass her on their way out of the room.

"Boone's a good man," he said as they walked out. "You could do a lot worse than him, sweetheart."

Sierra didn't look away from me. Didn't answer quite loud enough for the old man to hear as he and his son left. Just looked at me with that little smile of hers and said, "I know."

After serving me dinner in bed and tidying up in the kitchen while I lay here like a piece of meat, Sierra came into the room and picked up her pajamas on her way to the bathroom. The door clicked shut. One minute passed. Then another. She emerged in her pajamas, braiding her hair to one side as approached the bed again. Sinfully short shorts and a cropped top with thin little straps. What in the hell was I thinking? That little outfit would kill me if the concussion didn't. She picked up her pillow and tucked it under her arm.

"Where're you going?"

"I thought I should go sleep on the sofa. You know, since you need the bed."

"We can share," I said, patting her side of the bed. "It's big enough."

Sierra looked over her shoulder at the sofa, then back at me. After letting out a little hum, she set her pillow down again and left the room. For a second, I wondered if she was just going to leave me here. Padding footsteps sounded on the wooden floor as she reentered the room with the slim bolster pillows from the sofa, lining them down the center of the bed. I cocked a brow at her.

"I'm adding a rule," she said as she moved the pillows around until she was satisfied. "No crossing the pillow barrier."

I stifled a laugh, wincing at the pain in my side.

"Not only am I not in the condition to do a damn thing, but I wasn't raised like that. I'm a gentleman. You don't want me to touch you, so I won't touch you."

She cocked her hip to one side, chewing on her lip as she looked me over. I shifted under the weight of her gaze and tried to maintain eye contact with her, just to avoid looking too long at everything I could see in those pajamas.

"So if I tell you not to touch me, you won't touch me?" Sierra asked.

"No, ma'am," I said, holding my hands up in surrender.

Why I was talking her into sleeping beside me when I knew those pajamas would be the death of me, I had no idea. Maybe I liked the pain. Seeming to take me at my word, Sierra nodded. She sat down on the bed, feeding her legs under the covers and sliding down.

"Oh, wait," she sat up and stretched over me to turn the light off.

My eyes drifted shut as I let her brown sugar and rose scent flow over me with the movement. Resuming her position, she nuzzled into her pillow and sighed. Out here, night meant near-total darkness. For the first time I could remember, I cursed the lack of light as I wished I could watch Sierra fall asleep.

Twelve

Sierra

Once upon a time, I would have described myself as a princess. Daughter of a mafia boss who was a millionaire many times over, I wanted for very little. Except, instead of a castle, we lived in a large brick townhouse guarded by tall iron gates. It was both modern and timeless in its structure. White marble surfaces everywhere you looked. Pristine. Just as everything under my mother's relentless scrutiny was expected to be.

My existence wasn't that far removed from actual royalty, either. Live behind tall iron gates. Present oneself properly. Learn about the dynamics of our world. Dress in such a way that is stylish but not garish. Straighten my wavy hair. Wear enough makeup to look perfect but never more than is appropriate. Marry for political advantage and alliances. A golden collar and leash, never ever to be removed.

Everything was done for me. If it wasn't for college, I wouldn't have learned how to do laundry or cook for myself. When I returned after graduation, I wasn't allowed to continue the habit. I had everything I needed behind those high walls. The older I got, the more I felt like as much as they were there to keep enemies out, the walls were there to keep me in.

All of that preparation crumbled around me like the Roman Empire. My mother certainly wouldn't have expected what my days looked like now. Having to take care of a grumpy, injured cowboy in a house smaller than my bedroom instead was not exactly in my life plan. I'd expected worse for my life. The quarrelsome beast of a man was even kind of amusing.

"I told you, I'm fine," Alden protested as he helped himself out of bed. "I need a shower. I feel disgusting."

Dropping the basket of laundry onto the bed, I scuttled over to him, hauling a large arm over my shoulder to help him up. He did sort of stink in a bad way, but that was what happened when you didn't shower for several days.

"I don't care what you say, I'm helping you whether you like it or not," I argued, sliding myself against his chest. I helped to stabilize him as he stood.

An injured Alden Boone was an unhappy man. He didn't like asking for help. He didn't like needing me to get out of bed to use the bathroom. He didn't like asking for water or food. So I did those things without asking. Anticipated his needs. Between keeping the house clean and preventing him from injuring himself further, I had a pretty full day. By the time I got into bed with him at night, I was ready to pass out.

Okay, fine, I was failing at doing nothing but it wasn't my fault he came home with bruised ribs and a low-grade concussion. In all honesty, I was thrilled about the distraction.

Alden lifted his shirt, showing me his heavily muscled stomach and the bruise that had blossomed into an unpleasant purple. I wasn't sure which sight had stolen my breath. I swallowed and looked away, the image of that light trail of hair beneath his navel firmly in my mind.

"See, it's not that bad. I can do it," he grunted. "I'm going to shower and then you and I are going to eat dinner at the table like a couple of human beings."

He started stripping, shoving his lounge pants over his firm ass and thick thighs. The tee shirt went next as he entered the bathroom. Turning in the door, he looked at me expectantly. Waiting for my answer.

"Fine," I chirped, adjusting my tank top and jeans after they'd twisted under his weight. "I want to wash this bedding anyway."

Alden huffed a laugh and shut the door, turning on the water for the shower as he shouted from the other side.

"There's another set of sheets in the box under the bed."

Being cooped up with a man who looked like that twenty-four hours a day for several days was doing things to my brain. The passing idle fantasies I'd allowed myself were getting less innocent. Less innocent and far more frequent. What's worse was that now that I was sharing a bed with him, I couldn't do anything about it. All of that energy lingered.

So I stayed busy.

Stripping the bed to throw the sheets in the wash took only a minute or two. Hardwood bit into my knees as I knelt to peer under the bed. Gratitude washed over me as I found a footlocker and nothing else. No dust bunnies. Nothing gross. Sliding the black locker box out, I heaved it onto the bed with a grunt and to open it up. Metal snapped as I opened the closures and threw the lid open. There was bedding, sure. And magazines. Magazines with girls on them. In them. I sat down on the bed and flipped through one of them.

"Oh no," I giggled quietly.

Turning the magazine to the centerfold, I angled my head to take her in. A platinum blonde with big perky implants and arguably nice legs perched on a hot pink and white beach chair by a pool, baring it all with a big smile and matching pink lipstick. Was this his type?

The bathroom door opened. I looked at him over the top of the magazine, trying to fight the laughter bubbling up in me. Alden stood there with a hand on the towel around his hips and fear in his eyes. His wet hair dripped onto his broad shoulders.

"I can't believe you have these," I started.

"Sierra, I'm sorry," he blushed with a grimace.

"We are well into the twenty-first century, Mr. Boone. You have a smart-phone. You can see stuff like this online for free! Magazines? Really?"

Alden choked on a laugh, holding his side as he winced a little. His brows narrowed as he gave me a beseeching look.

"Come on now," he chuckled. "Don't kick a man while he's down."

I laughed. An honest-to-goodness laugh. The sound felt foreign coming out of my mouth, but it felt so good. Folding the magazine shut, I tossed it onto the bed so I could use my hands to brace myself through the laughter. Alden crossed his arms, waiting for me to finish as an amused look played across his features.

"This is from the nineties, Alden," I cackled, wiping tears away from my eyes. "Where did you even get it?"

"Hey," he argued, a big grin spreading across his face as he crossed the room to take the magazine from the bed. "Be nice to my girls. They've been with me for a long time."

"Gross."

"What can I say?" Alden drawled as he examined the magazine I'd been looking at. "I'm a loyal guy."

"Well, that's good to know."

Alden shook his head with a laugh and pulled on his grey sweats. I stood up, tossed the other magazines back into the footlocker, and began making the bed. When I finished, he stayed behind to presumably find a better place to hide his stash.

Chicken sizzled and popped in the cast-iron skillet. The sound filled the kitchen, leaving me unable to hear Alden as he entered the room on bare feet.

"Smells good in here," he remarked, causing me to jolt. "Easy now."

I peeked over my shoulder at him. In one of his white tee shirts, I'd learned while organizing his closet that he had many, and his favorite pair of grey sweatpants.

"You don't need to make me dinner every night."

"You're letting me stay here. It's the least I can do. Let me take care of it. To be honest," I sighed. "I like doing things for myself. I wasn't allowed to do it before."

Quiet footsteps crept up behind me as he peered over my shoulder to examine the fried chicken. With a little grunt of approval, he retreated a few steps.

"I had something else in that box you might want to see," he coaxed, the tone of his voice making the hair on my neck prick.

"Oh?"

I turned to see him proudly holding up the weathered looking box of a stacking block game with a big grin. The laugh I let out made my belly ache. He tucked it into his side and rounded the sofa.

"It's going to be cold tonight, so I'm going to get a fire going. We can play later."

After dinner, we sat on the sofa together and played as the fire snapped and popped in the black stove. Alden fed the flames every now and again with a bit of wood from the small pile beside it. His thick fingers made him terrible at the game, but I was a bad winner. Every time it toppled over, I rubbed it in his face. My stomach ached from laughing. I didn't know when it happened, but at some point during all of the taking care of him, I'd actually stopped thinking about my problems for a little while. I was just here. With a glance at the clock mounted over the bookcase, I blinked in surprise as Alden made his next move. It was almost midnight. We'd been at this for more than three hours.

"Alright," Alden huffed. "This is for all the marbles."

He slowly moved a brick from the center of a precarious tower. Carefully tugging it free, he held his breath. With a final tiny jerk, he succeeded in knocking the entire thing over. As the stack tumbled over on the coffee table, I snorted.

Alden threw himself back on the sofa with a defeated groan. I laughed, thrusting my arms up to celebrate another victory. Opening my mouth to brag, a yawn popped out instead as I reclined on the sofa. My hair pulled on my scalp. I took my hair out of the knot atop my head for some relief. We were both tired enough that the crackling embers in the stove had lulled us into a prolonged silence.

A tug, barely noticeable, pulled on my freed strands. Again and again. I wasn't sure when he had started toying with my hair, but it was making my scalp tingle. I hadn't realized we'd been sitting so close to one another. It dawned on me as I sat there, enjoying this new intimacy, that no one had ever touched me like this. Stroked my hair. There were no back rubs outside of a paid masseuse. Touches from other men were less about me and more about them. But this. I could get used to this. With a hum, I closed my eyes to better enjoy the feel of it. Tension I hadn't realized I'd been carrying melted from my shoulders. I took one deep breath. Then another.

"That feels good," I purred.

My eyes opened to find Alden staring at me. With a shallow breath, he continued sifting his fingers through my hair. The tension that had melted from my shoulders started building beneath my skin under his watchful eyes. Up this close, I wanted to pick out all of the different colors within them. Moss. Olive. Caramel. Coffee. We stared at each other, his hand working through my hair, my hand now drifting over his thigh as the crackling fire filled the silence.

I hadn't known what this felt like. When you feel attracted to someone and you want to know if you're imagining their interest or not. The others had pursued me. Their interest was obvious. Alden. The fleeting looks. They faded. He always looked at war with himself over it. Something was always holding him back. His eyes dipped to my mouth, causing me to pinch my lower lip in my teeth. Alden licked his lips. In the middle of the country, surrounded by trees and wide open spaces, there was no air in this room. My cheeks heated as my nerves prickled with that unfamiliar feeling. This thing. This entirely new thing was causing my breath to stutter and flutters to knot in my stomach.

We were seconds away. Seconds from the tipping point. I knew if I closed my eyes, I might feel his lips on mine. Because Alden was looking at me like he wanted to kiss me. Still, he wore that expression of internal debate. Eyebrows pulled together. Eyes hungry. Lips parted. Did I want him to? I glanced at his mouth. That cupid's bow.

Yes. Yes, I wanted it.

After everything we've done for you, you're going to throw it away on some rodeo reject?

Resentment burned like acid at my mother's phantom nagging. Everything they'd done for me. Nothing they'd done for me was actually for me. Not really. I'd done everything they asked of me. I would have walked down the aisle to marry a man who despised me. I would have had to do things I really didn't want to do with someone who didn't love me. To give him children.

For them.

I would have never known this feeling. The one that was making my fingers tingle. I'd only be trapped inside someone else's cage. Everything taken. Nothing given. But I could take something for myself. Right now. A small memory to keep. My hand found Alden's jaw, enjoying the soft scratch against my palm until my fingers found the chestnut waves at his neck. I sat up slowly, feeling the tug of his hand as it worked through my hair, and fell to the back of the sofa.

Nerves. I was just nervous. That's all.

"It's getting late," Alden breathed, his voice dropping an octave as I pushed myself closer to him.

"I'm not a good kisser."

Alden blinked. God, where did that come from?

"I haven't done this a lot. I feel like I have to warn you. I'm not. I might disappoint you."

The words had barely left my lips as I brought them to his. One kiss. Just for me. His mouth moved against mine in a careful, gentle caress as the hand that had been resting on the sofa behind me moved to gently cup my jaw. Letting me set the pace. Letting me decide how far to take this. Soft and warm. It wasn't fair. Completely unfair that someone who looked like him was as thoughtful and sweet as him, could also be such a master with his mouth. Light and sweet, one kiss turned into another, his movements like ice cream melting on my lips.

Tempting. Delicious. His mouth parted, sucking gently on my lower lip, pulling a mewling sound to break free from me. Warmth curled low in me as I savored the sensation. Tasting Alden felt like tasting chocolate for the first time. Part of me was uncertain that I should keep going. Another part begged me to take more, more, more.

This kiss. It had the feel of a first kiss. Not just with him. With anyone. Like it erased all of the bad kisses I'd had with anyone else because none of them could replicate the way this one felt. It felt like champagne foaming over in a glass. Like dropping from the top of a rollercoaster. Like being kissed awake after a hundred years of sleep.

The hand I'd placed on his thigh tightened as I fought the urge to keep going. Long fingers circled my neck, sending heat to my core as his calluses scraped over sensitive skin. A thumb skimmed my neck, the sensation tightening my breasts as I arched into the kiss. Humming against his mouth as it opened again, I wanted to feel his tongue against mine. Taste him. A lack of confidence in myself yanked at me. It felt too much like taking a leap. The ground was slipping out from under me and a fear of falling doused the fire in my veins.

Thirteen

Sierra

Our mouths still shared air as our chests heaved. Our eyes opened. Alden looked at me, eyes heavy-lidded as he moved the hand on my neck back to his side. I pretended to yawn and stretched.

"I'm going to clean the kitchen. All that oil from the chicken, you know? You should get to bed."

He blinked, then nodded as he coughed.

"Yeah."

I needed to douse this moment in ice water. Do something to take my mind off of wanting him. He was in no shape to do anything. He'd said so himself. And I was just distracting myself from the shambles my life had become. Just a spoiled girl looking for something to play with. Seeming to take me at my word, he rose from the sofa and cleared up the game. Tucking the box under his arm, he sighed as he exited the room.

I thought I could have one kiss. Just one kiss. I'd been wrong. Kissing him had been a mistake. A big mistake. Not because it was bad, but because it had been the kind of kiss I'd hoped to have since before I started kissing. The kind I eventually thought I'd never have because I had learned that in my world, it wasn't material goods that were luxuries. Love was the luxury.

Passion. Desire. My body was still screaming for more, demanding it from me, as I scrubbed every inch of the kitchen. The entire kitchen was sparkling by the time I came to bed, hoping he'd be asleep.

The gigantic cowboy was snoring. I'd grown used to the sound. It wasn't like a farm animal or anything. His snores were a gentle rumble, like a tired dog after a long day. Just enough to wake me up.

As soon as my eyes were open, my brain moved through thoughts like it was swiping through clips on social media. Alden. My family. Alden. My shattered life. Alden. I would not let myself lay here and wonder about that moment we had on the sofa. The anticipation. The want. The kiss. Because I did want him. It felt hard-wired into me now. I sat up and looked over at him. I could get up and read. Or I could do the thing I'd been thinking about for days.

Laying there in the dark, I started thinking about my family again. It had been a few weeks now. Surely someone had to know more. Unfortunately, I couldn't ask anyone without giving myself away. As long as I was missing, I was safe. Still, there was one way I could find out.

Bracing one hand on the headboard, I reached over Alden's sleeping body. Stretching my fingers toward the device, I grunted. The cowboy beneath me shifted, grumbling a little as he readjusted his position. I froze. Waited. Nothing.

With a sigh of relief. I grabbed his phone and opened an internet browser. Typing in my search, I waited for the screen to populate. There was barely any data signal here. After a minute, the search engine results popped up. I clicked the News button and waited again.

The first headline I saw made my skin go clammy.

Bruno Serpa Released.

Released?

I scrolled through the article that had been posted one week ago, reading nauseating details about the demise of my family. Where their wounds were. My father was holding my mother's hand. They were shot in the back of the head at point-blank range. Simultaneously. Which meant that they were killed by two people or one person holding two guns. My brother died shortly after. Goosebumps pricked my skin as I imagined Enzo's final moments, wondering if he'd known what was coming for him. If he had to watch our parents die.

After being fully autopsied by the city's medical examiner, their bodies were claimed by my father's lawyer. When asked for a comment, he only stated that he was waiting to hear from me and was going to proceed with family affairs as though I was still living. That gave me a small amount of comfort. I thought about reaching out to him. He had been one of my father's closest advisors. A good man I could trust to get some information. But as my eyes skimmed down the article, those ideas were dashed upon reading Bruno Serpa's statement.

"We are deeply saddened at the passing of the Volpe family. My son and I were not present at the time of their death. He was engaged to be married to Ms. Sierra Volpe. Antoni misses his fiancé and looks forward to seeing her again. I am using all of my resources to make sure that she is safely returned to us. If you have any information, please contact us."

Below his statement, there was a phone number. And a reward offered. He was paying a lot for information. For me. I didn't understand. With my father out of the picture, there was nothing I could offer him. I was no one. Nothing. So, what good would a price on my head be?

No one knows I'm here. No one knows anything about me. Mr. Weaver wouldn't sell me out. Right?

The thoughts pushed me out of bed as I closed the browser tab. After a few light steps, I set it back on Alden's nightstand with shaking hands. Water. I needed water. Padding out to the kitchen, I pulled one of the mismatched glasses from the cabinet and filled it, greedily drinking it down as if the solutions to my problems were at the bottom of it. I stood there in the quiet darkness, trying to get a handle on my fear. My disappointment. The rudderless feeling I'd been ignoring only for it to come back and swallow me whole. No. I couldn't panic. I just needed to breathe. Breathe. Breathe.

One deep breath followed another.

If I had gone back to Chicago, there would have been nothing waiting for me but a home full of things and memories. If there was anything left at all. My mother would never scold me for wearing the wrong thing. My father would never pat me on the shoulder after making him proud, even though he would never say so. And my brother would never wink at me when we shared an inside joke about someone in the room. There was no reason for me to go back. Nothing but death and the echoes of a shattered life awaited me there.

No. I couldn't go home. Not now. Possibly never again.

Fourteen

Alden

My ribs had healed enough to cause only fleeting moments of pain, but if that wasn't going to kill me, sleeping beside this woman was doing it slowly. She didn't snore. Didn't kick in her sleep or anything that would annoy me. She did talk a little. It was as if the words she kept bottled up during the day found their way out when her mind was unguarded.

Of course, none of it ever made any sense. They were random words. Things like "tomatoes" followed by "cashmere." Once she even said, "mash the bananas." I had no idea what any of it meant, but it was too adorable not to laugh.

Still, that wasn't the worst of it. The worst of it came last night when Sierra brought those full, delicious lips to mine for a kiss that made my bones turn to liquid. Her mouth. Her soft fucking mouth. The tips of my fingers burned with the feel of her skin beneath them. Even as I savored the way she tasted, like the first warm day after a long winter, it didn't feel like enough.

Fireworks cracked over every nerve in my body, forcing me to maintain control over the urge to take more. I had to focus on the moment. Enjoy it for what it was. Enjoy how pliant and warm. How gentle and sweet. For a few seconds, I could taste her in the air. Even if it took no small amount of restraint to keep my hands off of the rest of her. That and the painful, throbbing reminder that I was in no condition to do more than enjoy what little she offered.

Excruciating as it was, even that wasn't the only issue. It was also the scent of her. Sierra's goddamn brown sugar and rose scent that turned me into some kind of animal.

When she nestled in bed beside me, her head was right under my nose. Pillow barrier or not, her hair was there for my personal anguish. Those little pajamas. The fact that her body was mere inches away. All of it felt like some elaborate plot to turn me into a feral animal. Those were the moments I counted the wood planks in the ceiling. Recited every type of knot I knew. Anything to make my skin feel less tight. Among other things.

That scent was the reason I was having trouble controlling myself where this woman was concerned. That scent and the little blue pajama set that showed off miles of skin I wanted to worship with my mouth. It was enough to make me insane. Insane enough to imagine peeling those little shorts off her in the morning to bury my face between her thighs. The pink sundress she changed into after getting up this morning was even worse. It moved and swished around those thighs as she busied herself with cleaning up after making breakfast for me, French toast, and insisted that she liked having something to do even when I told her to stop waiting on me.

"Let me," she whined. "I keep telling you, I used to have a completely packed schedule. Without something to do, I feel like I might go crazy."

"Yeah, I know the feeling."

I picked up a book and pretended to read, instead watching her out of the corner of my eye. With a flick of her delicate wrist, she turned on the radio and got to work. Sierra shuffled around to the music, scrubbing out the pan she'd fried up our breakfast in. Washed the coffee pot, humming along to Johnny Cash. I slid my phone out of my pocket, needing distraction or I was going to crawl out of my damn skin. I fired a text off to Mr. Weaver.

Ribs are healed. The bruise is gone.

Can I come back tomorrow? I feel fine.

Don't need you yet. Come back on Monday. Tell the wife I said hello.

Fighting the irritation I felt at his denial, I had the sneaking suspicion that this was Mr. Weaver's way of doing his newlywed ranch foreman a favor by giving him some free time with his new wife. Little did he know he was helping send me to an early grave because Sierra was killing me. Squeezing the life from me with those sundresses and freckles. Sweet smiles. That hair. Those legs. That mouth. That delectable fucking mouth.

If he really wanted to do me a favor, he'd come in here with his shotgun and end me before I died at the lack of blood pumping to my essential organs from imagining what I could do to that soft mouth.

Sierra's tongue darted over her lips as she filled in an answer on an old crossword puzzle book I'd had lying around. The little wiggle of victory in her seat was too adorable. She glanced up from her book to catch me smiling at her like an idiot. Pink warmed her cheeks, long dark lashes fanned over them as she looked away. I returned my attention to the book in my lap, because if I didn't I was going to pounce on her.

This woman did not know what she was doing to me.

Glancing up from my book again, I noticed she'd gotten back to work on the crosswords. This time the pencil she'd been using was perched at the corner of her mouth, inside those perfect lips, just enough for her to nibble the end a little. Perched on that perfect lower lip I'd sucked between my own only hours ago.

I wanted to be that fucking pencil.

At least when I was on the ranch, I could distract myself with work. There were things to do. Horses to train. Fences to mend. Stalls to muck.

Equipment to maintain. Stuck here in this house with her twenty-four hours a day meant that I never got a chance to stop thinking about her. She was always here. Always available for me to kindle some new fantasy. So here I was. Fantasizing about her. Fantasizing about putting myself in that pouting, full mouth. Feeling that tongue slide over me.

Fuck.

Inviting Sierra to stay here may have been the biggest error I've ever made in my life. She was fully dependent on me. I couldn't impose myself on her. Making a move on her would be unfair if she didn't have anywhere else to turn. That would be wrong. Right?

Except for one thing. She kissed me.

Glancing over at her, I wondered. I could dismiss it as boredom. Sheer curiosity. Every once in a while, she looked over at me. A hint of a smirk would tug at the corner of that pink mouth. Then she'd go back to her crossword. But when her eyes were off of me, she'd shift in her seat. Different from the victory wiggle she did whenever she got an answer in the crossword. She eyed me and I didn't miss the way her cheeks colored. Again. Did she want to?

Kiss me again.

Inside, I was dying for her to take control of the situation like she had when she'd kissed me. Watching the girl out of the corner of my eye, I was too weak to resist imagining an entirely different scenario. Sierra setting down her book. Crawling the short distance across the sofa to me. Those appetizing thighs falling around my hips as she sits in my lap. Kisses me. Let me feel that tongue against mine. Grinding herself into me as I finally take hold of her, feeling every curve I'd sworn to myself I'd memorize if I ever got the chance.

Shit.

I stood and set down my book, leaving it spread out on the sofa so I wouldn't lose my page. I needed a break. A minute away from her or I was going to do something I shouldn't.

"Is everything okay?"

She looked up from the book of crosswords, batting those long lashes at me. I had to maintain eye contact with her because of that damn dress. The dress that was my fault. My fault. I should have bought her sweatpants. Coveralls. Even if I knew she'd still look cute as hell, at least there would be a little more distance between my imagination and reality. Sierra shifted a little, pink rushing to her cheeks as she waited for my answer. Oh god.

"Yup, I just need to, uh," I gestured toward the bathroom.

"Oh," she said, glancing downward for just a moment before quickly looking away. "Sure."

I strode toward the bathroom with purpose. One purpose. I had to tear my eyes away from her. Just to catch my breath. She was everywhere. In my bed. In my thoughts. On my sofa doing a great job of dismantling my sanity, one little sundress at a time. A problem I knew I'd created for myself when I picked up the damn things, but I didn't realize they'd be turning my brain to fucking mush.

Shutting the door and turning on the water, I splashed the cold tap over my face, then shut it off. My palms slammed down onto the vanity as I braced myself to take a breath. Every bit of me felt wound up and ready to explode. The reflection in front of me was unrecognizable. I didn't recognize myself.

"Get it together," I hissed at myself. "She's got nowhere else to go. You're not allowed to scare her off just because you can't control yourself like a fucking adult."

I took one breath. Then another. My heart still pounded in my ears. Blood thrummed in my veins as my brain flooded with ideas that would make me anything but a gentleman. At least my escape to the bathroom had offered a little reprieve. Enough for me to catch my breath. Until I noticed what exactly Sierra had glanced at straining against my sweatpants like a rock-hard red flag.

Somebody kill me.

Fifteen

Sierra

I'd woken up feeling optimistic. I got dressed, made breakfast, and kept myself busy all morning. Every chore I busied myself with carried the hope that we could get past that kiss and just move on. When I'd run out of tasks, I picked up an old book of crossword puzzles to keep my eyes off the broad-shouldered man lounging in sweatpants on the other side of the sofa.

It was peaceful. Quiet. An occasional smile passed between us. The afternoon became pleasant enough that I thought we could both move past my impulsive behavior last night. It was all going fine. Until I spotted what was standing at attention in his sweatpants.

Then I didn't think about anything else.

The man was attempting to read Great Expectations, which was not exactly salacious as far as I could remember. Between the glances in my direction and the way he rushed out of the room. Whether it was from the stringent "no sex" rule we'd set in place or from being so forward with him last night, I didn't know. Everything I knew about men could fit on an index card. A small one.

Alden barely said more than two words at a time to me for the rest of the day. Then it was time to go to bed. Still in his tee shirt and sweatpants, he'd decided to resume his vigil on the sofa without telling me. I caught him pulling the pillow off his side of the bed. Disappointment smoldered in my gut. I'd gotten used to him. His presence beside me every night had instilled a sense of security I hadn't known I'd been seeking. So much so that I panicked at the thought of sleeping here alone again.

"You don't have to go back out there," I blurted. "You can stay here. If you want."

Alden snorted.

"No. I'm going back to the sofa."

"Even your snoring was sort of pleasant. Like a living, breathing, white noise machine," I argued as Alden tried to take the extra bedding out to the sofa again. "We can share. I don't want to kick you out of your bed."

"Let me be a gentleman, Sierra."

"No, I," I choked out. "You've been a gentleman. You haven't crossed the pillow barrier once. Besides, I like it. Not sleeping alone. I'm asking you to stay." Alden stopped, setting his pillow down on the bed again so he could put his hands on his hips. I tried to ignore the way the motion drew attention to the pants that hung low around the arced muscles there, visible from the way his shirt puckered. Chestnut brows pinched together to complete the confused look he was giving me. "Please, Alden."

"You've never shared a bed with someone else?"

Shaking my head, I looked away to hide the embarrassment flooding my gut. Yet another normal thing I missed out on because I was locked away in an ivory tower. Graham and I shared a bed only once. The night he spent with me in that hotel. And snuck out before I woke up. After that, I wasn't in a relationship with anyone long enough to get that comfortable. In so many ways, I still felt like just a girl. Embarrassed didn't even begin to cover the way I was feeling now that I had to explain myself.

"I wasn't exactly allowed to date. There haven't been a lot of opportunities for me to do that. Except for college, I've always lived with my parents."

Alden made a thoughtful grunt, then pulled back the covers and climbed under them. Victory. He moved his pillow and laid down properly. I climbed into bed and laid down on my stomach as I tucked my pillow under my chin, squeezing it with both arms as I looked over the bolster pillow between us and up at him.

"What do you mean you weren't allowed to date? Your parents were that strict with you?"

He reached over and shut off the light, leaving us in near-total darkness. I considered not telling him. With people outside of our world, explaining how things worked felt strange. Even when I tried to explain it to my roommates in college, they never really got it.

Alden shifted to put an arm behind his head and even though I could barely see in the meager moonlight, I knew he was gazing down at me waiting for an answer. It could have been because I was tired. That was what I would tell myself. That I was tired and he didn't know my family, so I may as well be honest. At least a little. Keeping things to myself wasn't doing me any good. Keeping secrets from him was starting to feel unnatural. So I decided to tell him the truth.

"In Chicago, my family was very powerful. Very well known, too. My father owned a real estate development company, but that wasn't where all of our money came from."

"Are you going to tell me that you had a rich family? Because I already figured that out. The first time I saw you, I knew you came from money. Hell, that car is probably worth more than this house."

I buried my face in my pillow and groaned. Even in darkness, I wanted to hide.

"Yes," I moaned into the pillow. Tilting my face toward him again, I continued. "But not in a 'he bought stock in Apple early' way, so much as a 'he did a lot of crime and profited from it for generations' way."

"Okay," Alden paused on the word like it would normalize what I'd just said to him. "Like the mafia? I've seen the Godfather. All three of them. And Goodfellas. You mean like that?"

"Right. The mafia, yes."

The room grew quiet enough that I could hear something rustling in the brush outside. Telling him was a mistake. The thought repeated again and again in my mind for a long time before he spoke again. I felt the bed shift as Alden adjusted himself under the covers, laying down to face me fully. A silly thing to do in the dark.

"I'm sorry. I just don't understand what that has to do with you dating."

Well, here goes nothing.

"When you're a girl in a mafia family, especially a powerful one like mine, you're not a person. You're property. You have to get married for political reasons. It was my only responsibility. My parents didn't treat me like a child. They treated me like an investment. I was groomed for marriage my entire life. The day before you met me. I was dressed up because I was supposed to be getting engaged."

Alden went silent again. I wasn't sure what else to say. I hadn't faced that truth for most of my life. Saying it aloud felt like a mistake. For a long time, I thought maybe he didn't want to hear anymore. A long sigh loosed from him before he spoke, his voice deeper than it had been only a few minutes before.

"Sierra, do you have a fiancé waiting for you back in Chicago?"

I could have told him that I was a runaway bride. That the problem was just an arranged marriage. But that wasn't the truth. He knew my family was gone, but he didn't know why. He didn't know that Antoni and his father had plotted to destroy my family. My arrangement was a way in for the Serpas. And now there was a price on my head. They wanted me back. Probably to finish eliminating my family.

"You're just a spoiled bitch who needs to be housebroken."

Antoni's hissed words of cruelty had been enough to force me to excuse myself to the restroom. To stay in there until after the opera had started. The momentary slip of his icy mask had terrified me, but it had also saved my life.

Keeping the news about the reward from Alden felt wrong. Being here with him every day had stabilized me. Gave me a peaceful harbor when I felt lost at sea. He'd given me so much. Without my having to ask, he'd offered me his home. Even when he was a grumpy patient, he was good company. I'd started this confession because I'd intended to tell him the truth. Except telling him the truth could come at a cost. He could ask me to leave. I knew he'd help me find my way, but if he knew they were hunting me, my being here would come at too high a price.

"The man I was supposed to get engaged to was from a rival family. They met with my father and made the arrangements. Me in exchange for some development project. We were supposed to get engaged and then have our wedding a week later. The night of our engagement, my intended and his father killed my parents," I choked on the last word, my throat becoming tight with emotion.

My throat worked, and tears flooded my eyes. I sniffed. A warm hand brushed my cheek. He had a talent for wiping my tears away. How he knew where they were without light, I would never know.

"They killed my brother, too. My father was so desperate to solve problems with his business that he didn't see the trap they'd set right in front of him. I got lucky. They wanted to kill me, I heard them. And I ran," I whispered hoarsely, tears streaming down my face in earnest now. "That's what I've been running from. From them."

The bed shifted as Alden moved closer, warmth surrounding me as he pulled me into his chest. I let myself slump against him. Up this close, I could smell his soap and the bleach from washing his shirt. The fabric became damp with my tears as soft, gentle strokes moved over my back to ease my quiet weeping as he began speaking in low, soothing tones.

"No one is going to hurt you. You're not there anymore. Sometimes bad things happen and we just have to survive it." In the dark, I could barely see him. His voice was a low rumble as he spoke. "You're safe, darlin'. You survived it."

Late morning light trickled in through the cracks in the curtains. A heavy, muscular arm was thrown over me. A large, warm body was wrapped around me. I'd fallen asleep in the comforting presence he offered. Flat on my back, I saw Alden's head resting on my pillow.

His face was relaxed with sleep. In this light, I could see a few little wheat-colored hairs peppered into his chestnut stubble. It was always cropped close enough but never trimmed into any sort of shape. Functional, but not fussy. His lips were soft, full and pink with a nice cupid's bow to shape them. The bones of his nose were stately. Exquisite in their symmetry. Just as his eyebrows were. His thick and naturally well-shaped eyebrows. Alden Boone was rough. Rugged. And so, so pretty.

A hazel eye opened to peer over at me. He sighed through his nose as his lips curled into a lazy smile.

"Mornin'."

"Good morning," I half-whispered, turning my head to face him fully. I didn't realize how close we were until my nose brushed his. "Alden?"

Apparently, the pillows we'd used as a barrier were no longer an issue. The slim bolsters were now completely crushed beneath us after we'd rolled toward each other last night, both of us now in the center of the bed. So close. An arm was still draped over my stomach. He was so warm. So close. I'd only just woken up. How had I run out of breath so quickly?

"Hm?"

"You crossed the barrier," I whispered conspiratorially, nodding toward the pillows beneath us.

"We crossed it," he argued, his fingertips grazed the exposed skin on my lower back. "It doesn't count if we both break the rules."

"You're arguing that two wrongs do make a right?"

I glanced toward the arm over my stomach. It lifted as he remembered himself and started to retreat to his side of the bed. Losing his warmth had made my belly sink. Impulse had me reaching out to grab his withdrawing hand. I laced my fingers into his. Sleep disappeared from his eyes as they snapped back to mine.

"I want to touch you," I rasped, letting a thumb brush over his wrist.

Ladies didn't do this, I was told over and over. They didn't make passes at men. Ladies were meant to be chaste. Not chase. I wasn't supposed to encourage anything that would damage my reputation. It was easy to forget my reputation with a view like this. With him so close. No one was here to tell me not to. The heat of his skin under mine was too inviting not to try.

Summoning all the confidence I could, I nuzzled my nose into his again, both eyes pinned on his as I turned my body toward his. His breath was soft as it fanned across my lips. We stayed like that for what felt like a minute. Just staring at each other.

It felt like standing at the edge of a cliff. An intrusive thought inside me screamed at me to jump, jump, jump. Except I'd gone as far as I could push myself now. Too scared to close that final gap between us. What if he didn't want me? Or worse, what if he got what he wanted only to cast me out like Graham did? Of course, those worries didn't matter if neither of us was brave enough to take the leap. It was possible he didn't even like that kiss. I lifted my nose to brush his again, getting close enough to barely graze my lips over his. I hoped he'd see the gesture for what it was. Permission and invitation.

"Can I tell you something?"

After my chin dipped in the barest hint of a nod, Alden brought his mouth down on mine. Lush lips moved in tandem, walking the line between gentle and seductive. The hand holding mine slid until it pinned my hand beside my head. Alden's body rolled over mine a little more, his weight a pleasant pressure on top of me. The fingers of my free hand threaded into the hair at the back of his neck, enjoying the agonizingly soft feel of his curling locks. My body responded to him like a magnet, finally connecting with its opposite.

Snap.

We both felt it. An undeniable pull toward each other. Gravity overwhelmed me as my lips parted for him.

"Alden," I breathed.

"I've been dying to kiss you again."

The hand pinning mine slipped seamlessly beneath my head to knot into my hair, angling my head as he took the chance to deepen the kiss. Nipping my lower lip, sucking it just a little, he followed the bite with his tongue before moving inside to taste me. It was tentative. Sliding over mine with tantalizing tenderness, pulling away to gauge my reaction with a glance. I brought my mouth back to his to remove any question.

Each of his actions was thorough and unyielding like he was trying to memorize my mouth. It all added up to an irrefutable conclusion. Alden had wanted to do this. Each passing second proved I'd wanted it, too. With my hand free from his, I let it glide under his shirt. Up the broad muscles of his back and down to the waistband of his sweats. His body half-propped with his other arm afforded me the opportunity to explore him. The dip of his back. The curve of muscle over his hips that connected to the abdominals I'd only admired with passing glances. He shuddered as my exploratory touch wandered over his stomach. Lower.

Alden made needy little huffs and hums into my mouth. I arched into him enjoying the way he responded to me. My kiss. My touch. Powerful. That was what I felt. He groaned, kissing long and deep as my hand ventured down to find his arousal hard and insistent against my palm.

"Darlin'," he groaned, a vague tone of warning entering his voice as his eyes pinned me to the spot. "You don't know what you're doing."

He was right about that. I didn't know what I was doing. That didn't mean I didn't know what I wanted.

"Can I touch you?"

"Fuck," Alden panted, giving me one of those seductively firm kisses before answering. "Yes, Sierra. Please. Please touch me."

Heat bloomed low in me as curiosity made my hand skim over his length again. In grey sweatpants, men don't have any secrets. Alden had one big, insistent secret pressing through the heather grey fabric. Against my palm. I was dying to see him without any clothes because what I was feeling couldn't be right. It just couldn't. I stroked and explored everywhere I could as Alden's breath came in faster between kisses.

My thighs squeezed together as his tongue brushed mine in searing strokes. Hips undulated, seeking friction. Relief. I needed relief. Alden was kissing me like he'd gone without water for days and I was a river, except it was me who wanted to drink him dry. He hummed and growled as he savored my mouth. All the while, keeping some leash on himself. Some inner tether. I could feel it go taut between us as I acknowledged the unprecedented effect Alden had on me. His body. His tongue. The scratch of his stubble against my jaw.

One hand was in his hair as the other worked against him. Explored him. For once, I wasn't afraid. Wasn't worried about becoming the wrong kind of girl. I didn't care. For the first time, I felt almost grateful for what had happened if it had bought me this feeling. This sip of life.

I cursed the friction of the pajama top I wore, enduring the agonizing sensation of it grazing over the stiff peaks forming beneath. It was swiftly becoming too much. That coupled with the bottoms rubbing against the apex of my thighs as I shifted them together to seek relief was near blinding. That was what I needed. Relief. Relief from wanting to be touched. Because I wanted him to touch me.

"Alden," I purred against his mouth, hoping he would look at me as my fingers skimmed up his length through the soft fabric of his pants.

"Si-Sierra," he groaned, hand snapping to brace himself on the headboard as he swore.

Something warm and wet touched my hand as he buried his face in my neck. He panted rough and hot in desperate moans. I'd never heard a man lose control like that. It did nothing to cool my aching center. Alden stilled, breathing hard as he trembled.

"Shit, I'm sorry."

I opened my mouth to tell him it was alright. That I liked it. Only, he pushed off the bed and got up too quickly. My pajamas were a twisted mess. So was I. Wound up so tight. Alden threw me an apologetic glance, then looked to the damp spot on his pants. Swift steps carried him into the bathroom. The door clicked shut behind him.

Sixteen

Alden

With one more day of rest to endure, I spent most of it avoiding Sierra, which is hard to do in such a small house. She gave me a sympathetic smile every time she saw me, which made me want to walk onto the highway and await oncoming traffic. I'd finished in my pants like a teenage boy after she'd barely touched me.

Sure, it had been a little while since I'd been with a woman but this wasn't just some girl from the bar. It was Sierra. Like the falling star we saw that first night, she fell out of the sky and into my life. That first kiss had been just a tease compared to this morning. Kissing her, really kissing her, was like waking up from reality into a damn dream. It awakened a primal need in me. Those little noises she made were like fuel to the flame in my belly. When she asked if she could touch me, I was done for.

After everything she'd done for me this week, I felt like an ass for taking advantage of her. She waited on me hand and foot, even hauled my ass into the bathroom a few times that first day, and I thanked her by humiliating myself. No. She deserved better than that.

"Alden?"

Sierra poked her head out of the front door and examined me. I'd told her

I needed some fresh air and took a book outside to sit on one of the rockers and read. I'd not done one bit of reading and just watched the sun climb across the sky as I sat here with my thoughts. Now the day was nearly gone.

"Do you need anything?"

She held the door open a bit more. Today she was wearing that butter yellow sundress I liked. With the little sunflowers all over it. Her hair was a sheet of long, wavy dark brown over her shoulder. Like a waterfall made of the richest chocolate. The pale yellow fabric made her olive skin glow. My stomach knotted at the sight of her. Awestruck, that was the word.

"I'm fine," I muttered.

Her face fell a little. Shit. She liked being useful. Having a purpose. I'd noticed it while she took care of me. It was the quiet moments that seemed hardest for her. She needed a distraction. I eyed the curve of her ass in that dress as she turned away, an idea sparking at the sight. She deserved a proper thank you for taking care of me. I was going to give it to her.

"Let's pack up for an early supper," I offered. "I'd like to take you somewhere."

"Alden, I don't," she paused, worrying that full lower lip. "I shouldn't be going out anywhere."

I stood, tossing the book onto my chair as I approached her. Hell, I wasn't reading it anyway. She looked up at me with wide, curious eyes.

"Don't worry. We'll be alone where we're going."

I pulled the truck off onto the shoulder and put it in park. The field spread out before us in a blanket of yellow, gold and green. The vast pink sky stretched out over it. Sierra's eyes were wide with joy as she drank in the sight. I killed the motor and the radio died off with it. The old Chevy bobbed as

I hopped out and shut the door. Sierra began opening the passenger side to get out. I shut it on her as I reached it. She looked surprised, but amused, as she laughed a little. Then I opened it, stepping backward to let her pass.

"You wait for me to open this for you," I winked.

She laughed, smiling as she shook her head in disbelief. I extended a hand to help her down, enjoying the small thrill as she took it.

"Fine."

I grabbed the wicker basket from behind her seat and lead her toward the break in the flowers not far from where we'd parked. With tall stalks blocking the view from the road, I knew we'd be tucked away. Private. Just like I'd promised.

"Is it alright for us to be here?" She asked as I took her hand under the guise of leading her through the rows of tall flowers.

"It's the Miller family's field. Mrs. Weaver's people. What they don't know won't hurt them."

The wicker basket was a light load compared to the weight in my chest. An apology. I owed her that. From the smile on her face as we made our way through the tall stalks of flowers to the small patch of grass in the middle, she didn't feel the same way. Good. At least I didn't set myself back too far behind the starting line.

"When I was in college, I went to Amsterdam during a summer trip to Europe. It was this big art excursion. We were supposed to be seeing all these paintings by Dutch masters at museums around the area. They took us to see the tulip fields. They're kind of like this. Flowers everywhere, for as far as you can see."

"Are those your favorite?"

Sierra looked at me out of the side of her eye, smiling a little at my question. I couldn't help the smile that crossed my lips, despite myself. From the way that smile made me feel, I suspected that if this woman asked me for the moon, I'd find a way to pull it down.

"No. These are."

The heavy feeling in my chest lightened a little. Arriving at the patch of grass, I handed the basket to Sierra and untucked the blanket from under my arm to roll it out. She slid her boots off and sat down with the basket, opening it up to start serving the two of us. I opened a bottle of pop for her and handed it off. She nestled the bottle safely beside herself.

"I just wanted to thank you for taking care of me this week," I started.

"You don't have to thank me. But this is nice," she said as she bit into a strawberry.

I sat down, letting my legs extend before me as I leaned back on my hands. This was nice. I had taken one other girl here, but I didn't feel then the way I felt now. We sat there watching the sun crawl toward the horizon, eating in comfortable silence. Well, maybe she was comfortable. I was still trying to decide how to apologize. The right phrasing escaped me. After about ten minutes of not saying a word to her, I decided to just go for it.

"Anyway, I'm sorry," I started. "About this morning. I shouldn't have taken advantage like that. You're not a bad kisser, by the way."

Shit, now I was rambling. *Shut up, Boone.*

Sierra chewed on her lip, still looking out at the field of flowers that surrounded us. My gut dropped. I messed up. I really, really messed up. We were sitting on a blanket in a field of flowers. What was I thinking? This was a date. I'd taken her on a date. She must have thought I was trying to make another move on her. Then I felt her hand on mine. Sierra shifted on her knees until our thighs were touching and she was fully facing me. Gorgeous green eyes peered into mine, dipping to my mouth for just a moment.

"You didn't take advantage, Alden. I wanted to. To do that. I wanted you to kiss me."

"You did?"

It was my turn to look at those lips. Her tongue swept over them as she shifted her weight, the hand that rested on mine moving to my thigh. Those eyes bounced between mine as her teeth tugged at the corner of her lower lip.

"I do."

This woman. This beautiful woman wanted me. She wanted *me*.

"Come here," I ordered, tucking my fingers beneath her chin to bring her mouth to mine.

I wasn't a religious man, but kissing her this morning had been the closest thing to heaven I knew I'd ever get. Until now. I got the sense that every kiss with this woman would be better than the last.

Sierra's lips brushed mine as she carefully climbed into my lap. Then she looked down at me for a second. One long second. My chest ached at the sight of her. Those freckles. Those hypnotizing eyes. Then the most beautiful woman I'd ever seen in real life kissed me. Plush, pink lips covered mine in a soft caress that made my body tighten in intoxicating anticipation.

"Darlin," I huffed as I savoured her mouth with long, soft kisses. "You can kiss me any time you want."

Her answering hum was all I needed. Her hips ground into mine as she licked the seam of my mouth. I took hold of her jaw, moving my kisses to the space beneath her ear, my other hand fisted in the sleek fabric of her dress. She stilled. Sierra pulled away to gaze down at me as her hands braced on my shoulders, our chests so near to each other from heaving breaths.

"Touch me, Alden."

The plea was still fresh on her lips when she kissed me again. Her tongue tentatively moved into my mouth. Its warm slide against mine kept my blood rushing south as I relished the taste of her. Like pop and strawberries. Mixed with the flowers around us and her brown sugar rose scent, I could feel myself getting lightheaded. Sierra's body was all lush curves and muscle. My hands couldn't help but greedily covet every inch of her as they found their way to cupping her full, round ass. The muscles flexed and rolled from the way her hips made little seeking movements into mine.

It was my turn to pull away for a second. All I wanted was to get another look at her. Her olive cheeks were flushed with heat. Full lips swollen and rosy from our kisses. She was so beautiful. I couldn't resist her. She was a star and I was caught in her orbit. Without a second thought, my hand went to the buttons on the front of her dress and stopped. I wanted to see more of her. Touch more of her. Taste her.

"Can I?" I asked.

"I want you to," she rasped with a shallow nod, biting her lip as she watched me undo the top of her dress.

One tiny white button. Then another. A few more buttons and her breasts were exposed. Peaked from the chill in the air or her desire for me, I didn't care which. Not as she sat up on her knees to bring them closer to me. I still didn't care as I licked and sucked her pale brown nipples, especially when she softly whimpered as her hands fisted in my shirt. The sound was kindling to my need for her.

More. I wanted more of her. My blood pounded with it. Throbbed between my legs, aching with it. Needed it. Needed her. Pushing myself up with one hand, I let the other slide up between her legs. Except. Was she shaking?

"Are you alright, Sierra? We can stop."

"No. Don't," she breathed.

My hand continued moving toward her center, tracing the little scalloped edge of her panties. She was definitely shaking.

"I want to touch you here, Sierra," I groaned as I moved my tongue to her other breast, looking up to find her watching me.

"Do it. Please, Alden."

I wasn't ready. Not for one second. The little cotton underwear I'd bought for her, pictured taking off her, was already damp. Soaked, really. I let my fingers graze her over the fabric, where I knew she needed it. That sensitive bud was begging for it. She groaned. So responsive. Sucking and flicking her nipple with my tongue, I wondered what sounds she'd make if I gave that part the same attention.

Her face twisted as I increased the pressure, gliding over her center with firm sweeps of my fingers. Sierra tipped her head back, mouth open. I kissed the bare skin between her breasts. Her hips began pushing downward, seeking more of the friction I provided her.

"Come on, now. Let go. Take what you need."

If this was all I got, I would take it. She would be all I thought about every night I spent alone. Every time I had to sleep out under the stars, I'd keep myself warm with thoughts of this sunset and the sweet taste of her skin.

Then temptation took hold. Sierra's movements were growing faster. Her breath came more quickly as she kissed me. I wanted to slide the soaked cotton to the side and feel everything beneath. To know what she felt like. No. Not yet. This was enough. Eyes fixed on me as she flushed with color. Her breath was shaky. It wouldn't be long now.

"That's it, darlin'," I huffed between kisses. "Ride my hand."

She whimpered at the increased pressure of my fingers moving against her, her center flush with my lap as she ground into me. So sweet. Those noises tasted so fucking sweet on her tongue. As her head tipped back again, I moved my attention to her neck, licking and sucking the soft skin as she rode me harder. Her thighs tightened around me, hips franticly snapping against mine. It was all I could do to ignore my aching cock as I wondered what it would be like to feel her sweet squeeze around it.

"Alden, I'm..."

Surrounded by a wall of sunflowers, only I got the privilege of seeing this angel come undone. She and I were nose to nose as her mouth opened, eyebrows drawing together.

"Do it for me," I urged. "Come, gorgeous."

Green eyes went wide as the orgasm possessed her. I stole her scream and following whimpers as I took her mouth, plunging my tongue in to drink down her euphoria. Her pleasure took control as she shook and mewled in my hold, tongue thrashing with mine. Her hips continued moving against me as she finished.

Messy, loud, and fucking breathtaking.

When she finally stilled, a panicked expression crossed her features as she shoved me away. The hands that had been fisting my shirt buttoned the top of her dress as she closed her legs. My body immediately felt the loss of her heat, each nerve ending crying out for Sierra. I wanted more. Wanted to make her scream for me again. I moved toward her, eager to touch her. But she cringed away. My hand dangled between us as a pit opened in my stomach.

"What's wrong?" I asked.

"I'm sorry," she rushed out, straightening her hair. "I shouldn't've...That's never happened before."

My eyebrows shot up my forehead. She looked like she was shivering. I picked up my jacket and offered it to her. That panicked look softened as she pulled it on and skipped the buttons, choosing to wrap the jacket around herself instead.

"What hasn't?"

"That's never. Uh. No one has ever made me," she warbled. "Made me do that before."

Christ. What kind of guys has she been with? She'd told me about her first time, so I knew she wasn't a virgin. But never finishing with anyone before felt wrong in a different way. Irritation coated me in an oily sheen at the idea that any man had put himself before this beautiful creature.

"You've never had an orgasm before?" I asked, trying not to sound as surprised as I felt.

"No," she blushed. "I mean, yes, I have. I've just never had one with someone else around."

Regret and anger curled my hands into fists. This was so far from what I wanted her to feel. Hell, I didn't want her to be looking at me like a scared doe. Maybe this was going to be all she would give me, but I wasn't going to take this any further if she wasn't ready. Even if she would never be.

"Are you okay? Sassafras," I started, remembering the word we promised to use whenever we wanted the absolute truth.

"I'm fine, Alden," she rushed out. "Really."

It could have felt like a loss. Like a line I shouldn't have crossed. After this reaction, maybe she'd never let me touch her like that again. That was fine. Her discomfort with what had just happened was her business. Except she was beautiful when she came. Pink and green, like a field of sunflowers at sunset. She wanted me like I wanted her. Her body felt like sin and salvation rolled into one. All of it was incredible. That, I'd never regret.

Sierra's face was still pink as she finally looked me in the eye again. I silently thanked every deity known to man. Crawling toward her, I took her into my arms and rested my chin on her trembling shoulder.

"I'm sorry. I know that's not normal. I just...Can we go home?"

Her voice was small as she pulled away from me. She was embarrassed.

"Yeah," I sighed. "We can go home."

We packed up everything. The walk back to the truck was quiet. Sierra kept stealing glances at me. I couldn't say a word. After this morning, I knew how she felt. I just kept trying to imagine the kind of men she'd been with. None of them ever prioritized her. They didn't put her pleasure first. This morning was something else for me. An anomaly, even. I just couldn't imagine landing a girl like Sierra and not treating every part of her with the reverence she deserved. If given the chance, I'd do everything I could to make her come like that again. With the way she looked at me now, this might have been my only shot.

Still, as I opened her door, I couldn't help but smile a little. Not at what had just happened, though I couldn't imagine that I would forget the sight for as long as I lived. Nope. It was that she'd just called my house 'home.'

Seventeen

Sierra

I wanted to explode into ashes and rise like a phoenix from the embarrassment that was burning me alive from the inside. After all the times I'd been with other guys, which unfortunately hasn't been that many, I'd never come in front of a single one. Between Graham and the few guys who were ballsy enough to ask me out knowing who my father was, my small sampling of men seemed to all be completely inept when it came to satisfying a woman.

Alright, I faked it with them, so they thought they were getting me off. I'd seen porn. I knew what guys wanted to see and hear. Sometimes I just wanted it to end.

But that? I had absolutely no control over myself. As we rode back to the house, I wondered how he'd been able to make me feel that way so quickly when no one else had ever been close. Even when we were kissing, I could barely stand the touch of his hands on me without my pulse skyrocketing to a dangerous rhythm.

When I'd come by myself, it had never been like that. I lived with my parents, for god's sake. I wasn't exactly having screaming orgasms in my room. For someone like me, someone whose appearance was practically everything, losing control was a terrifying concept. What if I made a weird face? What if I made weird noises? I basically screamed into his mouth while I soaked his hand. I glanced at it again as he shifted the truck into gear. It flexed, long fingers fanning out around the shifter.

Alden had successfully wrung an orgasm from me more powerful than any of my toys at home. My mind temporarily wandered back to my bedroom in Chicago. Another small smoke bomb of embarrassment went off in me at the idea that some police officer could be going through my things, looking for some clue as to where I'd disappeared. Probably cataloging my small collection of vibrators. I really hoped my father's lawyer prevented that at least.

"You promise you're alright?" Alden asked, casting a sideways glance in my direction.

"Yeah," I lied.

The corded muscles in his forearm flickered as he flexed his fingers around the gearshift again. I pressed my knees together at the memory of what they felt like moving against me. Compared to Alden, the guys I'd been with before were pampered pets. Clueless and entitled. Between the things he did with his mouth and the way he played with my clit, it was like he knew exactly what I needed. It kept replaying in my mind, winding me up as my toes curled in my boots. He'd licked and sucked me. Kissed me. Gently coached me through riding his fingers.

"That's it, darlin'. Ride my hand."

Wanting someone this way felt foreign to me. Alden glanced my way again. His touch had awakened something in me. Before this, before him, I thought desire like that was pure fiction. That a connection like this wasn't real. I was wrong. After what had just happened and the thick length I'd felt grinding against my hand this morning, I wanted more.

When he looked at me again, I let my hand slip up my thigh to tug up my skirt. He tracked the movement out of the corner of his eye, his throat bobbing as he sighed through his nose. A hand flexed on the gearshift again. It was that movement that hit me with the truth. What we'd done had affected him, too. Primarily because this time it came with a shift of his hips in the truck's bench seat.

Alright, so, we were attracted to each other.

"Sierra," Alden rasped, glancing at me, but whatever he had to say died on his tongue.

We bounced as the truck started up the dirt road toward the house. My blood heated with anticipation. My stomach twisted. My fingers shook. I'd made a decision. When we got inside, all bets were off.

To hell with rule one.

If it took all the courage I could muster, I would tell Alden I wanted to keep going. To feel everything. Except, as the little red house came into view, we could see a beat-up red Toyota pickup parked in front of it.

"Shit," Alden muttered. "Eddie's here."

Icy realization that we would not be alone drowned any lingering flame, the shift so sudden that a chill went through me. Alden's movements became jerky and irritated as he parked the truck and walked to the other side to let me out.

"I'm sorry. He never gives me a warning," he groused.

"I remember," I chuckled, hopping out of the truck. "At least this time I'm wearing clothes."

Alden smirked, shaking his head while we climbed the steps. The front door creaked as it swung open. There he was, frosty blonde mullet pointing in every direction, sitting on the green sofa with a cup of noodles and no pants. I turned around quickly, but the pink pickle print underwear and cropped white Playboy tee shirt were instantly etched into my brain forever.

"Hey man," Eddie said with a slurp. "I need to crash for a while."

"Of course you do," Alden sighed at the ceiling. He rubbed a hand down his face. "Can you put some fucking pants on? There's a lady present."

"Foaling season, remember? Weaver called me." Eddie crooned as he set down his soup. I heard what sounded like a zipper and a jangling belt buckle. "I was crashing in town or I'd've been here yesterday. Apologies, Mrs.

Boone."

"It's fine," I shrugged. I'd been imagining shedding this dress and wrapping my legs around the broad-shouldered cowboy beside me, but sure, it was fine. He tapped me on the shoulder, giving me the all-clear. "How long are you staying with us?"

Eddie flopped back down onto the sofa and picked up the beer he'd been drinking. During my time in his home, I noticed Alden didn't drink much. He had a bottle of whiskey in the kitchen, but there was a layer of dust on it which suggested he rarely touched it. It may not even be his. Eddie had brought the stink of stale beer and body odor with him.

"With all the mares getting ready to drop, I'm thinkin' I'll be here for the next month at least. Maybe longer. Depends on how things go down. I'll probably stay on for chipping, too."

"Chipping?"

"We microchip the foals a couple weeks after they're born," Alden explained as he took his jacket off of me and hung it on the hook. "Let me get him set up on the sofa and we can go to bed."

He kissed the top of my head and approached the locked door beside the bedroom door that I had assumed was a closet. I tried to tamp down on my surprise at the casual affection as Alden whipped out a key and opened it. It was not a closet, but it might as well have been with all of the stuff that was in there. The small room was filled with boxes labeled with markers and a few pieces of furniture I couldn't quite make out. It wasn't disorganized so much as it was overstuffed.

"Are you a hoarder?"

Alden chuckled at my question as he dug around in a black rubber bin that had the word "camping" written on a piece of masking tape. He pulled out a pillow and a sleeping bag, tucked them under his arm, and walked out of the room. I lingered at the door, looking around at the boxes and boxes of things.

"This used to be Mr. Weaver's house when his dad was still alive," Eddie explained. "He and the Mrs. started out in this house. That used to be Junior's room. Then the old man's old man died, and he moved into the main house."

"Oh," I hummed.

"Most of this stuff is theirs," Alden explained, jerking his chin toward the storage room.

"Except for the books," I added.

"Except for the books," Alden smiled at me as he set the bedding on the sofa beside Eddie, then disappeared into the bedroom, but reappeared quickly as he tossed two more pillows at him. The bolster pillows from the bed.

When he returned to my side, he wrapped his arm around my shoulders and kissed the top of my head again. It was the second time in only a few minutes that he'd done that. Sure, we'd been all over each other, but this kind of casual touch wasn't exactly in my repertoire. Except now we had company. Eddie watched his friend squeeze me to his side as he took another sloppy bite of noodle soup.

"So," he slurped and chewed. "Tell me about yourself, Mrs. Boone."

"Uh," I stalled, trying for a polite smile. "There's not much to know."

"You know what, Eddie," Alden interrupted. "She's actually feeling pretty tired. We were going to get to bed."

Eddie chuckled as he sipped from his beer.

"Sure, buddy. Keep it down in there. I need my beauty sleep," he winked. "Good night, Mrs. Boone."

I huffed a laugh and went into the bedroom. Alden stayed behind, holding up his finger to indicate he'd be inside in just a minute. I took the opportunity to see to my needs in the bathroom and change into my pajamas. The door swung open while I was perched on the bed, braiding my hair. After what had to be almost two months away from home, it covered my breasts completely. It felt healthier and thicker, too.

"Sorry about him," Alden grunted, pulling his shirt over his head with one hand. He glanced at the hamper in the corner. "Do you mind if I sleep in my underwear? My pants are..."

He trailed off. His pants. Right. They were still dirty from this morning. For a second, I wanted to rewind our whole day and take advantage of being alone with him this morning. Because what I wanted now definitely wasn't going to be happening with his buddy sleeping on the other side of some very thin walls.

"It's fine," I shrugged.

"I'll stay on my side of the bed," he whispered with a wink. "Promise."

Alden unbuckled his belt and rolled the leather around his fist, his forearms flexing with the movement. Shifting his jeans down his thick thighs, I pretended to occupy myself with my hair again as I watched him from the corner of my eye. His boxers were blue and white striped. Bright against his tan skin. The tan skin shadowed by dark, curling hair on his chest trailing all the way down into those boxers. He adjusted himself and my stomach did one of those little flips with the motion. When the bed sunk with his weight, I looked over at him.

"You swear you're alright?" Alden asked as he propped himself up on an elbow.

Apparently, he wasn't going to be sleeping in a shirt, either. He absently drummed his fingers against his flat stomach, waiting for my answer. Right.

"Stop asking me that. I'm fine," I lied.

Someone kill me.

I shuffled under the covers even though my skin felt like it was on fire. I didn't need a blanket. I needed to swim with the penguins in the Southern Ocean.

Alden's hand slid to my waist beneath the sheets. Hazel eyes gazed down at me as he inched closer. A thumb began making idle circles over the tiny, lace-trimmed hem of my top. The lacey edge moving up and down with the touch, skin flicking against mine. Why did that small motion make my toes curl?

"So," he murmured. "I think we should keep things PG while Eddie is here."

My cheeks must have been so red because they felt like they were burning up. I wondered if he'd sensed the renewed direction of my thoughts. The list of rules that sat on the dresser. That first rule I wanted to strike out now that I'd had a taste of this new thing the cowboy beside me could make me feel. It was undeniable. A match had been struck. Fuse lit. Explosion imminent.

"Yeah," I released a frustrated sigh, trying to hide my disappointment. "This room isn't exactly soundproof, is it?"

"It ain't!" Eddie shouted.

Alden released a hearty chuckle, the sound warm in the waning evening light as his head angled toward the ceiling in exasperation. Then he rolled toward me, stubble grazing my cheek as he brought his lips to my ear. His voice became rough and low as he spoke, barely loud enough for me to hear.

"I can wait. If I'm the only man who's ever made you scream, I'm not sharing that sound with anyone. Your music is just for me."

I swallowed, barely able to stand his skin on mine as the rough pad of his thumb continued its idle strokes over my stomach. If I thought I had been attracted to other guys, I was dead wrong. This is what attraction felt like. His body felt so good, thick with muscle and a welcome weight even when it was barely touching me. Alden kissed the delicate skin beneath my ear, his breath warming the space as he spoke.

"I need to tell you something else," he whispered.

My skin pricked as the hairs on my neck rose. Alright, I was more than attracted to him. I needed him. With a sigh, I closed my eyes and decided this next month was going to be absolutely excruciating. Then Alden finished his thought, making things so much worse as his voice glided over my skin like the most expensive suede.

"You're so fucking pretty when you come."

Eighteen

Alden

Leaving a sleeping Sierra in my bed was bittersweet. I loved seeing her so comfortable in my bed. On our way back from the sunflower field, my mind raced with possibilities. Sure, I couldn't act on any of them, but I wasn't disappointed. Especially not as she drifted off, nuzzling into my shoulder as she held my arm against her. I'd take that over the pillow wall. The demolition of our very real barrier meant falling asleep with her scent right from the source. That I'd gladly take any day.

Sierra was already so different from the woman I'd met. When I first set eyes on the girl, it felt like I was looking at one of those models from social media. Airbrushed. Layers and layers of choices curated into an approximation of a picture-perfect, desirable woman.

Those things had started peeling away. The girl I saw underneath was thoughtful and sweet. Sierra's kindness and warmth made her tangible. Freckled and soft. I liked it. I liked her. I was still thinking about the freckle I noticed on the tip of her lip last night as I pulled the truck up to the barn.

Eddie was jabbering on about his latest conquest. The girl he'd been crashing with had had enough of him for the time being. The idea of anyone being attracted to the strangest man I'd ever known still baffled me, but women kept taking him home. He hopped out of the truck, tugging up his pants with one hand as he put on his hat with the other.

"So I told her you'd see her at her party."

"See who?"

Eddie chuckled, pulling a pack of Camels out of his pocket.

"Man, I knew you weren't listening. Natalie. I hooked up with her room-mate a few days ago. While I was on my way out the next morning, Nat invited us to a party at their house this weekend. I told her we'd be there."

My gut twisted.

"We?"

"What?" He shrugged as he stuffed a cigarette between his lips. "You said you told her you just wanted to be friends. This is friendly. It's a small town. You're going to have to see her, eventually. Rip off the Band-Aid, bro."

My breakfast went leaden in my gut as we entered the barn. A party at my ex-girlfriend's house sounded about as enticing as a kick to the head. How would I explain that to Sierra? Oh, Eddie accepted an invitation to a party at my ex-girlfriend's house on my behalf. Don't worry, we broke up three months ago. I hadn't told Natalie the reason before. I'd been ignoring her texts and calls for as long as we'd been apart. I sure as hell couldn't explain it to her now.

"I told her you were bringing someone."

"You what?" I seethed. She was on the run. *"People know me."* I couldn't put her in jeopardy for some party. Especially one that would have half the town on its guestlist.

"Oh, come on. It'll be fun. Sierra can meet new people, and you can show off your new little trophy wife to everyone," Eddie argued as he lit the cigarette between his lips. "This town is boring as shit without some drama."

"She's not a fucking trophy, Ed," I snarled.

Eddie shrugged as he made his way to his mount's stall, grabbing feed for the old boy as he passed me by. Annabel was waiting for me, as she always was. She anxiously mouthed for the apple I'd brought for her. As she chewed it down, I reached under my arm for the book. T.S. Eliot. Cracking it open at the page I'd marked off; I began.

I hadn't had a bad day in weeks. Not a single one since February. Today was the first. After spending all day trying to wrangle mares for the vet to give them their ultrasounds, some of them far less patient than others, I was spent. Eddie apologized for his intrusion by volunteering to make dinner at the house, so I had to drive the bastard to the grocery store before I got to go home.

While standing in the check-out aisle with a few extra things I thought Sierra might need, I realized I wasn't anxious to get home because I was tired or because it had been a long day. I wanted to get home to her. To see her smile. To take care of her. Taking care of others was a reflex for me. A habit learned after years of having to rely on myself and having others rely on me, too. But taking care of her didn't feel like something I was forced to do. I wanted to. More than all of that, I just wanted to be near her.

Eddie fired up the grill on my front porch upon our arrival and asked me to throw the frozen fries he bought into the oven. That guy knew he was skating on thin ice when he tossed me his signature shit-eating grin. I flipped him the bird as I walked in the door. His squeaky laugh followed me inside.

Poking my head around the living room and bedroom, I hunted for the woman I was dying to see. I slid off my boots and approached the kitchen. There she was. Sierra sat at the kitchen table with a notepad and pencil. Her hair was tied up in a messy knot on top of her head, dark tendrils twirling down to highlight her elegant neck. Tapping her toes along with the Fleetwood Mac song on the radio. She was wearing that blue dress again. It was quickly becoming one of my favorites.

"Hey."

Nothing, like she hadn't even heard me. I continued into the kitchen, telling myself I needed to start the fries. It was then that I noticed the book on the table beside her. The Hobbit. Her brows were drawn together in concentration, head tilted at an angle. I carefully set the grocery bag down on the counter, turned on the oven, and moved to look over her shoulder.

"What are you doing?"

Sierra jerked back in surprise. She hadn't heard me come in. Color rushed to her cheeks as she laid a hand over her work.

"Oh, nothing."

I looked at the paper she'd barely been able to cover, noticing a pretty decent rendering of the book's cover illustration.

"Did you trace that?"

Sierra's eyes lit up a little.

"No. I've been trying to pick it up again since I have time. I took some classes while I was at school."

She held up the notepad and flipped through the pages she'd folded back. The Sun Also Rises, the Great Gatsby, and the Hobbit. She'd even started on Frankenstein. There was so much detail. So much work.

"You drew all this?"

She laid the pad down on the table and shrugged.

"Yeah. It's nothing. But it's been giving me something to do."

With a glance over my shoulder, I realized the oven was ready for those fries. I pulled out a sheet pan and opened the bag onto it, then popped it in. Sierra picked up the pad, pencil, and book she'd been working from and set them on the windowsill. I kicked myself for not noticing this. Art. Art made her happy.

"Listen," I said as I stuffed my hands into my pockets.

"Hey, man. Can you bring those burgers out here?" Eddie called through the open front door.

I turned back to the groceries, getting out the beef patties he'd gotten and cracking the package open. When I turned around, she was gone. On quick feet, I brought the meat outside and went back inside. It didn't sit right.

"It's nothing."

"Sierra?" I called after her, knocking on the bedroom door as I entered.

The room was empty. Sierra stepped out of the bathroom, flipping the light off with one hand, a hairbrush in her hand. That long hair was down. Ignoring the urge to bury my face in it, I shut the door behind me and moved to sit at the foot of the bed. She leaned against the wall and began brushing, eyes on her hair.

"Do you want to go to a party this weekend?"

"A party?" Sierra chewed on her lip, sighing through her nose while considering my question. "I'm not sure that's a good idea. What if someone recognizes me?"

Sierra held some of her hair in one hand, brushing out the end with the other. She still wasn't looking at me. Why did that bother me so much?

"All these people care about are bull riders, barrel racers, and country singers. They won't know anything about you. It'll be fine."

And if anyone touches you, I'll beat their faces in.

"I don't know," she hesitated.

The sound of the brush going through Sierra's hair was doing something to my insides. This conversation was making my skin itch. Or maybe it was the fact that I was avoiding telling her where the party was. And who was throwing it.

Not going could be a good thing. If we could get Eddie out of the house for a night, that wouldn't be so bad. I could find my way back to where we'd left off. Because this feeling, wanting her without being able to do a damn thing about it, was rotten.

"Eddie told them we'd go. I wouldn't have accepted the invitation, so I can text them and tell them we're not coming."

I tried not to sound too delighted at the idea. Especially as I started picturing all of the things we could do with Eddie out of earshot. After making her come in that field, I wanted more. I wanted to taste her. The soft, supple skin on her thighs would feel so good against my ears. Sierra finally looked at me, green eyes weighing my expression for a long moment. She sighed at the ceiling, hands falling to her sides.

"If I weren't here, would you go to this party?"

She crossed her arms over her chest, brush in hand, as she awaited my answer.

"Probably," I confessed. I would go. I always went. Only because I was usually too polite to refuse.

"Then we're going."

I was going to kill Eddie.

Nineteen

Sierra

The last party I went to, the last one before everything happened, was at the Ritz. My father threw a massive spectacle for Enzo's twenty-seventh birthday complete with waiters in white coats and gold-plated flatware. Since he was a New Year's baby and was also basically the golden child of the family, my parents always made his birthdays a big deal.

This year the spectacle involved a troupe of French circus performers and a champagne tower. Both were my mother's ideas, of course. It was a black-tie affair. Also, my mother's idea. I spent the entire evening coordinating the event behind the scenes. She spent the whole time throwing back glass after glass of Bollinger. My father rubbed elbows with all of the business associates he made my mother invite. Enzo spent the whole night looking for the door. As he always did.

Eddie's truck was ahead of us, lighting the way to the house we were heading to. A party. I hadn't been to a party since that night. However, I had my doubts that this event would have flower arrangements and signature cocktails. Based on the fact that Eddie insisted on eating before we headed over, I didn't think they'd have passed hors d'oeuvres either.

I watched Alden out of the corner of my eye, picking at my nails as I tried not to stare and wondered if he realized how strange he was acting. Where he'd normally be warm and open, he was closed off and agitated. It almost seemed like he was nervous, which didn't make any sense. I had no idea what a guy of his size would have to be nervous about. Alden was bigger than any guy who ever worked for my father by a lot. He'd win in any fight he got into. He was even dressed differently.

Big hands squeezed the steering wheel as we pulled up to the house. Cars and trucks, mostly trucks, were parked all over the street in front of it. There were even a couple on the lawn. The little ranch-style house was bursting with people. People stood on the front lawn. People were milling around the gate that led into the backyard. They were all dressed fairly casually. Cowboy hats dotted the crowd.

Alden rounded the truck and opened my door, extending a hand to help me out. His face was tight with worry as his eyes raked over me. When I'd dressed, I worried I'd taken him too literally. Casual. He was wearing a pair of jeans and a grey henley under his shearling-lined coat with laced work boots instead of his usual pair, but instead of his dark brown cowboy hat, he wore the old white Broncos cap. It was backward, allowing the chestnut curls to peek out from the front. Oddly tempting, really. But not exactly fancy.

The light jeans and scoop neck white tee I had on were a far cry from the pale blue Amur gown I wore at the Ritz, but they were form-fitting enough for me to feel self-conscious. Everyone watched as Alden took me by the hand to lead me inside. My hair was in a loose braid, and I'd only used what little makeup I'd had in my clutch. I'd really tried my best to blend in and felt like I had succeeded. I didn't look much different from the other girls here. In fact, some of them were more done up than I was. So why did it feel like everyone was staring? Worst-case scenarios flashed through my mind.

Someone knows. One of them. They know who you are. This was such a bad idea. Go home. Go home. Go home.

Worry knotted in my throat, making it difficult to get down air. It was fine. Everything was fine. Alden wouldn't take me somewhere he thought I was going to get hurt. I squeezed Alden's hand as we worked our way through the dimly lit house, through the crowd, and into the small kitchen. He gave my hand a reassuring squeeze in return. Eddie had gone in ahead of us. We'd lost him in the mass of people, but I could already hear his boisterous laugh from wherever he'd disappeared.

"Hey, Boone!"

A guy in a black cowboy hat who was almost as big as Alden boomed as we arrived at the makeshift bar. The only light came from various neon beer signs sitting on top of the oak kitchen cabinets, illuminating the ice and sweating beer cans, all floating in containers of different sizes sitting on the white tile-covered counter. Alden lifted his hand in greeting, then let go of my hand to start looking around the containers for a drink. I stuffed them into my pockets and waited for him to introduce me. The guy in the black cowboy hat made his way around the counter and pulled Alden into a bear hug.

"It's been a while. Where've you been?"

"Oh I," Alden hesitated as he glanced at me. "I've been busy."

The guy in the hat looked at me expectantly, but Alden didn't say anything else. It was only then. Only at that moment that I realized I'd disrupted his life. A disturbance to his routine. I wasn't supposed to be here. This man had a life without me. Before I could wonder what that life looked like, the answer entered. A blonde girl with a too-white smile and pretty brown eyes ran up and threw her arms around Alden's waist. That tight expression remained, but there was an uncomfortable smile there.

"Hey, Natalie," Alden said warily.

She squeezed him and greeted him with a kiss on the cheek. Her hand remained on his waist, causing the hairs on the back of my neck to rise. It felt as if someone had taken one of those containers of ice and dumped it over my head. God, I should leave. I should hop in the truck and find my way home. How hard could driving a stick shift be, really?

"Hey, Boone. Have you been getting my texts? I was worried you wouldn't come. Eddie said you," she paused and looked at me, the broad smile turning into an edged blade in a way that made my stomach turn. Too many socialites had smiled at me like this before stabbing me in the back. This person didn't even know me. "He said you would be bringing someone. Is this her?"

Alden glanced at me and cleared his throat, brows furrowing. He was uncomfortable. I was uncomfortable. This was so uncomfortable. I let out a breath and forced an easy smile to my face. The blonde girl, Natalie, unwrapped herself from Alden and turned to face me. A few inches taller. She could probably take me in a fair fight. I held my hand out and tried for a friendly tone as I introduced myself.

"I'm Sierra," I shouted over the music.

"Sierra," she repeated as she took my hand, placing her other hand over her chest as she introduced herself as if I should already know her name, the smile gone from her face. "Natalie."

I glanced at Alden, who was watching us closely. Jaw tight. The people in the kitchen had gone quiet. They were watching us. It was then that I realized why this was weird. I understood exactly why everyone was staring at me. This wasn't just some girl's party. This was the party of someone who'd been with Alden. Recently.

Releasing Natalie's hand, that icy dread crawled through my veins like hoarfrost as I wondered if I'd interrupted a relationship already in progress. I had no right to feel ownership over him. He was helping me. Alden and I hadn't done much, but it was enough to break up a relationship. He'd seemed like a nice enough guy. He'd told me he was single. But maybe I didn't know him as well as I thought. Was he a cheater?

"When did you two meet?" She asked with that blade-like smile slicing through her face again, biting down on the last letter like she was a dog chomping through bone.

"About two months ago," Alden supplied.

Natalie snorted and picked up a beer from a nearby container. She cracked it open and slugged back a drink before placing her hand on Alden's chest.

The proprietary touch was getting under my skin. Just as it was meant to. He glanced down at the hand between his pecs and arched a brow at her.

The crowd watched carefully. Not Natalie. Me. They all watched me. Waited for a reaction. Well, they weren't going to get one. As far as they were concerned, I was just another city girl. Alden's new wife, if the power of Eddie's ability to gossip was to be believed. I reached into the nearest container and pulled out a canned margarita. Years of rubbing elbows with backbiting socialites had made my skin thick. Especially when I was never allowed more than two glasses of champagne at any event, so drinking my problems away wasn't an option.

Girls like Natalie always wore their emotions on their sleeve. All I had to do was wait. Everyone pretended to be occupied with other things, still watching the situation unfold. I popped the tab and took a sip, propping my hip on the counter.

Unbothered.

That wasn't what I felt. Not at all, but years of being forced to stuff down my feelings for the sake of others made me well-practiced at keeping things bottled up. Natalie gave me a pointed look, like I was the one who was intruding here, then returned her attention to Alden.

"Eddie told me the craziest thing. He's been telling everyone, but it can't be true," she laughed.

Natalie gave me another glance. A look of appraisal. By the set of her eyes, I'd come up short in some way. This woman was about as subtle as a flying brick. For a minute, I waited for Alden to say something. Defend the woman who was supposed to be his wife. His eyes softened sympathetically, but he remained silent. That gaze, the one I normally craved, made my stomach turn sour. I snorted and walked away. Fine. Let her throw herself at him.

The cold night air melted into my skin as I let myself out onto the little concrete patio behind the house. How my blood could feel so cold while my skin burned like this was a juxtaposition I couldn't explain. People were gathered around a large iron fire pit where a flame roared and popped over the music. Eddie was lounging in an Adirondack chair with a redhead in a printed Patagonia fleece perched in his lap, one boot propped up on the table.

"Hey, where's Boone at?" Eddie asked when he finally noticed me.

After setting my drink down on the table, I rubbed my hands over my arms, kicking myself for not stealing Alden's jacket. Inching closer to the fire, I held my hands out to warm them up.

"Inside talking to Natalie," I huffed. "Is she his girlfriend?"

Eddie snorted.

"Used to be. I was hoping she'd finally take the hint, but I guess not," he laughed with the redhead who rolled her eyes.

I huffed a frustrated sigh. I should definitely have taken the jacket.

"The hint?"

Eddie refocused his attention on me, puffing on the cigarette dangling from his fingers.

"She was always all over him. Constant calls and texts. Like flies on shit," he sighed and took a pull from his beer. "They broke up over three months ago. She just hasn't accepted it."

He tipped his hat up with a finger, looking at me with a secretive grin.

"I was hoping Boone's wife would set the girl straight."

"Boone's wife?" The redhead slurred, looking at Eddie with surprise. "Is she here?"

Eddie pointed at me with his cigarette between two fingers. The redhead looked at me with glazed blue eyes. Yeah, she was wasted.

"This is his wife, sweetheart. I told you about her. Mrs. Sierra Boone," he said with a wink at me.

The redhead made an "oh" noise that sounded like something from a sitcom. Alden had been right. Eddie wasn't much for keeping his mouth shut. He shifted in his seat, wrapping an arm around the redhead as he dropped the butt of his cigarette into his now-empty can of beer.

"I guess what I want to know is, are you going to do something about it or not?"

"I shouldn't have to do anything," I muttered. "No one should have to fight off other people for their partner."

Alden wasn't my husband in any real sense, but having to pry someone off of him still felt like a losing battle. If I had to fight for my husband, I didn't want him. Eddie shook his head, pushing the redhead off of his lap so he could stand up. His puffy orange coat was a strange choice with the pizza print button-down shirt he had on, but it sort of worked on him. Eddie approached, putting an arm around my shoulder.

"You're right. Except Boone already broke it off with her. He's too fucking nice. He never wants to hurt anyone's feelings. He won't let anything happen, but Natalie's like a dog with a bone when she wants something. Grew up wealthy. Daddy gave her everything."

Sounds familiar, I thought.

"She needs to hear the word 'no' from someone who isn't going to sugarcoat it."

"So, what am I supposed to do?"

Eddie leaned in, at almost the same height as Alden, he seemed to want to get down to my level. I couldn't tell if the look was patronizing or conspiratorial.

"Go force-feed that girl a taste of her own medicine."

I glanced at the glass sliding door, where I saw Alden still standing in the kitchen. Natalie was talking to him. His face said it all. Complete disinterest. But she looped an arm around his shoulder and started whispering into my cowboy's ear.

Eddie was right.

Alden was too damn nice. I could do him this favor because I didn't have to be. I didn't have to be nice. I didn't have to act like a lady. Not anymore. I picked up my drink and took several gulps from it, slamming it down on the table and shaking off the fact that I'd just thought of him as *my cowboy*.

"Fuck it."

Twenty

Alden

"We were barely broken up a month and you went and got married to some city girl?" Natalie barked. "She's just going to leave you when she gets bored with her little cowboy fantasy and you'll come running back to me."

This was exactly why I didn't want to come. Breaking up with Natalie hadn't been an impulsive decision. We'd dated for over three months. I'd wanted to break up with her for one of them. It was something that ate at me for weeks. I felt bad for dragging it out for as long as I did, so I tried to let her down easy. She was a beautiful woman. One of the most beautiful in town. And she had her sights set on me, whether I liked it or not. I liked it.

Until I didn't.

Natalie brought herself close to me. Close enough for me to smell the acrid scent of beer on her. The smell always made my stomach turn. Maybe because it reminded me of my parents. Her breath ghosted across my ear as she slurred, pressing herself into my side.

"Let's go to my room."

"No."

Fuck. I needed to find a way out of this. Where were her good-for-nothing brothers? I hated them as much as I hated the way she was stroking my chest but I'd do anything to make it stop right now, including dealing with them.

"Oh, come on. I bet I can still get you off," she said, hand fisting in my shirt. "Remember that time out at the springs?"

"I'm married, Natalie," I said through gritted teeth.

"I don't see a ring," she sing-songed. "You can't really be serious about her."

Her hand slid down my chest. Lower. Though it didn't reach her intended destination. Because it was intercepted by another hand as it hit my belt. Sierra's hand held Natalie's finger. Not her whole hand. Just a finger.

"Didn't anyone ever teach you to keep your hands to yourself?" Sierra sneered.

Natalie struggled, trying to free her finger from Sierra's hold. Natalie whimpered. Then Sierra's other hand snapped out until she had Natalie's face pinched in it like a vise. Though Natalie had at least four inches on her, Sierra's energy was ten feet tall. Green eyes flashed with ire as she spoke in a tone of voice I hadn't heard before. Icy and sharp.

"I know we don't know each other very well, but you should know I don't tolerate disrespect. Touch my husband again and I will break every bone in this finger. Actually, if you even think about coming near him again, I'll burn your fucking house to the ground. I'll find out where you work. I'll find out who your family is. All of it. I will ruin. Your. Life. Got it?"

Every consonant came out of her mouth with a snap, her words clear and cruel. She was fierce like this. Formidable. Natalie gave a small, jerky nod as she fought the iron grip on her chin.

"Good."

Sierra released Natalie's face and finger, pushing her away as she stepped into me. And then she kissed me. Sierra kissed me in front of everyone. This kiss was different. No tentative exploration. Nothing soft and sweet. It was dominating. Hungry. Almost as if I could taste the word *mine* on her tongue as it commanded my own.

Music dulled from the blood pounding in my ears. I felt dazed by it.

Wanted to take her home now and show her I was hers. Just hers. But when I looked down to take her in, I saw an expression I hadn't before. Brows drawn together. Mouth a tight line. Sierra was pissed. At me.

Two hours of ignoring me to talk to Eddie and three more canned margaritas later, Sierra was dancing through the front lawn on the way to my truck. Drunk people usually irritated me, but her terrible drunken two-step was sort of charming. I opened the door for her to get in. She'd demanded my jacket an hour ago. As she hopped into the truck, my scent and hers wafted past me. I bit down on a smile as I drank it in. Eddie slapped me on the back, bringing me out of my stupor.

"I'll see you back at the house in a little while."

"You're not staying behind? I thought you had something going on with the roommate."

Eddie shrugged, then sneered.

"I don't sleep with drunk girls. I'm going to make sure she's alright, then I'll see you in a little bit."

I nodded. Sierra pulled the door closed, slurring a complaint about it being too cold. I couldn't help but laugh. With the drive back to the house being as long as it was, I figured she'd be falling asleep soon. Maybe I should have grabbed a bag or something for her to throw up in. I'd never seen her drunk before and who knows. She might not be able to handle her liquor. Eddie made to turn away but pivoted on his heel to take my shoulder in his hand.

"Don't do that shit anymore," he ordered.

My rodeo hippie best friend had never looked more serious. Jaw hard, eyebrows flat. I was in trouble. I was also confused.

"What shit?"

"The nice guy shit," Eddie grunted. "You made a mistake with Natalie."

"I broke up with her months ago, Ed. We're done."

Eddie shook his head.

"That's not what I mean. You can't make everyone happy. For someone like her that means the door is open. You might think you're being kind by not flat-out rejecting someone, but rejection is kinder. When you're nice, they think they have a chance. That's worse."

"Why did you have me come here tonight?"

Eddie gave me a hard look, then pointed at the truck and the woman inside who was already nodding off against the window.

"Because you needed to see what being nice gets you. You got lucky. That girl is tougher than she looks. But your woman shouldn't have to fight your battles for you."

With that, he headed back into the house. As I circled the truck and hopped inside, I was forced to wonder when my friend had gotten smarter than me. Sierra curled up in her seat and let her head rest against the door. The drive back to my house was quiet except for the sound of her puffing breaths.

"No."

The syllable was so small and sad as it fell from her sleeping lips. I could look a bear in the eye. I could chase off coyotes or ride an unbroken horse, but I couldn't tell a girl *no*. One look at the peacefully sleeping girl had me deciding she'd never have to fight for me. She deserved a man with a backbone. It was time for me to grow one.

Sierra was still sleeping when I carried her into the house. Small, grumbled protests were warming my neck as I toed open the front door. With a few short steps, I placed her on the bed.

"Come on, darlin'," I murmured. "Let's get these clothes off so you can go to sleep."

Big green eyes blinked wearily as she looked at me. A little smile tugged at her lips. Here and gone in an instant. I was still grateful for it. She hadn't slept off the booze yet, but she'd at least slept off being mad at me. With a couple of jerky movements, Sierra shrugged off my jacket and handed it back to me as she yawned. I stood to hang it up, then came back into the room to find her sitting there in her bra. She laid back on the bed and began unbuttoning her jeans. I went into the bathroom to get a washcloth for her face as I looked around for her pajamas.

"Alden," she murmured. "Sassafras."

"Sassafras?" I echoed, still looking for those damn pajamas.

"Rule number three," Sierra slurred. "I have a question. You have to tell me the truth."

"Shoot."

I emerged from the bathroom and handed her the damp washcloth, then hunted around the bedroom. The pajamas weren't on the dresser. Or in the hamper. I looked at the bed again, this time finding Sierra in nothing but her bra and panties.

Someone up there hates me.

She tossed the bra well enough for it to land atop the dresser. I would have been impressed if I wasn't completely distracted by the most gorgeous breasts I'd ever had in my mouth. Strike me down with lightning and kill me where I stand. Sierra sat up on her knees and pulled something out from under her. The pajamas.

As she stood up and wobbled, I quickly took her side. She gave me a grateful little smile as she pulled the little blue shorts up. The top remained on the bed. I grabbed it and handed it to her, internally begging her to put it on and put me out of my misery. This had to be some kind of divine punishment for tonight. I was sure of it. Her question was muffled as she pulled it over her head.

"What?"

Sierra let out a frustrated huff and flopped down onto the bed, kicking the covers with a little grunt so she could crawl underneath them. Glassy green eyes looked up at me as she rolled to her belly and hugged the pillow beneath her.

"I said, why did you and Natalie break up?"

I squatted to meet her eye, pushing dark brown strands off her forehead. Alright. Sierra might not remember this conversation in the morning, but I could tell her. She'd asked for the absolute truth, so I'd give it to her.

"I broke up with Natalie because I didn't love her. We had a good time together, but she wasn't the one for me and I knew she never would be. It didn't feel right to waste her time."

"Why?" Sierra yawned.

My thumb skimmed her cheek. She was blinking slowly. The truth of it was right in front of me. I knew in my gut why Natalie wasn't the one for me.

"Sometimes things have to end in order to make way for something better."

She nodded, humming at my answer as the weight of her eyelids finally became too much. My hand made lazy strokes over her head as I watched her fall asleep. Once Sierra was talking in her sleep again, this time saying the word "pistachio," I stood and went to the kitchen for a glass of water. When I came back, I placed it on the nightstand beside her.

Ending things with Natalie had been tough. I felt awful about breaking her heart. Watching her cry after telling her how I felt had been one of the hardest things I'd ever done. But as I climbed into bed beside Sierra, I began to understand that I'd made the right decision at exactly the right time.

Twenty-One
Sierra

Alden's side of the bed was empty. Again. Neatly made, as always.

With a week having passed since Natalie's party, things had been fairly quiet around here. Lonely, if I was being honest. I was at the house, fending for myself while Alden and Eddie were at the ranch. The horses at Evergreen Springs were starting to give birth to their babies, which was supposedly timed with the ideal season for feeding strong offspring. Except, as Alden explained it to me, it wasn't all the horses on the ranch. Just a few. And for some reason, they tended to go into labor at night. This was the first birthing season for most of them, which meant they were basically being constantly monitored for health and safety.

Which left me alone. A lot.

With even more hours by myself than before, I had started to get cabin fever. Then I started to take walks around the property, going as far as I could while still being able to see the house. Every day my path got a little bit wider. A little bit further away. I found a trail that wandered along a creek and began to follow it. Each day I was shaded by pine, aspen, and oak trees as I wondered what was next for me. No matter how far I walked, I always arrived at the same conclusion.

I had nothing.

Nothing but a ranch foreman who was kind enough to open his home to me. To give me what little he had. He offered me kindness. This stranger opened his home to me and made me feel like it was my home, too. I didn't know how badly I wanted it. This absence of responsibility. This freedom to explore my own thoughts. This peace where before there was none.

I'd gotten used to Alden coming home at dusk and sharing meals with him. I'd even gotten used to having a mullet-bearing weirdo best friend around on nights they got home early enough to eat with me. Except it was often well into the night by the time I saw either of them. Apparently, it wasn't uncommon for horses to experience false labor, which was entirely new information to me. With almost no time alone together, Alden and I had gotten used to just existing in quiet stolen moments. A shared smile. Short conversations before falling asleep. A quick kiss before nuzzling into his shoulder, even though doing so made my skin ache.

On nights I fell asleep alone, I'd wake in the middle of the night to find Alden curled around me. His breath was a soft, even warmth against my neck as a heavily muscled arm held me against him. That part was my favorite. Last night I woke as Alden was crawling into bed. I had slept through his usual post-work shower. The fresh scent of his clean skin enveloped me as I backed into his warmth. I could still hear the midnight rasp in his voice as I stretched in the morning sunlight.

"I've been thinkin' about you all day."

Pulling his pillow toward me, I noticed a yellow folded-up paper resting on top. This looked like it had come from a sticky notepad somewhere. The paper stuck together. Definitely a sticky note. I peeled it open and read the message.

Birthday party for Mr. Weaver at the main house tonight. I'll pick you up at 5.

The note had a little heart doodled at the top. That little heart made the one in my chest give a small squeeze and my fingertips tingle.

That night at the opera, I'd been resigned to an existence devoid of connection. Wife of a man who would eventually be the boss of his family. It was all I was ever supposed to be. An asset to be traded for power. Property. A thing to be owned. I never allowed myself to dream of more because I never thought it was an option and dreaming had a way of making the soul ache. It was a useless pastime. I thought I would never get anything else, so why set myself up for heartache?

I set the note on my nightstand and got out of bed.

Every relationship I'd been in was designed to fail. With the guys I'd dated, if you could call it dating, I knew it was never going to work out. They were temporary. Just guys I'd spent time with. Graham and the others. They didn't mean anything to me. I was starting to wonder if they treated me the way they did because they felt that from me. Or if I picked them because I knew what kind of men they were. I knew I didn't mean anything to them and they would never ask for more. Neither option painted them, or me, in a very forgiving light.

I had been experiencing life on borrowed time. Every party I attended without my mother's knowledge. Every date. These were just a few of the handful of experiences I could steal for myself. The further away I got from that life, the more I realized that I didn't care about them at all. My hand was reserved, which meant no relationship could ever have a future. I locked away my heart and kept memories for myself like souvenirs. My first kiss. My first time. My first everything. When those men looked at me, they saw a spoiled princess. A socialite conquest. Never anything more.

That life scattered like ashes on the wind. I wasn't a prop in someone else's scheme anymore. Every day I heard my mother's voice a little bit less. Felt that pressure less and less because I wasn't anything to anyone. It was terrifying, but it was also liberating. Without my parents watching me constantly, I was free to fail. Free to relax without their expectations weighing me down. Without all of that, I was coming to know an entirely new feeling. I could dream. I could let myself imagine things for my life. There was no one here to tell me I was being selfish. No one to tell me I owed anything to the family because that obligation didn't exist anymore. I'd built a wall around my heart so high no man could ever climb it.

But it was starting to crumble. With every stolen kiss. Every night I spent in Alden's arms. It tumbled away, brick by brick. Without being required to marry for political gain, I was allowed to let myself feel. To free my imprisoned heart from its protective barrier. And for the first time in my life, I, well, *wanted*.

By the time I heard Alden's truck coming up the road, I was ready. Boots on. Pink dress on. Hair half up with a few loose tendrils, the best I could manage with what I had. I even put on a little blush and mascara. I went outside to meet him on the porch, trying to stuff down the excitement of seeing him in daylight. Alden was already showered and wearing clean clothes. A pale denim shirt and dark blue jeans with his normal brown boots and hat, a few of his chestnut locks catching the remaining light like little curls of wheat in the sun just shy of his shoulders. He looked up to see me waiting for him and smiled that brilliant smile that made my insides go wobbly. Hazel eyes flashed with appreciation as he feigned a pained expression and put a hand over his heart.

"Well, well, well. You're breathtaking, Mrs. Boone."

"You'd be proud of me. There weren't any chores to do around the house, so I did nothing," I blurted, ignoring how the way he was looking at me caused my stomach to feel like a shaken-up soda bottle.

"Nothing?" He feigned surprise, lifting his eyebrows like I'd just told him the most interesting thing in the world.

"Yup. Nothing."

I bit down on my smile as Alden took two steps up the stairs. Meeting him halfway, he reached out to tug me into his broad chest. I nuzzled my nose into his and softly kissed his lips. His hands fisted in my dress as he pulled me closer, huffing into my mouth as he deepened the kiss in a way that made my toes curl.

"I feel like I never see you anymore," I breathed.

"I know. I'm sorry you're stranded here," Alden sighed deeply as he rested his forehead against mine. "Are you sure you don't want to go bail out your car from the tow lot? You can drive around town. You won't be stuck here."

He leaned back a little to look me in the eye. We'd already discussed this several times since Alden discovered my father's car was no longer by the side of the road, having been towed to the impound lot.

"No," I sighed. "It's better if I don't use it. I told you if anyone working for the Serpas knows I'm here, it'll only be a matter of time before they find me. Someone could get hurt."

Alden stiffened against me, staring down at me with a strained look.

"Alright," he huffed, planting a kiss on my cheek before backing away to take my hand. That roguish grin washed away his more serious expression as he winked at me. "Your chariot awaits, gorgeous."

If Alden's house was Mr. Weaver's old love nest, then the main house was a whole coop. Alden hadn't exaggerated when he told me how close the ranch actually was to drive to, just a short trip around a larger hill and up a long dirt road that connected the two homes. With so much land, forest, and that hill between them, you'd never know the other property was there. Nestled up against the forest-covered mountains, the big blue house had creamy white shutters on the upper and lower windows and a wrap-around front porch with thick wood pillars that looked brand new. There was a gigantic white barn with a blue 'E' painted on it and big steel outbuildings scattered around that I couldn't quite identify. All of it looked well cared for. As Alden escorted me into the house, I glanced at him, knowing that he spent much of his time doing the work to keep this place in good shape.

"Smart men take care of the things that matter to them," my father had once told my brother and me.

While it was clear Alden took care of his home, it was also clear that his boss used what he had to take care of this ranch. Everything was either new or treated so well that it was as good as new.

Alden removed his hat as we entered the house, extending an elbow for me to take after he hung his hat and led me toward the dining room. Mr. Weaver and his son stood around a walnut dining table large enough to seat twelve people. A very large round iron chandelier hung from the ceiling to light up the space. Eddie and the redhead I'd seen at Natalie's party were standing on the other side of the table, ready to take their seats in simple but finely upholstered navy velvet chairs that complimented the large room's blue striped wallpaper. Some people I'd never seen before were waiting to take their place. A few of them had fiery red hair and freckles like Junior. All of them looked like ranchers. Probably the other hands. It was a full house tonight.

This might be a mistake. I squeezed Alden's arm. He leaned down to whisper into my ear.

"Don't worry, darlin'. These people are family."

"Mrs. Boone! Thank you for coming," Mr. Weaver said as he extended a hand in greeting.

I shook it gladly, taking the opportunity to give him a small kiss on the cheek. The old man was so kind, it was hard not to relax a little around him. Mr. Weaver blinked in surprise and chuckled as he glanced at his son, gesturing for him to join us.

"You remember Junior?"

"Of course, I do. It's nice to see you again, Sam."

The freckled teen gave me a kind smile while he shook my hand and returned my sentiment. Lifting a mason jar filled with lemonade, he arched a ginger red brow at me. Did none of these people own drinking glasses?

"Can I get you anything to drink, ma'am?"

I nodded and thanked him. Sam Jr. left the room as Alden shook his father's hand.

"Why don't you go help him out, Boone? I'd love to get to know the Mrs. better," Mr. Weaver said with a jerk of the chin toward the door his son had disappeared through.

"Don't try to steal her away from me now," Alden offered, kissing my temple before releasing me from his hold.

"There's no danger of that, I'm sure."

I watched him as he left to go help Sam Jr. in the kitchen, disappearing behind the swinging door. I turned to see Mr. Weaver watching me with a pleasant smile turning up the corners of his mustache. With a hand on my back, he guided me away from the dining room. This conversation seemed to be just for us.

"Boone knows this place as well as I do," Mr. Weaver offered as a means of explanation. "I guess he knows better than any of the other hands since this used to be his home."

At what must have been a look of surprise on my face, he hesitated. Whatever he was about to say was about Alden, not about me. I'd never met anyone's parents before, and I knew this man wasn't his father, but I had the strange urge to seek his approval. As soon as he deemed us far enough away from the others, the old man used his hand to smooth his grey mustache and went on.

"Boone has been working for me since he was sixteen years old. I'm sure he told you that. Did he tell you he used to sleep in the bedroom right down that hall?" he asked, pointing toward a hallway lined with photos. "Right up until he graduated from high school."

"He did?" I asked in an equally quiet voice.

The old man nodded. We stood there, and though I wasn't sure if he had guided me here to talk privately or examine Alden's old stomping grounds, I found myself looking at all of the framed photos on the wall. One of Junior holding up the biggest fish I'd ever seen with a braces-covered grin on his face. Another of him and his father standing shoulder to shoulder at his graduation with a little red-headed woman standing on the other side. And one of Alden, so much younger than he was now. His arms still packed with thick muscle, but his face was bare of stubble. His hair was short. He must have been a teenager. But there he was, sitting on the hay-covered ground with a foal in his lap and a bottle in his hand, smiling that sunshine smile at the little brown and white horse. Warmth flooded me at the sight. At the knowledge that he'd always been like this. Kind. Caring.

"He was a good boy then. He's a good man now," the old man said, noting the direction of my gaze.

"Why do I feel like you had a lot to do with that?" I said, finally breaking the hold the photo had on me to see the old man studying my face.

Mr. Weaver smiled at my implied compliment, though he immediately disagreed with me.

"Nah. He was a good kid. Took care of his parents better than they ever took care of him. His daddy and I were friends growing up. He used to work for me, so I've known Boone since he was a baby. That boy has always been a good one."

When I looked at Mr. Weaver, I could see that his pale blue eyes were lined with tears. He examined the photo that had caught my attention before he cleared his throat. I let my hand rest on his shoulder, giving it a gentle pat. This man cared about Alden. That much was perfectly clear. He cared more about him than my parents had cared about me. He only wanted happiness for him. Evergreen Springs wasn't just the place where Alden worked. These people really were his home.

Mr. Weaver gave me a warm smile and escorted me back to the dining room as the kitchen door swung open, his attention shifted to Junior and my cowboy. There was so much kindness in his eyes. His affectionate gaze was not just for his son, but for the man I'd come with. Alden was family to him too. Guilt dropped in my gut like a stone. I didn't want to lie to him about us. Or about why I was here. He was being kind to me because he thought I was Alden's wife and family by extension. The old man rushed out his last statement before Alden was within earshot again.

"You take care of my boy."

Alden approached with a glass of lemonade in each hand, extending one to me. Mr. Weaver gave him a polite nod and thanked us again for coming, then excused himself to check on dinner.

"What were y'all talking about?"

"He's feeling protective of you," I smiled, following him back to the table. Alden pulled out my chair. "He told me you used to live here."

"Yep," he huffed, his shoulders stiffening with the word.

Alden gave me a tight smile as I looked up at him while taking the seat he pulled out for me. Between his strained smile and Mr. Weaver's words, I was reminded that we'd only met a little over two months ago. There were still countless ways in which this man was a stranger to me. Sure, he wasn't around much these days, but I now understood that the cowboy I was spending time with hadn't shared much of himself with me. That was fine. He didn't owe that to me. I was just living with him. Even if curiosity about what had happened to his parents gnawed at me.

"They weren't what you would call good people."

"I hope everyone's hungry," Mr. Weaver boomed as he reentered the room, causing me to jolt a little. "We've got ribs, sausages, and all the fixings."

Platters of food came out on the arms of Junior and the man I assumed was the cook in charge, based on his apron. The man looked to be a relative of some kind based on how closely he resembled Mr. Weaver and Junior.

"That's Sawyer," Alden said, noting the way I watched them. "He's Mr. Weaver's nephew on his brother's side."

"Mr. Weaver has a brother?" I asked.

"Used to. Died a long time ago. Mr. Weaver is still close with his mom."

Alden pulled out my chair and then sat down beside me. Had anyone ever pulled out my chair before? Everyone was laughing and talking with each other as they took their seats around the table. The Weavers set themselves across from us. Alden took the napkin off of my plate and set it down in my lap, as Eddie started carrying on about a horse that had apparently been trying to buck Alden off a few days ago.

"That bronc wanted nothing to do with you," Eddie laughed, having seated himself on the other side of me. "You're lucky you're gigantic. She shook you like you were a can of paint in a damn paint mixer."

"Watch your language at my table, Eddie," Mr. Weaver said, tone exhausted like he'd told him that a hundred times.

"Sorry, Mr. Weaver."

The old rancher laughed, eyes crinkling at the bronzed corners as he speared a sausage onto his plate.

"Fuckin' cowboys."

Alden snorted as he picked up my plate and jerked his chin toward the food in front of us, silently asking me what I'd like for him to serve me. That was the other thing I'd been getting used to. There was no one here to watch my calories. No one was here to shame me for eating anything other than lean proteins and greens. God, if I so much as touched a carbohydrate in front of my mother I got long looks in public and a long talking to in private. It wasn't until I'd been here, being fed by this cowboy that I realized I'd spent so much of my existence in a constant state of hunger.

So, without anyone here to tell me not to eat the macaroni or the corn-bread dripping in honey butter, I knew my answer.

"I want to try everything."

Twenty-Two

Alden

Sierra was quiet on the drive home. Every now and then, she would steal a glance in my direction. As though she was trying to work something out.

Dinner had been a peaceful affair. With everyone curious about my new wife, she gracefully fielded several questions I wasn't prepared to answer. She seemed happy to talk with them as she enjoyed her food in that practiced fancy way of hers, even if she kept looking at me for reassurance. I nodded along. Only she could decide what to reveal. So she told them she was from Illinois. Went to college. Studied art. The basics. All of it true, as far as I knew.

I worried maybe I missed something. Maybe a question had made her uncomfortable and I hadn't caught on. I would have thought being cooped up on her own would make her anxious to talk to people. The opposite was true. As soon as we were back in the truck, her body relaxed. Still, her silence was making my skin feel two sizes too small. My headlights had just illuminated the road home when I finally had enough.

"Something on your mind?" I prodded.

She took a long while to answer me. So long I wondered if she'd heard me and prepared to ask again. Then she spoke.

"Mr. Weaver said you moved in with him when you were a teenager. And you said before that your parents were gone. What happened to them?"

My gut twisted. She'd laid everything bare for me. Told me all about the strange world she came from. This was something I should tell her. Everyone in town knew about my parents because their deaths had been all over the news when it happened. I hadn't had to explain this to people. They knew what kind of upbringing I had. Knew about my father. So I got looks of pity until I was a man. Then people mostly forgot about it. I pulled the truck off the road, angling us toward a copse of trees. I couldn't stand another look of pity. Especially from her. I didn't want this to change the way she looked at me, either. For a heartbeat, anger at my father flared. That even after all these years, his actions could mess something up for me. Opening my mouth to speak felt like nearing the edge of a cliff. If I told her this, there was no turning back.

Sierra reached out a hand, slowly placing it on my wrist. Her thumb brushed over my skin, trying and failing to ease my growing discomfort. I pulled away, grabbing the steering wheel as I focused myself. I needed to do this. I could tell her this.

"My dad, well. He and my mother weren't the most reliable people. Spent most of their days and our money drinking. My mom worked as a cashier at the market and my dad worked for Mr. Weaver. I think the old man gave him a job as a hand because they'd grown up together. My mom got fired for missing work one too many times. Then we only had my dad's pay to live off of. One day my dad wasn't paying attention to where he was riding and caused an accident that resulted in one of Mr. Weaver's prize mares to be put down. He let him go for his negligence."

I stole a look at Sierra. The dim dashboard light was enough for me to see her neutral expression. Not judging. Just turned toward me in the bench seat, hands folded in her lap, head angled to one side. Listening. I went on.

"That was when I was still in elementary school. They stayed home and did god knows what while I was at school all day. Ignored me when I was home.

It went on like that for years until I was in high school. I'd just turned sixteen and I got called to the principal's office. They informed me that our home burned down. My folks were asleep in the trailer when it went up around them. Mr. Weaver picked me up from school that day. He took me home. To his home. I lived with him and Mrs. Weaver, working on the ranch to earn my keep until I graduated from high school."

Sierra's eyes softened as her hand extended to me again. This time coming to rest on my thigh.

"Alden."

"I don't need you to feel sorry for me," I barked, shaking her off.

I regretted the words as soon as they came out of my mouth. Hurt clouded those eyes as her lips pulled down in a little frown. Sierra drew back a little, looking away from me. Her hand darted up to her face, trying to hide her tears. My reaction made her cry. I am such an unbelievable asshole.

"I don't feel sorry for you," she snapped. "I don't. It's just that."

A tear rolled down her cheek. I reached for her, taking her hand in mine. She fixed her gaze on our joined hands and let out a sigh, her tone softening as she spoke.

"I lost my family, too. I've only been able to survive it because of you. You gave me a safe place to land. You took care of me. I'm just glad that you had someone to take care of you then."

I lifted her hand to my mouth, kissing her knuckles before pulling her across the bench seat into my side. Sierra shifted, looking into my eyes as she brought her lips to mine, full and warm. One soft kiss. Then another as she sucked my lower lip just a little. Her breath warmed my mouth as she spoke.

"Thank you for taking care of me."

It wasn't temptation or need that made me kiss her. Whether she wanted to admit it or not, this woman cared about me. She cared about me before she even knew me. Coupled with the way my body craved her, it was fucking intoxicating. I took hold of her chin, curling my fingers beneath it as I dusted a thumb over her lips.

"I like taking care of you, darlin'."

A faint smile brightened her eyes as I brought my mouth to hers. Sierra welcomed my kiss, opening for me so I could caress her tongue with my own. My hand moved from her chin to cup her jaw, angling her head to take the kiss deeper. Her whimper alone would have been enough to heat my blood, but it was the hand that now feathered dangerously high up my thigh that sped up my pulse.

"We're alone, Alden," she said, her voice a soft purr as she peppered my jaw with more kisses, rubbing a hand over my thickening cock.

"As much as I want to, I'm not fucking you here," I laughed with a strained groan.

"I want to care for you now."

The hand that worked me lifted away, moving to join her other hand at my belt. My erection strained against my jeans because fuck, was she saying what I thought she was saying? Another kiss, this time to my ear before she gave the lobe a little flick with her tongue. My cock twitched in response.

"Sierra," I warned. "Someone will see."

"Who? The house is around the corner and Eddie left before us," she laughed gently as she tucked her knees under herself. Sierra tucked her hair behind her ears and looked at me with what seemed like nervous excitement. "Please, Alden. I don't have a lot of practice at this. Tell me if I do something you don't like."

"You don't have to do this," I breathed as she worked to unbutton my jeans and shift my clothes away from where she pushed them. First my jeans. My skin ached as I anticipated her touch.

"I know," she hummed, leaning forward to kissed me again. "But I want to. Let me make you feel good."

Sierra pulled my cock free from my jeans, her fingers barely able to wrap around me. Fire licked down my spine at the feel of her skin on my shaft. Fuck, how many times had I imagined exactly this? Her eyes went wide as they took me in. As she licked her lips, she gave it a firm stroke, prompting my hips to move with the motion.

"Alden," she croaked. "Wow."

I laughed and brushed a hand along the curve of her jaw.

"You don't have to do this. I know it's a lot," I choked on my words as her hand gave me another hard stroke and shifted her weight forward. My thoughts fizzled away into nothing as she followed her motion with a wide, flat lick over my moisture-laden crown. Conversation over.

I gathered her hair in my hand so I could watch as she took her time licking, sucking, and testing my responses. She began pumping me with her hand, barely able to hold me, and took me into her mouth. My hips pitched forward with the movement. Warm and wet, her tongue slid up my shaft, eyes on me.

"Sierra," I huffed.

She smiled a little and continued, taking me into her mouth. Deeper and deeper, she took me until I could feel myself hitting the back of her throat. We could have been there for five minutes or an hour. I wouldn't have been able to tell you. Every second was pure paradise. My hips arced off the seat as she worked her mouth and hand in tandem. I wasn't sure where she'd gotten the idea that she'd been bad at this, but she was dead wrong. People could probably hear my pathetic shivering, gasping moans a mile away. Looking to the roof of the truck, I bit down hard on my fist as I begged myself to find some self control because I was going to black out from this.

"Fu-fuck," I gritted out, squeezing my eyes shut to pull myself together.

There had been so many times I'd pumped myself in the shower these weeks thinking about some version of this. My hand stood in for Sierra's mouth. Those beautiful eyes staring up at me as I filled it. Every time, she begged me for more. Every time, I'd come hard enough to lose my breath a little.

As my eyes reconnected with hers, I decided the reality was so much better.

Those soft lips were making my toes curl as tears streaked out of Sierra's bewitching eyes while she looked up at me. Tension coiled low in my spine as

I felt release barreling toward me. My fingers twisted in her hair and I thrust into her mouth as my groin tightened, grateful that no one could hear us out here for all the wailing I was doing. Her answering hums were all the encouragement I needed.

"Sierra, I'm about to," I groaned.

She let out a noise that sounded like surprise as I felt myself spill down her throat. My hands went to both sides of her head, stroking her face as I pumped myself through an orgasm that felt like it lasted forever. Throwing myself back against the seat with a grunt, I looked down at Sierra with worry. Then she began sliding off me, her cheeks hollowed out, giving me one last hard suck before licking up the last of my spend. I cursed at the contact.

Sierra laughed a little as she took in my face, wiping her hand over her lips.

"Are you going to be alright to drive?"

"I may need to scrape the pieces of my mind back together first, darlin'. That was," I sighed, unable to think of a word for how she'd made me feel.

With a few quick adjustments, I tucked myself back into my jeans and buttoned up. Sierra flipped down the vanity mirror and ran two fingers under her eyes, getting rid of the little black smudges caused by her tears.

"Thank you," she smirked.

"Why on earth are you thanking me for that?" I laughed breathlessly as I started up the truck.

"No," Sierra said, taking her hair down. "Thank you for telling me everything. And for letting me take care of you."

She looked at me, eyes soft with gratitude. I smiled at her, enjoying the scent that released while she finger-combed her hair. This woman. I couldn't help but reach over and run a thumb over her full lips, grateful for the clear mind they'd given me.

Twenty-Three
Sierra

Alden didn't have any proper sketchbooks or anything around, so I'd taken ownership over an abandoned spiral notebook and some pencils that I had to sharpen with a pocket knife I found in a junk drawer. That wasn't something I'd done since the basic drawing course I took for an extracurricular in college, but I liked it. In a weird way, it almost legitimized the whole affair for me. I wasn't just doodling in a notebook. I was studying the craft. Well, sort of.

I was not going to think about Alden. After working out this morning did nothing to quell the energy coursing under my skin, I'd decided I needed to focus on something else. So I came out here. *Do not think about Alden.* No. Under the old oak tree, I nestled down onto the blanket I'd spread out and got comfortable in my little nook between two large roots. A fuzzy little bumble bee wandered into my eyeline, making itself comfortable inside a bloom on a spray of pale blue larkspur. Fine. A bee.

That fuzzy little bee was enough to take my mind off of the cowboy. The tall, tempting cowboy with a smile like sunshine. I wasn't going to think about last night. I was definitely not going to think about the way Alden gripped my hair as he thrust into my mouth. Or how the deep tones rumbling in him as he moaned mixed with the soft little noises in his whimpers. How those sounds combined with that needy look in his eyes made my skin feel like it was on fire.

My body ached for him. Wanted to do that for him. To see him come undone for me. To taste him. I didn't feel guilted into it or coerced the way the others I'd been with had. No one pushed my head down. No one begged me to do it because it would *make them feel good*, and *didn't I want to make them feel good*? It wasn't checking a box or trying to get him to like me. I just wanted to. I blinked away the thought.

No. I would definitely not think about that.

An entire morning spent thinking about it in my pursuit of *doing nothing* was already too much time.

No. Just the bumble bee.

My pencil moved, drawing as I got lost in thought trying to avoid thinking about that ludicrously attractive cowboy. There were the curves of his mouth. The upper lip that was as full as the lower, but still had a perfect Cupid's bow. The fact that they almost always had a little smile playing across them, even when he was being serious with me. As if everything I said amused him.

That near-constant smile lit his eyes. Hazel eyes. Sort of green. Sort of brown. I'd gotten such a good look at them before he kissed me that morning in his bed. Sunlight illuminated little olive splashes of color mixed with sepia-brown tones. All the slopes and ridges in his irises. Surrounded by long black eyelashes.

Alden was pretty.

Even with a stubble that was on just the longer side of things. It wasn't quite a beard. No. The hair stretched over his square jaw and down his neck, always just a bit too long to be considered a missed day of shaving. A bit too short to be a full-blown beard. Its texture was soft. Though its unrefined shape could scratch and scrape at the right angles.

That chiseled jaw. The flex of muscle beneath it as he tried to hold back laughter or bite back annoyance at his friend's crass jokes on the random days they came home in time to have dinner with me, flickering down the strong column of his throat down to his sculpted shoulders.

"You're so fucking pretty when you come."

His voice floated into my mind every time I let my guard down. Warm and soft. It wasn't the most poetic thing a guy had ever said to me. Once, while I was away at school, Graham actually wrote me a poem. He was fine to look at, very handsome, technically. He was a Comparative Literature major and wrote the poem in Old English because he was a total Beowulf groupie. I didn't understand a word. For all I knew, it could have been a recipe for chicken soup.

It was the way Alden said it. Full of reverence. Like he'd just seen the Sistine Chapel for the first time.

"You're so fucking pretty when you come."

Art. He was a work of... shit.

I surveyed the drawing I had done. The elegant rendering of a flower was not, in fact, a flower at all. It was a man. With a chiseled jaw. And a Cupid's bow. I slammed the notebook closed.

People did not do this.

No, correction. Adults did not do this. Girls with giant stupid crushes did this.

Sierra. You were a junior board member of several organizations within Chicago. You are a Volpe. Your name means something. We sent you for an Ivy League education so you could make something of yourself. And you're going to, what? Languish about in the country with some no-name roughneck? We've died and you're spending your days thinking about this instead of mourning us?

My mother. Right on time. The more I thought about Alden, the more her voice chimed in. It was like whenever I was enjoying something outside of my comfort zone, the zone she created to her comfort and not mine, her voice found a way to ruin it. She'd been gone for months. Months.

Wanting Alden felt like sneaking into the kitchen to eat raw cookie dough. Even though my mother told me half a dozen times not to do it. I still sat up in bed at night, thinking about how good it would taste. Grabbing a spoon and dipping it into the bowl while standing in the pristine kitchen of my parent's townhouse, I didn't care what my mother thought.

"A moment on the lips, forever on the hips."

Just like I didn't care now.

The sun had started to set by the time I traveled the long distance to the house again. Birds still chirped as the sun neared the horizon. Climbing the front steps, I noted the absence of my usual hunger.

Alden was completely unlike the men I'd dated before. Guys like Graham Johnson and the others, they were all perfectly coiffed and tailored. Their clothes were flawless. They drove expensive cars. Their muscles were from hours spent in the gym.

This cowboy was not like that at all. His truck was decades old. He was almost always dirty, but his hands were clean. And he didn't smell like cologne. He smelled like grass and sweat. Dirt and sunshine. He smelled like hours spent outside, which he did. Instead of working out at a gym, his muscles had been earned with hours of hard work. He even cut his own wood.

I didn't need him to take me on fancy dates or buy me fancy things. With him, none of the material things mattered. It was the safety he gave me that I cherished most. The way my body relaxed in his hold. In unguarded moments, I let myself fantasize about staying here. Being with him. Moments that came and went with a question that always came on the heels of those thoughts, disabusing me of the idea.

Did I want to stay here because I was too afraid to try something on my own?

As I crawled into bed alone again, I thought about all of the things he did that the others never bothered with. He held doors open for me. Made dinner for me. Listened to me talk and held me when I cried. The guys who came before wanted me for my appearance or my family's money. Not even my parents had provided for me what Alden did. Not one person before him cared about who I really was. He wanted to give me the space to figure it out.

The bed dipped as Alden crawled in beside me. My eyes opened at the small jolt, only able to track him from the pale light of the moon outside.

"Hey," he rasped as he noticed me watching him.

"Hi," I whispered, pushing up to my knees. "What time is it?"

"A little after eleven. Come here," he muttered, positioning himself for me to crawl under his arm. "I want to hold you."

I slid into his grasp, trying to make out his face in the dim light. I'd seen it so clearly in my mind. On the warm nights, he'd taken to sleeping in only his boxers. Alden was indisputably large. Tall. Packed with muscle. But there were parts of him that were soft. The place where his arm met with his shoulder, just above his pectoral muscle. That bit was soft enough to rest my head on.

"Did you do nothing today?" He whispered.

"Yup," I lied. *I definitely did nothing. I did not doodle in my notebook thinking about you like a schoolgirl.*

It was a crush. That was why my stomach filled with butterflies whenever he was around. A crush.

Just a crush.

It would be foolish to let it become anything bigger. I needed to figure out what my life looked like beyond being Sierra Volpe, daughter of Enzo Volpe. Someday soon, I'd leave to start that journey. But letting myself enjoy him wouldn't be the worst thing in the world, would it?

Alden wanted me, too. He'd kissed me. Touched me. Then there was what happened in the truck after dinner at the main house. No guy I'd ever done that for moaned like that for me. Desperate and wild. If I was being honest, and maybe just a little bit petty, none of them had ever been that big either. And I wanted to know how it would feel. How he would feel.

We were two adults. We were attracted to each other. It didn't have to mean anything. It certainly hadn't meant anything with anyone else. Feeling something for the people I was with wasn't supposed to happen to me. It was meant for normal people. People who were allowed to fall in love. But just as I'd tried things with other men, I could try this. Feeling something.

That first kiss had been just for me. The orgasm he'd wrung from me in the field of sunflowers, had been for me too. His hands. His mouth. His taste. I'd thought I could handle little bits and pieces. Take them for me. Sneaking a little bit of something I wanted. Except I didn't predict that I'd want more.

His breathing hadn't evened out, telling me he was still awake. I let the hand I normally let rest on his chest slide up to his jaw so I could turn it in my direction. I leaned forward and pressed a kiss to his lips. Soft and open. The hand at my waist firmed its grip, tugging me against him as his other hand slid up my thigh. It slid higher and higher until he was squeezing my ass. A low growl rumbled in his chest as my tongue caressed his.

"Sierra," he whispered. "What're you doin'?"

Despite his question, he rolled us to position himself over me. From the stiff evidence grinding against me, he knew what I was doing. Alden angled his broad hips to line up exactly where I wanted him. I hissed. He made a shushing sound into my neck as he moved his kisses over my pulse, to the soft skin beneath my ear. Tension coiled low in me at the combined sensations he was creating.

"Please," I panted, barely able to think around the way he was making me feel. "We can just kiss. Nothing serious."

Shifting his weight onto one arm, I wondered what he was doing until I felt his thumb ghost over my center as he pushed the fabric covering me to one side. His knuckle drifted over my exposed sex. I gasped at the contact. He chuckled, bringing his mouth back to mine for a quick kiss before speaking.

"Tell me something," Alden huffed, taunting me with calculated touches as he moved his mouth back to my neck. "Do you touch yourself when I'm not here?"

My hips rose to meet his efforts. He gave an approving hum before kissing beneath my jaw and grazing his teeth over the long column of my throat. I hadn't realized I was gripping him with my legs until my ankles joined at his waist. His hand glided over me in the dark, giving me just enough pressure to make my body hum with anticipation as I bit down on every little moan he wrung from me.

"I can't hear you, gorgeous," he huffed low into my ear before tugging on it with his teeth. "Do you?"

"Yes," I admitted.

Alden swore. The fingers gliding over me began making small circles at my clit, sliding back down. He repeated the excruciating motion. This man was taking me to the very edge of my sanity. I whined.

I could feel him watching me. Examining my features as he kept up his pace, my lower lip pinched in my teeth to keep from making a sound. I thought he'd given me a reprieve when the motion stopped. Only to feel a finger part me. Thick and rough, it slid inside of me. A moan lodged in my throat.

"Fuck, Sierra."

The finger was joined by another. My breath came in shorter and shorter bursts. He was trying to end me. There was no other explanation. My heart was going to give out and I was going to die right here in this room. Two fingers worked together, searching until they found the spot they were looking for and began to curl against it. I could feel my eyebrows pinch together as I stared up at him, pleading silently for him to give me more.

"Look at you so needy for me."

His whispered statement was almost lost to the lewd sounds of his touch and the raging beat of my heart as he brought me closer and closer to the edge. I could feel everything it did to me. Every zing of pleasure crackled over my veins like a surge of electricity. Something about Alden Boone turned me into a needy, panting animal. It was completely undignified.

"Tell me," he demanded, his nose brushing mine as we shared breath.

Close. I was so close to screaming if he was going to keep this up. My legs quaked as my body gripped his fingers. Oh god, I was so close. Then I was cold. Cold and empty as he pulled away. His voice was coarse and dark and I felt him looking down at me.

"I can taste it in your kiss, darlin'. But I still need to hear you say it."

"I want, fuck," I whined. "I need you."

A throat cleared on the other side of our closed door. Alden huffed a frustrated sigh, rolling back to his side of the bed with a laugh. I'd forgotten all about Eddie. The cowboy beside me released a breath as if he was trying to calm himself. I understood the feeling, internally cursing the couch surfer as we climbed back into our normal sleeping position.

Once the air had finally stopped buzzing with our frantic breathing, we settled into a comfortable, sleepy silence. I wasn't sure he was even still awake, noting his even breathing and relaxed body.

I, however, was a quivering mess. What just happened?

Twenty-Four

Alden

The west pasture was blooming with dandelions. That meant the remaining horses, the ones who weren't nursing new foals, were more fond of it than ever. I could hardly blame them. Wide open sky interrupted only by the black and white mountain peaks. Grass sweetened by the shade of proud trees. Wildflowers and dirt scented the air.

It was beautiful out here.

Driving them back through the pass along the creek was my favorite thing to do, so I didn't mind. The creek was deeper here. Colder. Dotted by boulders and little falls. Scattered blooms of bluebells bobbed in the wind beside it. It ran all the way back through the valley into my little holler. To the little house. To the woman there.

She wanted me.

My gloved hand flexed over the reins, remembering the feel of her squeezing my fingers. That look on her face as I took her to the edge of pleasure. So messy. So fucking perfect. After watching her become a trembling disaster for me last night, I was ready to beg Eddie to find somewhere else to sleep. This dance Sierra and I were doing around each other needed to end before I ground my teeth down to stumps.

"I love it when they run."

The old man looked at me in surprise and huffed a laugh. I didn't realize I'd said it aloud until he gave me that look. The one that said he knew exactly what I was thinking about. A warm smile crossed his face as we followed the herd through the rocky terrain.

"You know when that one was young," he started, nodding toward Annabel. "Mrs. Weaver told me you were reading poetry to her to calm her down. I didn't believe it until I saw it. Then I found you in the stable with her during the first storm of the season. She was laying down beside you and you were sitting down on the ground, reading to her."

I drew back, trying to get a couple of straggling horses to move ahead of me. Once I caught up again, the old man went on.

"From that day on, I knew you were a romantic at heart. Whether you let the rest of the world see it or not."

"I'm not sure I get your meaning, sir," I huffed, squinting up at him as he moved toward the top of the hill.

For a while, I wasn't sure if he would go on. Gravel scraped under hooves, filling the warm evening air. A warbler buzzed nearby. The old man heaved a sigh as we crested the peak, looking over the main house and stables as we approached.

"I never expected you to get married the way you did. I guess in a way, it makes an odd kind of sense. She makes you happy."

It wasn't a question and I didn't argue because he was right. She did make me happy. I felt myself smile and nod at the statement. I didn't bother to tell him that we were no better than a couple of teenagers or that I'd gotten so worked up last night that I had to recite the names of knots in alphabetical order in my head just to loosen up enough to fall asleep.

I didn't say any of that, but I let myself think about it because it was easier than thinking about the inevitable. She would be on her way one of these days and I would be left to wonder who could ever fill the void her absence would create. That worry ate at me every day and I kept ignoring it, hoping that it would just go away. No, that teeth-grinding agony was just for me. He went on.

"You treat that girl right and she'll keep making you happy for the rest of your life. I promise you that, son."

Annabel huffed her agreement. I gave her a rub on the neck, followed by a firm pat.

"Hey!" Eddie shouted on our approach. "Auburn is getting ready to drop. She's restless as hell, and I think I saw milk a few minutes ago."

The old man gave me a look. He didn't need to spout orders at me, but he still rattled them off. Old habits die hard, I guess.

"Alright. Boone, settle these girls for the night. Eddie, get the stall ready. It's going to be another long one, fellas."

The old man had been right. He was always right. After another long night bringing on a foal who was as fiery as his mother, I was glad to be home again. This house never really felt like mine. Still, as I walked up the front steps, they felt like my steps. The door felt like my door. And the bed? That was *my* bed she was sleeping in.

I never made any plans for myself. Growing up, it was just a thing that people talked about. The future. I spent so much of my time worrying about getting through every hour of every day that I didn't plan for the future. Living, for me, was just about survival. When the Weavers gave me this house to live in, I thought that was it. It was a place to stay so long as I worked at the ranch. Without a plan for the future, I thought I was going to be here for the rest of my life. Before I met Sierra, I didn't mind that thought.

It was a nice enough house. Nicer than the trailer my parents died in because my father couldn't be bothered to put out his cigarette before he passed out watching game shows in the middle of the day. Before his negligence killed my mother, it almost killed me. He didn't buy food. Mr. Weaver did. He didn't clothe me. Mr. Weaver did.

People thought Mr. Weaver was enabling my parents by taking care of things the way he did. But he paid the bills because he knew that my father wouldn't and I would freeze to death without it. He didn't call child protective services because he still cared about my father and he didn't want to break up a family.

Sam Weaver showed up for me when no one else would. Made me feel like I mattered. My eyes skated over the woman tangled up in my sheets. Dark hair tangled around her as she lifted her head from my pillow to look at me. She'd taken to sleeping next to it like it was serving as a substitute for me. I wanted to matter to her because she mattered to me. I imagined she mattered to me a hell of a whole lot more than to the people who considered her their property. The words she used still made me flinch. Not family. *Property.*

"Alden?" Sierra muttered sleepily.

I shucked off my clothes to grab a shower before bed, wishing I could just climb in beside her.

"Yeah, darlin'. Sorry, I woke you."

I didn't have a family until after my parents died. Well, except for Eddie. The Weavers were more like parents to me than my parents ever were. Even if I was just working for them. I slept in a spare room. That's what they called it at first. After a while, it became "Boone's room." They bought me clothes. They fed me. Mr. Weaver even helped me fix up my father's truck so it ran like it was new. He still helped me out with it when I needed it.

Then I graduated from high school. Mrs. Weaver made me my favorite peanut butter pie. Mr. Weaver gave me the keys to this house. But even after eleven years, it didn't feel like it belonged to me. No, this little red house didn't feel like a home until the girl in my bed made it worth coming back to. Even if this wasn't going to be her home forever.

Twenty-Five
Sierra

Sunlight filtered through the leaves of the old oak tree, casting a pale green glow over me. Spring was giving way to Summer, burning away the cool spring air to make way for summer. Reclining against the thick trunk, I shut my eyes and tried to imagine what I'd been doing this time last year. I went to summer fundraisers for local after-school programs. Attended garden parties in uncomfortable heels. Went to baseball games with my brother at Wrigley Field.

My brother. I tried to breathe through the pain of his memory. Of seeing his smile. His laugh. On a day when he was just trying to make me feel better. It was the last real conversation I'd had with Enzo. I was supposed to be putting the finishing touches on my makeup for the opera benefit when he found me crying in my bathroom.

"Are you crying because of how amazing you look? Do you think you've topped out and you'll never look this good again?"

Enzo leaned in the door with a big grin on his handsome face. His dark brown curls were tamed. The tuxedo he wore was flawless. His tattoos were covered. He looked exactly like the golden boy my parents believed he was. Everything was perfect except for one thing. The neck of his shirt was still unbuttoned, and of course, his tie was still untied. I met his eye in the vanity mirror as I dabbed away my tears with a tissue.

"You need me to tie that, don't you?" I sniffled.

He gave me the big-eyed puppy look he always gave me before asking for a favor. With a watery laugh, I stood from my vanity bench, smoothing the front of my black Saint Laurent dress before approaching him. Taking both ends of the silk black tie in my hand, I started working on it. He never could do them up.

"I won't be here to do this for much longer," I warbled. "You'll have to figure it out. God, I feel like Wendy getting kicked out of the nursery. I won't be able to go to Neverland with you anymore, Peter."

Enzo huffed an indignant laugh.

"First of all, I'm not a child. And second, you're getting married. It's not the end of the world."

Nope. I was not dying. I didn't get married either. But he was gone. My brother was gone. Tears stung my eyes. One more minute. Coming out here every day to sit with my thoughts, to think about what my life had become, everything came down to one thing. After weeks and weeks of thinking about what had happened, I wasn't sure I even missed my parents. They never told me they loved me. They never got to know me. I was never in their hearts, just stuck under their thumb. But Enzo. I missed him the way you miss a limb. His absence weighed me down every day because he wasn't just my older brother. He was my only friend.

I would give anything for one more minute with my brother.

But under this tree, I missed him less. It was here for every walk. Every afternoon I wandered out here. Sometimes to draw. Sometimes to read. I wanted to linger somewhere away from the house. Here. This tree was here to support me as I worked my way through things. Just as Enzo had been in my toughest moments, it was here for me to lean on.

So I started talking to it. Talking. To a tree. To Enzo. I found myself talking about the one thing I'd been dying to talk to him about for months. Well, not a thing. A person.

"He didn't go to college, but he loves to read. He has almost no money at all. And he stinks at the end of the day. Every single day. Which I sort of love. When he's covered in sweat at the end of the day, I love nothing more than to sniff him. I love his house. It's so cozy. Everything is worn and comfortable. Mom would hate it."

I spilled my guts to a tree. Ate the lunch I'd brought with me while I talked, tearing off little pieces of cheese sandwich and stuffing them into my mouth. One of the benefits of sitting under a tree, listening to a creek in the middle of the forest, is that no one can see you when you act like a lunatic.

"I like him."

The confession floated away on a warm gust. Another breeze rustled through the long grasses as I finished my lunch. I brushed the crumbs off of my lap and shook out the handkerchief I'd wrapped up my sandwich in.

"I'll be back tomorrow."

Pushing up off of the ground, I tucked the square of fabric into the pocket of my jeans and started walking back to the house. Without a book or my little spiral notebook to keep me company, I could only be left alone with my own thoughts for so long. The conversation with the tree was pretty one-sided. Obviously.

As I walked back to the house, I ruminated on the things Enzo would like about Alden. He would like his truck. And his collection of books. They were both complete nerds about Tolkien and the Lord of The Rings series. My brother would probably have bullied Alden into getting a television and internet just so he could make him watch the Rings of Power series.

Then they would argue about the merits and shortcomings of the adaptation.

The thought made me chuckle to myself as I climbed the front steps, but the sound died in me when I saw what was waiting by the front door. I'd told the tree that I was confused about my feelings for Alden. I was worried I was diving into something just because it felt good. Were the feelings I had for him real, or was I using him to distract myself from grief?

What was waiting for me at the house wasn't an answer. It was a gift. I'd spotted it from the bottom of the steps. I would have wondered how he'd gotten them here if I hadn't seen horseshoes in the dirt leading up to the house. Which meant my cowboy got the items waiting for me and rode here on the back of his horse with these things in his arms. I could feel the smile spreading over my lips at the thought.

It was a set of watercolors and brushes sitting on top of a dark green leather-bound notebook. And three sunflowers with a pink ribbon tied around them. I scooped the items into my arms and flipped open the notebook to take the dense paper inside between my fingers. Paper made for watercolor painting.

Walking in the front door, I brought Alden's gift to the kitchen table and put the flowers in a white glass pitcher. As I threaded the ribbon through my fingers, I thought only one thing.

I shouldn't care what my mother would think of a man who knows me better than she ever did.

Before that night in his truck, I'd been falling asleep to thoughts of home. Thoughts of everything I'd left behind. Now I fell asleep with my hand between my thighs to thoughts of him. His smile. His kiss. The way he moaned as I swallowed him down. I'd barely been able to manage it. Though a very real part of me was shocked at his size, I lay awake wondering what it would feel like. It was that thought that occupied most of my imagination. Alone in the house with no one to hear me, I fantasized about what it would be like to be full of him I pleasured myself into a dreamless sleep.

That was all I had to look forward to. Fantasies. Because sleeping beside

Alden had become an experiment in overstimulation. With Eddie still staying at the house, we spoke to each other in whispers. Our late-night kisses had become more frantic. Begging him for more was becoming my routine. Every time, Alden would insist that we'd be alone together again soon. That things would go back to normal. Whatever that meant. We hadn't been around each other for there to be a 'normal' state of being and the 'normal' that I knew left me a long time ago. My skin ached. My nerves sparked like downed powerlines. So I let my hands take care of the growing ache between my legs, hoping to soothe the frustration building under my skin for long enough to fall asleep.

A thud woke me as a half-naked Alden looked over his shoulder, hissing through his teeth.

"Sorry," he whispered.

"It's alright," I sighed, rolling over to look at him.

In the waning moonlight, the room has been cast in shades of blue. Alden pulled his boxers on under the towel wrapped around his hips. With the nights becoming warmer and warmer, he often came to bed this way. I didn't have it in me to complain about the gigantic, rugged rancher who made my stomach go fluttery, sleeping half-naked beside me. Especially as he flopped into bed and opened his arms for me to enjoy the freshly showered scent of him, straight from the source.

"How was your day?"

His voice was a tired whisper as he kissed the top of my head, letting me know Eddie was already asleep on the sofa. The muffled snoring coming through the door was a more obvious clue. I nuzzled under Alden's chin to take a long sniff, scratching his stubble with my nails as he gave a tired sigh.

"Why don't you grow this in?" I asked. "It's always in between stubble and a beard."

"I do when it's winter. Too warm out right now. I trim it but not much because growing a beard takes time and I don't like to start over. But you didn't answer my question."

I wasn't sure I wanted to. We'd just started to explore what we felt for each other. All the casual touches. The way he treated me like his wife when Eddie was around. It was a strange tightrope to walk between finding comfort behind closed doors and being familiar with each other to put on a show. The nights I ate alone. Read alone. Went to sleep thinking about what I would do when we were finally alone together. Those were a mercy.

"It was alright. Your gift made it brighter. I can't wait to use the paints and the flowers are beautiful. I'm flattered that you remembered my favorite."

"Darlin', you and sunflowers are forever linked in my mind."

Shifting away as I stifled a giggle, I looked at him. I propped myself up on an elbow and tried to think of a way to say what I needed to without adding more to his plate. He worked so hard. For so long. And I was just here. Floating.

Ungrateful.

When more elegant phrasing escaped me, I decided to go with something simple. Something honest. And I tried to soften that honesty it with a kiss.

"Alden," I breathed against his mouth. He groaned as I gave his bottom lip a delicate suck, his hand a warm weight as it drifted to the space between my shoulders. "I miss you."

A large, rough hand cupped my jaw as he looked up at me with hazel eyes that were warm and gentle. Alden brushed a thumb over my cheek, nudging my nose with his before he spoke.

"I'm sorry, darlin'. We'll be done soon."

He sat up and kissed me, mimicking the way I'd sucked his lip into my mouth. Then nipped at it. I stifled a whimper, deepening the kiss as I straddled him. These were the moments I let myself imagine. I'd imagine one thing leading to another until we let our growing need for each other take control. His length was already hardening beneath me as he grabbed my ass and pulled me down to feel all of him with a roll of his hips. God, I wanted to know the feel of his skin on mine. To know the feeling of his lips on every bare inch of me. After another rough kiss, he spoke against my lips.

"I don't know how much more of this I can take," I purred, nipping at his lip. To emphasize my point, I ground my hips into him and enjoyed feeling the evidence of what he wanted. He sighed through his nose, arcing himself up against my core.

"Fuck," he groaned. "You're killing me."

"The feeling is mutual," I whispered playfully, rocking myself over him again. "We could always be quiet."

Alden shot up, pulling my top down as he licked up the expanse of my neck. He loved to do that. Lick me. Like he was memorizing the way my skin tasted. My blood roared with hope and anticipation. Hope that he'd finally had enough. Hope that we would find some relief from the anguish we were both feeling. A work-roughened hand squeezed at my exposed breast forcing me to suck in a sharp breath. My teeth sunk into my lower lip in an effort to muffle the whimper that snuck past them. The soft scrape of his beard was tantalizing against my shoulder as he kissed the bare skin. His low voice became rough with promise.

"No. You don't know how to be quiet," he said with a kiss on my breast before he covered it again. "And the first time I'm inside you, I don't want you to be."

Twenty-Six
Alden

"How much do you know about her?"

I was sitting on the front porch, about to tuck into my meal, when Eddie flopped down beside me. The old man insisted on feeding us as a perk of the job and his cook Sawyer did a hell of a job in the kitchen. The big guy still had some venison sausage he'd made, so today he cooked that up with some cheddar grits. So far, I'd only gotten a bite.

Eddie had been poking at me with questions for weeks, every day since the first morning after he started crashing on the couch. Trying to needle everything he could out of me. Admittedly, not telling my best friend I had gotten married was very out of character for me so his curiosity was not surprising. That didn't mean it wasn't irritating. He made it his mission to find out everything he could about Sierra. The questions had started out as annoying. Now they were getting to be exhausting.

"She could be a grifter, you know. Moving from town to town, shaking down unsuspecting men. A con artist with designs on milking you for everything you're worth."

"Sierra's not an idiot, Eddie. We've been living together for months. There's no way she hasn't figured out I've got no money. She wouldn't be milking me for anything."

Not that there was much of that going on either, thanks to him.

Eddie scooped grits into his mouth and chewed, looking around for listeners as he geared up for his next question. I braced myself as I watched the wheels turn in his mind. Before I could let him get out another question that would get under my skin, I told him a small truth. Something I knew he would understand.

"I know she doesn't have any family left."

His eyes softened under his sandy blonde eyebrows as his mouth quirked to one side. With a heaving sigh, Eddie nodded his head in defeat.

"That sounds familiar."

Scraping down the rest of his lunch, he took the last few bites in silence. I finally tucked into my own, hoping the conversation was over. Eddie slapped his thighs and stood up with his bowl, getting ready to take it back into the kitchen. Then he paused and gave me a stern look.

"I know you care about her. I'm not fuckin' blind, Boone. She's your wife. I'm just trying to look out for you, buddy."

He left me with that thought, proceeding into the house. While eating what turned out to be a delicious meal I didn't mind grabbing second helpings of, I thought about how much I really knew about the woman living with me. Sierra had told me the basics about herself and her situation. Her family was gone. That family had been in the mafia. They'd been wealthy. They'd been killed by a rival family.

While the rest of the hands were enjoying their lunch at the wooden table nearest the barn, laughing amongst themselves. I slid my phone from my pocket, choosing to remain in my usual spot hidden away on the porch steps.

It could have been that Eddie's concern had finally sunk in. Some sort of self-preservation instinct finally taking hold. Because with a few minutes left to enjoy lunch on the old man's porch, I took advantage of my time. And his wi-Fi.

"Where I come from, people know me."

Sierra Volpe. Chicago. I'd thought it would be hard to find her. That I'd have to wade through a few different Sierras before I found mine, but there she was, smiling back at me at the top of the page. Clicking over to the images, I scrolled and scrolled. God, she was fucking stunning. She always seemed to be walking a red carpet. Cutting a ribbon. Standing there with an older woman who was definitely her mother based on the almost identical green eyes and bone structure. Beautiful like her daughter, but in a superficial way. And there was something in Sierra's face when she was beside her. She seemed smaller. Cowed. It gave me a rotten feeling in my gut.

Most often in the photos, Sierra was dressed the way she was when I first met her. Hair completely straight if it wasn't up, makeup on but polished. She looked like a doll dressed up in expensive-looking clothes. A polished figurine. Manufactured perfection with an emptiness in her smile that made my chest ache.

I knew this was her. That these were pictures of the woman living in my house. But this wasn't the girl I couldn't stop thinking about. The one I wanted to laugh with in bed at the end of the day. To hold until she fell asleep. My Sierra was a different creature entirely.

"Whoa. Is that her?"

Eddie peered over my shoulder. I tried to hide my screen, but it was too late. His hand shot out and held it up to take a closer look, tapping on a photo as he grabbed the phone.

In this shot, it was unmistakable. Green eyes. Dark brown hair pulled away from her face. She was even wearing that black dress I'd first seen her in. The image he'd clicked on opened a link to an article published a few months ago in the Chicago Examiner. The headline knocked the breath out of me.

The End of an Era: Volpe Family Slaughtered.

City in mourning as a night at the opera led to devastating tragedy. Enzo Volpe, owner and CEO of Volpe Development, Catarina, and son Enzo Volpe Jr. were found dead in their private opera box at the City Opera Benefit Friday night.

Fuck. Sierra's whimpered confession rushed back to me. That dress. The date on the article. This was what she'd been running from.

"They wanted to kill me, but I ran."

Lead tugged at my gut as I scrolled down. There wasn't any hiding it from Eddie now. My eyes skimmed the article, Eddie reading over my shoulder from beside me. We clicked link after link, learning about the girl who'd been living in my house for a couple of months. Learning about her family. But most of all, learning who she was desperate to escape.

"So, what does that mean? Is that why you married her?" Eddie uttered as he looked around to make sure we were still alone.

I shook my head.

"No," I said. The syllable felt wrong on my tongue. "We're not married. I found her when her car broke down. She just needed somewhere to hide. That's the truth."

"Not the whole truth, though," he argued.

My phone slipped from between my fingers as Eddie took it, tapping on a link I hadn't yet seen. An accompanying article on the paper's site about Bruno Serpa's release. The man who'd killed her family got released? Confusing as that was, that wasn't what made my blood go cold. It was the seven-figure reward he was offering for information on Sierra's whereabouts.

"That's a lot of money," Eddie said with a low whistle.

"It doesn't make any sense," I said, rubbing a hand down my face. "She's not in their way. Why would they pay so much to have her back?"

"I guess they don't like loose ends," Eddie shrugged. "Sounds like she's the last of them."

The rest of the hands were heading out to the barn to start their chores for the afternoon. I took my phone from Eddie and tucked it back into my pocket, standing to take my bowl back into the house. My friend looked up at me expectantly.

"Please, Eddie. Promise you're not going to say shit to anyone. As far as you're concerned, she's my wife in every way that matters."

"Yeah, yeah. I hear you. What are you going to do?" Eddie asked as he stood up and stuffed his hands into his pockets, arching a brow at me.

"I'm going to keep my gun loaded."

No one was going to take her from me. This woman came to me for help. I told myself it didn't matter how I felt about her. That aching to see her at the end of every day wasn't the reason for my loyalty. Because the money didn't matter. Keeping her safe was the right thing to do. She was just property to them. To me, she was so much more than that. I wouldn't turn her over for anything. And I would kill anyone who did.

Eddie gave me a short nod, standing up to get back to his mount. As my boots clopped onto the steps, I knew he was right before. I hadn't told him the whole truth. The truth was I felt something for Sierra I couldn't explain. I hadn't even said that out loud. Or allow myself to think the words. I just knew what I felt the way the sun knows to rise.

The girl I had those feelings about was making dinner in the kitchen when we got home, a welcome sight. She turned where she stood, beaming at me from over the stove as she greeted us. That silent part of me strained inside my chest at the sight.

"Everything alright?" Sierra asked, eyebrows high.

"Sure," Eddie chirped. "We just had a long day is all."

As though that were answer enough, Sierra nodded and returned her attention to the stove. Long hair braided down her back, wearing jeans and a tee shirt that belonged to me. My Highwaymen shirt practically drowned her, but she knotted it up at her belly button. She looked relaxed. Peaceful. I gave her a hug around the waist, kissing her temple before heading into the bedroom to rinse the day off.

"You're a good cook, Mrs. Boone," Eddie offered as we ate the meal she'd prepared. Mashed potatoes with what tasted like butter and seasonings I didn't even know I owned. "You don't have to cook for me, you know. I've got about thirty packages of noodles tucked away here."

"I don't mind," she smiled.

I knew she didn't. That cooking gave her joy because she hadn't been allowed to do it for herself. To anyone looking in, it would seem like she'd been domesticated. That she was filling some archaic requirement. But I knew it for what it was. A small act of rebellion. A declaration of her independence.

After that, dinner was quiet. Eddie watched Sierra carefully as if trying to judge what sort of person she was now that he knew more about her. It was not lost on her. Sierra shifted in her seat under the weight of those looks, glancing at me for an explanation. I couldn't give her one, so I just gave her a smile.

All I could think about was her family. Her mother and father. Her brother. She'd lost all of them in one night and tumbled into my life on the other side of it. They looked so much like her and not at all at the same time. Except for her brother. In the few photos I'd seen of them together, Sierra looked different. Happier.

"They killed my brother."

Those people. The Serpas. The man in charge, the father, had looked like a mafia cartoon. Balding but somehow hairy everywhere else. Gold jewelry and a snakelike smile. His son, though. The tall, lean Antoni. His suit and jaw were sharp. Brown eyes dark with cruelty. The sight of him had chilled me to the bone.

One million dollars. That's what they were offering to get their hands on this woman. If they'd wanted her dead, they wouldn't be asking for her safe return. If I thought too long about what they wanted from her, I'd get sick all over the damn table.

Sierra was carefully pushing potatoes onto her fork with her butter knife. She couldn't break the habit of her ladylike upbringing. Green eyes flicked up to mine. She smiled gently. I smiled back. No, the Serpas couldn't have her. They'd have to kill me first.

The idea of this sweet creature being married to a guy like Antoni Serpa nauseated me. He would never have appreciated the little things that made her special. Because she was. There wasn't a star in the sky that shone as brightly as she did when she smiled. Really smiled. He couldn't appreciate the little wrinkle between her brows when she was focused or the adorable way she chewed her lip when she was working out what she wanted to say.

That snake could never deserve her in a million years. I knew that down in my bones. It was why, as I looked at her now, I knew I had to treasure every second I had with her. Eventually, she would go back to her life. To the riches. To find a man who could give her everything she deserved and treat her right.

"Is something wrong?" Sierra whispered as she dragged her nails through my chest hair, looking up at me from where she was nestled under my arm. The sensation sent ripples of pleasure down my spine. "You were really quiet at dinner."

Her long tresses were tangled around my fingers. I loved how long and thick her hair felt in my hands. The awkwardly silent dinner led to everyone heading off to bed early. Sierra crawled over to me, happy to rest her head on my body as we embraced in dark silence. With a sigh, I nodded.

"It was just a long day."

Seeming to accept my answer, she kissed me on the nose before rolling over and throwing herself over her pillow with a sigh. Her soft breaths filled the room as she drifted off. The soothing sound sent me off to sleep.

I dreamed of the girl who lay beside me being carried away in another man's punishing grasp. Long nails dug into his arm as he pulled her away. Blood leached down over his skin from where she marked him. Sierra screamed for me. Reached for me. Cried. Kicked. Eyes wild and desperate as she screamed my name again and again. Then Antoni threw her in a cage, shoving the iron box into a deep and endless ocean with a satisfied sneer.

My eyes snapped open. I rolled over, needing to feel her in my arms. To bury my face in her hair to smell that tempting scent. To know that she was safe. Instead, my hand met with cool cotton and empty sheets.

Sierra was gone.

Twenty-Seven

Sierra

I needed air.

For the last few weeks, I found myself in a dreamless sleep. I'd sleep all night without issue. Except every so often, I had the same nightmare. As a little girl, I used to hide in a crawlspace in our house. It was in the back of my mother and father's closet. Just a small door hidden behind a Burberry trench coat my mother almost never wore. I'd found it during a game of hide and seek with my brother and claimed it for myself in perpetuity. I'd even hidden a blanket and flashlight inside for reading when I just wanted to be left alone. Every time I was scared or in trouble, that's where you could find me.

The nightmare always started with me being chased. We all know it. That unmistakable feeling. Someone coming after you. Fear that you'll be caught. Your feet betraying you because you know you can run faster than you're going. You're not going fast enough. This is what I felt. Running from Antoni through the vast expanse of my parent's palatial home. Slipping on marble floors. Unable to get a grip on myself as I sprinted as fast as I could in those stupid stiletto heels.

Each of my family members stood alone in a room as I sped past. Sounds of my mother's screams followed me down the halls. My father asking to be reasonable. My brother begging them not to hurt us as a wet squelch stopped him mid-sentence. He followed, but couldn't catch me. Just kept chasing me. Following me up the stairs. Through the bedroom. Until I was crawling into the hole to hide away. No one could find me there. I only watched with horror, quieting my breath, as blood seeped beneath the door.

I woke with a start, shoved on my boots, and crept past Eddie on the sofa to leave the house. The full moon lit my path well enough. With Alden's jacket thrown over my pajamas, the cool night air wasn't even much of a bother. My feet carried me into the woods as I tried to steady my breathing, boots crunching on leaves and twigs in the otherwise silent air. The tree. I needed the tree.

The creek babbled, the noise so familiar that I welcomed it. I hadn't realized how quickly I'd moved until I found myself beside it, the oak tree rising strong and steady in my view. Standing proud in the moonlight. I stopped and closed my eyes. One deep breath followed another. Out here, the pleading voices of the people I loved melted into nothing like the vapor of the breath from my lips. With one hand over my heart and one over my stomach, I let the air soothe my frayed nerves. Only, it wasn't just my breath that I heard.

Yipping pierced the night. Loud. Nearby. Turning where I stood, I carefully searched around me for the source only to find darkness. Another yip. The sound was sharp. Closer. I kept searching until I met with a pair of yellow eyes flashing at me from the brush. The owner of those eyes crept toward me, illuminated by a shaft of moonlight from the forest canopy. A coyote.

A sharp inhale popped out of me. No. This was not okay. This was bad, right? My boots were frozen to the ground as I stood there, trying to decide what to do. Trying to remember what Alden had explained to me about how to get rid of these things. Now that it was in front of me, my mind was blank.

"Hey! Get out of here! Go ON!"

Yelling. Waving his arms over his head as he charged forward in nothing but his boxers and boots. Alden was still yelling as he rushed toward me. Past me. The coyote ran away as my gigantic cowboy chased it off, roaring at it until he was certain it was gone.

"Are you insane? Do you know what could have happened to you out here? Why would you come out here alone?" Alden growled as he stalked toward me, eyebrows drawn, jaw clenched.

"I couldn't sleep," I muttered sheepishly.

His chest was heaving, covered in a light sheen of sweat. His eyes were wild as his hands roamed over me, searching for any sign of injury.

"I'm sorry," I babbled. "I just had a nightmare. It was about my family. I needed to get some air and I didn't want to wake you."

"Darlin', I don't care if you wake me. I care if you're hurt. I care if you're safe."

His boots bracketed mine as he took me in his arms. It wasn't until he'd wrapped himself around me that I realized I was shaking. A curse whispered into the night as he pulled away, taking my hand in his to lead me back to the house. We walked in heavy silence for a while, both of us coming down from what had just occurred. When the house came into view, Alden gave my hand a squeeze before he spoke.

"Do you want to tell me what this dream was about?"

"No. I just want to take my mind off of it."

I didn't want to explain about the nightmare. Not now. Alden nodded and squeezed my hand again. We climbed the front steps on careful feet.

"Take your boots off," he whispered as he slipped off his own.

I did as he asked, taking his boots in my hand when he handed them to me. Before I could ask why, Alden swept me into his arms and carried me through the front door. Remembering the couch-surfing cowboy, I stifled my giggle until we were safely behind the bedroom's closed door.

Alden sat me down at the end of the bed like I was a breakable thing. He took our boots and set them down. Then he took his jacket, draping it over the dresser with care before returning his attention to me.

"You scared the hell out of me. I woke up and you were gone," he whispered.

"I'm sorry."

Alden sighed deeply as he got to his knees before me. Thick arms wrapped around my legs as he let his head rest in my lap. I combed my fingers through his hair, relishing the feel of the thick chestnut waves moving through them. A minute passed without a word. Then, with a decisive breath that fanned over my thighs, Alden looked up at me.

"Next time you need help to take your mind off of things, tell me. I can help."

His voice was a dark rasp and a plea. I reached for his face, scratching his bearded jaw with my fingernails. Alden leaned into my touch as he looked up at me with pale moonlight gleaming in his eyes.

"Help me how?"

A wicked grin pulled across his lips as his fingers hooked around my bottoms. A brow arched in question. I nodded, laying back and lifting my hips to help him remove them. His hands shook, his eyes begging me for this as they betrayed the smile on his face. Like he needed to feel me as much as I did him. Soft breath danced over my thighs. Lips gently kissed my hips where my bottoms had been. Alden's mouth moved over me as his hands slid the garment off of my legs, stubble brushing where my skin was softest.

Awareness tightened every part of me as anticipation welled low in my belly. I'd never had a man touch me this way. Worshipping. Tender. Thorough, as though he was trying to memorize the way my body felt as his callused hands roamed back up to part my thighs. Warmth washed over me, taking all he had to offer me. Protection and care. Affection and this. I'd come out of a nightmare only to fall into a dream. A cowboy who would do anything to make me feel safe. Whether he knew it or not, he made me feel other things. Things I couldn't explain. Alden shifted, placing one of my knees on his shoulder. Then the other.

It was an entirely new thing to have a man so close to me in this way. None one else had even bothered with this. Not really. There had only been a few men, and they certainly hadn't bothered to return the favor when I'd given them oral pleasure. Now Alden stared at my sex like he was trying to appreciate a work of art. Under the weight of his expression, I felt the urge to pull my legs together, nervous from what seemed like an assessment. But his tongue ran over his lips as he braced my legs apart. Hazel eyes lifted to me.

"Don't hide from me. I've been thinking about this for longer than you know. Now be quiet, darlin'."

Warm lips kissed the insides of my knees. The effort was slow and deliberate, working his way up my inner thighs with his lips and tongue as his short beard scratched the sensitive skin. His eyes fixed on me, Alden sucked and licked his way toward my center. An involuntary rocking, small and needy, had started in my hips as I grew impatient. I wanted him to touch me. Fill me. My hands fisted the comforter beneath me as his mouth finally made contact with my core. One flat lick all the way up. One lick and I muffled a gasp. He was right. I couldn't stay quiet.

"Uh-uh. Make one sound and I stop."

So unfair. So unfair to make that demand when he pushed his tongue into me. The hands that had spread me open for him now squeezed me, touched me. Slid over my thigh to thumb the bundle of nerves that ached for his touch. Biting hard into my lip, I looked at him. Tried to beg him silently for what I needed. Rubbing over my swollen flesh, only enough pressure to make me squirm. Alden growled into me as I arched into his touch. I relished the sound, even if he wasn't exactly being quiet.

More. I needed more.

As if understanding my silent command, Alden moved his mouth to replace his thumb. He massaged the flesh with his tongue as he parted me with two fingers, burrowing inside further until he found what he was looking for. The fingers curled to match the rhythm of his mouth. A sharp inhale slipped from my lips at the intrusion.

"Hush," he scolded, looking up at me through the dark hair falling over his forehead. "Quiet or I won't let you finish."

"Please," I begged.

Alden's other hand wandered up my body, slipping beneath the cotton of my top to toy with my breast as he smirked up at me. Right. Quiet. I had to stay quiet because I did not want this to stop under any circumstances.

He returned to his task, fingers, and tongue working me in tandem. Winding my pleasure higher with every fervent lick and suck. If I thought I'd felt pleasure riding his hand, this was another thing entirely. Biting my lip was not enough to stop the tiny distressed noises escaping me. Fisting the soft bedding beneath me was not enough to keep control over what was happening to my body. My hands franticly searched for something to hang on to until they moved into his hair, angling his mouth exactly where I needed it as my hips bucked into him. He grunted as I pulled, part of me worried I was hurting him with my grip.

Then it happened again. It happened because I realized he was taking pleasure in this. A distraction as much for him as it was for me. That understanding coupled with his sinful tongue caused my spine to bow. Pleasure snapped at me like a flaming whip. The feeling of his rough hand on my breast. Curling fingers inside me. His mouth. His mouth. His deliciously devious mouth.

Oh. My. God.

I hadn't realized I'd closed my eyes until I heard Alden speak against my sensitive flesh.

"Look at me. I want you to know who makes you feel like this."

Devilish hazel eyes peered up at me as he continued. We were still looking at each other when I started to shake around him. Choking back a sob, Alden's name fell from my lips in breathless whispers as my sex clenched around his fingers with another climax. He didn't stop. Didn't withdraw until he was certain he'd wrung every ounce of pleasure from me.

Alden gently kissed my inner thighs, then my knees, closing my legs with a feather-light touch as he stood. I was still catching my breath when he climbed onto the bed and used a massive arm to drag me up toward our pillows. Crawling beneath the covers, he wrapped himself around me and kissed my temple.

"Better?"

I nodded.

"Now go to sleep like a good girl," he whispered into my hair. "Don't go wandering off into the woods again."

"I wasn't wandering. I was going out to my tree."

"Your tree? That old oak tree is your tree now?" Alden chuckled. He kissed me again, his lips lingering against my hair. "It's not safe out there at night. Not by yourself."

We didn't say anything else for a long while. I felt my body giving up on consciousness and I yawned into the dark.

"Good night, cowboy."

"Good night, darlin'."

Twenty-Eight
Alden

Annabel huffed as we walked along the pasture, vapor curling from her nostrils in the frigid morning air. Only a few hours ago, I'd been on my knees watching an angel shatter on my tongue. The memory played on a loop. Fingers curled into my hair, pulling hard enough to make my scalp sting as she tried to stifle those harmonious little whimpers behind those perfect lips. Fuck, the way she tasted...

"How are things with Sierra?"

I blinked. Eddie looked at me expectantly. I'd forgotten he was out here with me. I huffed a sigh, looking for an answer I didn't have. Between learning about the riches she'd come from and fulfilling my need to taste her, which only made things worse, my head was a damned mess. I wanted her. I didn't just want to sleep with her; I wanted to keep her, which was a problem. A big fucking problem. Even if holding her while I slept was becoming second nature to me now.

"For the record, Boone, I know things are good. She woke me up when she left last night and y'all were not as quiet as you thought when you got back," he snorted. "You've been quiet all morning so what are you torturing yourself about?"

"Nothing," I grunted.

Eddie rolled his eyes, urging his mount forward to leave me with my thoughts. We rode in silence for a while, checking fences for when the new foals were ready to transition out of the stalls. By the time we found a broken rail the sun high in the sky and beating down on us in earnest. Summer was almost here.

"Boone," Eddie grunted as he lifted part of the rail free from the post. "Tell me what's up your ass. You're a quiet guy and I accept that about you, but this is just ridiculous."

"It's nothing, Ed," I huffed as I lifted the other end free.

We dropped the rail to the ground and I scrubbed a gloved hand down my face. There wasn't a good way to explain the way I was feeling. The words. I didn't have them. How was I supposed to explain that this woman was changing everything for me? From the way my life had gone so far, it was hard to believe that something as good as Sierra Volpe would just fall into my lap. Good things don't just happen to me.

I'd thought my life was going to go one way. That I was going to find some local girl, get married, and eventually have a family. I didn't make much and we'd struggle to get by. That was the life laid out before me and I thought I had accepted that. There are plenty of people in the world who are happy living that life.

Except I hadn't. I hadn't because if that's what I wanted, I would have stayed with Natalie. I'd broken things off with her because I wanted more. I wanted something crazy. Something I couldn't explain. Actually getting a shot at it was something I didn't expect. Just like I didn't expect to fall for a girl I found on the side of the road. A girl with a whole life I didn't understand. A whole life I didn't fit into. A life filled with fancy clothes and jewelry. Sierra deserved those things. She deserved a man who could give her everything. I wanted her to have them. To have stability and someone to protect her. The thoughts warred in me, making my whole body ache with the urge to run to her.

Eddie pushed up his hat with a finger and wiped his face with a forearm, squinting at me. With a shake of his head, he pulled out a cigarette and lit up.

"Boone, you're all twisted up over this woman. Why?"

A puff of air blew out of me as I weighed my options. I could keep my mouth shut. Keep torturing myself with this eventuality.

"Sierra is," I sighed. "You know she's just staying with me until it's safe to go back to her real life."

"Ok," Eddie shrugged. "What if that's never? What if she never goes back?"

I tried to shrug and approached my saddle, opening the bag to get out my clippers and 9-gauge wire. The wire would have to do as a temporary holdover until I could get the Polaris out here with a replacement post.

"You saw what she came from, Eddie. I can't give that to her."

Eddie snorted, rolling his eyes at me again as he took a long drag from his cigarette. Flicking the ash away, he waved his hand, urging me to go on.

"She's," I huffed, wrapping one post with the wire and pulling it tight before I uncoiled it to extend to the other.

"Goddamnit, Boone," Eddie heaved with an exasperated sigh.

"What?"

"Just say you're falling for the girl! It's not rocket science. I know you've got this hangup like you think you're not worth caring about, and you can thank your fucking parents for that but shit. You're living with a gorgeous, sweet girl who takes care of you. And you let her, which you don't let anybody do. It's so fucking obvious!"

"What I'm feeling doesn't matter, Ed. Someday she's going to go back to her real life. Even if we do eventually," I stopped myself before admitting the rest to him. "She told me she spent her whole life being groomed for a political marriage. She deserves the chance to find something better. Do you think she's willing to give up all that to be with a nobody like me?"

Eddie stubbed his cigarette out on the top of the fence post, spitting into a napkin he carried in his shirt pocket as he tucked the butt away. Shaking his head at me again, he let out a long breath as he hooked his thumbs into his belt.

"Can I give you some advice?"

"Am I going to be able to stop you?"

Another snort-laugh. He picked up his hat and rubbed the business part of his blonde mullet, looking around to make sure we were still alone, even though we both would have heard someone approach. Annabel puffed, waiting patiently for us to move on from this task.

"Pull your head out of your ass. Be in the moment and enjoy the time you have with her for as long as you can. You don't know what she feels for you, and she won't know unless you tell her."

Eddie and I mounted our horses, continuing down the line of fencing. Hoofbeats thudded on the ground as we wove through the trees.

"Enjoy the time you have with her."

Terrible advice. That was the easy part. Whenever I was around her, I forgot my troubles. Her smile washed my fears away. Sure, I craved her. Repeatedly fisted myself in the shower just to get through the primal need that made my body scream for her. But as soon as I walked out the front door, my brain went into overdrive. It listed all the ways I wasn't good enough for her. It went to work dreaming up exactly how it would feel when I eventually lost her. It wasn't just a possibility. It was a foregone conclusion.

Eddie hopped back on his mount and began walking the fence line again. I followed. His constant yammering was replaced with thoughtful silence and the occasional glance in my direction as we rode through the rest of our task. The fucker was letting me stew.

As I brought the Polaris back to the barn after using it for evening feedings, the old man informed me that one of the two remaining mares had started labor. This was her first birth. Being new to the process meant we could be in for a long night. Sable, a pitch-black Quarter Horse, whinnied in discomfort while I wrapped her tail.

"How's she doing here?" Mr. Weaver asked, sticking his head into the stall.

"Poor girl's probably in for a long one like you said. I texted the vet just to let him know that things are moving along, just in case he needs to head over. I just finished adding some fresh straw in here, but I'll get some more in here if I need to."

The old man nodded as he let his eyes roam over the black horse. Even if her stall was large enough for the both of us, he stayed outside. His hands made a decisive pat on the door as he stood up straight. Routine.

"Why don't you go on into the house and grab some dinner with Junior? If we're in for a long night, you need to eat. I can keep an eye on her for a bit," the old man offered.

"Yes, sir," I agreed as I finished wrapping her up, tucking the roll of wrap under my arm after cutting the end.

"You know, son. I don't care how many times I've done this. It never gets old. Even the hard ones."

Rolling the door open, I let myself out of the stall. The old man gave me a solid pat on the shoulder and looked me in the eye. His mustache partially covered the smile I knew was there. He did love this part. The foals coming into the world.

"At my age, you come to realize you've got to hold on to the good stuff when you can. You never know when it's going to be taken away from you."

Twenty-Nine

Sierra

The front door slammed closed. 6 o'clock. They were home early. Excitement pulsed in my veins as I shot up from my seat at the table to greet them. Eddie was hanging his hat beside the front door. No Alden. The hippie cowboy tossed me a half-sympathetic glance as he shucked off his boots and approached the kitchen. I tried to hide my disappointment.

"It's just you and me tonight, honey."

"Where's Alden?"

I tried to sound breezy as I asked the question like I didn't care that the only person I wanted to see was still not here. Tugging my jeans up and smoothing my shirt, I headed back into the kitchen. Dinner for one was about to be a dinner for two.

"One of the horses is giving birth. The old man and Boone are handling it, so I snuck off. Only one more to go now. You making dinner?" Eddie asked as he eyed a pot of water I'd set to boil.

"I was just going to make some pasta with butter and parmesan. I can make some chicken or something if you'd prefer."

"Nah," he shrugged as he sat down at the table. "I know I'm crashing. I won't make you cook anything extra for me, but I'll take some of that pasta if you don't mind."

Nodding, I looked around, not really knowing what to do with myself as I stood there. He'd always been friendly to me, but this felt odd. Then it dawned on me. Eddie and I hadn't really ever been alone together. When he was here, Alden was here. I found myself missing my cowboy even more when Eddie's normally friendly demeanor seemed to melt away as he took me in. My hands fisted at my sides at the frank look of assessment in his blue eyes. Unable to take another second of it, I turned away to start grating cheese.

"So how long are you planning to use my friend for shelter before you go back to living the high life in Chicago?"

Metal clacked onto the butcher block counter as I dropped the grater. I hesitated before turning to face Eddie again. The hard set of his jaw made it clear he wasn't kidding. I didn't say anything. My mind raced. How he knew about me or Chicago, I didn't know. I doubted Alden told him. Even if we barely knew each other, I understood that much about him. Unable to answer his question or take the weight of that unnerving blue stare for much longer, I picked up the grater and started shaving the block of cheese again.

Relax. You haven't done anything wrong.

I knew I could trust Alden and he didn't seem like the type to break a promise. But this was his best friend. He could have told him and kept it from me. I opened the package of spaghetti to dump into the boiling pot of water. Tipping the package over, the noodles fanned out and forced me to grab a spoon and stir them into the bubbling liquid.

"I'm not using him," I protested. "It was his idea."

"Of course it was. He put clothes on your back and a roof over your head. He put this food on the table for nothing. You're not using him?"

Frustration tightened my hands into fists as I turned to face him.

"How much do you know?" I sighed.

"I know your name. I know where you came from. And I know who's looking for you," he said, now leaning against the wall beside the bedroom with his arms folded over his chest. "You didn't answer my question."

"I'm not using him, Eddie," I snapped. "I would pay for everything if I could, but I can't access my bank account right now because the resources of the people looking for me mean that I can't even get a dime without them figuring out where I am. Those people want to kill me. If they find out where I am now, I won't be the only person they hurt."

Eddie snorted and walked to the fridge to grab one of his light beers. He cracked it open, cocking his hip as he lifted the can to his lips. Silence. Eddie waited for me to go on.

"Once it's safe for me to access my account, I'll give everything back. With interest."

He set the can of beer on the counter and walked away. The bedroom door closed, informing me that he'd decided not to continue this conversation until after he'd bathed. I hoped that in the time it took him to get washed up, he'd decide I was telling the truth. Minutes passed as I thought about what he'd said. He thought I was using Alden. His best friend. Water sizzled on the burner as it boiled over from the pot. I poured the noodles into the colander and heard Eddie's advancing footsteps.

A sharp intake of breath told me I'd been foolish to hope that he would just drop it and move on. He was just getting started, only now he was wearing that cropped Playboy tee shirt and a pair of blue banana print pajama bottoms.

"Alright, Sierra. I need to know something. And don't lie to me."

I scooped pasta into two bowls, dropping a knob of butter into each nest of noodles. Handing him one bowl, he sprinkled grated cheese over the pasta and dusted on some pepper, then took a seat at the table. I followed. Eddie stirred his pasta with a fork, letting me sit in agonizing silence.

"What?" I snapped, tired of waiting for his looming question.

"Do you have feelings for him? I've seen the way you look at each other. Is it an act?"

I bit my lip, trying to find a way to say what I felt. To define what was happening between Alden and me. I couldn't explain how our shapes matched, even though we were from entirely different puzzles. How could I explain that puzzle piece feeling? I didn't fit into his picture, and he didn't fit into mine. Each of them was beautiful on their own, but incomplete. Saying that out loud meant acknowledging something that I wasn't sure I was ready to confront in myself, let alone to someone I barely knew. No, that was insane. Instead, I just kept it simple.

"No."

"No, you don't have feelings for him," he monotoned.

"No, it's not an act," I sighed, my fork hitting the bowl with a clink as I dropped it. "I couldn't fake that. I wouldn't even know where to begin."

Eddie eyed me for a long moment, clearly trying to decide if I was being honest. The pause was as irritating as his questions since I realized I was being a little too honest. He took a forkful of food into his mouth, then washed it down with a swig of beer.

"Then I need to explain something to you. It's about his parents."

"He told me about the fire," I offered, relaxing enough from the change in subject to start threading noodles through the tines of my fork. I spun them in the bowl and hoisted them into my mouth.

Surprise lit his eyes for a moment. Then he nodded as if that had answered some question he didn't ask.

"I've known Boone for almost my entire life. I mean, we met in kindergarten. He's the way he is because of the way he grew up."

"Because his parents were," I struggled to find a kind way to explain.

"Drunks," he interjected. "Sorry. But they were. There are the kind of alcoholics that don't do any harm to anyone but themselves. The kind that are functional. People who get help and live happy lives. But the Boones...They weren't like that. They were barely semi-functional for most of his life, but it got a lot worse when we were about ten years old. Mr. Boone lost his job, but it didn't stop him from drinking. Mrs. Boone wasn't any better. Soon Alden was doing laundry. Keeping their home clean and picking up after them. The only thing he couldn't do was get a job, but he did what he could. That's too much responsibility for a fucking kid."

I pretended to focus on eating as I let that mental picture destroy me from the inside. A chestnut-haired little boy left to fend for himself because his parents were too busy ignoring him to care. Memories of my privileged childhood coated my tongue with acid. I was spoiled and placated by my parents with material things while I was cared for by household staff. Nannies. Housekeepers. Bodyguards. I had no shortage of people making sure all of my needs were met.

"My mom helped out a little, but if it weren't for Mr. Weaver, I don't think he would have eaten."

With that, my appetite left me entirely. Not only did Alden grow up with none of the same resources as I did, he grew up with almost no one to look out for him. Everything had been decided for me while he was left to twist in the wind. The thought of a child enduring that kind of isolation was awful. Knowing it had been Alden's reality made an unbearable weight settle in my chest. As if sensing the direction of my thoughts, Eddie went on.

"Boone takes care of people because that's what he does for the people who are important to him. It's how he's built. He thinks I stay here because I need it and that's only half true. I stay here to take care of him because I hate the thought of him being out here alone."

Eddie twisted noodles around his fork, stuffing his mouth with them before speaking.

"He cares about you. A lot. We both know it. He's like a brother to me, so if you're using him for a safe place to stay, then I'm sorry, but you have to get out."

I set my fork down on the table, not realizing I'd been clutching it so hard, and took a breath.

"I told you I'm not using him. I'm not trying to take advantage of him," I said hoarsely. "I couldn't have planned this if I tried."

He went silent, thinking over what I'd said as he finished his meal. As he cleared the final bit of pasta from his plate, he stuffed it into his mouth. I watched, having completely lost my appetite. The can of beer tapped against the table with a hollow clack as he finished that off, too. Finally, Eddie spoke again.

"Boone's on his way to falling hard for you, Sierra. A little closer every day. The guy's such a fucking mess over it that if he hadn't told me so himself, I would have figured it out anyway."

A foolish flutter flickered in my chest at that. I knew he cared for me. It wasn't because he looked after me. The look in his eyes when he watched me was enough. The way he held me. I'd never felt anything like it. I just wasn't sure if it was because of him or because I'd never allowed myself to feel it. If what Eddie said was true, this careful maneuvering we were doing around each other was likely going to result in heartbreak. I blinked the thought away before it could take root.

Picking up Eddie's dish, I shuffled over to the tiny ancient dishwasher and shoved the bowls inside. All of the energy I'd had was drained out of me by this conversation. Thoughts weighed me down, exhausting me with a heaviness I now felt everywhere. I wondered if that was the plan as I finished cleaning up and went to the sofa to pick up the book I'd been reading and walked to the bedroom. Eddie had gone to the sofa and sat down, immersing himself in whatever was on his phone. Before entering the bedroom, I turned back to him.

"You know, I didn't ask for any of this."

Eddie's gaze softened, but his words remained hard.

"Neither did he, Sierra."

Thirty

Alden

The trail through the woods was a rough one. Through some parts, I had to take the truck over the terrain very slowly. Very carefully. It was through those parts that I knew Sierra was holding her breath.

"Where are we going?" she asked again, eyes bright with curiosity. "This is like, deep in the forest. There could be bears."

"You'll see," I said. "I've got bear spray under my seat. And the revolver's in the glove box."

"Okay," she huffed. "But if a bear attacks us, I'm letting him eat you."

I would have smiled at that if I wasn't already grinning from ear to ear. I'd thought about bringing her up here a dozen times. The minute the old man gave us the go-ahead to pack up for the day, Eddie and I hauled ass home. I basically threatened my best friend my physical harm if he volunteered to go with us. It was a rare thing to get to go home early and I wanted to spend every second of it enjoying time alone with her.

The forest parted ahead, illuminating the path with waning sunlight. We were almost there. Sierra sat up a little taller, trying to see what was coming. That adorable curiosity made my lips pull into a smirk. I hadn't told her a damn thing. Just told her to get in the truck because I had a surprise as I grabbed some towels from under the sink. She'd looked as confused then as she did now.

Pink sunlight washed over us as we exited the forest, pulling up to my little surprise spot. Steam lifted from the gathering of rocks ahead. I was relieved to see we were the only ones here. Gravel crunched under my tires as I parked the truck off to the side. Sierra's eyes narrowed as she looked at the rock formations.

"Wait. Are these hot springs?"

"Yup."

Opening the door, I hopped out and went to her door, opening it before returning to the driver's side to start getting undressed. Sierra watched as I unbuttoned my shirt, shaking her head with a smile.

"I don't have a bathing suit, cowboy," she laughed.

"You don't need one, gorgeous," I winked. "But if you want to, you can wear your underwear. I'll keep mine on."

She nodded, more to herself than to me, and climbed out of the truth. Nimble fingers started unbuttoning her jeans. I watched the denim slip over her the sinful sweep of her hips and thighs, taking in her olive skin. Next came the top. My gratitude for our solitude grew as each lush inch was revealed. I'd kill anyone who laid eyes on her. I pretended to focus on undressing myself as she folded her clothes and put them on the seat of the truck. That green gaze traced the length of my body before Sierra blushed and closed the passenger door.

Clad in only our underwear, I took her hand to help her the short distance from the truck to the pools of water. Surrounded by stone, the river flowed behind them as steam rose from the natural stone bowls.

After placing towels on a nearby rock, I picked my way into the hot spring to show Sierra the safest places to step. Once I was waist-deep, I held out a hand for her and watched her follow my footsteps as she carefully entered the water.

"This is so nice."

Sierra moaned deeply at the warm water, letting her eyes fall shut as her head tipped back. Ignoring what that sound did to my dick, I watched her recline in the steaming water.

"How did you find this place?" Sierra asked, face angled toward the pink and purple sky.

"Me and Eddie used to come up here in high school," I paused.

She lifted her head from the water, a teasing smile on her tempting lips. The plain white cotton bra and underwear clung to her, barely covering what they were meant to. Sierra looked like a creature meant to lure sailors to their watery deaths. I tried to maintain eye contact as I wondered what the hell I'd been thinking bringing her here when I was faced with a view like that. Mouthwatering. That was the word.

"With who, Alden?"

A roaring engine split the quiet air. Hoping to see Eddie's truck, I looked to where the road parted the copse of trees. Big and black, basically brand new. Not Eddie's. I recognized the truck as it pulled up, a sinking feeling swallowing my gut. Sierra stood on her toes, trying to peer over my shoulder at the new arrival. If they saw her, they'd be more of a problem than I had the patience to deal with.

"Who is that?"

Shit.

"We need to go."

There were a few ranches around here. Most were small. Some were empires. One of the biggest ones was owned by the Thompson family. Two of the four brothers were on the rodeo circuit. The other two, the twins, worked on the family ranch. They got out of the truck. Their sister, Natalie, hopped out behind them.

"Well, if it isn't fucking Alden Boone," Natalie's brother Trent grunted as he strode toward us, pushing a hand through his close-cropped sandy blond hair. He was always the talker.

I held out a hand, trying to silently command Sierra to remain behind me as the biggest Thompsons came to the edge of the water.

"Natalie told us you got yourself married. Is this the little woman?" Brandon, Trent's mirror image, mocked. Only a few inches and twenty pounds smaller than me, they wouldn't have been a problem individually. Together, they were almost impossible to take on. These guys always got under my skin. From the shit-eating grin on his face, Brandon knew it. "Come on, sweetheart. Don't hide. Let me get a good look at you."

I reached out for a towel, only to be foiled by a big black boot as it pinned them. Sierra slipped around me, her arms crossed in front of her. Covering what she could. Fuck, my anger was already slipping its leash.

"Well, well," Trent grinned. "Hello, honey. Now I get it. You broke our poor sister's heart for a sweet little piece of ass."

Sierra grabbed a towel, Brandon lifting his boot to let her remove it. I didn't miss the wink he tossed at her with that shit-eating grin. Ten seconds. They had ten seconds to get out of here before I caved in their skulls.

Motion around their truck caught my attention. Natalie was now leaning against the grill. Watching with an impassive look on her face. They may have had the same brown eyes and blond hair, but that was where the similarities ended. This wasn't her. The girl I knew was nice. Welcoming. This. This was them. They'd been like this in high school. Aching for a fight wherever they could find one. Not a damn thing had changed.

Trent extended a hand to Sierra, who took it with a wary look in her eye as she stepped out. With his other hand, he snatched the towel away before she could wrap it around herself.

"Hey!" I barked, trying to climb out of the water only to be foiled by Brandon's looming presence.

The brothers surrounded Sierra, caging her in between their broad forms. I moved toward the back edge of the pool, needing to find a way out of this fucking hole.

"Let's take her to Paris," Brandon smirked over her shoulder as he tucked two fingers under her chin.

She looked at me. I hated the helplessness I felt as she covered herself as best she could. Nervous. The sight made rage boil low in me. Wet stone scraped my skin as I climbed out of the water from the other side.

"Have you ever been with two guys at once, sweetheart?"

Sierra shrunk away, bumping into Trent as she stepped backward. He took her hips in his hands, grinning from ear to ear. She tried to push his hands away and he didn't move. That was it. That was fucking it.

"Brandon, stop!" Natalie called from behind them. "Leave them alone."

"Get your hands off her," I fumed, wedging myself between them as I pushed Sierra away. From the corner of my eye, I could see her backing toward my truck. Good girl.

"What did you just say?" Trent seethed.

"Don't fucking touch my wife," I snarled.

Blinding pain lanced through my cheek as a feminine scream sounded. Sierra. Between the fully dressed twins, my feet scraped on rock as I braced them to defend myself. Their blows rained down on me.

"Stop!" Sierra shouted frantically. She pulled on my shirt, hastily buttoning the pearl snap buttons as she stuffed her feet into her boots.

I threw an elbow into Trent's nose, satisfied with the sound of cracking bone as I dodged Brandon's next blow. A knee to his gut knocked the wind from him. Trent threw his arms around me, pinning my arms to my sides as he tried to pull me off of his brother. I threw my head back, seeing stars as it connected with his.

"Just stop it!" Natalie seethed. "Brandon. Trent. Stop or I swear I'm telling Daddy."

A loud shot snapped in the evening air. Brandon and Trent went still as they held me between them, looking over to the source of the sound. Sierra had gotten my revolver from the glove box and was now holding it over her head.

"Let him go," she ordered, her voice trembling as she brought the gun down to aim it with both hands.

"Sierra," Natalie said carefully.

"Sweetheart, you can barely lift that thing. I doubt you'll hit one of us. Let alone both of us," Trent sneered.

My woman aimed the gun at their truck and blew out one of their headlights. Alright, so she did know how to use a gun. Then she cocked the revolver as she trained the barrel on Natalie.

"I don't need to hit either of you. Just her," she shouted. "Let my husband go."

Trent released me with a growl. Brandon put his hands up, walking toward the truck to put himself between Natalie and the gun.

"This ain't over, Boone," Trent barked as he climbed into the driver's seat of their truck.

I strode toward Sierra, taking the gun from her as I pulled her into my side. The feel of her trembling body against mine did nothing to temper my anger. I decocked the revolver, trying to stifle the urge to use it.

"Yes, it is," Natalie snapped. "Let them go."

Thirty-One
Alden

Eddie was already snoring on the couch with one hand shoved down his pants when we got back inside. Sierra stifled a laugh at the sight while she slipped off her boots to leave them beside the door. I followed her into the bedroom after doing the same.

Adrenaline was still riding me hard. Tremors wracked my hands. Just as they had for the entire drive home. I sighed through my nose. This was not how I wanted this night to go. Shutting the door, I turned to see Sierra stripping. One article of clothing after another was tossed with a wet thump into the hamper until she was bare from top to tail. If I'd been in trouble at the hot springs, I was done for now.

"Are you coming?"

I felt my eyebrows shoot up. She crossed her arms over her perfect tits and propped her hip on the doorframe of the bathroom. I did my best to keep my eyes on hers, even if my self-control was threadbare at the moment.

"I'm not rewarding you for that ridiculous fight. I just want to save water."

"Right," I smirked as I undid my belt.

Sierra blushed as she watched me.

"This is strictly about getting clean."

"Yes, ma'am."

I nodded, sliding the belt free from its loops. Her eyes tracked my hands as I wrapped the leather around my fist. I relished the way her throat bobbed at the flex of my forearms. Her eyes dipped to my jeans. Before I could start taking them off, she turned around and fired up the shower.

Undressing was an effort. Just getting clean. Right. Get clean and ignore the most beautiful woman I've ever seen in real life completely naked in my shower. Every ounce of energy I had left was focused on deescalating the thickening problem between my legs.

Steam billowed out of the bathroom by the time I opened the door, ready to get in. Sierra had stepped inside of the tub, holding her hand out to test the temperature of the water as she moved forward. Picking up the soap I bought for her, the one that smelled like roses, she began making a lather with her hands.

Attempting to keep some distance between us, I entered the tub and drew the shower door closed. If I got any closer to this woman in this state, all bets were off. Terrible timing, really, since we were now in a tiny glass box together.

"I'm not going to touch you," she declared as she soaped herself up. "Or kiss you."

No, I wanted to say, *you're just going to torture me instead*.

I wouldn't touch her. Even if every cell in my body had turned into screaming cavemen begging me to do something about this. My hands flexed at my sides. Sierra's soapy touch smoothed down the plane of her stomach, the suds washing over the swell of her hips and down between her thighs making my knees go weak. She was right. This was not a reward. This was punishment.

Sierra finished cleaning herself, allowing me to watch as she rinsed every inch. Fucking hell. By the time I got out of the shower, taking a few extra minutes to think about day-old roadkill and horse manure in order to navigate the problem watching her had created, she was in her pajamas. If I hadn't just come out of a box of pain, I would have enjoyed the sight of her perched on the bed beside the orange case containing my first aid kit. With visions of decomposing animals still dancing in my head, I pulled on my boxers and sweatpants and then sat down beside her.

"I'm assuming that's for me," I said, nodding toward the box.

"That's right, cowboy," she smirked. "Let me clean you up."

Elegant fingers soaked a cotton ball with alcohol. Sierra got to her knees, hair resting over a shoulder in a damp braid as she reached for the gash in my cheek. I hissed at the sting of the cleanser on my wounds.

"Not so tough now, are you?" Sierra laughed, placing a hand on my knee to balance herself as she reached for a bandage.

"Where did you learn to fire a gun?"

"My family was mafia, Alden," she monotoned. "I went to the range with my brother all the time. I can probably hit targets better than those assholes."

Sierra's face fell as she went still. She'd told me about her parents. About her overbearing mother and her stern father. But her brother. I knew that wound stung more than the others. Hell, a small part of me was glad her mother wasn't around to make her feel like shit about herself. But I never had a sibling, so I'd never know what it would feel like to lose one. Paper crinkled as she opened the bandage wrapper, and then removed the backing. With a cautious and precise touch, she applied the bandage over my wound.

"There's something else," Sierra rasped, reaching behind herself to fetch something from her nightstand and lift it in a closed hand between us.

She opened her hand, revealing a pair of pearl earrings with white gold and little diamonds on them. The earrings she'd been wearing when I found her by the side of the road.

"I'm really more of an emerald girl," I joked.

"Take them," she laughed, reaching over me to place them on my nightstand. "Sell them. They're worth more than some people make in a year. That money will go a long way."

I eyed the earrings a moment before returning my gaze to the girl sitting in front of me.

"I had a jewelry box filled with things exactly like those earrings back home. Granted, my mother picked all of them. But I didn't think twice about it. Hundreds of thousands of dollars just dangling on my ears. I was just a stupid, spoiled girl. I don't want you to think I'm using you."

Sierra let out a sigh, taking my hand in hers as she cleaned the scrapes I'd completely forgotten about. None of it hurt because I was transfixed by her face. Her brows furrowed as she took another breath. Was she trying not to cry?

"You didn't have to defend me, Alden," she scolded. "I didn't want you to get hurt. It's not worth it."

"Yes, you are," I rasped.

Before she'd fired that gun, I was willing to take a beating. Willing to go to jail for what I'd do to the twins. I was more than happy to give them the punishment they deserved for touching her. For putting that fear in her voice. In her eyes. A few cuts and bruises were nothing compared to what I was willing to endure to protect her.

She shook me off and packed up the first aid supplies, but I saw the way her lips tugged up in a weak smile she was trying to hide. Quickly, Sierra hopped off of the bed to stash the kit back under the sink. But she didn't go to her side of the bed. Didn't get under the covers or pick up the book she was reading. She resumed her place beside me.

"Are you still mad at me?" I asked.

She smiled, that real smile that melted my insides, and shook her head. I reached out to push that hair I couldn't keep my hands off of behind an ear. Peering up at me through those long lashes, she laughed.

"Yes," she lied.

"Fuck it. I'm kissing you anyway."

Her mouth was warm and welcoming as we toppled over, her body soft and enticing beneath mine. I tried convincing myself that this was enough. That kissing this gorgeous creature in my bed was as good as things were going to get for us. Because if I'd already been willing to go to jail for her then crossing that final line would be the last nail in my coffin. Instead, I coveted the rosy scent of her skin and the feel of her body beneath me. Dreamy green eyes peered up at me from the rumpled sheets, pupils blown wide with a thirst I wanted to slake.

"Alden," Sierra panted as she stared up at me. "I don't know how to explain the way you make me feel."

"I know."

I shut my eyes, letting out a breath. For just a second, I wanted to forget that this was temporary. The day would come when she would go back to her life and I would be left with mine. Her smile would be a memory. Her scent would linger on my sheets and I'd be left with only the ghost of these moments.

"We should go to sleep," I said as I got up and moved toward the headboard, kicking the covers down.

Sierra sat up and looked at me, then at the earrings on the nightstand.

"Alden. Sell those earrings."

I simply nodded at her, just to let her know I'd heard, and opened my arms to welcome her. Sierra settled into my grasp and released a sigh. This routine of ours was going to do more damage to me than the twins ever could have. I took a deep breath of my own and wondered how long it would take me to recover from the shattered heart she would leave behind when she walked out my door.

Thirty-Two
Sierra

The fight. Alden's bruises and scrapes. I never would have shot Natalie. But I knew how protective older brothers were. Enzo would have killed anyone who pointed a gun at me. As I fixed lunch for myself, I thought about everything that had happened the day before. I'd been impressed that I'd made the shot with a revolver. I'd never fired one of those before. The last time I fired any gun was the day my father informed me of his arrangement with the Serpas.

The day he told me about my engagement to Antoni.

People don't tell you that days that change your life always start like any other. Wake up and go to Pilates. Eat breakfast. Come home and get cleaned up. Work until the afternoon, when my parents expected us home for family dinner. I was breaking the rules, working in the kitchen when I heard my mother's heels click on the polished floors.

"Sierra, your father needs you in the study."

I looked up from my laptop to find my mother standing on the other side of the large white marble island. Lifting my coffee from its saucer, I took a sip as I crafted a response in my head.

"Let me finish sending this email and I'll be right in."

My mother gave a reluctant, terse nod and placed her palms on the island in front of her. Green eyes moved down to my laptop as she arched a brow. Waiting for me. Placing my cup down again, I typed as quickly as I could to send out the report I'd been consumed with for the last month. Standing from the upholstered stool, I smoothed my hands down my cream shift dress and slid my heels back on.

"Don't you think that's a little inappropriate?"

"It's Prada," I argued, looking down at the little flared skirt.

"It's too short."

My mother sneered as we approached the doors of the study. She reached a hand toward the knob, waiting to open it as she took me in. Her lips pulled into a tight line as she released the knob and took my face in her hands. Her eyes softened. For a moment, I had the foolish notion that she'd tell me she loved me. That she was proud of me. It was fleeting and ill-advised, as that hope would always be with her. She smoothed her hands over my hair, pushing it out of my face before speaking. Moment over.

"Don't disappoint me."

My mother retreated from me, moving to open one of the white double doors to my father's study. Icy dread crept over me as I entered the room. The floor-to-ceiling shelves lined with books pressed in around me. My Mary Jane heels clacked on the wood floor until they hit the expensive wool rug. Enzo Volpe stood behind his antique wood desk, wearing a grey suit and crisp white shirt unbuttoned at the collar. His jaw was tight as his blue eyes shifted to examine me, quickly returning to his guest facing away from me in one of the two leather armchairs across from him.

"Bruno, this is my daughter, Sierra Briar Volpe."

The man rose from his chair, turning to extend a hand to me in greeting. Cold dark eyes raked over me, taking their time on the more intimate parts. I wanted to run away. To hide. His hand felt clammy in mine. Sweaty as it gripped me too hard. Hard enough to hurt. I let go, folding my arms over my chest, and tried to muster a polite smile.

"Sierra, this is Bruno Serpa."

Understanding teased the edges of my mind. No. I glanced at my father. Everything I needed to know about what he expected from me in this moment was in his eyes.

Don't disappoint me.

"It's a pleasure to meet you," I smiled.

Twisting anxiety moved through my gut like a snake. This wasn't right. Nothing about this was right. Bruno Serpa was the head of our family's most violent rivals. They burned our businesses. Blocked deals. Killed our men on sight. Now he was sitting in my father's office. For what?

"Have a seat, Ms. Volpe," Bruno offered, tugging me toward the chair beside his.

"That won't be necessary," my father interjected. "You've seen her. I trust that is satisfactory."

Bruno's gaze trailed over my body again.

"Oh, absolutely," he grinned. "My son will be very pleased."

The words felt like oil on my skin. I forced the polite smile to remain on my face, trying to fight the confusion and fear I felt. His son? The purpose of this meeting was finally clear to me. My father stood from his overstuffed leather office chair, rounding the desk to escort his guest out.

"Mr. Serpa, I'll see you out," he said, pausing beside me to mutter his instruction to stay in his office.

That wouldn't be a problem. My feet felt like they were filled with lead. If I took one step, my heart would collapse. His son.

"It was nice to meet you, Ms. Volpe. You'll make a lovely addition to our family."

I swallowed and nodded.

"The feeling is mutual, Mr. Serpa."

I couldn't tell if it was what I'd said or the nausea threatening that brought the bitter taste to my tongue. Metal clacked as my father pulled the door open. My mother was waiting on the other side, ready to finish escorting

Bruno Serpa out of our home. With a quick click, the door was shut again. My father turned on his heel, approaching me with the ice-cold face of the Volpe patriarch. All business.

"You and Antoni Serpa will be married before the end of the month. Following the nuptials, you will move into their family home. I've informed the staff that they will need to pack your things."

"That's in three weeks," I croaked, nausea shortening my esophagus. "It's too fast. We can find someone else. Not them. Not him. Please."

His hands flexed in irritation before he stuffed them into the pockets of his slacks. The muscle in his jaw flickered at my watery voice. Though they were near mirror images of each other, there was nothing of my brother's kindness in our father's face.

"This is not up for negotiation, Sierra. Your marriage to Antoni and subsequent heirs will help to cement our alliance with their family and eliminate the roadblocks our developments have been hitting with the city council."

Every day of my life had been leading up to this. An arranged marriage. I once thought my parents would take my happiness into consideration. That they'd at least consider my safety. I'd been so wrong. They wanted me to marry that monster's son, a man I'd only heard of in passing but I couldn't imagine he was kind. The Serpas were notoriously cruel, and they hated us. I couldn't decide which was worse, that my father was giving me away for business or that he didn't seem to care what happened to me.

"You're selling me to those sadists for a fucking building? I'm not a goddamn cow."

I wasn't ready for it. The back of my father's hand connected with my cheekbone hard enough that I could feel every bone in his knuckles.

"Watch your mouth. Never forget that you exist by the grace of me. I am your father. You do not question me. You do not argue with me."

"No," I sniffed, fighting the tears that rushed to my eyes. "I won't. I won't do it."

Another slap seared my skin with its swift brutality. I bit back the urge to scream, unable to stop the yelp that slipped out at the blow that was harder than the first. Arguing would do no good. I didn't know why I was trying. My father looked down his nose at me as my nose dripped blood onto the twill, cream-colored fabric of my dress.

"As I said, this is not up for negotiation. We will announce your engagement in two weeks at the opera benefit and your wedding will occur on Saturday the following week. I expect you to smile and act the part of the happy bride-to-be."

With that, he turned and left. Alone in the spacious study, my heart thundered in my ears. The enormity of my situation tumbled onto my shoulders like a pile of stone, my knees collapsing under the weight of it. I crumbled to the floor and let the tears I'd been holding back fall.

Antoni Serpa. I didn't know anything about him. I'd only seen one or two photos and while he wasn't bad looking, he frightened me. The sharp angle of his jaw. His black eyes. Not brown. Black. Cold. Just as his fathers were. His father who'd looked at me like I was a piece of meat. A piece of meat that was going to be delivered to his doorstep in three weeks' time. Kept in his house. Another cage. One I'd never be allowed to leave.

"Sierra?"

My brother's voice filtered into the room. Afternoon light had faded from the big windows behind my father's desk. I wiped my tears. I hadn't even heard him enter. Enzo knelt beside me, lifting my chin with his hand. His dark brows furrowed as he took in our father's work.

"I'm engaged," I said weakly. As if saying it out loud made it real, I choked on a sob. Tears spilled down my cheeks. Enzo put his arm around my shoulder, rubbing a circle into my back as he let me cry.

"I know."

I drew back, anger temporarily replacing misery as I took in his face. My brother's face was filled with regret.

"Why didn't you tell me?"

"You know how he is," Enzo sighed. "He only told me yesterday. Father took me with him when he met with the Serpas at their house. Your new bedroom is going to be very nice."

I shook my head at him. No. He knew about this whole arrangement and didn't say a word to me. Enzo pulled me up from the floor, wiping my tears away.

"I was going to go to the range for a while. You should come with me. We can get a pizza on the way back," my brother slung his arm over my shoulders as he escorted me to the door.

"You know mother will never let me eat it. Especially since I apparently have to fit into a wedding dress now," I groused with a sniff.

"They have a dinner with the Capriottis tonight. She won't be here by the time we get back. I'm thinking something with lots of meat."

He mussed my hair and I whined. Enzo laughed as I pulled away to fix the damage.

"Lots of cheese?"

"Lots of cheese," he promised. "But only if you make three bullseye shots. Headshots. Not center mass."

"Fine."

Firing that shot the first shot had been strange. The blast reverberated into my bones, making my skin prick with memory. Memories of Enzo standing in the next stall, laughing as I made my shots with ease. He'd made a joke about all bets being off when cheese was on the line. I was trembling so hard by the second shot that firing the gun again had been a relief.

I flipped my grilled cheese in the pan, listening to the butter sizzle as I smirked down at the sandwich. My brother would have never have guessed I'd end up here. Still, Enzo would've been proud of the way I handled those men roughing up Alden. Even if I'd been shaking like a leaf the entire time.

Thirty-Three
Alden

Primrose looked up at me from the thick layer of hay she'd nestled into, her foal nuzzling at her side. She was the prize. The award-winning mare whose brand-new baby boy would sell for seven figures for his legacy and eventual breeding potential. For now, his biggest problem was trying to figure out how to feed himself.

Regret at missing his arrival stung like a fresh wound. Of all the girls giving birth this season, Prim was my favorite. I'd been stuck working on fixing broken heads on the irrigation system in the pasture out by the highway. The birth went smoothly, Eddie had handled everything just as I would have. He had started chipping the first arrivals with the other wranglers in the other stalls. I could hear him laughing at something one of the Miller boys said. Mr. Weaver chuckled as he peered in at Prim's young black colt, scratching at his mustache as he took up a place at my side.

"He came out quick," I marveled.

"Yep," the old man agreed. "She labored all morning."

"That's it, then," Mr. Weaver grunted. "We'll have the vet out to look at them as soon as he can. The Thompsons are calving now."

The Thompsons. I cringed at the memory of the twins. The way they touched my woman. Intimidated her. It had only been a few days, but the anger stirring in me felt fresh. Flexing and releasing my hands I huffed a sigh through my nose. The old man arched a brow as I backed away from the stall and tugged off my work gloves.

"You good, son?"

I nodded, coughing to clear the irritation lodging itself in my throat.

"Yeah, I just have a lot on my mind."

Eddie's laugh bounced off of the walls again from a few stalls away. A couple of others followed. Mr. Weaver smiled at the sound.

"You know, this is the best part of the season. There's not much to do with the little ones but enjoy them until they're old enough to move out to the pasture. All the other horses have to do is stay healthy and happy."

That was an oversimplification of the coming weeks, but summer was always less about the horses and more about maintenance on the property to prepare for fall and the next round of dams. But the old man was right. With foaling finished for this year, we could all breathe a little easier.

"Sawyer's got some burgers going today," the old man crowed loud enough for all of us to hear. His favorite thing in the world next to sunrise on a spring morning was a cheeseburger. "I'm going to get inside and get my plate. Y'all come up to the house as soon as you're done in there."

His direction was heard loud and clear by everyone. Eddie hummed his agreement along with a few appreciative grunts from the others. Mr. Weaver turned and left while I headed toward them. The little brown filly had flopped down in Eddie's lap, sniffing and snorting at his mullet as she tried to take bits of it into her mouth. Auburn's baby girl was turning out to have just as big a personality as her mama.

"Always the ladies' man, huh?" I snorted.

The other two wranglers saw themselves out, anxious to get to lunch. The smell of charred beef was already making my stomach growl. How I hadn't noticed it before, I wouldn't know. Eddie pushed the filly off of him, carefully moving her onto her feet as he got to his.

"Lunch?"

"Yeah, man," Eddie huffed. "I'm starving. I left my phone in my truck, though. Let me grab it."

His boots clopped on the barn's wooden planks as I followed him out. He'd left before my feet had even hit the floor this morning. Granted, I'd been dragging myself out of bed later and later since I'd started sharing it with Sierra. It was so damn hard to leave warmth and comfort her nearness provided. This morning she'd had her leg thrown over me and whined when I removed it with a muttered "five more minutes."

Eddie threw open the passenger side door, rummaging through his center console for his phone. The old red Toyota had been the first thing he bought for himself, and he'd told me he'd never let her die. She was newer than my truck by about twelve years but looked just as old since he practically lived out of the thing. I crossed my arms and stayed a step back, eyeing the state of his interior when I noticed his bags packed behind the passenger seat.

"You going somewhere?" I asked, jerking my thumb toward the bags as Eddie looked over his shoulder at me.

"I'm moving on to Coldwater," he grunted, pulling his phone out of the driver side door's compartment. "They're a few weeks out from calving but they've got about a dozen more."

Eddie shoved his phone in the front pocket of his mud-stained jeans. He was moving on to another ranch. He was off of my sofa. Out of my house. The house I was sharing with Sierra. My palms started to itch. With the birth of Prim's colt this morning, I hadn't even thought about what came next. It was time for him to move on. Time for me to get my house back. Junior walked out from inside the house and shouted to us that lunch was ready.

"You're going to Coldwater?" I asked, trying to mask my excitement. "When?"

My friend snorted, glancing at me sidelong as we made our way toward the front steps. With everyone gathering around the cooler stuffed with Sawyer's jars of lemonade, I paused and waited for Eddie to see that I'd done so. He noted my absence and turned to face me.

"I'm sure you're heartbroken I'm cleared out of the house, but I'll only be a few miles away. Besides, I'll be back before you know it."

"Right. But you're heading over there today?"

Eddie slapped his hand onto my shoulder, giving it a squeeze as he gave me a lupine smile.

"Yup. Packed up this morning."

Thirty-Four

Sierra

Solitude had become a more comfortable concept with each passing day. Walking through the woods. Teaching myself to paint. Reading. It was as if my body had finally detoxed from a lifetime of living on a tight schedule. Without the pressure of living up to someone else's expectations, I was starting to get used to the idea of doing nothing.

Evening light filtered in through the large living room windows. I reached to turn on the table lamp, perched on the sofa with another book from Alden's Tolkien collection. I was nestling back into my seat and turning the yellowed page when I heard his truck roar up to the house. Six o'clock on the dot.

Heavy footsteps rushed the porch steps. The front door opened with a slam into the wall that made me jerk in my seat. Alden's chest was heaving. With a glance at me, he took his hat off and set it on the shelf before shutting the door with his foot. He backed himself against it, flexing his hands at his sides with a little chuckle. Strange energy radiated from him. It wasn't anger. Or fear. Alden watched me from beneath lowered brows. The look made the butterflies in my stomach take off in a frenzy.

"That was the longest afternoon of my life."

"What? Where's Eddie? " I asked, folding the book shut and setting it on the end table. "His pile of clothes is gone."

Pins and needles pricked over my skin at the way his eyes trailed over every part of me. Then he smirked. Smirked as if he was aware of some joke I hadn't heard. It was a confusing combination that was making me nervous. Was there any oxygen in this room?

"Eddie moved on to another ranch," Alden rasped, hazel eyes filled with heat as he drank me in. "He's gone."

Oh.

It felt like I was trapped in the house with a wild animal. Any sudden move and he would, well, I didn't know what he would do. Part of me was terrified. The other part of me desperately wanted to find out.

"We're alone."

He licked his lower lip. Boots clopped on the wooden floor as he took slow, deliberate steps toward me. I shifted onto my knees, trying to slowly move from the sofa. He'd warned me about wild animals. Explained how to behave when one was staring me down. Except this was uncharted territory. Alden wasn't a coyote. Or a wolf. That didn't mean he wouldn't swallow me whole.

"I love that blue dress on you," he said, his voice a low growl. "But if you don't take it off now, I'm going to tear it to pieces."

The dominance in his voice had my hands moving. There, on my knees with a slight tremor in my fingers, I unbuttoned the dress down to my waist. Alden watched me with a starved expression, waiting to pounce. I slowly slid the straps down my shoulders. Then off of my arms. Hazel eyes tracked everywhere the fabric slid over my skin until the dress dropped to my knees.

Alden drank me in. Not an assessment or even ogling. Just hungry appreciation. Trailing over my face, my pebbled breasts, down my stomach to the white cotton panties I still wore. He reached for my face, a callused thumb ghosting over my lip. The green in his hazel eyes burned into me, the air between us crackling with months of anticipation.

"Have you been tested?"

I blinked.

"Have you?"

"Yes. All good."

"Me too," I nodded.

"Good. Stand up and turn around."

I stood and turned to face the sofa, instinct forcing me to cover my breasts with folded arms as my dress dropped to the floor. Alden's rough hands bracketed my waist and smoothed down to my hips as he slipped his thumbs into the waistband of my panties. With heartbreaking gentleness, his calluses rasped over me as he tugged the garment down with a light kiss on my shoulder. Then another on my hip. My thigh. Until he was kneeling behind me. Those calluses scraped over my softest parts as appreciative hands coasted over my hips and thighs.

"Beautiful."

The sound of Alden's belt unbuckling was almost lost to my thundering heart. If I'd known this had awaited me at the end of the day, I might have hidden in the woods. Even if the idea of him chasing after me did nothing to cool my blood. Soft kisses moved up my legs. Everywhere his lips touched me felt like he was throwing gas on an already raging flame. Lips. Tongue. Teeth. They skimmed one thigh, then the other. Higher. His tongue glided over my core as he hummed with approval.

"Get on the sofa. On your knees for me."

I obeyed, watching him strip the rest of his clothes off as I turned to brace myself on the arm of the sofa. Alden's nakedness had an astounding effect on me. No one I'd been with before had dark whorls of chest hair or a treasure trail like he did. They didn't have dense muscles packed on from hours of work. Golden skin that wasn't a result of expensive tanning cream, but hours working in the sun. Those boys sure as hell didn't look at me the way this man was looking at me now.

There had been nervousness before. Fear of doing something wrong. Not being perfect. Not being what my partner wanted. Not living up to someone else's expectations. None of that explained how I felt now. The way I shivered wasn't from the fear that I would disappoint him. I knew exactly where I stood. When Alden touched me, it was with reverence. His kiss was a prayer on my skin. Every time I felt him, I understood. This wasn't something I had to do. It wasn't a box to be checked. It wasn't an experience achieved for the sake of having it.

This was being alive.

Alden climbed onto the sofa behind me, moving my now waist-long hair aside to lavish my spine with more kisses. The heat of his mouth on my skin sent another shiver through me. An appreciative hand ran down the length of my back before he knocked my knees apart with his own.

"You know what's about to happen, don't you?"

The question was a rumble against my back as his chest pressed against me, his mouth a breath away from my ear. He followed his question with a soft kiss just below it.

"Yes."

Alden buried his face in my neck, inhaling deeply before speaking again.

"You can tell me not to, Sierra. Tell me you don't want this and I'll stop. Right now."

Over and over again. I had imagined this so many times. Not once had I realized how it would feel. How much I would hate the waiting we'd done because I'd been deprived of this feeling. I thought I'd felt desire for someone before. With Graham. With the others. I hadn't realized there would be such a difference between being interested in someone and craving them like I'd been dying and he was air. Because I had no idea it could feel like this.

I turned, bringing my mouth to his. Never had I wanted anyone or anything the way I wanted him right now. My skin ached with it. My blood screamed for it. I let him taste my answer. Let him feel it in the movement of my lips. With the slide of my tongue. Then, with that soft kiss, I begged.

"I want you. Please, Alden. I can't wait anymore."

He huffed a sigh of relief as that sunshine smile spread across his mouth.

The dense length of him brushed through my center as he wrapped an arm around my waist. His other hand grasped my hip with a gentle, squeezing touch before moving between my legs. A kiss pressed to my shoulder as he lined himself up at my entrance.

"I don't want to hurt you. We're going to take it slow. Take a breath now."

Even as I sucked in a puff of air, I was not prepared. Not for the stretch of him as he pushed his thick crown past my entrance. My hand flew to the arm at my waist, clawing at him as he moved slowly, searing me from the inside, inch by punishing inch.

"It's too much," I whined.

Alden let out a surprised laugh as my nails dug into him. Pushing my head back to his shoulder, I looked up at him. Nothing I could have imagined compared to feeling this. That first time with Graham came to mind. It was my first time and he hadn't taken half the care and patience Alden was taking now, even though I could feel the large cowboy shaking against me with restraint.

"It'll fit," he panted, a hot breath against my ear. Then kissed my neck. "Relax for me, gorgeous."

I wasn't prepared for the way my body screamed for more of this delicious agony as I trembled in his hold. In a little more. Overwhelmed wasn't the right word. There had to be a better word. A drowning word. Something that would explain this crushing breathlessness I felt.

"Alden," I mewled with a strangled yelp.

"I know, darlin'. You're doing so good. Just breathe. I'm almost in."

This was excruciating. Utter torture. In and in and in. Until I felt his hips pressed against me. We both groaned when he was finally fully seated. His body went taut as a bowstring. Waiting. Breath sawed out of me at the staggering sensation of finally crossing this boundary. Of being so impossibly full. Full of him. The hand between my legs slid over my sex as Alden felt where he was embedded in me as if needing to confirm this was really happening before moving it to my hip.

I turned, needing to see his face. We looked at each other and I felt something I'd never had, not with anyone. Felt it snap tight between us. Something so real, I felt like I could almost touch it. Alden moved to kiss me again, closing his eyes with a steadying breath.

"I'm sorry. I want to take my time with you," he panted as he drew out of me, then pushed in with a slow thrust.

Breath whooshed from me in a helpless exhale at all of the new sensations his movement stirred in me. My nails dug into his skin again and he let out a sharp moan. Shaking. I was well and truly shaking now. He withdrew from me, almost completely.

"To worship you like you deserve and learn everything that brings you pleasure."

Another thrust. This time, harder. Faster. Full. So unbearably full. I whimpered. Alden pulled me against him, nipping at my ear before his deep and rough declaration rattled into it.

"But right now, I need to fuck my wife."

With another thrust, he moved both hands to my hips and began driving a steady pace into me. The burning stretch of him. The way he rotated his hips so I would feel it all. It was too much. So much. The helpless noises that came out of me were nothing compared to the powerlessness I felt, submitting wholly to the pleasure that welled within.

Alden's face buried in my hair as he shifted to brace his hands on the arm of the sofa, caging me in with his large form. The flex of his hips into me transitioned to deep, thorough thrusts as he began moaning and panting my name. Ecstasy licked every inch of me as I let myself get lost in this. This feeling he stirred in me had me grinding my hips back into his.

Boys. All of the ones who'd come before were boys. Alden Boone was a man. A man who was giving me everything he had, overpowering my ability to think clearly as sensation crested with every stroke. Each hum of pleasure that came from him. The hard length of him. Shaking breaths. I did that to him. Me.

"Come here."

He sat up and yanked at my waist, pulling me against his chest as he quickly shifted to wrap an arm around me, sitting on his heels as he pulled me into his lap. Alden kissed my neck, giving the skin a hard bite as he sucked it into his mouth with a growl. The sweet cowboy who'd come to my rescue had been replaced with this wild creature. A predator marking his prey.

His teeth distracted me long enough to be surprised by his hand. Work-roughened fingers toyed with my clit, testing and moving until they found a rhythm that made me squeeze around him. I loosed a helpless wail, throwing my head back against his shoulder as his cock brutally ground into that leg-wobbling inner spot.

"That's it," he growled between moans. "That's what she wants. Don't you dare make a noise that I didn't earn."

A tiny pit of dread opened in me as I wondered if this was a mistake. Sure, the others who would follow him couldn't measure up. Not physically. That was trivial compared to the way he made me feel. He was setting the bar in the sky with the way he moved and the sounds he made like he was enjoying my body as much as I enjoyed his. The dominance in his touch, his words. He didn't just take control of me. I gave it to him.

"Please."

Begging. I was begging him. For what, I didn't know. More of this may very well kill me. Of course, if this was how I was meant to die, I'd take it. It was a far better way to go than a bullet in an opera box.

Alden played my pleasure like a master. He was a musician and I was his instrument. I bared down on him, ready to explode as breath became harder and harder to come by. It was all too much. His body dominated mine. The stinging pleasure of his size. His fingers moving against my sensitive flesh. The filthy, pretty words he spoke.

"Yes. Come, gorgeous. Be a good wife and come on my cock."

As if on command, my head whipped to his. Nose to nose, wild hazel eyes watched me shatter. My brows tugged together as I choked on a silent scream.

Alden's breath was fighting through clenched teeth as if it took all of his focus to continue working me through my orgasm. Hips drove up into me at an unbroken pace, fingers stroking exactly where I needed them.

A sob shuddered out of me as every feeling collided into a deafening crescendo. The field of sunflowers. That night after the coyote. Toying with me. None of it prepared me for how this would feel. Wanting him had been foolish. If I wasn't careful, this would ruin me. My name was a rough prayer on his soft lips as he gripped me hard enough to bruise. The arm at my waist tightened around me. Then I felt it.

"Fuck," he roared as his hips stuttered.

Alden pulled my body flush with him, swelling inside of me with his release as he panted through it. He held me close as I braced an arm on the back of the sofa, still shivering with euphoria. Nuzzling into my neck, he breathed me in with a satisfied hum. The hand he'd used to pleasure me slipped down to where we were joined. I jerked in surprise as he chuckled, then swept two fingers around my entrance. I watched him give one a lick. Hazel eyes tracked the other as he placed it on my lips.

"We taste so fucking good together."

Thirty-Five
Alden

Holy. Shit.

I'd never gone all night with a girl. Not before her. Never felt like I'd lost all impulse control. Rational thought was a distant thing when this woman was in my arms. There was only the way she felt. Her mouth. Her everything. Shit, with Sierra it all felt brand new. Those first few moments were excruciating. Taking it slow when I wanted to do anything but. It was an agonizingly exquisite fit. After what might have been the closest thing to experiencing heaven that I'd get while I was still breathing, I decided I didn't want to be anywhere else.

Eddie hopped into his truck at the end of the day, and he knew exactly what I was thinking. He slapped me on the shoulder and said goodbye.

"Just leave the sofa out of it, man. I sleep there."

Whoops.

I'd buy a new sofa. I'd buy ten new sofas. It was all worth it to see the look in her eyes as she finished all over me. Her trembling body pressed up against mine as she moaned my name. The way her face twisted in divine agony. That might be the last thing I think of before I die. At least, I hope it is.

Once I regained feeling in my legs, I scooped Sierra up from the sofa. She squeaked with delight, slapping my back as I threw her over my shoulder to carry her to the bathroom. Another squeak popped out of her when I set her on the counter to turn on the shower. I knew I reeked from a long day of work and I'd done her no favors by wrapping myself around her. Even if she still smelled delicious.

Sierra piled her hair atop her head, and we hopped into the steaming water. We laughed and toyed with each other until getting clean moved to the back of my mind. I bent down to kiss her. Then we were consumed with each other, kissing and touching each other as if tonight was all we had. I was ready to go again when I heard her stomach growl, otherwise, we wouldn't have taken a break for dinner.

I cooked an evening breakfast with a towel slung around me. Scrambled eggs eaten on top of pieces of buttered toast. We sat next to each other on the counter. She was wearing one of my tee shirts. It was comfortable perfection.

Upon finishing the dishes, she found me star-fishing on the bed, hard and waiting for her. Sierra gave me an arch look as she climbed into my lap, placing herself just above my hips. My woman bent over, licking and kissing my stomach until she planted a kiss over my heart. I hooked a finger into the knot atop her head to see her hair spill down around her.

"I fucking love your hair," I huffed, taking a moment to breathe her in.

She sat up and pulled my shirt off herself, looking down at me. Her hand wandered back, taking me in a long stroke as she studied my face. There was something new in her eyes. A fledgling confidence that simmered like an ember. An ember I wanted to nurture into a roaring flame.

"Can I?"

Shoot me if I ever say no to that, I wanted to say. I nodded with a smirk, letting my hands knead her thighs as she shifted her weight. Sierra slid down my cock, squeezing me into oblivion as she winced at my size.

"Damn," I gritted out. "You feel so good it just might kill me, darlin'."

Sierra watched me for a minute as she panted a little, waiting to move as she adjusted to me. Then she braced her hands on my thighs and rolled her hips until it was me who couldn't breathe. Her lips curled into a smile as she moved again with more confidence. I couldn't help but grin up at her as she began.

My hands roamed over her, taking in the silken feel of her olive skin against my palms. The weight of her full breasts in them. The light brown buds made my mouth salivate. The more I touched her, the more she arched into me. Taking. Relishing being touched as much as I relished touching her.

"Look at you," I marveled.

"I've never been on top before," she breathed, head angled up at the ceiling.

Idiots. Those other guys had been absolute idiots to deprive themselves of this spectacular view. This woman was a fucking goddess.

"You're doing so well. Put on a show for me, gorgeous," I winked. "Show me how good I feel inside you."

Sierra took things slow. She rolled her hips nice and easy, taking her time. Her cheeks were flushed pink. Beautiful. Lips swollen from my kisses. Beautiful. Dark hair cascaded over her in an ethereal mess. Beautiful. Perfect tits bounced with every movement. I sat up, not wanting to wait another minute to taste them. Her voice went thready with my mouth on her.

"Alden."

Goddamn, I loved my name coming out of her mouth.

"Alden, I'm not," she gasped as I nipped her nipple. "Fuck. I don't know if I'm still protected."

I grabbed her hips, stilling her motions. She gazed down at me, hands meeting around the back of my neck.

"Do you want to stop?"

I hadn't bothered to think about it. After weeks of being cooped up without being with her in this way had given me a one-track mind. I should have kicked myself for being so reckless. The funny thing was, I really didn't care. The train had already left the station, but if she wanted to stop, we would stop. Sierra's eyebrows drew together.

"I'm sorry. If we," she paused, dark brows furrowing. "If something happens."

"Then I'll spend the rest of my life taking care of you," I promised, kissing her hard. "If you want. I don't care."

It was an easy promise to make. If it was up to me, I would never let her go. Her tongue licked at the seam of my lips. I opened for her, relishing the feel of her sweet invasion. As I drank in her sighs, tongue languishing mine with savory strokes, she began working herself on me again and started moaning into my mouth.

Asked and answered.

Three times. Three fucking times. After she rode me, coming undone with wails that hit my ears like the sweetest melody, she explained her worries about protection.

Being sold off in marriage to the Serpas also made her a fucking brood mare for the guy she was supposed to marry. She'd only used condoms with men she dated and had never been allowed to go on anything before. She was expected to provide an heir, so she'd secretly gotten the shot to ward off a pregnancy too early in the marriage. It made an odd kind of sense. She wanted to get to know the guy before having a baby with him. I understood her motivation, but the idea of someone like that Antoni guy using her in that way made my blood boil.

She counted the weeks on her fingers as she leaned on me, my back against the headboard, and our legs tangled together. With days melting by so quickly and no way to track them, she'd forgotten how long ago that had been. I made a mental note to finally pull the trigger and get her a phone.

"I don't even know how long I've been here, so I don't know if it's still good or not. I'm sorry. I've never had to think about it before."

"Does it matter?" I asked.

Sierra shrugged, blushing a little. I smiled at her, taking her hand in mine as I kissed her knuckles.

"We can figure out the protection thing later. Right now, I want to be inside of you, and I don't want to feel anything else."

It started sweet and slow. A kiss. Then another. Then I was laying her down, entering her as I tasted her whimpers of ecstasy. The ones that were just for me. I enjoyed each note as I drove in slow and deep. Skin on skin. Breath mingled in frantic puffs. There's not a moment of hesitation from one movement to the next. Especially when she begged.

"Alden, please."

"What, gorgeous?"

I'd never forget her sweet sounds as I drove into her, clutching her ass as I threaded my arm beneath her knee. Her other leg wrapped around my hip, barely able to hold on. She looked up at me, biting her lip, blushing like she was afraid to tell me what she wanted. I slanted my lips over hers, breathing hard as I spoke against her mouth between kisses.

"Tell me."

"I want to feel you come. Please, Alden. It feels so good."

Fuck.

We stared at each other as I moved inside her, squeezing that round cheek in my hand. My other hand moved between us, pulling a gasp from Sierra as it made contact with her swollen bud. Her body seized up around me as I continued my pace, rolling deep as I worked her with my hand. Angelic cheeks turned pink and green eyes flared amidst a field of dark brown hair. She screamed as she came, squirming as I buried myself to the hilt with my release.

"Darlin'," I said as I withdrew from her, watching my spend trail out with me. "You're so much filthier than that angel face lets on."

She blushed. I kissed the swath of skin covering her pounding heart. After she went to see to her needs, I welcomed her into our bed with open arms.

Sierra rolled over, resting her head on my chest with a contented sigh as I stroked my fingertips over the long swath of supple skin. We stayed like that for the rest of the night. I watched her, unable to get my heart to stop racing long enough to drift off. Sierra was smiling in her sleep when morning peeked through the curtains. Dawn. I'd only just shut my eyes, but I wasn't tired. Not one fucking bit.

My heart was still crashing into my ribs. Her sweet little moans still echoed in my ears as I admired the dip of her waist climbing into the curve of a well-formed hip in the meager sunlight. Sleep was overrated. I was glad I didn't miss one second of taking in the masterpiece that was this woman.

As I peeled myself out of bed, the thought of Sierra walking away from me was a distant worry. I dressed, unable to take my eyes off her. She was draped over my pillow, sheets gathered around her waist as one perfect leg dangled from them.

Beautiful.

Every night I'd gone to bed alone in this old house, I wondered what it would be like to finally find someone to share myself with. To want a woman down into my fucking bones. To need someone so much that I felt her in my blood.

Asked and fucking answered.

Thirty-Six
Sierra

I woke up alone. I'd expected it. It happened every day. The difference today was the little white chamomile flower bathed in a shaft of sunlight, waiting for me on Alden's pillow.

The first time I'd ever slept with anyone, it was with Graham at the Gramercy. He'd set up a nice private dinner. Roses and candles were everywhere. The stereo played sensitive indie rock. It was a nice gesture. But all of his romantic gestures were undermined by the fact that I woke up alone. He didn't return my text messages for almost a week afterward. Graham had even left me to figure out a way back to New Haven by myself. I was so embarrassed that when my roommate asked how the night went, I told her everything was fine.

It made me wonder what I'd done wrong. For days, I replayed everything that happened that night. Then he responded to my text to thank him for a lovely night with a message that told me everything I needed to know.

Before that, I got poetry. Before that, I got flowers after our dates. Before that, he responded to me within an hour, if not immediately. Virginity was just a social construct. Sure. Yes. Of course. That didn't mean I was crazy for wanting my first time to be special. To be with someone who cared about me. I thought he did. I didn't know what someone caring about you felt like and he did all of the right things leading up to that point. After that night together, Graham felt that I didn't even warrant an actual text message. Just two letters. To him, I was just a goal. I'd heard my brother's friends talk about "body count." But how was it fair for them to judge women when they would so easily discard them? To him, I was disposable. Goal accomplished. Time to move on.

Then there was Alden. I picked up the little white flower and held it between my fingers as I sat in bed, unable to stop thinking about the differences between a spoiled Ivy League trust fund baby and the cowboy who had almost nothing and made me feel like I was worth everything. A knight in cobbled-together armor. Those hazel eyes stared up at me as I rode him. His large, work-roughened hands were so gentle when they touched me. Alden Boone was so many things I didn't expect.

I took myself to the kitchen to make breakfast. Coffee, now cold from Alden's cup this morning. Poured it over ice into what was now my favorite jar. Egg on toast. Before I sat down to eat, I found an empty Coke bottle and filled it with water. I set it in the center of the table, dropping the bloom inside.

Sitting down to eat, I was met with a soreness I hadn't expected. Even though I'd seen him beforehand, I wasn't ready for how good the pleasant pain would feel. He'd been so gentle. So careful not to go too far, even when his patience was excruciating.

"You're doing so good. Just breathe."

A shiver rushed through my body at the memory. I wanted more. Sitting here at breakfast after spending all night with him, I wanted more. I could still feel his hands on my hips. Feel the bruises from where he gripped me so tight. Hear his filthy words and desperate moans as he climaxed.

With Graham, it had just been cold and awkward. For me, at least. He'd asked me if I was okay two times before about ten minutes of grunting and finishing. Everything about it was so...Underwhelming. I lay there wondering if I'd made a mistake. Since him, there had been two more. One guy at school who'd been equally uninterested in getting me off and another who'd been an investment banker who was so far off the mark that I faked it just to get it over with.

Alden was a caring, attentive man. He was the kind of man who made sure I came before he did. Literally. And after rolling around together all night, he'd left me a flower as he was heading out for work. That meant he walked outside to the little field of wildflowers on the other side of his barn and picked one just for me. Before the sun came up. The man had barely gotten any sleep, and he was still thinking about me. The epitome of 'if he wanted to, he would' behavior.

It was the kind of thing a girl could very easily become addicted to.

A terse knock sounded at the front door, followed by footsteps that trailed away and down the stairs. I got to the door in time to see a delivery truck rumbling off down the road. Looking down at the welcome mat, I saw a package. A small brown box with a name printed on the shipping label.

Mrs. Sierra Boone.

There was only one person in the world who called me that. Curiosity took hold as I shut the door and strode to the kitchen. It was the work of a moment to find the scissors in the junk drawer. I set the box down on the kitchen table and slid an edge of the blade through the tape, then peeled the flaps away to look inside.

Another box. And a note printed on a bit of paper with the receipt.

Dear Mrs. Boone,

I'm tired of not being able to talk to you all day. Please use the number below to get in touch with me.

Your husband,

AB

His phone number was printed at the bottom. I set the note down beside the bottle with the flower and pulled the shiny white box out of the brown cardboard. He bought me a phone. There were several cards tucked in beside the box, clearly some sort of pay-as-you-go plan. A burner, my brother called them. He always had a few. Repeating the process with the scissors, I examined the object within. A little flip phone. A pink flip phone.

I rushed to the nearest outlet beside the coffeepot and plugged it in to charge. A phone! It was amazing I'd gone so long without one. I wondered how many messages my old phone had on it. The Serpas were likely checking them. That's what my father would have had one of his men doing. Reading my messages. Returning them. Hunting down people I knew for information. Hunting me.

I supposed it was lucky for me that the only people who mattered to me in the world were now long gone.

Except for one.

The screen on the front of the phone illuminated, showing me the time. Noon. Wow, it was that late in the day already? I'd gotten so disconnected from the world that I rarely checked the time. The only time of day I noted was when Alden arrived at the house at the end of the day. I flipped open the phone to look for the calendar.

May. May? Had it really been three months since I left home? Walking to the table, I retrieved the note with Alden's number on it and punched it into the phone as I typed out a text message.

> Thank you for the phone. You didn't have to do that.

It was almost an hour before his response pinged through. I wondered how much reception he could possibly get riding around the mountainous property all day. I jerked at the sudden loud chirp, turning the blue brushstroke I had been practicing at the kitchen table into a splotch. Quickly crossing the kitchen, I picked up the phone off the counter and read Alden's response.

> You're welcome. Sorry it took so long.

It was quickly followed by another message.

> I can't stop smiling.

A quiet laugh huffed out of me. Graham couldn't be bothered to send me a text message and Alden got me a phone just so he could say that. They were not the same. Then I considered his apology. Sorry it took so long. I hadn't been waiting for him to give me a phone. I hadn't even asked for one, since I was already a drain on his resources. A drain on his income. And there was no end in sight, not with the Serpas putting a price on my head.

Sorry it took so long.

It took so long for him. It took so long because he had to save up for the phone. He went out of his way to make me more comfortable, offering what little he had and I couldn't even be honest with him about why I was still here. Why I was terrified. If that wasn't enough, things between us were getting more complicated. What happened last night complicated things. Confused them, really. Confused me. Because I didn't know how to understand the way I felt about him.

Realizing I hadn't sent him a response and he'd soon be out of range, I shook the thought out of my head as I tapped out my best flirtatious response. God, I was never very good at this part.

> We better take it easy tonight or you're going to fall off your horse again.

His response was almost immediate.

> Fuck no.

My thighs squeezed together at his protest. I'd thought that when I finally had him, I'd get it out of my system. To stop thinking about him all day. Except Alden hadn't been what I imagined. I didn't realize how incapable of imagining this I had been. How sheltered I was. There was no way I could have dreamed of what had happened between us. I didn't know I was able to feel those things with another person. Sure, I'd read about it in books. But if I was being honest, I thought it was fake. That no one felt like this ever. Everyone was just fooling themselves into thinking they felt something like this and that eventually everyone would settle for their best option.

I was so wrong.

Last night had awakened something inside me. That part of me that could indulge in pleasure without worrying about what my mother would say. There was no shame in feeling what I felt. No reason to protect myself from wanting more.

Except for one.

Just thinking about his heated hazel gaze last night had me hopeful for another eventful evening. I unbuttoned my dress and sent him another message. A photo. Another speedy response followed.

> Those are the most perfect breasts I've ever seen. You're lucky I just had lunch, or I would come home to feast on you.

The smile that crossed my lips was completely involuntary. I needed to tell him about the money so that he could protect himself. People around here knew about me now. They didn't make the connection yet, but if they did he would be in danger. I owed it to him to tell him everything. I sent him another tease.

> More perfect than your magazine girls?

> Absolutely.

Thirty-Seven
Alden

Last night was a mistake. A big mistake.

If I thought letting this woman go would be difficult before, it would be impossible now. She was all I thought about all damn day. Every time I had a second to myself, I was met with memories of her riding me. Moaning my name. Looking at me with that little line between her brows like she couldn't quite believe what was happening as she came. There was no need to daydream anymore. Not with the reality I'd enjoyed. The rational part of me knew this was why I shouldn't have done it. I shouldn't have crossed that line. We crossed it and it was far better than anything my imagination could have dreamed up. It was that same imagination that was teasing me with little moments I'd savor forever.

I might actually be falling for my wife, which is possibly the stupidest mistake I've ever made. That small voice that was begging her to go. To protect myself. Protect my big, stupid heart. It's the same voice that remembered what it was like when I realized I couldn't rely on my parents.

This isn't permanent, it said. *Don't get attached.*

Eventually, she would leave, and I would be alone. Only now I'd be worse off than before because I knew Sierra Volpe was walking the earth. Nothing, not a single damn thing, would ever be so sweet. And that picture?

Shit. Put a fork in me. I was done.

"Boone."

Junior was gaping down at me, an irritated look on his freckled face. Had he asked me something? I screwed in the plug, then moved the oil pan out of the way to roll all the way out from under Mr. Weaver's truck.

"Sorry. What did you say?"

"I said my dad wants you all to come over for a big barbeque on Saturday. The whole family is coming over."

I sat up and looked him over. No wonder he seemed irritable. Junior wasn't exactly a social guy. The cousins. Aunts and uncles. Everyone. All those people. I'd been hustled into taking Sierra to Natalie's party, but these people were different. They were protective of their own. They'd ask questions. Wiping my hands off on a rag, I noticed Junior was still there. Waiting for my answer. Right. Shit.

"What's the occasion?"

Junior watched me with a flicker of confusion in his eyes, as I stood and started gathering the discarded materials from the oil change on his dad's truck. He huffed a sigh and muttered his answer.

"It's for my birthday."

"Right," I laughed, trying to cover the mess that was happening in my head. I'd forgotten the kid's birthday, for goodness sake. "Sorry, Junior. We'll be there."

I was still thinking about how to explain the barbeque by the time I got home. Except Sierra wasn't on the sofa. Or in the kitchen. Worry started gnawing at me as I looked around the house. Nothing. There was nothing.

Panicked, I ran out the front door. Then immediately ran into the woman I'd been looking for. She let out a yelp of surprise as she collided with me. The watercolor palette and notebook I'd purchased for her were tucked under one arm and the jar with her brushes fell out of her hand, clattering on the wood porch planks.

We both crouched to pick them up. I took her jaw into my hand. That sweet smile coupled with her hitched breath made my panic ease with each passing second. If that wasn't enough, the way she hummed a little when I kissed her did the trick.

"I've got this," I said against her mouth. "I'm sorry."

Scooping the brushes into the jar, I stood and opened the door for her. She hurried into the house ahead of me, a hand sweeping over the skirt of her yellow dress. I'd learned that though the blue one was my favorite, this one was hers.

"I haven't started dinner yet," she huffed. "I wanted to get the sky right on the sunset over my tree."

Right. Her tree.

"I'll make dinner," I offered. "But I need a shower."

"Okay," she chirped, setting her things down on the kitchen counter.

Something about her voice was odd. Off. I reached out, taking her hand as it came into my path.

"Everything alright?"

She nodded and plastered that fake smile onto her face. I hated that. Something was eating at her. Warning bells rang in my mind. No. *Please don't let her think last night was a mistake. Please don't push me away.* Without another word, I twirled her where she stood, eliciting a small giggle from her as I went to the bathroom to shower. I let that sound drown out my worries.

"Can I jump in there with you?"

I'd just stepped under the hot water when I heard Sierra's voice on the other side of the frosted glass. The doors clattered together loudly as I slid it open for her and waved her in. Long dark hair hung over her chest as she stepped in, giving me a sheepish little smile.

"I forgot it's a little tight in here."

God, help me.

"We've been in here together before," I laughed.

"I haven't showered yet today, and I need to wash my hair," she frowned as she looked at me as I crouched under the head. "But I didn't think this through."

"I'll do it for you."

"You'll wash my hair?"

Dark chocolate hair fell down her back as she pushed it over a shoulder, long enough now to skim her lithe waist. I started reciting state capitols in my mind just to keep myself under control.

"Darlin', I would love to wash it. I told you, I fucking love your hair."

I moved to let her stand beneath the spray. Sierra shuffled under it and let her head fall back, water sluicing over her face as she soaked her hair. Denver. Sacramento. Streams of water coursed over her perfect tits and down her stomach. Boise. Tallahassee. Springfield. I reached over her shoulder for the shampoo sitting on the rack, brushing a kiss over her exposed collarbone.

"Turn around."

Squeezing some shampoo into my palm, I slid it over the crown of her head and placed the bottle back on the rack. My fingertips plunged into the thick brown strands as I got to work. Suds bubbled up around my fingers as I worked them into her scalp. Sierra let out a little hum of pleasure as her shoulders slumped with relaxation.

"I think I could get used to this," she giggled.

Honolulu. Topeka. Little Rock.

"Rinse," I commanded as I finished, giving her ass a little slap.

She turned to dip her head under the stream. As she tipped her head back to wash the shampoo from her hair, she closed one eye and eyed me with the other. Graceful hands slid through her silky strands as she made sure it was good and clean.

"Alden," Sierra sighed. "I need to tell you something." Her voice was strange again, tight and serious. Sierra shifted out from under the spray and squeezed the excess water from her hair before picking up the bottle of her conditioner, not meeting my eye as she applied the product to the long ends of her hair. "It's about the people who killed my family."

Shifting positions, I stood under the spray to wash my hair as she wrapped her arms around herself. I watched her, lathering up my hair as I waited for her to go on. While I was grateful she was actually going to tell me what was bothering her, I worried about what was coming next. What was the worst way this could end?

They were caught. I'm going home.

"God, there's no good way to say this," Sierra huffed, looking down at her feet. "Well, when you were on bedrest while your ribs healed, I sort of used your phone to check up on them and found out that they're looking for me."

"Okay," I acknowledged. So far, not bad. "You said they would be."

"Yeah," she sighed, still not meeting my eye. Her discomfort was making me uncomfortable. Fuck, just say it. "Except, I didn't tell you they offered a reward."

That was it? I schooled my face into neutrality because, goddamn, I thought that would be so much worse.

"I know."

That got her to finally look at me. If she was being honest, so would I. Full lips popped open as if she was ready to say something, but then they shut again. I continued washing up. Only the sound of water hitting the tub broke the silence as she watched me.

"How do you know that?"

The question was low. Irritated.

"I read about it," I muttered, placing my soap back on the rack. "There was an article about that Serpa guy getting out on bail and he offered a reward for information on you."

Sierra's jaw flexed as she pinched the bridge of her nose between her thumb and forefinger. She sighed and looked at me, irritated.

"Is that why Eddie told me to leave? So he could collect?"

"He did what?"

She snorted, pushing me out of the way to grab her soap as she hastily washed herself.

"Yeah. The night he came home without you, he basically told me to get out of your house. He said I was using you."

Note to self: kill Eddie. Rage worked its way up from my feet, tightening every muscle along the way. I flexed my hands and shook them out to release some of the energy building there. Using me?

"Hey," I rasped, reaching out to place a hand on her waist. "I don't think that."

Realization tightened my shoulders.

"That's why you gave me the earrings. Fuck, I don't need the money, Sierra. I can take care of us on my own."

"I know," she croaked. "I just. I wanted to do something."

Sierra rinsed herself off, then climbed out of the tub. I shut off the water and pushed open the doors, filling the room with the clattering glass as I got out to grab her towel. An appreciative but weak little smile bloomed over her lips as she took it to wrap around herself. As I dried myself off, it occurred to me. She'd been sitting on this for weeks and I wasn't sure why. So, I asked.

"Why bring it up now? The reward."

"I just thought. I don't know," Sierra muttered, sitting on the closed toilet as I slung my towel around my hips. When she wouldn't look at me again, I took her jaw in my hand and directed her gaze up to mine. "It's a lot of money. I don't want you to get hurt in case anyone else finds out about me. Natalie and her brothers know about me. And Eddie. And because now I feel, well... I just. I don't want you to get hurt."

The stammering. Babbling, really. Not meeting my eye. There was even a bit of pink creeping over her cheeks. The words she was trying and failing to put together. The combination made my lips tug into a smirk as I looked down at her.

"Are you trying to tell me you care about me, darlin'?"

First there was a small laugh of casual disbelief. Sierra's eyebrows drew together as she gazed up at me, I let my hand fall from her jaw and circled her throat as I bent over to kiss her gently. She didn't have to say anything. I knew.

"Do you remember how much they're offering?"

She stiffened, pulling back to give me a wary look. Then she picked up her hairbrush and started pulling it through the long, wet tresses. Not looking at me again.

"One million dollars."

A laugh burst from me. I couldn't help it.

"It's not funny, Alden."

Sierra gave me an admonishing look as I shook my head at her. My hands cradled her face as I forced her to keep her eyes on me.

"Oh, darlin'. I don't know a lot about money, but that's a hell of a lot less than you're worth."

If my words weren't enough, I let my kiss tell her the rest. She hummed into my mouth as she relaxed in my hold, hands gliding over my stomach as her nails grazed damp skin.

"Does that mean you care about me, too?"

Her question warmed my lips. Warmed me everywhere. You care about me, *too*. I looked into those gorgeous green eyes, the sight causing that ache in my chest to burn, and smiled.

"Yes, darlin'."

I tasted the lie in it as soon as I uttered the words. It wasn't half of what I felt. I'd been worried I'd let myself get caught up in wanting her, but I hadn't anticipated this. *You care about me, too.*

If I thought I was in trouble before, I was in deep-fried shit now.

Thirty-Eight

Sierra

When I graduated from college, my parents threw a massive party for me. I'd arrived home from New Haven on the morning of the party, only to find a surprise when I got to my bedroom. My mother was practically vibrating with excitement. Her perfect ivory nails dug into my hand as she dragged me upstairs to my bedroom. The door swung open, and we entered.

"Don't you like it?"

During my last semester at school, my mother made my room into an ivory box with little accents of pink. All of my things had been moved into a gleaming white closet, shut behind frosted glass doors, or lined up to look pretty on every shelf. This wasn't me. It was her. When I didn't say anything, she turned on her heel and looked at me with disgust.

"You're not going to thank me? Do you realize how much time I spent on this? This was a lot of work, Sierra."

A sinking feeling soured my stomach. I'd been anxious on my flight home, something I'd attributed to being a nervous flyer. Now that I was standing beside Catarina Volpe in one of her moods, I understood the real reason. I was back home. Back in my place under her thumb. I sighed. It was too late for me to smooth this over.

"Thank you, Mother. It's beautiful. I was just surprised, that's all," I smiled.

"Ungrateful, you mean," she snipped, turning on her kitten heel to head for the door. "Alright. I'm going to leave a dress and shoes for you in the closet. The party starts at five o'clock. Please be downstairs no later than a quarter after."

She made to leave my room, pausing with her hand on the antique crystal doorknob, another Catarina touch.

"I expect you to look your best, Sierra Briar Volpe. This party is important. Do not disappoint me."

As I unpacked and got ready for the evening, I'd mistakenly thought I'd known what to expect. Parties for me or for my brother were always thinly veiled networking opportunities for my parents. Something to seal a deal. To rub elbows with someone powerful. Everyone coming to this affair would be someone my father worked with or someone my mother was trying to impress.

The new bedroom was only the beginning of the surprises that awaited me. The next surprise was the dress I'd been given for the event. While I'd been in the shower, fixing my hair, and putting on makeup, my array of sundresses and clothes I'd acquired had been removed. Even my school sweatshirt. They were all replaced with designer pieces. Pieces that were beautifully constructed, but lacked my taste. My colorful items and jeans had been swapped for neutrals. Beige. Camel. Blush. Grey. All except for one item.

An ivory dress was displayed alone on a rack, with little gold sandals sitting beneath it. It was unlike anything I'd been allowed to wear before. The top showed more of my chest. The skirt hit above my knees. The material was a soft chiffon. At first, I'd thought this was my mother's way of showing me that I was a woman in her eyes. Even if it cost me my entire wardrobe.

Then I got to the party.

I'd walked down the stairs, through the kitchen, and out into the backyard where the party was being held, pausing on the last step down to the terrace. Not only had I been wrong about the guest list, but I'd been wrong about my mother's intentions. There were no family friends. No members of my mother's organizations. Only members of my father's organization.

"Sierra, come on," my mother clucked as she tugged me down the final step, wearing a flawless black shift dress which didn't seem more party-appropriate than the skirt and silk blouse she was wearing earlier. "We need to introduce you to everyone."

The guests were strange. Some of them I knew. Some were new to me. Most of them were men. They eyed me from head to toe as each of them congratulated me on my recent graduation. I thanked them politely, hoping no one could feel my trembling hands as they shook them. They stared. Actually stared at me. My mother and father made the rounds. No one attempted to converse with me. Not until I found my older brother drinking with his friends at the table on the side of the house where no one could see them.

"Hey," he greeted me, lifting his tumbler of whisky. "Nice dress."

He hadn't even bothered to get out of his uniform of Air Force Ones, jeans, and some sort of Chicago team jersey. Since we were entering summer, he was wearing a white baseball jersey that displayed his full sleeves of tattoos. Another thing I'd never been allowed.

"Thanks. This is the worst graduation party ever," I muttered, grabbing the glass and tossing back the tawny liquid. I hissed at the burn and handed it back to him. One of Enzo's friends stifled a laugh.

"This isn't a graduation party," Enzo snorted, dark brows pulling together as he gave me a worried look of assessment.

"What?"

He threw a heavy arm around me, ushering me to peek at the crowd eating from trays of passed hors d'oeuvres in our backyard. So many people wearing smart suits. Not talking with each other so much as with my parents. And looking around for someone.

"Look at them," Enzo said, pointing with his tumbler at the gathered guests. "Most of those guys are made men. Or they work at the company. They're either married and here with their sons who are your age, widowed, divorced, or single."

Enzo's friends went silent as I looked over my shoulder at them. My gut turned at their pitying expressions. I was the last to know something, that was for sure.

"This isn't your graduation party, Si. It's a marriage market."

Returning my attention to the crowd, I saw them for what they truly were. Not suitors. Not men looking for love. No. They were buyers. Men assessing my value like they were making an investment.

My mother stood at the edge of the crowd, speaking with one of the wives. The woman she was speaking to spotted me, forcing my mother's attention to land on us. Catarina politely excused herself. Her heels clicked on the large pavers as she made hurried steps toward us, dodging guests with a graceful smile. The smile fell away as soon as we were Louboutin to Louboutin.

"Sierra Briar Volpe, this party is for you. It is rude to hide from your guests."

"What is this?" I snapped.

"It's your graduation party," she cooed, nervously checking over her shoulder to make sure no one was watching because of course that's what she was worried about. Not me.

"Oh, come on. That's bullshit," Enzo interjected, pushing a hand through his dark brown curls. "These guys are looking at her like she's fucking cattle. She doesn't even know any of them."

"Because she's hiding in the corner with you like a child," our mother snarled through gritted teeth, green eyes flaring. "Be a good older brother and escort her back."

Without another word, she turned on her little heel and left. My father was the boss of the family, but she was the boss of this household. Her word was final.

"I'm sorry," Enzo muttered, scratching his brow with a thumb as he looked back at his friends.

"I know," I sniffed.

We'd both known this day was coming. My parents never hid my purpose in this family from me. While my father mostly ignored me, my mother treated me like her project. She always made sure I knew where I stood. But this felt like the rug being pulled out from under my feet.

That night I met twenty different men looking for a wife. All of them seemed unimpressed with my education. Completely uninterested in my love of fine art or my desire to continue working in the field. They all ended up married within the year to other girls. Nice, vanilla girls. Which was fine. I was thrilled for them at the time because, at the time, I thought I'd dodged the proverbial bullet. As I showered in a cowboy's house hundreds of miles away from that backyard, I thought maybe the temporary freedom I'd won had been at the cost of my family's lives.

If I'd been more welcoming three years ago, maybe I'd be in a marriage with one of those men right now. I'd probably be a mother. Probably live somewhere near my parents' house. And they would still be alive. Enzo would still be alive.

Working out. Taking walks. Painting. I'd gotten in the habit of keeping myself busy. All to keep my mind off the truth that burned like acid. Its corrosive bite seared every spare moment. I blinked the thought away as I loaded clothes into the old washing machine in the laundry closet next to the kitchen. The front door swung open.

"Hey, gorgeous," Alden smiled as he tipped his hat at me, a brown box under his arm. "You hungry? The old man sent me home with some beef from the cow he bought from the ranch down the road. There's like ten pounds of it here."

I hadn't even heard the truck pull up to the house.

"Sure, that sounds nice," I said weakly.

He took the package into the kitchen, storing it in the refrigerator before approaching me for a kiss. The warmth of his mouth soothed the sting of my thoughts. And that smell...There were the self-obsessed men drenched in Dior cologne and then there was this filthy, selfless man. Sweat. Grass. Dirt.

"Let me grab a shower and then we can get cooking."

"Okay."

Alden pulled back, looking down at me with furrowed brows. His hand tipped my jaw up as his thumb brushed over my cheek in a tender caress.

"What's going on?"

"Nothing," I shrugged, biting down on my lip. I thought he accepted my answer, bending down to kiss me again. The arm that had been squeezing me relaxed as he rubbed his palm between my shoulders, the calluses scraping over my bare skin soothing the raw edge of what I was feeling.

"Don't lie to me, darlin'," he muttered between soft kisses. "I've got you."

Unable to speak past the tight knot in my throat, I hummed my agreement, only to be betrayed by the crack in my voice. Alden released me only to smooth my hair away from my face with both hands.

"You don't have to be okay," he said, staring down at me. "I mean it. I've got you."

I had always been treated like I was a doll. Dressed up like a doll. Bought and sold. A small and breakable possession. Valuable as long as I was perfect. Antoni had wanted to break me. Even if the Serpas hadn't destroyed my family, I knew marriage to him would have destroyed me.

That wasn't how Alden saw me. He took care of me because he wanted me to feel cared for. He sheltered me because he wanted me to have a safe space. He comforted me now because he knew the sharp sting of loss I felt and wanted to dull the edge of that burden.

"I need you to season a couple of steaks for us while I get a shower. You do it better than me," he smiled, finally releasing me with a quick kiss on the tip of my nose. "Then we're going to talk about what's bothering you."

Thirty-Nine
Alden

"I don't think this was a good idea."

Sierra chewed on the corner of her bottom lip, watching the Weaver's house come into view. Alright, I shouldn't have waited until this morning to tell her. I should have given her time to think about it. I probably should not have used the fact that I'd already told Junior we were coming to get her to agree.

Yeah, I know that wasn't great but here we were.

I parked the truck in my usual spot near the barn and waited. Sierra scratched one thumbnail over the other as she stared down at her lap, a nervous habit I'd noticed early on. I knew she was uncomfortable being around other people.

"Darlin'," I sighed. "Junior asked me to be here, so I'm here."

"I know," she winced. "I know they're important to you. I'm just worried about. Well, you know."

"No one here reads Chicago newspapers. All they'll be thinking is that I landed myself a wife who's way too pretty for me."

I gave her a wink and a smile. She smirked down at her lap.

"Fine," she huffed, reaching for the door handle.

It swung open before she could do it herself. Mr. Weaver stood there, smiling at her. Sierra hopped out, smoothing her dress as I rounded the truck.

"Welcome, Boones! Listen, I'm going to be honest with you. The Millers brought some booze. Some of the guys are already pretty tipsy."

The old man cringed in my direction. I knew he was trying to protect me. Still, the warnings were unnecessary. It didn't bother me to be around people who drank. My family history wasn't something I needed to be reminded of and I sure as hell didn't want my girl thinking about it. I heaved a sigh, hoping we could just move on from this.

"I'm pretty hungry," Sierra smiled up at me as I took her side. "Let's join everyone!"

Bless her for changing the damn subject.

Junior was right. Everyone was here. My name rose from the tables in a cheerful chorus of greetings. Red hair and freckles were scattered through the crowd. Millers everywhere. I squeezed Sierra's hand as I escorted her toward the crowd. Mrs. Weaver's sisters were seated nearest to us, both of them turned on the bench with cans of beer in their hands and matching expressions on their freckled faces.

"Is this the wife?" Harriet, Mrs. Weaver's older sister asked, gesturing toward Sierra with a beer can. "We've heard a lot about you."

She turned to her sister, pumping her red eyebrows suggestively. If I hadn't spotted Junior cringe and walk in the other direction, I would've wondered who'd said anything about the girl at my side.

"Sit down, sweetheart," Mary, the younger Miller sister crooned. "Tell us how you two met."

Sierra gave me a beseeching look as the Miller sisters scooted down the bench to make room for us. I held out a hand to help her into her seat and then took one at her side. The large wooden tables lined up off of the Weaver's back porch were illuminated with string lights for the festivities. Everyone was already seated for dinner, chatting over their food and drink. Mary and Harriet watched Sierra, waiting.

"Well," she started. "I was driving down the highway and I ran out of gas. Alden saw me pull over and offered to help."

Sierra turned in her seat, smiled at me, and patted my hand as if that was the end of the story. We both wanted this conversation to be over.

"So, it was love at first sight for you two, huh?" Mary grinned.

"Oh yeah," I said, throwing an arm around Sierra. "One look into those big, beautiful eyes, and I was done for." I gave her a good, long kiss to wrap this interrogation up. When the ladies decided to refocus their attention on someone else, I tugged Sierra close enough for my lips to brush her ear as I whispered into it. "What did I tell you about cowboys and city girls?"

"Yeah, yeah," she rolled her eyes playfully. "Happens all the time."

"That's right. Now let's get some food in you."

She watched me pile her plate high with everything on the table. I knew from Sam Sr.'s birthday that she loved macaroni. That was the first thing she'd finished. Honey butter smothered cornbread. All of it.

"I can't finish all that," she whisper-shouted at me, looking up at me with fear in her eyes. "I don't want them to be insulted."

So polite, my girl. I laughed.

"Eat what you want, gorgeous. Anything you don't finish, I'll eat," I chuckled, sucking a bit of sauce off of my thumb as I picked up my plate to start serving myself. Sierra's eyes went wide with surprise.

"You can eat all that?"

I brought my mouth close enough to speak nice and low, my words easily disguised in the mass of her hair.

"You know I love to eat, darlin'."

Sierra's hand slapped my thigh as I pulled back to grin at her again. To see those cheeks go rosy at my words. More likely at the memory of only an hour ago. That little blue sundress she had on did me in every time. It was why we'd been late for the party, really. Because when she walked out of the bedroom in it, smiling that smile that did something to my insides, I hoisted her onto the kitchen counter and used my mouth to make her scream.

I didn't have to play a part with her. Didn't need to put on the act of a fool obsessed with his wife. When it came to Sierra Volpe, I was a hungry man. I'd never felt this way about a person before. Insatiable. But if she was food, I was starving. If she was water, I was the thirstiest man alive.

As predicted, I finished her food. There wasn't a whole lot left, though. Sierra lazily leaned into me as we chatted with Junior's cousins about the warm weather we were having, sated and happy. I could still taste the honey butter on her lips as I kissed her. Blush crept onto her cheeks again, darkening the olive skin beneath her freckles.

"Not used to public displays of affection?" I muttered.

She leaned into my shoulder, wrapping an arm around mine for stability as she whispered low.

"Not used to affection."

"Alright," Mr. Weaver clapped his hands loud and hard. It was his way of getting everyone to listen. It always worked. "Junior didn't want a cake. He didn't want candles. He didn't want attention so I don't know where he's wandered off to. Sawyer's started a fire for us over there. He's made some graham crackers from scratch. And we've got marshmallows and chocolate, so you know what that means."

"Come on, I want to show you something," I whispered into Sierra's ear as I laced our fingers together.

A few steps away from the table, I shrugged off my jacket and held it open for Sierra to slip into. The pearl snap shirt I had on was plenty against the cool night air, especially when she looked chilled. Fuck, why didn't I buy her a jacket? Grass crunched under our feet as we walked away, lacing our hands together again under the night sky. I looked up. Couldn't help it. I glanced over at Sierra, who was doing the same thing.

"I've never seen so many stars. All those purples and blues. The stars scattered everywhere like diamonds on a dark blanket. It's the most beautiful thing I've ever seen," she said, practically whispering as she returned her attention to me. "Isn't it?"

I turned to look at her and arched a brow. Without light from the barn or the string lights by the tables, it was harder to see her here. Green eyes. Even in the dark, I could still see them. They blinked up at me. Did she ask me something?

"Isn't the sky the most beautiful thing you've ever seen?"

"I used to think so," I said, tucking two fingers under her chin. "Now it's got competition."

Sierra went quiet, biting down on a smile as her gaze moved away from me. She didn't know how to take a compliment. I firmed my grip on her, forcing her to look at me.

"That voice in your head that's telling you not to listen to me is a fucking liar. The first time I saw you, I lost my breath a little. Leaving you every morning has been torture. Not just because I love looking at you but because I like talking to you. Stop thinking you're not good enough. You're better than I could have ever hoped for."

A glint of light caught on her cheek. Tears. I used my free hand to wipe them away and brought my forehead to hers.

"Who do I need to kill that made you feel that way about yourself?"

I was joking. It was a joke. But her answer. Fuck.

"They're already dead."

She started walking away from me, but in the wrong direction. As we walked away from the house I took her hand again and started pulling her toward the barn. She turned on her boot, narrowly avoiding Junior's cousins scampering by in a fit of laughter. One of them shouted about s'mores as they sped toward the fire.

"Do you want kids?"

I gestured toward the children who ran toward the table covered in chocolate and marshmallows. Their parents chatted loudly with Mr. Weaver and Junior, all of them sitting around on stumps as they sipped lemonade and whiskey. Sierra's brows tugged together as she angled her head, looking at me instead.

"You know, I don't think I ever thought about it. It was always something I was supposed to do. Get married. Produce an heir. I guess I always assumed I would."

She whipped her hand through the air like she was checking imaginary boxes. I nodded, giving her other hand a squeeze as I tried to ignore the way the thought of her doing those things with Antoni made my skin crawl.

"Alright. But now that you're on your own. No obligations. No one telling you what to do. Do you want those things?"

For a while, we just walked. It could have been ten seconds, but it felt like ten minutes. She didn't owe me an answer. If she'd been sold like a broodmare, then she might not want that. Hell, I wouldn't blame her. But this girl had me dreaming of picking out rings and saying vows. Dreaming of the future. If she couldn't go home, I foolishly hoped that she'd want to build a life with me. We were almost at the barn door when her shoulders popped. She glanced sideways at me.

"Maybe. With the right guy."

Our boots thudded on the floor of the barn, drowning out the thoughts racing through my mind. The right guy. The right guy was a man who could give her everything. That wasn't me. But fuck, did I want it to be. Sierra gasped as she stopped in her tracks at the first stall, spotting exactly what I wanted to show her. I yanked her hand, pulling her closer so she could get a better look.

"That's Copper," I said, pointing to the near-red Quarter Horse mare who gave us a bored look. "And that's Eloise."

Her foal huffed as she guzzled from her mother, ignoring us completely as she filled her belly. My girl folded her arms over the stall door, standing on her toes to get a closer look. I braced my hands on either side of her, giving her neck a swift kiss.

"How old is she?"

I counted the weeks in my mind. Eloise had been born two weeks before Eddie headed home. Eddie, who had not answered a single text message I'd sent him about his conversation with Sierra. I leaned into her and took a deep inhale of that scent that heated my blood, then pointed at Eloise.

"She's about a month old now."

"She's only a month old?" Sierra said, turning surprised eyes on me. "They can walk that young?"

"Yep," I smirked. "They can stand and feed. Walk. Hell, they can even run the day they're born if they need to."

Sierra blinked in surprise.

"How many did you deliver?"

"I don't deliver them by myself," I laughed. "There are usually a couple of us around."

"Fine. How many did you help deliver?" Sierra asked nose scrunching in feigned annoyance. She couldn't hide her amusement as she turned back to watch the little brown foal.

"Almost all of 'em."

She huffed a laugh as I tugged at her waist to continue to the next stall. Sable stood there, beautiful and dark as night as she ate her dinner. She was always a slow eater. I watched Sierra take her in. The matching black foal sleeping at her feet made my woman take a breath. She looked back at me with excitement in those greens. I laughed and took her waist again, wrapping her up as we looked into the stall.

"She's beautiful," Sierra gasped. "Do you want a family?"

Her question was quiet. Unsure. Like maybe she didn't want to know my answer.

"The truth is, I'd never thought about it much either," I sighed. *Until you*, I wanted to say. "With my parents being who they were, I never thought much about becoming one myself. It's hard to dream about having a family when you weren't part of one."

One of the horses nickered in their stall. Probably Annabel since she could hear me. A brown and white face poked out to confirm my suspicion. Sierra nodded her understanding, still watching the black horse in front of her.

"Yeah," Sierra agreed. "I know what you mean. I didn't have great role models for parenting, so it's hard to imagine what being a good mother would even look like."

Her shoulders lifted and slumped with a heavy breath. She turned, eyes soft and a hint of a smile playing over her lips.

"So where do all the horses go if you guys are breeding new ones every year?"

The change in subject didn't surprise me one bit. Talking about family was always uncomfortable for me. I avoided it when I could. If my family had sold me off to the highest bidder and then been killed in the process, talking about them had to feel like broken glass on her tongue. I obliged her, wanting to move on myself.

"We only breed a few a year. Gives them a chance to recover. Some of them we breed only once, depending on how healthy they are and if the old man has sold them off or not. Most of the foals get sold as yearlings, eventually. When they're about two or three years old."

"Where are their fathers? All I see are females."

"We don't keep the studs around here, gorgeous. We get different studs for different rounds of breeding. The old man pays a stud fee and then, when two horses love each other very much, they make a baby."

Sierra laughed, pushing me with a half-hearted slap in the chest as she turned around. Sable had approached the stall door, curious about the woman looking at her. Sierra opened her palm in front of Sable, laughing a little as the horse sniffed her. The mare nudged her shoulder, huffing a little as Sierra stroked her muzzle.

"This has all been so disorienting. I don't think I ever dreamed about my life before," Sierra said, her voice hoarse as she stroked the animal in front of her. "I was given everything I could ever need or want. It was like they gave me material things to placate me. Now I feel paralyzed by it."

Sable huffed again, pushing her face into my girl's shoulder. Sierra cradled the horse's head, resting her own against the lone white star on her forehead as she stroked a shiny black cheek. Letting her eyes fall closed, she just stood there. The black mare blew softly.

"I know I was lucky in a lot of ways," Sierra sighed. "I just I feel like I was raised in captivity. Even the most beautiful cage is still a cage. Now that I'm free, I don't know if I'll fly or fall."

Forty

Sierra

Crisp spring air was melting with the warmth of an oncoming summer. My boots crunched on bits of grass and stone. The sound eroded the anxious cabin fever that had gnawed at me all morning. I couldn't sit still, so I left the house on my morning walk. Except this morning, instead of stopping at my tree, I kept following the creek.

The BBQ had been a breath of fresh air. I'd been so nervous. Not just because I was scared someone would sell me out. Or recognize me. Deep down, I knew the Weavers wouldn't do anything like that and Alden wouldn't let anything happen to me. The fear, my real fear, came from not knowing how to talk to people. To socialize without my family's agenda. To be judged as myself. Not a name. Just me.

Meeting so many kind, friendly people all at once was staggering. All of them spoke about how much of his mother Junior had in him. Family members on both sides greeted Alden as if he was one of them. While he was introducing me to them as his wife, I wondered what it would be like to have a family like this. One who cared about you no matter what. A family who supported you so long as whatever you were doing made you happy. That's how they treated Alden. As one of their own.

I followed the creek, enjoying the sound of its rushing waters as I walked and walked. Stuffing my hands into my pockets, I tipped my head back to take in the cool breeze that rushed over my bare arms and took the edge off the summer air.

Ever since I was in kindergarten, I was required to know my place. Instead of greeting potential suitors or serving as my father's publicly perfect ambassador, I was conditioned to behave as a perfect child would. Take dance lessons, tennis lessons, swimming lessons. Conduct myself politely. Always eat what I am served, regardless of whether or not I like it. Speak only when spoken to. I was absolutely not allowed to cry under any circumstances, so I always cried in the bathroom. Alone.

That extended to when I was away at college. I was expected to conduct myself in a certain way. But no one was there to watch me. I wanted to have fun. So I began lying to my mother about where I was. I wasn't at a party; I was studying late with friends. I wasn't on a date. I was having coffee with a study partner. Between my classes and my family obligations, I didn't have much freedom. Almost none, actually. I was required to show up to all the family events my mother required, which meant that sometimes I missed classes I didn't want to. Every second of fun was stolen.

Her priorities superseded my own.

When I'd told Alden I didn't know what to do with myself now that I was free of them, it was true. My family, especially my mother, had trained me to worry only about her needs. Her goals for me were the only goals that mattered. It was all for the family, she'd tell me. Wanting anything for myself was, well, selfish.

Without family obligations, the absence of a forward path was a palpable one. One that I tried my best to ignore. With a cowboy. With painting. With working out in my underwear. With walks that took me so far away from the house that I looked at my phone to realize that I'd been walking for an hour.

A big blue house with a wraparound porch and white shutters rose up before me. The blue lap siding looked almost cerulean in the bright sunlight.

The white barn and steel outbuildings sat off on the northern side. Paddocks of various sizes were lined up in front of them. I'd walked all the way to Evergreen Springs.

Horses were gathered in two of the paddocks. Most of them had beautiful rich brown coats. One or two were black like Sable. Alden had given me the name of the horse. She was so beautiful and gentle, nuzzling the small animal she now shared a stall with. I marveled at how naturally motherhood seemed to come to her. I'd stayed to watch her nurse her foal. After that, we'd walked around the barn to see all of the fuzzy little foals that had been born this season before going back to make s'mores with everyone.

When I realized how far I'd come, I decided it couldn't hurt to walk a little further. The smiling faces of the other wranglers greeted me as I got closer. Colton and Louis, both red-headed Miller cousins I'd met at the barbeque and permanent residents of the bunkhouse, tipped their hats at me.

"What are you guys up to today?" I asked curious about all the commotion.

"Everyone's getting checked out by the vet," Colton, the older cousin said from where they leaned against the fence. "He's here to make sure the mares and foals got through alright and he's updating the vaccines of our mounts."

I nodded, taking in the large trailer that was parked in front of the barn. A traveling veterinary service, based on the colorful information graphic wrapped around it and the assistants walking around with the logo embroidered on their scrubs.

"Boone! Get Annabel in here," Mr. Weaver shouted from the big open door of the biggest steel outbuilding, looking to the paddock behind me.

There he was. My cowboy. Dark leather chaps, a white tee shirt covered in dust and sweat, jeans, and that dark brown hat covering his chestnut hair. He whistled, taking Annabel by the bridle with glove-covered hands as he spoke in low tones to her. She nudged his shoulder with her muzzle and he laughed, the sound causing a straining sensation in my chest.

"Let's get this over with."

I hadn't seen him interact with Annabel much except for that first day. It was only now that I realized how much their energies matched each other. She didn't just belong to him. They belonged to each other.

He tugged her toward the building's entrance. I followed, not wanting to take my eyes off of them while also trying to give them enough distance. I didn't know a lot about horses except that standing behind one was probably a bad idea. There was a metal structure that looked like it was there to barricade a horse inside. Annabel tugged at her bridle, whinnying softly in resistance.

"I know," Alden murmured, his voice low and gentle. The way it sounded when he held me as I cried. "I know, sugar. You got this."

"Come on now, Annie," the vet, a kind-looking man in his 40s with short black hair in the same scrubs as the others, said to the troubled horse.

Alden gave him an irritated look and whispered something to Annabel, who calmed at his voice enough to be ushered into the barricade. He and Mr. Weaver took positions to keep her settled while the vet did his work. It wasn't until they were finished and walking out of the building that Alden noticed me standing there.

"Hey," he grinned, leading Annabel toward the door. "I've got to put her in her stall for a bit." He paused, kissing my temple before nodding toward the door in a silent request to follow him. "How'd you get out here?"

"I walked."

"Long walk," he huffed with surprise, the corded muscle of his forearms flexing as he tugged Annabel along beside him. I trailed along behind him, examining the fit of the leather around his thighs. How anyone could look so good in a pair of chaps was beyond me.

"I guess my feet wandered with my mind today."

"Got a lot going on up there?" Alden asked, giving me a look of concern over his shoulder as we entered the barn.

I nodded, chewing the corner of my lip as I adjusted my ponytail. Alden led Annabel into what must have been her stall since I recognized his gear tossed over a low wall. He gave her forehead a few strokes and reached into a saddlebag that was hanging with his other things to pull out a pink and yellow apple. Once Annabel was happily chewing her treat, he leaned against the wall behind him and returned his attention to me.

"What's wrong?"

"Nothing really," I said, not believing the word as it left my tongue. "I was just thinking about what we talked about the other day. About family. The future and everything. I sort of feel like I don't have one."

"A family or a future?" Alden angled his head, lifting his hat to wipe at the sweat at his brow with a forearm.

"Both," I shrugged with a humorless laugh.

He looked at Annabel in a way that reminded me of the night I'd met him. Some conversation passed in silence. These two had a relationship I would probably never understand.

"I think I know how to make you feel better."

"I don't think that's a good idea. Your boss might catch us."

He tilted his chin up with a laugh, giving me a look at the strong column of his throat as it worked with the sound. God, he looked good today.

"Not that," he chuckled as he gestured for me to come closer. "It's something I do to calm Annabel down. Well, one of the things."

I came to the side of the horse, where he'd indicated with a nod. He came around, giving Annabel a little rub to her muzzle as he got to the side I was standing on.

"Put your hand here," he said as he took my hand in his and moved it to Annabel's side. For a second, I hated the feel of leather on my skin, missing the way his rough hands felt on me. He rested his other hand against her side. "And lay your head there."

I bent forward awkwardly. Alden huffed a soft laugh and corrected me as he used his body to push me into Annabel's side. His breath was a warm caress on my ear as he used those low tones to speak to me.

"Let her take your weight. Just a little."

"Are you really telling me to hug a horse right now?"

"Yeah, kinda."

I gave him some incredulous side eye as I let my head come to rest where he'd directed, wrapping myself around the side of the horse. Alden gave a gentle chuckle. I only worried about my white tank top for a second. Just a second.

"Listen to her."

Her heart. It beat, loud and strong. Thud. Thud. Thud. Breath wooshed from her. I breathed a deep sigh and closed my eyes.

Thud. Thud. Thud.

Woosh in. Woosh out.

"Don't listen to the worries, Sierra. Just the beat of your heart. The air in your lungs. Everything else is just noise."

The warmth of her body. Her sounds. The steady beat of her heart. I wasn't sure how long I stood there, but I felt myself relaxing. Coming to center. With every passing second, uncertainty's cutting edge was dulled by her stability. Annabel let out a long breath.

Big woosh in. Big woosh out.

"She's got you."

I wasn't sure whether he was addressing me or the horse. I opened my eyes to see Alden stroking Annabel's muzzle. Watching me with soft eyes that looked more brown than green in this light. I started stroking her side, enjoying the feel of her support as I did so.

"Why doesn't she look like the others? The rest are all entirely brown or black. She's different. Beautiful, but not like the rest."

Annabel chuffed like I'd insulted her. I laughed at the rush of sound. I patted her side with an apology, telling her she was still beautiful, and let my hand rest at her side. Alden covered it with his own.

"She was a rescued foal. One of the nearby ranches closed after the owner died. The family couldn't afford the taxes on the property and sold everything off, but they couldn't find buyers for all the horses. This one's mother got adopted by another ranch, but they didn't want to take her. So, Mr.

Weaver took her in." Alden laughed a little, looking down at his boots as he rubbed the back of his neck. "He's always taking in strays, I guess."

"Seems like all the good men do," I said, offering him a small smile of my own.

"Anyway," he smirked, blushing a little. Had he ever blushed before? "She didn't do too well being separated from her mother so young. So, I stayed with her for a while. But that didn't seem to help. Mrs. Weaver suggested I read to her. And that didn't help much either."

Annabel snorted, startling me enough to stand up. I giggled at the surprise. Alden took her face in his hands, rubbing the white stripe down her snout.

"Nothing helped until I started reading poetry to her."

"Poetry?" I asked, angling my head at him with the question. Then I remembered his shelf full of books at home. "Oh. That's why the poetry books."

"That's why the poetry books," Alden murmured, more to his horse than to me. "Her name came from a poem. I was reading a lot of Edgar Allen Poe to her at the time. Now she likes the more romantic stuff."

He reached into the saddlebag hanging from the wall. Digging around for a moment. Alden pulled out a little green paperback collection of love poems by Byron. I stood back to watch him, immediately missing the feel of the horse's warm belly. He flipped the book open to a random yellowed page. As if the action summoned her, Annabel pressed her head into Alden's chest as he rubbed her neck, giving her a soft pat as he murmured soft words to her.

"She walks in beauty, like the night

Of cloudless climes and starry skies;

And all that's best of dark and bright

Meet in her aspect and her eyes;

Thus mellowed to that tender light

Which heaven to gaudy day denies."

There was a warm timbre, a gentleness to his voice I'd only heard when he was whispering sweet things to me. My shoulders slumped as the sound filled me with quiet. Apparently, it had the same effect on his horse. Annabel puffed into his hand as I smiled at them both.

"She loves you."

Alden lifted his gaze to mine, hands still on the piebald mare who was crazy about him. The green in his eyes caught a shaft of sunlight as he looked at me with a soft smile on his face that made my stomach warm and fluttery.

"I know she does."

Having a sweaty, chaps-wearing cowboy drive you home in his truck felt like something from out of a bodice ripper. The wind rustled his hair through the open window. Sunlight brightened his smile when he glanced over at me. I wanted to crawl into his lap and figure out how to undo all of those buckles and straps. But I would settle for this. Sleeping in beside him on a Sunday.

"Go back to sleep," Alden mumbled, rolling over to draw me into his arms as he spooned me.

For the last few days, I'd peppered him with questions about the ranch. After seeing the place on a normal workday, I was curious. The ranch had been in the Weaver family for three generations. Junior wanted to do something with cyber security, so he was going to school for that. The horses they sell usually go off to work because they're from award-winning stock in that area, though Sable had come from another breeder that shuttered. With every detail he shared and every story he told me, I could feel more of what Evergreen Springs meant to him.

I could understand it. Someone taking you in and making you feel safe. Making you feel like you were home. As we went to bed, Alden pulled my body against his, curling himself around me as we fell asleep. That was how he made me feel. Being physical with him was about this, too. This sense of comfort.

That first time with Alden felt like so long ago now, but that step had been a welcome relief. Like cracking your neck. Or popping a champagne cork after weeks of buildup. Since then, I'd developed an addiction to his body. The feel of him. It was so luxurious in the way it moved. My big rancher was a man who seemed to know exactly how to give me what I needed. I couldn't fight it. So, I didn't.

Alden ran the blade of his nose up the length of my neck, grinning against it when I gasped at the tingle it left behind. His stubble scratched against my collarbone as I slipped my hand into his boxers to tease my fingers along his length.

"What are you doing?" He smirked into my shoulder, kissing the bare skin he found there. A low curse soon followed.

Easy. So easy, it was like breathing. I let him take down the strap of my pajama top. Let him kiss the skin beneath it. He pulled my top up over my head, letting me enjoy the feel of his chest hair brushing against my bare back. My hand shifted in his boxers to take his arousal in it, giving it a firm stroke. The rumble of his bare chest against my back paused as he dragged my bottoms off to wedge his length between my curved cheeks.

"Take that hand off me and touch yourself," he ordered, his voice still husky with sleep.

I obeyed, relishing in the feel of his mouth on my neck. Rough calluses scraped over my breast; the delicate flesh tightened in response. With him, I could let my mind be free. Free from worry. Free from the confines of who I used to be because every cell in my body cried out for him. Needed him like a plant needs sunlight. In these four walls, that was all that mattered.

"That's it," he urged as I whimpered. "Give me more."

Alden's hips rocked into my backside as I brought myself closer and closer to the edge. At some point, he'd shed his boxers. I bathed in the feel of all of his skin against all of mine. My legs squeezed together, trying to heighten what was already stealing my breath. Stilling my motion, Alden shifted his hips to line his broad crown up to my entrance.

"Does this pretty cunt need me?"

"Yes." The word was more of a whine than an answer.

"You know what to do. Take a deep breath for me," he instructed as he fed me the first few inches.

Slow and steady, he moved in and out, a little more each time until his hips were almost flush with my ass. Getting used to his size would be an ongoing effort. One arm snaked beneath me, holding me close to him. The other moved over the length of my body. It took inventory of every curve and edge until it hooked under my leg for purchase, using the hold to bury himself completely. Alden's unhurried mouth licked, kissed, and sucked at my neck and shoulder. Nibbled at my ear as he whispered filth and sunshine into it.

"Goddamn. You take me so well, gorgeous."

Alden covered the hand between my thighs with his as he began moving, my body following his in perfect harmony. I didn't recognize the noises coming out of me at the sensation. Euphoria spread through every limb like the sunlight gradually warming the bedroom, spreading out to my raw edges, making every hurt and worry disappear. Here there was no pain. No grief. Only this. Only him.

"Fell out of the sky, didn't you? Just for me."

A work-roughened hand caressed my breast as he panted and moaned into my neck, the other hand taking control between my legs. Turning my head to meet his gaze, I saw bliss and anguish. Ecstasy and something else. I knew it. That feeling.

I pushed away from him, feeling the temporary loss of his warmth as I climbed onto his body. Alden smiled up at me, hands bracketing my hips as I lowered myself onto him again.

"Fuck," he sighed. "Yes. Let me look at you."

This was quickly becoming one of my favorite ways to enjoy him. On top. In control. Alden's hands circled around to my backside, rocking me into him as I braced myself with both hands on his chest. The way he looked at me was the way I always wanted to be looked at. The deep groans that thundered in him with every movement that satisfied him was the way I wanted to be praised. And when he sat up and brought his mouth to mine as we both went over the edge together?

That was the way I wanted to feel forever.

Sunlight warmed the bed as we melted into each other. Toying with each other. We remained like that, kissing and touching while letting unspoken words evaporate between us. I never had a safe place. Not with friends. Not at college. Definitely not at home. Nowhere to cry. Nowhere to be vulnerable. But if a safe place could be a person, I was starting to think maybe Alden could be mine.

Forty-One
Alden

ays off were rare for me. Mr. Weaver always gave me Sundays off because I was the ranch foreman, but I disliked time to myself. It gave me too much time to dwell on things I didn't want to think about. Before Sierra came along, the old man actually had to force me to take Sundays off. I wasn't religious, so I usually took care of things around the house. The first few Sundays after foaling had me running out as far as Jackson to pick up things for the ranch. Orders the old man placed or parts I needed to repair equipment on the ranch. But now that we were back to our regular schedule and I wasn't spending my days alone, time off didn't sound so bad. Starting my day with Sierra on top of me was the cherry on top. After a long morning of enjoying her, it felt impossible to get out of bed. I pulled Sierra into my side, still too breathless from our coupling to speak.

"What do you want to do today?"

I huffed a sigh, trying to even out my breathing as a curious finger trailed down the crevice of my stomach to my navel. Groaning at her tentative exploration of me, I took a lock of Sierra's hair into my hand.

"Well," I started. "I was thinking we could teach you to ride today."

"Didn't I just do that?"

Her giggle was short and sweet. I squeezed her, bringing her close to kiss the top of her head. Fuck, I could get used to this. Before I let that thought take root, I went on.

"We can go over to the ranch and grab Annabel. Get you set up in the training ring. She won't mind getting a little exercise. It'll be fun."

Sierra tensed but didn't say anything for a long moment. Then her hand ventured south.

"I think I'd rather stay in bed."

That hand wandered dangerously low. Fingertips skimmed the muscles limning my hips, tracing their path all the way down. It was low enough to pique my interest, but even I wasn't able to bounce back that quickly.

"Are you trying to distract me?" I laughed.

"No," she cooed as fingernails grazed my inner thigh.

I snared that wicked hand and brought it up to rest against my stomach. She was trying to distract me.

"What's the matter, darlin'? Are you afraid of horses?"

Sierra huffed, rolling onto my chest to prop her head on her hands. Staring up at me with those big green eyes that looked close to moss in this light, she chewed her lip a little before answering.

"They're just so big. I was never allowed to have a pet, so I'm not really used to them. Or, like, any animal. I love Annabel, but the idea of actually riding her is kind of intimidating."

I arched a brow at her, unable to help my smirk. She huffed a little sigh, causing hair to fall over her face. Reaching out to move it out of her eyes, I let out a breath.

"I'll make you a deal," I soothed. She pouted. Actually pouted. I laughed. "Listen. If you agree to let me teach you how to ride a horse this afternoon, I'll teach you how to ride my face right now."

She blinked and released a startled laugh.

"I'm sorry. Ride your what?"

"You heard me, gorgeous," I said, unable to keep the grin from taking over my smirk. "You ride this." I tapped my lips with my index finger. "Then you ride my horse."

Sierra sat up, looking down at me. It was impossible not to enjoy the sight of her. Since she'd arrived, there was a softness to her that hadn't been there before. Something she'd been holding onto that drifted away. Only a complete moron wouldn't appreciate it. I winked at her.

"You are unbelievable," she laughed. "Fine."

"Good girl. Get up here, darlin'. Hang onto that headboard," I said, drinking in the sight of her as she climbed over me. Dragging my stubbled jaw along her inner thighs, enjoying the sight of her shiver at the contact, I gave my first instruction. "Now sit."

"Don't be nervous," I murmured into her ear, enjoying the feel of her leaning against me. "I've got you."

We'd come out to the ranch. After tacking up Annabel, I led her into the indoor arena. With everyone else out tending to their business, it was just ours today. Sierra looked up at me, hair piled on top of her head, spilling down in little pieces that feathered over her collarbone in that white tank top she had on. I put my hands on her waist, enjoying the feel of her ass in those jeans.

"You do?"

Smiling down at her, I dipped my chin in confirmation.

"I'd never let anything bad happen to you, gorgeous."

I helped her into the saddle, instructing her to get one boot in the stirrup and swing her leg over to the other side with a kick. After I was sure she was securely in the saddle, I turned my ball cap around and smiled at her. She shifted in her seat, eyeing me with a mischievous grin.

"What's that look about, darlin'?"

"Nothing. I just," she paused, biting the corner of her lip. "I just like that hat on you. I can see your face when you wear it like that."

Clearing my throat of the temptation to tell her exactly what that kind of look did to me, I refocused my attention on why we'd come here in the first place. The blood rushing south argued that maybe I'd been a complete dipshit to ignore her request to stay in bed all day.

Adjusting the stirrups for her much shorter legs, she looked around the arena. Corrugated steel walls tipped up to a pitched steel roof. Not the fanciest looking arena, but it was nice enough to show the horses for sale to the buyers. Usually, it was other ranchers who paid in advance because of Evergreen's reputation. Returning my attention to the woman in the saddle, I continued my instruction.

"Sit up straight. Keep your heels down. Try to relax."

Sierra did as I asked, throwing her shoulders back and rolling her neck. I gave her the reins but kept hold of the leather in one hand.

"Alright, we're going to start with a walk. Give her a soft tap with your heels."

Sierra did as she was told and squeaked as Annabel moved. With one hand on the halter and over a decade of training this horse, I was more in control than she was. But she didn't know that.

"She can feel your nerves, darlin'. Just breathe. I've got you."

Hoofs plodded on the soft dirt as we walked together. Sierra's posture was tight. Uneasy. From the look on her face, she seemed ready to jump right off of the horse. In an attempt to take her mind off of the worst-case scenarios she was undoubtedly imagining, I started talking.

"How's the painting going?"

Her eyes shifted from the back of Annabel's head to me.

"Good. I've been trying to teach myself different brushstrokes. I might actually be able to paint something that resembles an actual picture soon," she laughed.

"Is that what you want to do?" I peered up at her.

She angled her head at me, brows furrowing.

"What do you mean?"

It was just the two of us here. There was no reason to lie or beat around the bush. Though I was trying to take her mind off of her worries, my curiosity was entirely selfish. With the way I was starting to feel for this woman, I wanted to know what she saw for her future. More importantly, I wanted to know if there was a place for me in it.

"If you had nothing standing in your way, no limits, what would you do with your life?"

There was a long pause. Only Annabel's hoof beats in the dirt filled the air.

"I don't know what I want," Sierra released a heavy sigh and looked up at the ceiling. I nodded. She went on. "Until I met you, everything in my life was decided by someone else. They decided what school I'd go to. The job I'd have. The guy I had to marry. Everything I ever did was to make someone else happy. To make my parents happy."

We'd made almost a complete lap around the arena. I stroked Annabel's neck for being so patient with my woman. Glancing up at Sierra, I gave her a half smile.

"It sounds like you need to find something that makes you happy."

Her lips curled like she was fighting a smile.

"You make me happy, cowboy," she smirked. "But I don't know what's next for me."

"What if you stayed?"

Sierra looked down at me in surprise. Hell, I was surprised I'd even said it. I wasn't used to asking for what I wanted. The things I wanted had a way of being out of reach for me. Sierra staying here. With me. That was out of reach. But when that star fell over us the night we met, it was like it took root in me. The idea that maybe she'd come to me for a reason. It wasn't a rational thought.

Just a wish.

She released a breath, not answering my question. I shouldn't have said that. Her silence felt like a kick in the gut. The uncomfortable tug in my stomach had my hand brushing over my tee shirt to try and ease the ache. Deciding I may not want to hear her answer, I forced a smile onto my face.

"Alright, we're going to trot now."

"What does that mean?"

"That means hold on."

Sierra squeaked as I clicked my tongue at Annabel, a sound the horse had learned well as she started moving more quickly.

"Keep your weight centered, heels down, but move your hips with her," I directed, watching as Sierra followed my instruction. "Atta girl."

I took a few steps back, watching my girls trot around the arena together. She smiled back at me, laughing and bobbing in her seat like I'd shown her at Annabel's steady pace. That tug in my gut collided with the ache in my chest, creating a sinking feeling that felt a lot like fear. One that told me to enjoy this moment because my days with Sierra Volpe were numbered.

Forty-Two

Sierra

No one was telling me what to eat.

No one was scolding me for being late.

No one knew where I was.

Wind rustled through the trees. Water rushed through the creek beside me. Somewhere a bird chirped. Every day I spent under this tree allowed me to memorize the sounds around me until the music of this little clearing became a familiar song.

There was no one. No calendar alert flashing on my phone. No side eye at the dress that showed more of me than my mother would like. Only me and my big oak tree. I dipped my paintbrush into the little jar of water I'd filled from the creek, then moved it to my palette of watercolors. Little brush strokes filled the page of my notebook in various shades of green. I'd been practicing the techniques I'd studied in college.

A warm breeze rushed through the leaves, causing little drips to scatter across the page. I didn't cringe or panic. No one was here to tell me I'd made a mistake. To let me know how much I'd disappointed them with a tiny misstep. Instead, I let it dry.

It was like the more time away from my old life I had, the more I didn't care. I could make my life look exactly the way I wanted it to. I didn't have any choice in it. I couldn't go back to Chicago. So, I may as well enjoy it, I thought.

The first night Alden and I had acted on our attraction to each other didn't seem to scratch the proverbial itch. If anything, it had doused my need for him in kerosene and lit a match until we spent almost every night of the last several weeks enjoying each other. Sometimes all the way into the sweet blue light of dawn. Craving him became a habit. A roaring truck engine heated my blood as much as the feel of his stubble scratching over my skin.

Most nights, he took his time with me like he'd said he wanted to. Touching and teasing me until I was a quivering mess. Waiting until I was a disaster for him before he slid inside. The way he treated me like I wasn't some doll but a woman to be worshipped. Every second I spent with him, I learned more about myself until losing myself in his attention had become all too easy.

Setting the notebook and paints aside on the blanket I'd laid out, I dumped out the water and nestled into the base of the old oak tree. The rush of the warm summer wind was a serene lullaby as I let my eyes drift close to listen.

"Hey."

My eyes opened at the feel of soft lips on mine. Alden was kneeling beside me, brushing the hair away from my face. The dark brown cowboy hat was pushed up like he'd moved it to get closer to me. He smelled like sweat and hay. A bead of sweat rolled down the thick column of his neck, disappearing beneath the collar of his white tee shirt.

"I didn't expect to find you here," he smiled gently, speaking in a low rumble like he didn't want to disturb the trees around us.

"Aren't you still on the clock, Mr. Foreman?" I asked, blinking at the golden afternoon sun. How long had I been asleep?

"Told the old man I needed to check on some trees over here before the storm tomorrow," he winked, shifting to sit down beside me. "Annabel is over there."

He jerked his chin toward the other side of the creek. There she was, nibbling on the grasses that grew on the bank a few feet away. Annabel looked up like she knew we were talking about her, twitched an ear, and got back to her afternoon snack.

"You don't need to tie her up?"

"Nope," Alden smirked, lowering his head to my exposed shoulder. "She knows she's got a good thing with me. She'd never run away."

I breathed a laugh and grabbed his hat to place it on top of my head. His smirk remained as he shook his head, shaggy chestnut locks bobbed with the movement. A large hand reached out, turning my chin to meet his hazel gaze. Those eyes were so nice in this light.

"You know, in some circles, it means something when a girl wears your hat."

"Oh, really?" I rolled my eyes. "And what does it mean in those circles, cowboy?"

"Well," Alden huffed, kissing me quickly before crawling from his spot beside me to kneel between my legs. "In some circles, it means that you belong to me."

Rough palms skimmed up my legs. My breath hitched at the touch. Alden's mouth transformed from a teasing smirk to a roguish grin as he continued traversing my skin. The higher his hands moved, the closer he crawled. Then my back was pressed to the tree as I peered up at him, his hat now pinned beneath me.

"Do I?"

I'd meant the question as a joke, but I'd been made so breathless by his touch that the words sounded more like a whisper. Up this close, I could see the little gold flecks in his green and brown irises. The ever-present stubble on his jaw was a little thicker. His sun-bronzed skin was pink around the cheeks, almost as pink as his lips. Alden Boone was made of beautiful colors.

"Only if you want to, darlin'."

His mouth captured mine in a searing kiss. Strong hands moved, one bracing on the thick trunk over me as the other cupped the back of my head to protect me from the hard surface. Alden sucked my lower lip, tracing it with his tongue, causing my skin to tighten everywhere. I whimpered, digging one hand into the grass to keep myself steady as I let the other go to his jaw.

That first morning at the breakfast table with him, he'd told me city girls ended up out here all the time. They got caught up in the fairy tale. The fantasy of being with someone who was rough to the touch, but soft for them. Between his smile, his scent, and the way his powerful body made me feel, I understood why those girls fell in love with cowboys.

Being with Alden felt like I was living in a different reality. That smile of his lit up the dark corners of my mind like the sun that trickled through spaces between the leaves to warm our skin. When I was with him, I didn't feel like I wasn't enough. I wasn't trying to be perfect. With him, I was whole. An anxious part of me wondered if I was going to wake up in a cream and pink bedroom, having dreamed him up after reading a romance novel and this escape from my life would be over.

Alden consumed me. Drank me in. Hummed approvingly as my nails scratched through the stubble. I took the opportunity to lick at his parted lips. He welcomed me, meeting my tongue in a stroke that sent a zing of awareness through me. I didn't recognize this girl. The one who took what she wanted. Who didn't apologize for feeling what she felt. Threading my fingers into his hair, I pulled him toward me. But he didn't move. Instead, he sat back on his heels and heaved a frustrated sigh at the sky.

"I need to get back. If I don't get Annabel in on time, I'll be late getting home to my wife," he said, winking at me as he stood.

"We wouldn't want that," I teased, sitting up to grab his hat from behind my back.

I brushed it off and lifted it for him to take. Alden took the hat by the brim, giving it a little flip as he rested it on top of those thick, shaggy curls that glinted in the warm afternoon glow. He grinned that roguish grin as he gave the hat a little tip in my direction.

"No, we wouldn't."

Ignoring the way that grin made my insides go molten, I watched as his long legs strode over a narrow part of the creek. He mounted his horse, winking at me again before turning Annabel to disappear between the trees like I really had dreamed him up.

I packed up my things and walked the long way back, hoofbeats and heated kisses under the oak tree filling my head. By the time I got to the house my cheeks ached from smiling, having spent the entire walk home wondering who wouldn't want to belong to that man.

Forty-Three
Alden

After mentioning that I had to secure the house and barn for the oncoming storm, Sierra volunteered to help. We'd finished closing up the shutters. All that was left was to board up the windows on the storage side and tie down the doors. It was a task that wouldn't take long, since it was only large enough for two horses anyway.

When Sam Weaver and his wife started out in this house, they'd kept their horses with them on this side of the mountain. The road hadn't yet been cut to the ranch, so they'd ride their mounts to the main house and back. It wasn't a long stretch, but the stalls at the main house were much nicer, which was why I felt better about leaving Annabel there than here. That and it saved me from having to get up even earlier for a long ride.

Sierra looked around the small tack room. There was a tool bench and the rack for my saddle. Some bridles hung on the wall along with some rope. Just the essentials. She rubbed her arms to ward off the chill as her eyes returned to me. I picked up a small piece of plywood and walked to the tool chest to grab my hammer.

"Go inside, gorgeous. I don't want you to catch a cold out here."

"I'll be fine," she said, following me outside to watch me hammer the wood in place over the small window. "Besides, don't you want company?"

I snorted, hammering the next nail into the frame.

"With you around, I might drive a nail straight through my hand."

Securing the last corner, I looked over my shoulder to see she'd gone. Shuffling down the ladder, I hunted for her. Did she go back in the house? Worry ate at me as I searched. I would have heard her go up the porch steps, wouldn't I?

"Sierra?"

"I wouldn't want to break your concentration."

Her voice fluttered out to me on a cold wind. She'd gone back into the tack room. I followed the sound of it through the open door. There she was, perched on an old wood crate I used for storage. Stuffing the hammer back into the tool chest before crossing my arms over my chest to scold her.

"The only thing that breaks my concentration is you disappearing on me like that. Don't do that again."

"Oh, I'm sorry," she smirked, standing up from the crate to close the distance between us as her boots crunched on strands of hay and gravel on the wood floor.

I looked down my nose at her, trying my best to remain serious as she stared up at me with mischief in her eyes. My pulse jumped as I felt her fingers trace up the front of my jeans. She did it again, grazing her nails over my length as she nibbled her lower lip.

"Alden," Sierra started. "Can I?"

Her hands were on my belt, unbuckling before I could give her an answer. My cock twitched at the way her tongue wet her lips with anticipation. I gave a small nod. All I could manage and all the permission she needed. Sierra plunged a hand into my pants and stroked me. I swore. She let out a soft, breathy laugh as she pumped me. Then she was about to drop to her knees when I stopped her. For a second, she looked disappointed. I reached up for an old saddle pad hanging on the wall, folding it over to drop it in front of me. For her. She smiled and got down on both knees for me before tracing her palms up my thighs. If I didn't see the way she looked at me, I'd think she was trying to kill me.

My belt buckle clacking against itself and my hard intake of breath were the only sounds as she shoved my pants down around my hips to free my erection. Wasting no time, she took me in her hand and pumped. A long lick up my shaft and I almost blacked out.

"Darlin'," I panted. "You don't have to."

Sierra's mouth closed over the head, giving it a teasing lick over the crown. Then a hard suck as she moaned around me. Her cheeks flushed as looked up at me through long lashes. She liked this.

"Have to what?" She said, stroking her hand up and down before taking me in her mouth again.

"Never mind."

I watched myself slide into those perfect lips, taking me deep as her eyes teared. Her hand moved to my thighs, pulling me forward. For someone who claimed not to be good at this, she sure knew how to make my knees buckle. If I watched her for another second, this would be over too quickly. Hell, those little moans vibrating against me were enough to do it. My fingers plunged into the waves of her hair as my hips started to move. The walls of her mouth fluttered around me, sending that familiar zing to the base of my spine.

This afternoon, I'd found her asleep beneath the tree. Her tree. It was like something from a fairy tale. She could have been asleep there for years. I'd expected to find her at the house. Seeing her there, surrounded by flowers and the sound of the creek babbling. It made me wish I had an artistic bone in my body, just so I could capture it. Because a picture could never do justice to this thing I felt.

It was a step beyond need. Beyond desire. Every nerve in my body lit up with the drive to claim her. There was lust, and then there was this. Except this wasn't me taking from her. No, she was taking from me. Every kiss, every touch, every furious joining. Every fucking time, Sierra took little bits of my soul. It didn't matter. I'd let her have every bit of me if she'd asked. Hell, I'd give it to her anyway.

I opened my eyes to see her almond-shaped gaze on me as I thrust into perfect pink lips, one hand working to make up for what she couldn't take while the other had settled between her legs. With a view like this and that heavenly mouth, I wasn't going to last long. Glancing at the saddle stand beside the stall, an idea snagged on the corner of my mind.

"Get up," I ordered as I pulled myself out of her mouth. "I want you to lay over that rack and put your hands behind your back."

Sierra stood, wiped at her mouth, and turned on her boots. The saddle stand was just a little too high for her, which was perfect for me. At about a whole foot taller, I didn't exactly line up. She struggled, standing on her toes as she giggled a little, hands on the rack in front of her. Fucking hell. Who was this woman? This confident woman who had insisted she was bad at kissing. Bad? No. She wasn't bad at any of it.

Her ass wiggled against me as I pressed myself up against her. A little excited noise came from her. Something between a giggle and a whine. I had to suppress a groan of my own. Instead, I kissed the space between her neck and shoulder.

"Do you want me to fuck you, Sierra?"

"Yeah," she sighed.

I kissed her shoulder and stood upright again. This was too good for me. This woman. This view. That sinking feeling in my gut telling me that this would end came and went with a flicker. A better voice, a louder one, told me to stop getting ahead of myself and enjoy this. So I did. I pulled her panties down, slipping them over her boots as I lifted each of her feet to tug them free. Sierra's breath heaving breaths were all I could hear over the sound of my blood pulsing in my veins. These would do.

"Do you want it nice or rough, darlin'?"

Sierra nodded, looking over her shoulder at me as she bit into her lip. I ran a finger through her glistening sex. She was already so wet. My woman liked sucking cock.

"Let me hear you say it, gorgeous. How do you want it?"

"Rough."

Her voice was soft but the word was an order. My wife gets what she wants. My imagination always ran wild where she was concerned and, based on the way she was worshipping me with that mouth only minutes ago, my woman felt the same way.

"Hands behind your back."

Sierra tried to balance on her feet, leaning forward to give the rack her weight as she did what I asked. The white cotton panties were stark against her warm olive skin. I took both wrists in one hand, letting that dumb animal male part of me enjoy how small they felt in my hold as I started looping her panties around them. I twisted the fabric until I was sure it would hold. As Sierra looked over her shoulder at me, that beautiful face pulled into a little worried expression. But I could tell by the way she smirked a little, bouncing on her toes, she was intrigued. Excited, even.

"That's my good girl."

My obedient little wife. I kneed her legs apart and ran my fingers through her again. My cock was still slick with her saliva as I lined it up with her before burying myself inside her with a brutal thrust. She yelped at the sudden intrusion. With one hand on her bound wrists and the other plunging into her hair, I pounded into her as she screamed my name loud enough for the whole valley to hear.

If she wanted it rough, she would get it rough.

The decadent feel of her wrapped around me. The way my blood hummed with electricity. Embedding myself in her was a tempting and treacherous action. It worried me. Ate at me every day because I knew that this was as good as things would get for us. Since that first night and all the trysts after, I'd give up anything to be with her. Nothing mattered but this. Her. Sierra Briar had already turned into an irresistible obsession, which meant I was completely fucked.

"Who do you belong to, darlin'?"

This afternoon, I wanted her to say yes. To tell me she wanted to be mine. Not like this. The little blue dress was such a bad idea. I should never have bought it. Every time she had it on, I was taken back to the first time she wore it. I knew in that moment I was in so much goddamn trouble.

"You," she gasped.

The syllable felt wrong. At that moment, I realized I didn't want to hear it. I released her wrists. When it came to this woman, my imagination was limitless so long as I could stay in the moment because everything else I dared to dream about burned away in the light of day. I stared down at where I slid into her, noting another space I wanted to fill. Spitting onto my thumb, I circled the tight ring of muscle. Massaged it as she whimpered.

"This is mine, too," I growled as I bent over to meet her ear, barely recognizing the sound of my voice. "Tell me."

"Alden," she squeaked my name in surprise as she clenched hard around me.

My thumb pushed past the entrance. That zinging feeling returned to my spine. I massaged that ring of muscle as I let my thrusts turn deep and thorough, rolling my hips as I moaned at the crackling edge of my oncoming release.

"Oh my," she whined, surprise turning into pleasure as she arched into me. "Don't stop."

She turned, eyes wide as I worked her. That little crease between her brows. My woman was close. I released her hair and brought my hand up between her thighs. Sierra cried out at the contact. Her eyes fluttered closed as I felt her clamp down on me.

"Fuck," I grunted. "You feel so good, gorgeous. So fucking good."

My knees went weak as I came hard enough to see stars. We stilled, the sound of our heaving breaths the only noise. I withdrew and examined the work of art before me. Sierra was a beautiful disaster. Hair stuck to her sweaty, flushed cheeks as she caught her breath, hands still bound.

"Perfect."

Squatting to examine her gorgeous pink cunt, I watched my spend leak out of her and pushed it back inside with two fingers as she trembled at the contact.

"Alden!" Sierra panted. "Can you untie me?"

"We're not done yet," I said as I turned myself around and sat down.

Grabbing hold of her thighs, I lined her up with my mouth and went to work on that swollen bundle of nerves. I licked at sucked at her, teasing and torturing her until her legs were shaking again. Then I sucked it into my mouth until she screamed so loud, they probably heard her in the next county.

Forty-Four
Sierra

The sky turned from shades of grey to nearly black. It was only two o'clock in the afternoon. Were it not for the nearing booms of thunder, I'd think we were in for a lot of rain and nothing more. With all of the windows shuttered, I could only stand on the front porch to watch. And wait.

"Stay inside. If you hear the wind kick up, get in the tub. I'll be home as soon as I can."

Alden's order still rang in my ears as I watched the swirling clouds. Rain fell in fascinating sheets. Here one second. Gone the next. Branches undulated with the wind. Lightning cracked across the sky, a bright skeletal arm with bony white fingers reached for the mountains. Then another. I flinched. The wind gusted hard and fast, howling through the trees. The sudden warmth chilled my bones, causing my skin to prick and my fingers to tingle.

Time to go inside.

I opened the door and rushed inside, closing and locking it up as Alden had instructed while we were in bed last night. Climbing in with him had become so normal for me that it hadn't been strange when he lifted his arm, extending it for me to slip underneath. Positioning myself to lay across the broad expanse of his thickly muscled chest, I draped a leg over his and nestled my hand between his pecs. It was our everyday. Our pattern. Our normal.

"Have you ever seen a tornado?" Alden murmured his question in the dark, fingernails ghosting over the skin of my thigh and up to my ribs in a soothing caress. The touch made me feel like a contented housecat, tingles running down my back in that way that made all my nerves unwind.

"No," I'd whispered. "Have you?"

His hand stopped, settling at my waist before he answered.

"When I was a boy. They rarely happen this close to the mountains. But my parents' land is further out. Closer to the plains. It skipped over us, which was lucky because my father didn't do a damned thing to... Anyway, I was about eight at the time. Ran outside in time to see it rolling away from us."

He let out a long sigh as if remembering that day brought him pain. Tension coiled the muscles beneath me. There, in the darkness of Alden's bedroom, I remembered what it was like when my mother was like this. She would clam up. Refuse to talk to me. Punish me in some way, like withholding food or taking my car away. My father, well. He didn't keep his anger pent up. He would rage. Hit me. Even if I was just a bystander. For some reason, I knew I didn't have to feel afraid. I just had to be patient. I used my hand to make soft circles in the space between his pecs. The tight feeling beneath me eased. Another sigh loosed from the man beneath me, this one more relaxed than before.

"What did it look like? When you saw the tornado, I mean."

"Like the sky was reaching out to have a closer look at everything and throwing it back down to the ground."

That description stayed firmly in my mind as I fell asleep on top of him, his soothing touch resuming along the length of my body. It was with me when I woke.

It was with me now as I gathered a throw blanket collected the copy of Crime and Punishment from the bookshelf and sat on the couch to begin reading. Thunder crashed overhead, loud enough to shake the house a little. If that weren't evidence of the storm growing stronger, the sound of the shutters tapping against the side of the house was doing the trick. My shoulders tightened as another thunderclap sounded.

Sierra, you're a big girl. You can handle this. It's just a storm.

The voice wasn't my mother's. It wasn't bored or irritated. It was mine. Raindrops fell onto the house like nails onto the metal roof. Loud enough to drown out my fears. At least, that was what I thought until my phone chirped at my side. I jerked at the sound, not realizing I'd been on edge.

Doing alright?

No, I thought. *I keep thinking about that tornado you told me about and I'm wondering if I should just set up shop in the bathtub so I don't have to worry about being sucked out of the house.* But of course, I didn't say that.

Fine. Just reading. You?

Good. We're bunking down the horses. I'll be home in a bit. Keep the phone handy.

I set the little pink phone down and tried to resume reading. My eyes bounced from the top of the page to the bottom over and over again. Either this literature was dreadfully boring or the storm was at its peak because I couldn't focus on the words in front of me. The insistent tap, tap, tapping against the home's windows was winding my anxiety higher and higher. I just wanted to tell Alden to come home and wrap his big body around me because I knew I'd be okay as long as he was here. Rain hammered the roof. The wind was still rattling the shutters. Loud. Everything in here was so loud. Was this a tornado or was I just being a baby?

No, I was not being a baby. I wasn't. I was a totally rational human who was afraid of the storm raging outside. That was fine. Picking up the phone I started to type out a message stating that I was *actually not okay* and *could you please come home to protect me* when a loud crack snapped the air in two, followed by a crash.

It had come from outside. Outside. but the crash had startled me enough to rocket up from my seat. Now was the time to get to that tub and hope for the best. But my feet didn't move. Instead, everything went fuzzy as I lost my balance. And pitched forward as everything went black.

Forty-Five

Alden

Annabel picked her way over the stony trail, wisely avoiding the stones in our path as was made our way back toward the house. This was as fast as we could go in this terrain. I cursed myself for letting these animals get this far out when we knew a storm was coming. I had no one to blame but myself.

A boom of thunder rattled my ears. The sky was turning black.

"Shit," I grunted.

The old man looked up, giving the air a sniff. A whorl of dark clouds let the light in, showing a bit of green at its edges.

"We need to hurry up and get them down to the riding hall now."

Lightning whipped across the sky in a bright crack. Thunder roared overhead. Another immediately followed. Annabel whinnied as I gave her a squeeze, urging her forward. She hated this kind of weather. Mae started running ahead of us, having popped up on the grassy bank of the hill. Mr. Weaver's horse never liked thunder.

Only half a mile away. We could see the building, standing on the other side of the barn with its doors wide open. Junior was in the doorway, huffing from having done the job quickly.

Mr. Weaver whistled through his teeth, shouting commands at the herd and the hands ahead of us. I followed suit. Just as the first horse crossed the threshold, an icy sheet of rain fell down on us. The old man shouted at his son as we dismounted.

"Get inside!"

I hopped off Annabel, grabbing for Mae's reins to usher both horses to the barn. The rain shifted with the wind, stinging like needles everywhere that my skin was bare.

"That all of em'?" Mr. Weaver called to me.

"Yeah! I'm going to get these two to the barn."

"It's too late for that. They can ride out the storm in here with the others."

Pulling Annabel and Mae into the building, I cringed at the sound of the door slamming shut behind me. Both the Miller boys were there to secure the opening. Junior was shaking the water off of his blaze orange slicker as the old man wiped the rain from his face with an arm.

"I'm sorry, sir. I should've gotten them in here sooner," I breathed, removing my hat to dry my face.

Mr. Weaver gave me a hard look. The kind I saw when I got in too late or failed a test. Every time I got that look, I was sixteen years old again. I didn't want to fail him.

"You may be foreman but it's still my ranch, boy. Did you make sure the barn was secure for the foals before we set out to move the herd?"

"Yes, sir."

"Then you did your job. Everyone's safe."

Little hairs on the back of my neck stood up at his statement. Rain hammered down on the steel roof at a near-deafening volume. Both of the Sams and I were staring up at it as if we could all see the storm going by through the thick sheets of metal. I checked my phone again. Sierra hadn't responded to my last message. Normally, I'd let that go. It could have been the rain. Or the thunder. The signal wasn't exactly reliable out here. But it ate at me. Made me uneasy. I dialed her.

"Come on, darlin'," I snarled. "Answer the goddamn phone."

It rang. And rang. And rang. Then it went to voicemail.

"Not answering?"

"No," I grunted.

"Maybe the storm is messing with reception. She might not be getting the call," Junior offered.

I dialed again. Nothing.

"It's not the signal. It would go straight to voicemail," I grunted. "She's in trouble."

The grind of dirt met with my boots as I strode toward the doors. I'd told her to answer the phone if I called. Told her I'd only call for an emergency. I was fine. The horses were fine. Everything here was fine. Her not answering the phone? Not fine. Worry snagged at my mind, pulling every thread of rational thought loose as I imagined all of the worst possible scenarios.

A board came loose and a window broke, leaving her bleeding on the floor. She didn't listen to me about staying indoors and got caught in the storm somewhere I couldn't find her. Someone from the Serpa family found her and used the storm as an opportunity to sneak up on her. I just kept picturing her helpless, hurt, and alone. I needed to know. Needed to see her. Needed to put my hands on her and know she was okay.

A hand slapped onto my wet shoulder. Mr. Weaver's blue eyes were filled with iron where there was usually kindness.

"Boone, there's no sense in leaving. You're not going to beat the storm. You're just going to get yourself hurt and then you won't be able to do a damn thing for her. Stay inside until the worst passes."

My teeth ached as I ground my molars together. There was no room for argument. He was right. I knew he was. I let my chin dip at his order. She was alone. She could be hurt. She could be-

"Alright. Let's get them dry and hunker down."

Even though busying myself was the best thing to do, time seemed to drip by as I dried the horses and waited for the wind and rain to stop. By the

time every horse was dried and covered, I was still wound up tight. Every few minutes, I checked my phone for anything from Sierra. Thought about how last night she used her hand to circle my heart in small, careful touches. It soothed an old ache. Thought about how I'd kill for that touch now.

She needed me. I could feel it in my gut.

An hour. A fucking hour. By the time the worst of it had passed, my jaw was tight enough to crack my teeth. As soon as Weaver gave me the nod, I sprinted for the door, my jeans and chaps restricting my movement after taking on so much water. The old man followed me to the door, calling after me as I leaped into my truck.

"Careful, son!"

Get to her. Get to her. Get to her.

Careful wouldn't get me to her. No, I was fishtailing all over the road home. My windshield wipers were almost useless in this kind of rain, but it didn't scare me. I could drive this route with my eyes shut. The gaping maw of fear I was feeling wasn't from the storm or the rain. It was from wondering what was waiting for me when I got home.

Forty-Six
Sierra

"**S**ierra! Sierra, darlin', wake up. Shit."

I blinked. Alden was squatting over me, one hand braced on the sofa to keep himself upright. Water dripped off of his face, caught in little drops on his stubbled jaw as others rolled down the golden column of his throat. His black tee shirt and jacket were soaked, along with his chaps. The dark brown hat on his head dripped onto me. I was on the floor. The floor?

"Thank fuck," he puffed, extending his other hand to help me sit up. "What happened?"

Pushing myself upright, leaning into the sofa as I sat on the floor, I rubbed my forearm. I'd at least had the failing presence of mind to throw it out in front of me as I went down, but it felt bruised.

"I, uh," I blinked again, still feeling lightheaded. He was here. "I think I stood up too fast. Something crashed outside and I thought I should go to the tub, like you told me. But I didn't make it, obviously."

I let out a little laugh. Alden didn't. He just sat there, dripping onto the rug, staring at me. After he seemed to process what I'd said, he picked up the arm I kept rubbing and took a look at it. Rain still poured onto the roof above us, flooding the room with its white noise. The wind had quieted. Or maybe that was me. He was here. He was here and I was safe.

"You fainted," he said, digesting the information as he searched the rest of my body for signs of injury. Then he sighed, speaking more to himself than to me. "Which explains why you weren't answering the damn phone."

He called? He must have called a lot, which was why he was here when he should have been at the ranch. Oily guilt pooled in me at the thought of him rushing over here just to find me out cold on his floor. Even if I had only been seconds away from begging him to come home. He was here.

"What crashed?" I asked, cradling my arm against myself.

"A branch came down on the barn awning. Took the whole thing down. I can fix it easily enough with a little help. Come on," he said, standing as he reached his arms out to help me up. "I'm going to go out there and check it out. But I need for you to lay down here. I don't want you getting hurt again. Does it feel like you hit your head?"

"No. I just fell on my arm. Really, I'm fine."

Without missing a beat, Alden scooped me up and placed me on the sofa. I rolled my eyes at him. He stared down at me. The way he looked at me. It was strange. Like he was searching me for an invisible aggressor. Something else to fight on my behalf.

"Listen, Sierra," he ordered, the muscles in his stubble-covered jaw ticking with his gritted teeth. "Don't you dare move your ass from this sofa until I'm done out there. I don't want this happening again."

"Okay," I muttered. Alden looked me over again, as if I was going to get up from the sofa just to defy him. Had he ever sworn at me before? Instead, I pulled the blanket over myself and folded my arms. "See. Not going anywhere."

He grunted at me. Grunted. Examined me again. Then left. Rain was still falling hard outside, splattering against the windows in hard taps. But at least the thunder had stopped. Alden headed for the door, his boots thudding on the wood floor as he stomped off. The front door slammed behind him.

I fainted. I actually fainted. People don't faint. I'd never fainted in my life. Of course, I'd also never spent most of my nights rolling around the sheets with a cowboy. Was I really that tired? Deciding a nap on the sofa was probably for the best, I curled up under the blanket. Listening to the rain and Alden moving around outside was enough to soothe me as I let my eyes close. This day had officially worn me out.

I woke up on the sofa to the sound of the closing front door. The floor lamp was on. I checked the time on my phone. Hours had gone by. I didn't realize I'd been asleep for quite so long. Alden walked into the kitchen with a little brown paper bag and what looked like a takeout bag, noticing me stirring from the corner of his eye.

"You feelin' better?"

He set the bags down and approached the sofa, brushing a hand through my hair. I looked up at him as I reached my arms over my head to stretch.

"Yeah," I yawned. "How long have I been asleep?"

Alden chuckled dryly. He was actually all dry. He was wearing clean, dry clothes. He'd come in here and changed and I hadn't even noticed.

"Since the last time I checked on you? About two hours."

Alright, so I *was* that tired.

"Where did you go?" I asked, jerking my chin at the bags.

"I, uh, went to the drugstore," he said, shoulders straightening.

I gave him my best confused look as he took a few steps away, toward the kitchen. Alden reached past what was definitely a takeout bag and grabbed for the brown paper bag. His large hand reached inside and removed a pink rectangular box.

"You'd better take this," he said as he set it down on the counter.

A pregnancy test.

"Oh, come on," I laughed. "I don't need that. I fainted. That's all. It was probably just a blood sugar thing. I haven't been feeling sick at all, and I just had my period two weeks ago. Remember?"

I started counting the days on my fingers. It had been light, but it was there. Cramps and everything. Alden squatted to meet my eye.

"Darlin', we've been going at it like rabbits for weeks and we both know we haven't exactly been careful. Now let's just make sure or I'm going to keep worrying about you."

He gave me a soft smile. Worried about me. He was worried about me. It was an irritating kind of thoughtful. I let out an annoyed groan and stood from the sofa, snatching the test from the counter as I made my way to the bathroom. Alden followed me, boots thudding on the floor until he stopped to take them off.

I shucked my pants down my legs and sat on the toilet. Alden entered the bathroom and ripped open the box to hand me the test.

"Excuse me," I barked. "I don't pee in front of people."

Alden gave me a flat look and fished out the paper with the instructions. He read them to me as I peed.

"Says we should know in three minutes," he said as he looked at his phone.

There was no way. Just no way. My cousins had a hard time getting pregnant. Most of them took months. Some even took years. My mom took years. Besides, I felt fine. I felt normal. Aside from passing out cold after standing up too fast. But that could happen to anyone.

I placed the test on the counter and watched the window fill. Pulling up my pants, I washed my hands and flipped the toilet seat down to sit on it. Waited. Waited. Waited. One line showed up.

It was negative.

"See? It's not that." I held the test up victoriously.

He took the test from me. Stared at it for a minute. Chestnut brows drew together as Alden gave me an odd look. A heavy sigh followed.

"We should get you to a doctor."

I huffed. This was getting ridiculous. I was fine.

"It's only one line."

"It's two," Alden sighed, showing me the test as he held a finger up to the little window.

One blue line. And a thin little nothing line.

"No, it isn't," I argued.

Alden scrubbed a hand down his face, sighing through his nose as he looked at me with worry still in his eyes.

"Fine. But I'm getting you in at the women's center. It's confidential. No one will know but us. Just to check."

That night we split a tuna melt from the diner and some fries. Well, I ate half of my half and he ate the rest. Despite being a horrifyingly large sandwich dripping in cheese, it was delicious. Alden watched me take every bite. Maybe he'd come around on my theory that the fainting had been blood sugar related. Because I was fine.

Completely, totally fine.

Forty-Seven

Alden

I didn't sleep a wink last night. In fact, I don't think my heart rate dropped below a hummingbird's pace from the moment I saw that test. And while Sierra seemed to decide not to acknowledge it, my brain was going a mile a minute.

We'd spent so many weeks circling each other like prey that when we'd finally gotten together, we didn't think about what our actions might lead to. Actually, that wasn't true. I'd be lying if I said I hadn't thought about it. In an abstract way. Not a "let me knock this woman up and trap her in my house" sort of way. I wasn't a caveman.

If she wanted to deal with it her way, that was her business. I wouldn't hold it against her. None of this was planned. Not her showing up in my life. Not us spending all of our spare time intertwined in each other. Not me falling for her. Sierra was more than the girl of my dreams. She was untouchable. A star that fell out of the sky. I knew that. I sure as shit wasn't going to use this to keep her here.

I kept thinking back to Mrs. Weaver, who had given me the sex talk after I'd gone on my first date with Clary. She'd explained the technical details of how this would happen, sure. I'd wanted to die right there in my room as she showed me pictures from an anatomy book while telling me about how fun it could be. Except that wasn't the part of the conversation that stuck with me.

"If you're two consenting adults, you don't owe anything to each other, Boone. You don't have to put a ring on her finger. If you're still getting to know each other, don't rush into anything just because you feel obligated. I know that's not what everyone else is teaching around here, but a baby doesn't equal marriage."

Then she gave me a gigantic orange box of condoms with that gladiator icon on the side. I wondered how and where she bought them because a box that big could have only come from the big box store over in Hoback. It was impossible not to picture dainty little Maggie Weaver dropping a gigantic box of condoms in with all the other goods she'd likely picked up.

I wished she was here now to tell me what to do. Sierra didn't owe me a damned thing. I knew she had feelings for me. I hoped they were the same as what I felt for her. That didn't mean we had to jump into this together. We could move on from it and continue forward. Figure out what we were to each other without this complication. Or not.

This wasn't my fucked up way of trapping her. That was for damn sure. She could do what she wanted. She didn't belong to me. Even if I wanted to keep her, this wasn't the way. Every minute I had with Sierra was borrowed. I knew that. There was really only one thing repeating in my mind again and again: I didn't do this on purpose.

"You alright?" Mr. Weaver asked as we approached the house for lunch.

"Yeah," I lied. "Sierra and I have some business in town tomorrow. Is that alright?"

Mr. Weaver nodded, leaving me on the porch as I pulled my phone from my pocket to send a text I'd been dreading.

The response took a while to come in. Three dots popped up and stopped a few times, telling me she was typing responses and deleting them. I felt like a fucking asshole for asking, but this needed to happen.

A confirmation for the appointment came through by the time I was getting in my truck to head home. Making my way around the property and back to the house wasn't a long drive, but it felt longer without the radio on. The chatter of my restless mind was enough to fill the air.

That first night felt so long ago now. We'd spent all of it consumed by each other. Letting our worries fade into the background as we acted on everything that had built up between us. Attacking each other. After that, there was no way I could keep my hands off of her. I mean, I didn't. At all. Shit, I didn't want to. From that day on, we'd been all over each other.

When I was away from her, it wasn't the sex I was thinking about. It was the way her eyebrows furrowed right before she laughed. Or the way her foot tapped when she was pretending to be patient while watching me do something when she knew she could do it better.

"Hey."

Or the how, after letting our guard down around each other, she would smile at me at the end of a long day.

Anxiety loosened its hold on me as soon as I set eyes on her. Sierra was sitting on the front porch in one of the rocking chairs with a book in her lap, wearing that blue sundress. I grinned back at her.

"Hey, gorgeous. Hungry?"

She nodded, folding the book closed and standing to kiss me hello. Saying

Sierra was the girl of my dreams was like saying the sun was just a star. There was so much more to her than I could have ever thought up. She wasn't just a rainbow, she was every color. Scooping her up, I hauled Sierra into the house. Legs wrapped around my waist as I walked through the house to get to the kitchen. Her laugh filled the space as I placed her on the counter.

"Alright," I huffed as I examined the contents of the refrigerator. "We have leftover chicken. Some pork. Or we can make spaghetti."

"I can make something with the leftover chicken if you want to grab a shower," she offered, gently tapping her heels against the cabinet door.

"You sayin' I stink?" I said, closing the refrigerator to get good and close to her.

Placing my hands on either side of the counter, I leaned in until she was giggling at the feel of my breath on her neck. God help me, I loved that sound.

"Yeah," she giggled. "You do. But I like your stink."

She took my hat off, placing it on her head as she grinned up at me. I kissed her. Those giggles. That smile. I couldn't help myself. As I left her there to clean myself up, I couldn't help but imagine how pretty any child of Sierra Briar would be.

Forty-Eight
Sierra

Between the drive from the house into town and the drive through town to get to the clinic, we had been in the truck for almost an hour. The women's clinic was a small office building on the other side of town, so I got to see it all.

I spent the drive taking in the sights, if you could call it that. Compared to the sprawl of Chicago, it was hardly anything. Still, after spending several months cooped up in a little house in the mountains, it looked like a thriving metropolis. There was a movie theater that looked like the town had been built around it. Something that must have been a bar at the end of the block. Alden pointed out a diner across the street from the clinic building as we pulled into the little parking lot. The small building looked more like a log cabin than the diners I'd seen in the city.

"That place has the best burger you'll ever get your mouth around."

It hadn't occurred to me until he was holding the door open as I walked in to wonder why Alden knew about this clinic in the first place. Once we got into the small reception area, I had my answer. Natalie was sitting behind the desk. Dressed in yellow floral scrubs with her hair in a tight ponytail, she looked more professional than she had when she was hitting on Alden at her party or hoping I didn't shoot her at the hot springs.

Determined to make the best of an annoying situation, I strode up to the desk, holding Alden's hand as I painted a big smile on my face.

"Hi," I crooned. "I have an appointment. Mrs. Sierra Boone."

Natalie said nothing as she marked something down and typed something else into her computer. Alden removed his baseball cap and took my hand, pulling me toward the row of navy blue guest chairs lined up against the wall. As my legs met with the upholstery, a flutter tugged at my stomach. This was nothing. Nothing.

A friendly face of another nurse popped out of the door beside the reception desk, where Natalie peered at us from over the raised counter. The petite black-haired nurse who looked about ten years my senior held up a clipboard and called out my name, which was odd because I was the only one there. Alden stood up with me.

"Actually, can you wait here?" I asked.

"Fine. I'll be here," he agreed, giving my hand a soft squeeze. Then he directed his attention to the nurse at the door. "Come get me if you need me."

The exam room was cold and florescent the way all exam rooms at doctor's offices always were. The last time I'd been in a doctor's office was in Chicago, but it still felt like this. After the nurse took some blood, she told me to change into a gown and hop onto the exam table. This was ridiculous. So ridiculous.

A quiet knock tapped as I situated myself. A white-haired woman in pale blue scrubs walked in. This woman looked old enough to be my mother, but not much older. For a fleeting moment, I wondered what my mother would have looked like with white hair. I'd only ever seen a tiny hint of white roots before she'd have it covered by her colorist. The woman's face was kind as she introduced herself with a hand over her heart.

"Hi there, I'm Dr. Riggs, Mrs. Boone."

Somehow in the short amount of time I'd been in here, I forgot that little detail. I gave her a polite smile.

"Hi. Sorry, I'm still getting used to that."

She nodded as she pulled up a seat and flicked on a couple of monitors. Rolling a condom down a long wand thing. My eyebrows shot up.

"Not married long?"

"Only a few months. I'm on the shot but my husband is a worrier. Also, I had my period like two weeks ago. What's that?"

I sat up on my elbows and pointed to the wand. I didn't feel it was necessary to mention the test. The totally negative test.

"It's for the ultrasound. It's the best way to see what's going on in there."

Ultrasound? I examined the condom-covered wand-looking thing again.

"And that goes where exactly?"

Her dark eyebrows rose as she gave me a sympathetic look. Oh.

"When was the last time you had your dose?"

"February," I said meekly.

The doctor's expression flattened as it returned to me.

"Honey, the shot only works if you're getting it every twelve weeks. We're in June now. It's almost July."

"I know," I muttered.

Doctor Riggs shook her head a little as she turned on the machine and rolled her chair to sit beside my propped-up leg. She glanced down at my exposed rear end and shook her head.

"Alright honey, scoot your butt to the end here. I'm going to do your pap smear, and then we'll get a look."

I did as I was told, suddenly feeling a lot more nervous than I was before. The pap was unpleasant, as they always were. Like having a skinned knee, only somewhere more sensitive. She bottled up my sample and placed it on the little medical tray. Then she sat down on her stool again and moved to the machine.

"Okay, Mrs. Boone. Everything looks good here, so I'm going to start the ultrasound now."

Five months. It had really been that long? Days had slipped by. Melted together. It had felt like time stood still with Alden, but I'd been wrong. So wrong. My toes curled in the stirrups as my heart thudded in my ears. She slid the wand in as the screen remained dark.

If that was right, then Alden and I had been completely reckless. Still, I'd had my period. I'd used that little cup he got me and everything. It had been short. Light. But it was definitely there. Racing thoughts landed on my motivations for getting the shot in the first place. I'd been only a week away from being engaged to Antoni. Two weeks from being married to him. I'd wanted to prevent having a child with someone I didn't know.

I'd wanted to give myself time to get to know my new husband. For us to learn about each other.

"Just relax, honey. You're all clenched up."

I took a deep breath and looked away as the wand pressed into me. Cold and weird. Uncomfortable as she pressed it up. A small, annoyed part of my brain dwelled on how uncomfortable it was just to exist as a woman. I distracted myself by focusing on the screen. A big grey area. Nothing. Nothing. Random dark circles. Then a pat on my knee.

"Yup. Congratulations, mama. You're pregnant."

My stomach bottomed out.

"What."

"See?" The doctor pointed with a latex-gloved hand to a tiny flicker in the mass of grey. Circles. A little blob. Barely anything. "That's your baby. Right there."

"That's impossible."

It wasn't. I knew it wasn't even as I said it.

"Like I said, the shot is only effective for twelve weeks. From the look of it, I'd say you're about six weeks along. That bleeding you saw was probably implantation given the timeline."

Six weeks. I did the calculations quietly as the doctor waited for me to seem excited. My mind finally arrived at the date in question and I let out a laugh of disbelief. That night. It had to be.

"I'll spend the rest of my life taking care of you."

That night, when we'd spent hours kissing and enjoying each other, it had led to this. When we'd finally acted on our attraction to each other, neither of us had been thinking. Not really. We hadn't just thrown caution to the wind. We'd thrown it into a freaking hurricane. Repeatedly.

"It was the first night."

I hadn't realized I'd said that out loud until the doctor replied with a reassuring pat on my knee.

"That's all it takes. Some people are just more reproductively compatible than others and you two knocked it out of the park. Alright, do you want me to get Daddy so he can see?"

I must have nodded because the doctor racked the wand and stood up, leaving me alone in the room with my thundering heart.

A baby.

Guilt opened its mouth and swallowed me whole. God, I was an idiot. I'd just ruined Alden's life. I showed up in this town and ruined it. I worried about how he would feel. Surprise! Here's a child you didn't ask for from a girl who's been nothing but a complete burden to you from the moment you met.

As I waited for the doctor to return with him, I tried to calm myself. We could work this out. People dealt with this all the time. People in much worse positions than me dealt with this. I was educated. I was capable. I could handle it. That first night. Everything had felt so good. So right. Then every night after. In a strange way, it was a comforting thought. At least I knew that part wasn't a mistake. I wouldn't trade it. Even if it had only taken one night with Alden Boone to change everything.

Forty-Nine
Alden

"Let's get a picture of the little one."

Sierra's hand was squeezing mine hard as we watched the black-and-white shapes on the screen. Circles. Black and grey circles. The doctor seemed all worked up when she asked for Mrs. Boone's husband. Me. I practically ran into the room as soon as I thought something was wrong with Sierra. Then I got in there and saw her with that smile that didn't reach her eyes as the doctor explained everything to me.

I was going to be a father.

That hummingbird heartbeat feeling went away. Maybe it stopped entirely. Except, it wasn't from disbelief. On some level, I knew we were playing with fire. I just didn't care. From the look on my woman's face, she'd known it too. Now that I was seeing her. Seeing that. It didn't change anything for me. Except for regret. Because I didn't like that look on her face. That frightened look. I didn't want her to be scared of anything.

The doctor pulled the wand out and removed what looked like a condom from it. I glanced at Sierra, who still wouldn't quite meet my eye. A tear rolled down her cheek as her lips wobbled. A black and white sonogram popped into my view. I took the paper from the doctor and gave her a polite nod.

"There's your baby, Daddy. Like I told your wife, it looks like she's about six weeks along," she smiled. Then she clocked my woman's face. "A honeymoon baby. I'll, uh, give you two a minute."

I kept Sierra's hand in mine. Six weeks. That was all it took. It's funny because as soon as I realized what might be happening, I thought the time on the kitchen counter was it for sure. I wondered which time that first night had sealed it for us, which was a stupid thing to be thinking about. Especially when she was crying.

"Darlin'," I prompted once the door shut. I took the doctor's seat and waited for Sierra to look at me. I hoped this baby would have her beautiful eyes as they fixed on me, even if they were rimmed with red at the moment. I let the thought go. "Talk to me."

"I didn't think it would happen so fast. I know it's stupid, but I thought we'd have like a grace period or something."

The laugh that came out of me was involuntary. Really. I was still coming down from learning what had happened. This woman came into my life from out of nowhere and now we were here. Coming home to her, getting to know her, sleeping beside her. It all felt like a gift. This was unexpected, but not a surprise. Not for one second did I want Sierra to feel trapped. She had told me on the first day that she couldn't be my wife forever. This felt like a forever decision.

"We don't have to keep it and we'll make it work if that's what you want to do. This doesn't change anything between us. We're still figuring things out and that's fine with me."

She nodded, listening to me, but not really. Her hands pulled away to wipe at her cheeks. Picking up the sonogram, she eyed the picture in front of her. My chest ached at the sight of her worry. Her pain. This felt so much like that night I found her on the side of the road. Just as I had then, I wanted to fix it. Everything in me just wanted to make her feel better.

"Do you believe in destiny?"

Her eyebrows drew together as another tear rolled down her cheek. Setting the picture down, she didn't say anything as she focused on me.

"The first time I saw you, I think I knew you were going to change my life. You and me," I smiled, placing a hand on her belly. "We crashed into each other like shooting stars. Whether we do this together or not doesn't change a thing. I'd give you the whole universe if you let me."

She wiped her tears away with both hands, letting out a long shaky breath. Muffled voices fluttered in from the other side of the door, filling the air that had become heavy with unspoken worries. Sierra sniffed, wiping tears from her chin before she spoke.

"I always knew I'd be a mother. Someday. I didn't think it was going to happen like this," she said, then followed it with a humorless laugh. Sierra lifted a hand to wipe away her tears again. "I don't even recognize my life anymore."

"Sierra," I soothed. "This is just biology. It was always going to happen like this. But your life can be anything you want it to be now. You're resilient. If this is something you want to do, I'll be here to hold your hand. I'm not here to force anything on you. The world is still wide fucking open for you, gorgeous."

I smiled. I should have been terrified. I didn't have much, but I wasn't lying to her. I knew I wanted to give Sierra everything. She let out a wet laugh as she looked down at the sonogram in her hand.

"You shouldn't swear in front of the baby."

A laugh burst from me as I stood up to kiss her, my star. Her lips were salty with tears. She was shaking. I wanted to get her out of this damn exam room and hold her until she stopped. Maybe even get some food in her.

"I do believe in destiny," Sierra whispered, her words warm against my mouth as she looked up at me, my hands bracketing her face. "I know what I want to do."

Sierra let out a long breath as her eyes fell closed. Placed her hand over herself, she nodded.

"So, we're doing this?" I asked as I let my forehead drop to hers, trying not to let anything but support enter my voice.

"We're doing this."

Fifty

Sierra

It had only been five months ago that I was sitting in a different doctor's office for an entirely different reason. The day after I'd been informed by my father that I had no choice in my future. Only a week away from meeting Antoni for our engagement, I'd booked an appointment for the shot and made sure to do so while my mother would be busy. If I wasn't allowed to choose who I would marry, I could choose this.

I'd told my mother it was a checkup to make sure everything was alright. To make sure I was able to provide an heir when it came time to do so. It was rare for me to do anything on my own outside of going to the studio for a workout or to work for menial tasks. When she asked to reschedule the appointment so she could accompany me, I declined.

"It's just the gynecologist. It'll be fine."

My mother nodded absently, sitting at the large marble island in the kitchen as she typed away on her phone. She'd been busy enough as it was planning the big day. Our wedding was only a few weeks away. There was my dress to order. The flowers to arrange. Everything had to be perfect, and I didn't have a say in any of it. I didn't even know what my wedding dress looked like. But I could claim this for myself. Even if I had to lie.

I'd driven myself. Parked the coupe in the private lot and walked into the doctor's office on my own. Though it was a more luxuriously outfitted office than the women's clinic, it felt the same. Brochures everywhere. Large exam table. Person in a white coat.

"This shot will last you twelve weeks. Then you'll have to come in and get another."

At the time, twelve weeks seemed like enough. I'd be expected to give the family an heir. Based on what I knew of Antoni, it didn't seem like he'd be the type to wait. He'd been the one to insist on our speedy nuptials. I couldn't imagine he'd be gentleman enough to sleep on the couch on our wedding night. Nor did I want to broach the subject with his father, who I'd only met once and scared the wits out of me. No, this was my only opportunity to buy myself a little time. I would take all the time I could get to learn about Antoni Serpa before letting him father my children. No, not father. What's the word the ranchers use?

Sire. That's it.

Antoni wouldn't have been a father. Not in any real way. He would likely have acted just like my father. Or worse, his.

Alden waited for me to say something. Anything. I was too lost in my thoughts about where I had come from and everything that had led up to this to get out anything beyond single-syllable answers. Otherwise, our drive home was nearly silent.

Inside, I could hear my mother screaming at me.

You have no money. Nowhere to go. Now you're having a baby. With a nobody you met on the side of the road. You barely know him. That is not a life plan, Sierra. That's a cry for help.

It was easy to argue with the ghost in my head. I knew him better than the man who they were going to shove me down the aisle with. The one who'd helped murder them all. If they hadn't carried out an assassination on my family, it could have easily been Antoni's child instead of the man who'd done everything he could to take care of me. To make me feel safe and wanted. I couldn't imagine feeling about Antoni Serpa the way I felt for Alden Boone.

Sure, it wasn't a plan. I still didn't have a plan. Not even a hint of a plan. Just because I was having a baby with Alden didn't mean I had to stay here with him. Women raised children on their own all over the world. I could be one of them. I was smart. I could do it. He said it wouldn't change anything between us.

It was strange. As I lay there after seeing our baby for the first time, looking down at the sonogram, I had a sense of calm wash over me. Logically, I knew I had options. There was more than one way for this story to end, and in any other situation, I might have chosen something different.

As Alden spoke with me, that calm feeling that started in my gut crystallized into a decision. Sure, I'd never chosen anything on my own in my entire life. That didn't mean I wasn't capable. I was so aware of how alone in the world I felt now that my family was gone. It was just me. The last Volpe. Well, with this baby, I wouldn't be.

All those months ago, I'd been scared. Terrified of having a baby with a man I didn't know. Someone who could hurt me. Treat me like property. Alden was not that man. He was so much more than I could have hoped for. He listened. Protected me. Cared for me in little ways I'd never imagined. I knew him.

Laying there in that office, as I looked at the big bear of a man who wanted nothing but my happiness, I realized I'd already made my decision. This was my baby.

"Are you feeling alright?" Alden asked around a bite of burger.

"Yeah."

"Sassafras, Sierra. You had a load of bricks dropped on you today. I wouldn't be surprised if you were feeling a little flat."

"Was that a pun?"

"Yup," he smirked.

The dinner we'd picked up from the diner was a small luxury, but he'd insisted. Just like he was insisting I tell him the truth now. I dipped a fry in some ranch and tucked it into my mouth as I tried to think about how to bring up the other thing I'd been mulling over.

"I don't want you to think you have to support me. And, I guess, the," I hesitated. Even though I'd acknowledged the existence of this child in the office, it still felt strange to say it out loud.

"The baby," he finished. "I told you I'd take care of you. That wasn't bullshit. We'll figure it out. Don't borrow trouble, gorgeous."

Alden took a gigantic bite of burger and smiled at me with cheeks full like a chipmunk as I burst out laughing. He reached a long arm across the table, gently touching the tip of my nose with his index finger. A few seconds passed as he worked to swallow his bite, picking up his soda to wash away the rest.

"I feel like I ruined your life," I muttered.

Alden choked on his drink.

"That is some old-school bullshit right there," he choked out, giving one good cough before he continued. "I work on a ranch. I see pregnancy all the time. This was no great mystery to me. I knew exactly what could happen and I didn't care. Not for one second, darlin'. Stop worrying about me."

He reached across the table and placed one giant paw of a hand over mine, brushing his thumb over the back.

"Let's be honest," he chuckled, lifting both our hands to kiss my knuckles before setting them back on the table. "We didn't do a damn thing to prevent this."

"No," I said with a grimace. "We didn't."

I knew exactly what could happen and I didn't care.

I'd known, too. I mean, I made straight A's in school. I wasn't an idiot. I just didn't think about it, so it was still a shock. My life had changed in the span of a few hours only a few months ago. Then I got mixed up with this grinning bear of a cowboy and everything just kept changing colors until I didn't recognize the picture anymore.

As I went to bed with Alden, tucking myself under his arm to let his big heart sing me to sleep, I decided that change might be the only constant in my life now. That and the beat of a cowboy's heart.

Fifty-One
Alden

I'd spent so much of my life just surviving from minute to minute that I didn't think much about the future. In some distant way, I thought I'd end up with a wife and kids. People do that. They meet someone. They get married. They have babies. But I didn't think much about the how or the when of it.

Until I met Sierra.

We'd started out protecting her identity under the guise of being husband and wife only to fall into the habit. Being with her was all I thought about all day. I wanted to make her happy. Wanted to see that beautiful smile light up her face with something I said or did. She wasn't my wife on paper, sure, but she'd become my wife in every way that mattered. She was who I worked hard for. The woman I came home to at the end of the day. The one I wanted to fall asleep beside every night.

Now we were going to have a baby together.

I stared at the little black picture pinned to the refrigerator with an old letter S magnet. It was just circles and darkness on a piece of paper.

A baby.

Of course, I knew how this happened. Hell, it wasn't even that much of a surprise. Natalie had told me once about all the strangest signs of pregnancy a woman could miss. Fainting was one of them. I'd arrived at the possibility while I took care of the wrecked awning on the barn, worrying about all the reasons she might have fainted so that I could prevent it from happening again. Then I started thinking about how careless I'd been. Six weeks of not being able to keep my hands off her. Six weeks of enjoying every second together. Six weeks of treating her exactly like my wife. It was bound to happen. She knew it too. I know she did.

This was the beginning of an entirely different chapter of my life. I could let myself be terrified by it. This baby, the person we were going to bring into the world, was going to rely on me. That was a terrifying thought. A terrifying thought for someone whose parents had essentially ignored me while they drank themselves to death. I could have let myself be terrified by that. Only, that wasn't what scared me. The uncertainty of my future with Sierra, however.

That scared the shit out of me.

Tugging open the refrigerator door, I grabbed the creamer for my coffee. Doctoring the cup as quietly as I could in the darkness of my kitchen, I thought about everything that could be.

On socked feet, I walked to the bedroom to take one last look at Sierra before starting my day. She'd taken my pillow, hugging it to her body to replace me. The blankets had shifted down, exposing the length of her body. Tiptoeing into the room, I crossed to my side of the bed and used my free hand to tug the blanket over her. A quiet hum slipped out of her as she nuzzled into the blanket.

"Are you leaving?" Sierra turned over, looking up at me with the fog of sleep in her eyes.

"Yeah, darlin'. I've got to get to work," I smiled down at her.

"Kiss me goodbye," she said, turning her head up to face me fully.

I braced a hand beside her head, bending over to brush my mouth over hers. Her kiss was soft and sleepy as her fingers threaded into my hair.

"Stay," she begged. "Please."

"You beg so pretty, darlin'," I sighed, savoring the luxurious feel of her mouth as I kissed her again. "But I have to go."

"Fine," she huffed, rolling over again with a yawn. "Goodbye, cowboy."

"See you later, gorgeous," I said, kissing her bare shoulder.

I'd been leaving her in that bed every single day for weeks. Every day, it got a little harder. I wasn't lying to her about the baby. We'd figure it out. If she stayed. She'd decided to keep this baby. I knew she hadn't decided on me. On us. Not really. It wouldn't be fair to pressure her into telling me how she felt, and I didn't want to rush her. We were good. That was enough for me.

A bit of light caught on the jewelry I'd been ignoring until now. Those expensive earrings of hers.

"They're worth more than some people make in a year."

Swiftly picking them off of the table, I tucked them into my pocket and headed for the door. I didn't know how I would go about selling something like this, but I was sure I could figure it out. This was something she'd asked me to do, and I would do it. They didn't belong here. But she did. She belonged here. With me. In my bed. Glancing back at the girl, an idea took root.

Sierra was everything I could ever want. I didn't want to shackle her to me. Not when she'd never had a chance to create a life for herself. I wanted her to know what she meant to me. Even if I was still too big of a chicken shit to say it.

Things were quiet this time of year. This in-between time. Mr. Weaver went into town to take care of business, taking the Miller boys with him to pick up some feed and other things. With them gone for a few hours, I was alone for lunch. After scrounging up a couple sandwiches in the kitchen, I took myself to the porch. The glass of water I had was sweating in the early summer sunlight. The sparkling condensation reminded me of the valuables in my pocket.

Diamonds glinted in the sun. Pearls that were so white and perfect, that they reminded me a little of Sierra's teeth.

"I was just a stupid, spoiled girl."

Hundreds of thousands of dollars dangling on her ears without a second thought. And she hated herself for it. She wasn't selfish. She wasn't using me. She took care of me. She did it without my having to ask. She did it because she wanted to. The same way I did for her. Blind, stupid hope made me want to get rid of these things.

"What've you got there?" Junior asked.

I jolted and closed my fist around the jewels, panicked about dropping them. Junior arched a red brow at me, stuffing the last of his sandwich into his mouth. Without Sawyer here to cook, it looked like we'd both had the same idea.

"Earrings. They belong to my wife. She wants to sell them."

"Oh," he squinted at me, some question flashing over his features as he spoke through a full mouth. "Well, I can help you with that."

Wiping the crumbs off of his hands on his pants, he stuffed them into his pockets and leaned against the pillar beside me.

"You can?"

"Online, man. Sell them online. Start a bidding war. I was able to get enough from some of my mom's old vinyl records to pay for some computer parts. You'd be surprised. You might get more than you expect."

"I don't know anything about that," I sighed.

"Here. Let me get a picture," Junior said, sliding his phone out of his pocket. "Lay them on the deck so we can get some nice shots with this light."

I did as he said, and Junior snapped a few pictures with the camera on his phone. Freckles scrunched together as he examined his work. I started on my second sandwich, waiting.

"Alright, I'm just going to image search them to see if we can find a brand. That'll help us set a price," Junior said, his voice trailing off as he scrolled through his phone. He paused, looking down at me in confusion. "You want to explain to me what you're doing with twenty-thousand-dollar earrings, Boone?"

"They're Sierra's," I huffed. The Weavers were good people. Trustworthy people. That didn't mean I wanted to tell them all about how my woman really came to me. That she was wealthy beyond even their well-off understanding.

"Did she steal them?"

"No. They belong to her. She came from a family with a lot of money." Before Junior could say whatever he'd opened his mouth to ask, I added. "It's complicated. She asked me to sell them a while back. I just forgot."

Lying to Junior felt bad enough, even when I was trying to mix lies and truth. I hadn't forgotten about the earrings, that was for sure. When she gave them to me, I wanted to show her we didn't need it. That I could take care of her. Provide for her. And I could. So I left them there. I still wanted to prove that to her. But now I wanted them gone. To forget that there was another life she could return to.

A deeply selfish part of me wanted her to forget that, too.

"I'll get them sold for you. It's better if you're verified. Don't want anyone to look like you stole it and are trying to pawn them off on some unsuspecting stranger on the internet."

I thanked Junior and stood from the porch, wanting to busy myself with other things. To shake off the sick feeling I got whenever I thought about Sierra leaving. My boots ate up the distance between me and the barn. I hurried inside and grabbed the toolbox along with everything else I'd need to tune up the Polaris along with the ATV. Work helped keep my mind off things.

Except, today it didn't help. Nothing helped. Complex little tasks weren't enough to distract me from the things I still needed to let go of. The fears I had about what was coming. The worry that I wasn't ready. I didn't know how to be someone's father. I wanted Sierra to let go of the things that she'd left behind, but there was so much still holding me back. Two people I needed to forget, because forgiveness wasn't an option anymore. Two people I needed to let go of. For good.

By the time I was cleaning engine grease off of my hands, I knew what I had to do. I sent Sierra a text, letting her know I'd be home late. It had been a long day. I desperately wanted to see her. Wanted to feel her warmth against me. It would have to wait. Because instead of going home, I dialed the phone and headed in the opposite direction. I was finally ready to take care of the other thing I'd been thinking about. Something that had been coming since the day my parents died.

Fifty-Two
Sierra

Pregnancy was already doing strange things to my body. It was like as soon as I acknowledged that there was a baby in there, my body decided to show off and reduce my daily activities to three things. Food. Sleep. Sex.

"Do nothing."

Now I didn't have a choice. It had only been a week since discovering our activities had created a little result and I'd spent most of that time asleep. Just like every other day, I awoke in the early afternoon. Sleeping in was never an option for me before I got here and now I was doing it constantly. The old me would be appalled at how much time I was spending in bed. Sleeping or...not. When I complained about not being able to keep my eyes open, Alden simply smiled at me from across the table.

"Making a person seems like tiring work."

Tiring and hungry work, more accurately. I spread some peanut butter over a slice of toast, cut up a banana, and sat down with the Hunchback of Notre Dame, having given up on Crime and Punishment. Even with almost nothing else to do, I couldn't make myself read that depressing tome.

I took a sip from my tea. Tea. I had been reduced to herbal tea, upon Alden's request.

"I'll buy you all the coffee you want when it's over, but just try the tea. If you hate it, I'll get some decaf."

So, yes. Fine. I was trying the tea. For him. It was so hard to say no to him now. No to the smile he seemed to wear constantly now? No. I couldn't do that. It was too sweet. Too charming. The way his lips curled so slightly that no one else might notice. I did. That ever-present smirk lit his eyes. Softened them. And for as much as we might still be strangers to each other, I knew one thing about Alden Boone now. He was happy.

"Stop worrying about me."

I wasn't foolish enough to think he was happy about this change. I wasn't. Well, I wasn't *not* happy. It just didn't feel real yet. Still, his happiness grew more and more evident by the day. Not for this baby. For me. I felt his affection in every action. And while the girl who never knew a day of real love in her life ate up every bit of it when he was here, the woman who'd only experienced loss wondered when it would all come crashing down when he was gone.

Because it would.

Alden has a book of Robert Frost's poetry. Frost was the one who said that *nothing gold could stay*. Every day I spent with him felt like something leafed in gold. Each moment was a precious thing to keep for myself. He told me not to worry about him. That we would figure this out together, but that didn't mean he should have to. That didn't mean I wanted him to.

We'd only just found each other. Only just started to explore the things we felt for each other. I knew that it was more than a physical connection. Alden made me feel so safe. So at ease. It was also possible that it was nothing more than that. I'd never felt safe or secure with anyone. Not even family, because at the end of it all, they were always looking out for their bottom line. Even my brother.

But not Alden.

He was looking out for me. Protecting me. Caring for me. He'd welcomed me into this house. Gave me his bed to sleep in. Now he was planning to care for this baby. All because I wasn't strong enough to stand on my own two feet.

I tried reading the page again. I'd only made it to Esmerelda's entrance and I'd been attempting to read this book every day for a week. Feeding myself. Sleeping. Enjoying Alden because being with him felt like basking in the sunshine. All of that helped to silence the torrent of voices in my head telling me I was wrong to be here. Wrong to choose a safe life instead of carving my own path. Wrong to thrust this responsibility on someone I cared about without worrying about how it would affect him in the long run. The voice that sounded so much like my mother's would try to convince me that eventually, he'd see the error of his ways.

I knew enough about Alden to know his feelings for me wouldn't tarnish quickly. He was kind enough to care for me for years. Decades, even. We were still strangers to each other. Eddie's sour words repeated in my mind.

"He put clothes on your back and a roof over your head."

If his best friend thought that, how long would it be before Alden felt like I was using him? I hadn't earned this. Earned him. Just because I'd decided to keep this baby didn't mean that we needed to be together. I heaved a sigh and laid the book across my lap, placing a hand over my still-flat stomach.

"I promise I'll figure my life out before you get here."

I couldn't leave. Not with the Serpas still looking for me. It wasn't just my safety I had to worry about anymore.

Ungrateful.

The word followed me everywhere, throughout my life. Always uttered by my mother whenever I was faced with something I really didn't want to do. She would hurl that world at me any time I performed below her standards. That rotten word. It was the same word I'd hoped Alden would never think about me. Sitting on that sofa, I made my first parenting decision. No matter what happened, I was never going to use that word.

Fifty-Three

Alden

Going home used to be the worst part of my day. At the end of the workday, I just washed up and ate alone. Fell asleep on the sofa reading, then shuffled off to bed when I eventually woke up. I hadn't realized how much I despised it until those days were behind me. It took Sierra's company for me to see how lonely I truly was. It was that same company that changed how I felt at the end of every day. The sinking feeling of returning to an empty house was replaced with urgency. Anticipation because I knew she was there.

As I pulled up to the house, I saw Sierra seated on one of the rockers out front. She was wearing that pink dress today. The fading sunlight illuminated her olive skin in beautiful gold tones. She lifted her head, looking up from the book in her lap, and smiled at me. I practically leaped out of the truck just to get to her.

"Hey," she greeted as she folded the book closed and set it down on the porch.

Sierra's feet were propped up on the chair she'd angled to face her. I lifted her feet and pulled them into my lap as I sat down in it.

"How was your day, gorgeous?"

"I started a painting and had a nice walk, which I'd heard is supposed to be good for girls in my condition," she sighed, stroking the still flat plane of her belly. Between her fuller breasts and the belly soon to come, that dress wasn't going to fit for much longer. "But Alden, I have a question."

"Hm?" I hummed, rubbing her feet in little circles.

"Where am I supposed to have this baby? I can't go to a hospital. Do they even do that at the clinic?"

"I don't know. But that's alright. I'll deliver it."

She laughed, tugging her feet away as she gave me a little kick.

"You're not serious."

"I've delivered plenty of foals."

She rolled her eyes and crossed her arms. I got on my knees and crawled to her. Parting her thighs, I smiled up at her. Sierra covered her mouth, trying not to laugh at me as the book she was reading fell down.

"The baby comes out here. Right?"

"You're an idiot."

"Maybe," I joked. She covered her mouth with a hand as she tried to stifle a laugh. "But don't worry. I've got you, gorgeous."

I kissed the inside of her thigh and noted the way it made her skin prickle. She hummed as my mouth moved over her soft skin.

"You look good all covered in dirt," she rasped. I kissed her other thigh, higher. "Alden. I need you."

Without a moment's hesitation, I slid my arms beneath her thighs and yanked her forward until her arms flew around my neck. She yelped in surprise. One arm wedged beneath her ass, I stood up and took her with me.

"What are you doing?"

The question was a tremulous giggle as I strode across the porch, flinging the door open with one hand and kicking it shut behind us. I slid off my boots, walking toward the bedroom. With one hand, I tossed my hat onto the sofa.

"Alden!"

She bounced as I tossed her onto the bed. I used one hand to tug off my shirt, enjoying the undiluted hunger in her eyes as she watched me. Sucking her lower lip into her mouth and pinching it between her teeth, her eyes tracked my pants as I shoved them down my legs.

"Sierra."

Those eyes snapped up to my face.

"Take your fucking clothes off," I winked.

Rosey pink flooded her cheeks. She got to her knees and pulled her dress over her head. Dark hair covered her breasts. She looked like a goddess. How? How had I gotten so lucky? Sierra sat down again, then reclined to take her panties off. I climbed onto the bed, slipping my fingers around the fabric to finish the job. A blind throw had them flying toward the hamper as I climbed on top of her.

"Alden," she breathed. I loved the way my name sounded on her perfect lips.

I crooked a knee under one of her legs, using the other leg to drive myself forward. Her lips parted with a gasp as she felt my erection glide over her, covering me in her arousal. Satisfaction and need warred in my veins at the knowledge that she was already so wet for me. Sierra's arms circled my neck.

"You said you needed me," I pushed forward again. Another gasp. I grinned down at her. "I'm here."

Arcing my hips as I drove forward again, I slowly buried myself in her. Sierra cried out, eyebrows drawing together as her legs tightened around me. Pressing in inch by inch, I nudged her nose with mine before kissing her. Fuck, I loved kissing this woman. Her moans tasted so sweet as I began to move inside her. Perfect fingers looped into my hair, pulling a little. Her eyes opened, staring into mine with that little line between her brows.

"That's all I have to do, huh? Tell you I need you?"

"Yes, ma'am."

The oncoming evening had darkened the room enough that the color had left her green eyes. Only shades of purple and lavender and grey. The warmth of her hair had now turned to night dark strands spilled across my bed. Her body tightened around me with the promise of her release, the sounds of her pleasure growing more feral. More desperate.

Nothing would ever be as sweet as this. Sierra's frantic tugging at my hair. Her skin. The way my name sounded when I hit that spot. The way she begged when she was getting close.

"Oh god, Alden. Please."

I couldn't count how many times we'd tangled together since that first night. Couldn't tell you exactly how many kisses or touches there had been. I only knew I could remember the way each of them felt, as I knew I'd remember the way her hips lifted to meet mine. And the way she looked at me as she shattered beneath me.

I sat up, moving my arms from where they'd propped me over her to loop beneath her body and pull Sierra into my lap. Her legs wrapped around me, arms still around my neck as we stared at each other.

I wanted it all. All of this. With her. I wanted everything. To stay here and raise our child together. To have more babies together. To keep laughing together. Get through the hard days together. To grow old together. All of it.

An expression I didn't recognize crossed her features. Something like pain flickering in her eyes. I stilled.

"What is it?"

"No one's ever looked at me like that before."

"Like what?" I asked, trying to stuff down the overwhelming urge to spill my guts.

Like I want to ask you to spend your life with me?

"I don't know," she breathed, beginning to move on me again. "But I liked it."

My hands kneaded her ass, rocking her against me as my lips dotted kisses over her shoulder. Sierra moaned as she took her pleasure, grinding into me where she needed as she tightened around my cock. Those moans. Little whimpers as she drew near. They undid me. Some purely male satisfaction kindled in me the moment I learned I'd been the only one to do this to her. To make her feel what she was feeling now.

Her next climax was swift and sudden as she kissed me. With the way my toes were cramping as the base of my spine tingled, I wasn't far behind. My hands pressed her down, pulling her tight against me as I came. As the sensation overwhelmed me, the urge to confess everything I was feeling about her dissolved. Our heaving breaths filled the room, drowning out any lingering thought.

When I finally regained my ability to move, I lifted Sierra off of me and headed to the bathroom for a washcloth to clean her up. She closed her eyes and lay back on the bed, humming like a satisfied cat as she stretched out. I braced an arm on the doorframe and watched her.

So fucking perfect.

Crossing the room again, I climbed onto the bed with the damp washcloth in my hand. Sierra opened her eyes, the almond-shaped beauties going round at the feel of the cloth sliding over the apex of her thighs. I smirked.

"I need to feed my woman. What are you hungry for?"

My hand took its time cleaning her up. There was no hurry. Not when I saw her nipples furl at my touch. Skin exploded with tiny goosebumps. We weren't done here.

"You. And nachos."

I obliged her.

There were a few things I was certain of. The first was that my woman was going to eat her weight in tortilla chips before this pregnancy was over. The second was that I wasn't just falling for this woman. I was fucking done for.

Gone. Dead and buried.

I had asked her to stay. Those weeks ago, riding with Annabel in the arena, I had asked her. When she didn't answer, I dropped it. We couldn't make the argument about not knowing each other well. Not when we'd shared so much. The request was on the tip of my tongue every time my chest gave that familiar tug. The one that knew this was more than a passing fling.

Sierra sat with me and discussed books. We talked about paintings she loved and artists who meant something to her. She told me she loved Von Gogh the most because he was a romantic at heart. That even though she loved sunflowers, her favorite work of his was Starry Night Over the Rhône.

"With the water and constellation in the sky, it feels timeless. We could stand right there and look at the stars. We could be standing right beside him and see it all."

She loved seeing the world through the eyes of people who felt things deeply. I wanted to see the world through her eyes. I wanted to finally step foot out of this state and learn about things from her. To see those fields of flowers on the other side of the world. To hold her hand and walk with her anywhere. I'd told her the world was wide open for her, but the truth was that it had never been that way for me until she was in it.

With a belly full of cheese and chips, Sierra was sleeping soundly on the sofa by seven o'clock. Normally, I would have left her there until I was finished cleaning up the kitchen and was ready for bed, but tonight was a little different. I scooped her into my arms, earning muttered gibberish as I carried her to bed.

"Good night, gorgeous," I said, kissing the top of her forehead after tucking her in.

"Ma-night," she half mumbled as I shut the door.

Opening the door beside ours, I surveyed the shelves, boxes, and disassembled furniture in front of me. There was so much in here that I needed to take up to the main house, but we could still use some of it.

"Alright, Boone," I said, trying to pump myself up. "Let's do this."

The storage room had been Junior's nursery when the Weavers brought him home so many years ago. Some of his things were still in here. I was determined to spend my night finding them. So I did. About halfway through the project, my phone buzzed in my pocket. I pulled it out to see a text from Junior.

Earrings sold. For a nice chunk of change, too.

This night just kept getting better and better. As if I needed a sign to move forward with the wild idea that had taken root as we sat on my sofa together eating the chips I'd dumped grated cheese and chicken over and microwaved. We had time, sure. Months of it. But I wanted to show her that I was in this with her. That this was not all on her shoulders. Maybe I couldn't find the courage to tell her how I felt right now, but I could show her. I didn't have a lot, but I was going to make this a home for us. All three of us.

Fifty-Four
Sierra

Aloud chirp woke me. With my body going from out of control horny to needy to hungry, I was on a hormonal ride that took all of the energy out of me. That meant I was waking up in the middle of the day. Again. I hadn't realized what time it was until I looked at my little pink phone.

Noon. Noon? I saw the message from Alden. Propping myself up on Alden's pillow, I looked around the room. Usually, if he was leaving something for me, it would be right here where I could see it.

I tapped out a response and hit send, then swung my feet out of bed to start my day. Or so I thought. As soon as I stood up, a wave of nausea washed over me and sent me running for the bathroom.

Pregnancy had been a breeze so far. Okay, I'd been completely unaware of it for the first six weeks, and I've been asleep for most of it since then. But I thought I'd gotten lucky. That I was one of those women who just didn't get morning sickness. I. Was. Wrong. My body wrung itself out like a rag.

Food? After about twenty minutes of vomiting, I peeled myself off of the floor, attended to my needs and got dressed. I was still brushing my teeth when his answer came through.

> I should have guessed you were still asleep. Go check the den.

"The den?" I wondered aloud, mouth full of toothpaste.

What den? Braiding my hair away from my face, I walked out of the bedroom. My eyes snagged on the only closed door in the house. The closed door that had a sticky note posted on it.

I know you'll make it beautiful.

Another little heart was doodled into the corner. Pressing the note to my chest, I opened the door to the storage room. All the shelves were gone. Boxes and old cans of paint were piled into a corner next to a window I hadn't even noticed before since it had been blocked by the shelves. There was sunlight pouring in through sheer olive-green curtains.

Entering the room, the den, I realized it was larger than I'd thought. Not exactly a full room but much bigger than a closet. Well, bigger than a normal closet, anyway. All the clutter had made it seem smaller. Now that the boxes and things were almost gone, likely thanks to Alden's hard work, it didn't feel like a storage room anymore. As I turned to see his second surprise, I let out a laugh.

It was small and simple. A little over three feet wide and made of pale birch wood. It looked lighter than air sitting in all that sunshine. My fingers skimmed the barrier as my lips pulled into a soft smile.

A crib.

The little wooden crib must have belonged to the Weavers. Alden told me their son had been born while they lived here, and it seemed they'd left the baby furniture behind. A petite dresser sat behind me, a pale green painted thing with little brass knobs shaped like acorns.

It's perfect.

I typed the message and sent it off, unable to say anything more. Though I knew I'd made the decision to keep this child, the reality of it still evaded me. But there it was. A crib. A place for the child to sleep. In this house. Because this was happening. I was going to be someone's mother.

Nausea tightened my throat as I sprinted to the bathroom. Logic begged my body to explain what I could possibly have left to vomit since I hadn't eaten yet. My mother would tell me I was being a cliché and say that she had two children without being so theatrical.

Grow up, Sierra.

I was grateful my mother wasn't around to witness this. She'd have no problem telling me all the ways I was failing at being pregnant. Like it was some skill I should have miraculously acquired.

Sierra, you're not reading the right books. Why haven't you gotten the nursery together yet? That crib is too old. Are you taking the right supplements? Don't gain too much weight, you wouldn't want to get fat. You'll need to bounce back. You're not actually eating for two, you know.

The thought forced me to dry heave long enough to make my abdominal muscles ache. When I was done, I let my head rest against the wall behind me as I sat on the floor in front of the toilet. My gaze trailed over the tiny bathroom. Everything in it that had been added just for me. Shampoo. Conditioner. Little pink bars of rose soap with tiny, dried petals. A towel on the bar next to his.

So many months ago, this man had made room in his life for me. A stranger. He'd gone out of his way to make sure I was comfortable and gave me space to figure out what I was going to do next. Now he'd created an entirely new space for this baby. He seemed happy to do it. I was still reeling from how everything in my life could change so quickly. The decision to keep this baby had felt abstract in the clinic, but this gesture had made it feel so real. I couldn't tell if it was nausea or guilt that made my stomach tug.

I'd completely upended this man's life. I know it takes two for these things to happen. But if I hadn't shown up and taken advantage of his kindness, he wouldn't have to make space for me now. He wouldn't need to worry about any of this. He could just live his life.

The thought nipped at my heels as I stood. Padding into the kitchen to brew some tea and put some food into my stomach, I sighed. No. That thought would have to get in line with all of the other things I didn't want to think about.

Lunch wasn't with me for long. If you could call dry toast and chamomile tea "lunch." At one in the afternoon, it felt odd to call it breakfast and it was one frittata and several mimosas short of being brunch. It left me quickly as I vomited for the third time. Again, for no reason. Literally no reason at all except for the vague scent of a meat package from the garbage. That was all it took to send me running to the bathroom again.

At this point in my life, I was the closest thing to a wild animal I may ever be.

"Kill me," I whined at the toilet as I flushed and tried to stand up, only to be hit with another purge.

After I finished hurling my guts up, I dragged myself into the kitchen for some water. Alden had obliged me and bought a filtered pitcher since I complained about the water having an odd smell. Why he laughed when I mentioned it, I had no idea. He just kissed the top of my head and rubbed my back.

"I'll take care of it."

I filled the jam jar, which was now my favorite glass, and grabbed a handful of tortilla chips to fill the stomach that now ached with hunger. But instead of sitting down, I wandered over to the little room and leaned in the doorway. The tower of boxes niggled at my mind like a problem. And an opportunity.

Mr. Weaver didn't need any of these things. They'd been in here for years. If Alden had helped himself to the crib, I could help myself to some of the things in here. To do what I'd been asked to do.

Make it beautiful.

Several of the boxes were unlabeled. I tugged them into the center of the floor onto the little yellow braided rug Alden had laid down in the room. In the first box there were cleaning supplies. A large package of sponges. Some powdered cleaners. Gloves and other things. I set that aside. Then there was a box with sewing supplies. Embroidery hoops. Twine. Thread in every color. A spool of what looked like fishing line, clearly thrown in here by accident since it had nothing to do with anything else in the box.

Crafting décor for the den was a much better distraction than imagining how disappointed in me my parents would be. After snagging one of the paper shopping bags from out of the kitchen, I set out on my usual walk. Today it was a walk with a mission. In place of my usual leisurely pace, I strode through the area with purpose. Instead of taking in my surroundings as I usually did, I was hunting for something I'd seen scattered all over the place.

My next task included cutting fishing line, pouring paint into some paper cups, and sorting through the embroidery hoops until I found a big enough option. With all of my materials laid out on the table, I sat down and got to work.

Fifty-Five

Alden

The room was aglow with blue light as the sun began to crest over the horizon. Dawn wasn't far off now. I pulled on my pants and buckled my belt, looking at the woman I shared my bed with. Dark hair a mess from sleep, face peaceful with dreams.

I wasn't a religious man, but there was no eternity better than every night spent beside this woman. Crossing the room on quiet feet, I took her in. This sight had become a daily torment, causing an ache in my chest that felt like it was never going to go away. The blankets had fallen down to her waist. A slight chill in the room was enough reason for me to tug them over her. Sierra smiled sleepily and sighed. I bent over and kissed the top of her head, following it with a stroke of my hand over her hair.

My wife.

In name only. For now. We'd fallen into everything. Into each other. As if fate's intention revealed itself through accidents and coincidences. It was hard not to believe in that kind of thing. Not when I had this. Her.

I finished dressing myself, unable to take my eyes off of her. We'd talked long into the night until our words turned to whispers and eventually, she fell asleep tucked under my arm, one leg thrown over me. She and I had so much to say to each other, but those three words still eluded me. It wasn't that I didn't feel them. Hell, I'd known for a while now. It was that ache that stayed with me every time I left her.

I was in love with her.

Real love. Not lust, though that was there too. I couldn't deny the way I craved her. Walking down the steps toward my truck, all I wanted to do was climb back into bed with her and wake her with my mouth. But that wasn't what I thought about all damn day.

It was all those damn little things. Her scent. The quiet smile on her face while she listened to me. How excited she was about the den, even if she wouldn't allow me in there until she was finished fixing it up. How she spoke with her hands when she talked about the people and things she loved. How I hoped I was lucky enough to be one of them. Every night she fell asleep beside me, I kicked myself for not saying what I felt.

I want you to stay.

Mr. Weaver was already in Mae's stall when I arrived. Dragging my feet out of the house each morning was starting to bite me in the ass because it was the third time this week he had beat me to the tacking up. I picked up a brush and feed, then headed into Annabel's stall. Looking around, I noted that we were the only two in the barn. Brushing Annabel's coat, I wondered how long it would last.

"Mornin'," the old man grunted.

"Mornin', sir."

"How's the wife?"

Perfect. Amazing. Lying to him about who she was had begun to feel wrong to me. I wanted to tell him I wanted to spend the rest of my life with Sierra, but it wouldn't make a whole lot of sense to say that about my wife now, would it? As far as he was concerned, we were already doing that. I was only hoping for it. Instead, I thought about how to answer his question like a sane person when I realized I hadn't told him about our recent news.

"She's, uh," I started, pausing my work. I chuckled, glancing at my boots as if it would give me better words than the simple truth. Mr. Weaver set down his brush, folding his arms across his chest as he waited for me to finish. "We're having a baby, sir."

The old man laughed and picked up his saddle pad. He shook his head, grinning as he eyed me from the other side of her flank. With a swift motion, the pad was over the horse's back.

"Congratulations, son. I wondered how long it was going to be before y'all got around to it. How long?"

"About three months, almost four," I said, stowing the brush and grabbing my gear.

"Ah," Mr. Weaver nodded with a knowing smile. "That explains why you've been walking around here smiling like an idiot with your head in the clouds these days."

I threw my saddle pad over Annabel's back, eying the old man as he slung his saddle over Mae. He was smirking at me like a cat now.

"I still remember the day we found out about Junior. I thought I was going to pass away from shock. But I suppose I shouldn't have been surprised," he sighed. I felt my eyebrows shoot up. My face must have shown enough interest because he went on. "Mrs. Weaver and I were all over each other from the minute we got married. I don't think that poor woman got a minute of peace from me."

A barked laugh burst from me, startling Annabel. I reached out a hand and gave her an apologetic pat.

"Yeah, I know the feeling," I chuckled, placing the saddle over the saddle pad.

"I bet," Mr. Weaver snorted.

Boots thudded on the floor, alerting us to the arrival of the boys from the bunkhouse.

"How's it going, Boone?"

I looked up from buckling the saddle to see Eddie hanging off the stall door. It was nice to see my best friend's smiling face. Especially since I'd sent him on an errand for me.

"Did you sleep here?"

"Yep. Thought I'd give couch surfing a rest and offer you and the little lady some privacy," he winked.

Mr. Weaver snorted from his stall. Eddie was always his favorite comedian. Junior walked in, blowing into his hands. Even on a balmy morning like this one, the boy always ran cold.

"You going to tell them the big news?"

My head whipped toward the old man. I wasn't sure. From the minute it was official, I wanted to scream it from the rooftops. But the doctor had told us most people kept it quiet because of the risks early on. Her second term was here, and we'd made her next appointment to check in. I weighed the odds. Screw it.

"Boys," I grinned. "I'm going to be a father."

Eddie whooped loud enough to make Junior drop his hat. I couldn't help but laugh, even though I was still mad as hell at him for trying to get her to leave.

"Good god. Y'all didn't waste any time. Come here, you dog!"

My best friend pulled me into a hug as he yanked me out of the stall. Patting my back firmly, he was still laughing when he asked when the baby was due.

"Valentine's day," I said with a smile.

After announcing to the crew that there was a little Boone on the way, I pulled Eddie aside outside of the barn for a conversation. He piped up with an apology before I could even open my mouth.

"Look man, I was just trying to look out for you. But as long as you're happy, I'm happy.

"If that's how you feel, why didn't you just text me back?"

"I wanted to give you time to cool off," he laughed with a slap to my shoulder. "You weigh almost a hundred pounds more than I do. I'm not winning that fight."

A chime went off in my pocket. I didn't have to pull my phone out to look at who was texting me. Returning my attention to the woman in front of me, I nodded as she spoke. My hands shook a little. I was really doing this.

"Just sign where the little flags are. I'll take your fingerprint and then we'll be all set."

What was left of the trailer my parents died in had been cleared up after the fire. I'd made a small amount of money off leasing the land to neighboring farms for them to graze their cattle. It wasn't much. Enough to pay the taxes on it, and never much more. But I had never been ready to let it go.

Until I realized I was starting a family of my own, I didn't understand why. I'd told Sierra that sometimes we mourn who we wish people were instead of who they had been to us. That was true for me. I'd wished I'd had parents who loved me more than the bottle. I'd wished they were the kind of people who could stay sober for the son they regularly left at the store or forgot to feed for days at a time. I wished that they hadn't died in that fire. That I'd gotten to know who they were beyond what they weren't to me.

Now that I was going to be someone's father, I could forgive them for who they weren't and accept them for who they were. It was time to let them go for good.

I picked up the pen and clicked it, readying to sign the documents that would free me from the last remaining dregs of Boone history. The woman pointed out areas I'd missed with the date or places I needed to initial. Scratching my name next to every little yellow tab, I flew through the contracts.

"Everything alright here?" Mr. Weaver asked as he entered his dining room with a pitcher of sweet tea.

He'd looked over the paperwork for me. Contacted a realtor friend of his and strong-armed them into not taking a commission. Made sure I was getting the best deal possible. The old man refilled my glass and held up the pitcher to ask the notary if she'd like a refill.

"No, thank you. Alright, Mr. Boone. Everything is all set here. Congratulations."

The woman straightened her blue blazer and ran a hand through her bottle blonde hair. I gave her a tight smile and stood from the table to shake her hand.

"I'll see you out," Mr. Weaver offered, setting the pitcher down to round the table.

Sensible low heels clopped on the floor as Mr. Weaver and the notary made their way to the door. I took my seat again, looking over the contracts in front of me. Twenty acres. My father had foolishly purchased the land in the hope that he could make a rancher of himself, not realizing he didn't have the constitution to see that dream through. Dreams without work are just fantasies and my father spent his life living outside of reality.

I'd just sold his fantasy for about half a million dollars. It was the only good thing to ever come out of that shit existence. I was going to use every cent of that money to build a better life for my family. And it was going to start with buying a ring for the woman I loved.

Fifty-Six
Sierra

This baby better be really freaking cute.

Laying on the floor with my legs bent over the sofa seemed to be the only way to make the vomiting stop. So that's what I did. For two hours.

Dipping a saltine into my glass of ginger ale, I nibbled at the cracker as I shut my eyes. Halfway into month four, I was barely able to move without getting nauseated. I lay there wondering what Antoni would have been like with a sick wife. He seemed like the type to lock his spouse away and forget about her completely until he was presented with his child. The thought made me try to focus on something nicer. I had nothing around to distract me. Since I'd finally finished all of my projects for the den, I was not going to move from this spot. Nope.

Someone was knocking at the door.

"Why?" I whimpered as I swung my legs off of the sofa.

The person at the door knocked again. By the time I actually opened the door, I decided I was going to give this person a talking to. Except, when I opened the door, I found a sixty-year-old cowboy standing on the other side. Still wearing a pearl snap shirt, which seemed to be his uniform, he was holding his hat in his hand.

"Mr. Weaver?"

"Call me Sam, please," he laughed.

I angled my head, uncertain as to why he would come here. Worry hit me like a bus. Was it worse than falling off Annabel?

"Is Alden alright? Is he hurt?"

"No, no. Boone's fine. I thought I might take you out for some lunch. And if you needed anything in town, we could pick it up."

I took a step backward, opening the door for him to come inside. He didn't.

"That's generous of you."

"Well, I'd like to get to know you better. Come on. Put on some shoes and we can get going."

Mr. Weaver escorted me to the passenger side of his truck. I could see where Alden got his manners as he opened the door for me to hop in. He made his way to the other side and hopped in. Alden's truck was decades older than this one. It didn't have heated seats or a wood and leather accented dashboard. It definitely didn't have a display screen with satellite radio. I still liked his better than this one. The thought surprised me.

"Don't worry," he offered. "Your husband knows I'm stealing you away for the afternoon."

Cars went by and the wind tumbled the cab, adding their sound to the quiet ride. I wondered if he was waiting for me to say something first. I wasn't really sure what to talk about with him. As far as he knew, I was Alden's wife. Just a city girl who broke down on the side of the road and fell in love with his ranch foreman. That wasn't too far from the truth anymore. But the how and why of my presence here was still known to only a few people.

"So, Boone told me the good news," Mr. Weaver said, breaking the silence between songs on the radio.

"Good news?" I asked, settling into the passenger seat.

"The baby, sweetheart. He told me you two are expecting a little one."

"Right. Yeah," I sighed. "It was kind of unexpected."

Mr. Weaver huffed a laugh, nodding a little.

"Junior was a surprise, too. Of course, the wife and I were only blessed with one. Lucky for me, I have a lot of nieces and nephews to spoil."

I laughed. He wasn't wrong. I'd met most of them at the barbeque. There were so many Millers and Weavers around, that I couldn't keep them straight.

"We brought him home to the house y'all are living in now. It was a nice spot for a growing family. Quiet. Of course, you'll probably want to get into something bigger if you two decide to have any more."

"Any more?"

"Have you and Boone talked about how many you want to have? The Mrs. and I were only blessed with Junior, but you and Boone will probably have better luck."

"We haven't really talked about that," I faltered. We hadn't really talked about the future. Like, at all.

Mr. Weaver's hands flexed and settled on the leather-wrapped steering wheel. The old cowboy looked like he'd seen a lot of hard days, but there was still joy in those eyes. The look of a man who was doing what he loved. I examined the shirt he was wearing. A pearl snap shirt. Faded blue to match his eye color. Alden had a few like it. Watching the expression on his face, thoughtful but relaxed, I realized I'd come to know it well. It was then I realized how much my cowboy had come to take after this man. He'd told me his parents had died in the fire, but it seemed like Mr. Weaver was the father he had all along.

"Alden told me you helped take care of him when he was little. How you helped his parents and, uh," I paused. I didn't know Mr. Weaver that well. But knowing the man I'd been sharing a home with, the man I'd been falling for, I thought maybe he'd gotten his warmth from him. "Thank you. For raising a good man, I mean."

Mr. Weaver's lip wobbled below his grey mustache. It was quiet for long enough that I thought he wouldn't speak. Not until he let out a wet puff of a laugh.

"You know, I think Boone nearly bankrupted me eating all he did. You can't imagine what it took to feed that boy as a teenager. He was a black hole."

"He finishes my dinner basically every night," I chuckled. "He is without a doubt the biggest man I've ever seen."

"Built on ten thousand bowls of cereal, I'll tell ya."

Lunch was supposed to be at the deli in the grocery store, but I just watched him eat while I sipped a ginger ale. I'd told him I had already eaten, but the truth was I was fighting nausea from smelling the meat counter. What it was about smelling chicken that made me want to heave, I had no idea, but I couldn't stand it.

Strolling down the white linoleum aisles beside Mr. Weaver, I wondered when the last time I'd set foot in a grocery store was. College, maybe. Even then, I ordered groceries to my dorm more often than I shopped for them. The housekeeper at my parent's home did all the shopping and meal planning after that. A friendly older woman with red hair greeted Mr. Weaver. He dipped his chin at her and continued pushing the cart.

People seemed to like the man. I understood why. Being in his company was easy. He didn't expect you to talk to fill the silence. Just went about his business, enjoying the pleasure of my company. I was putting a bag of tortilla chips in the cart when he piped up.

"Junior doesn't want to run the ranch after I retire," Mr. Weaver started, throwing a few bags of jerky into the cart. He loosed a heavy sigh before continuing. "Boone doesn't like taking handouts. Mrs. Weaver always sweet-talked him into taking things. But I want to give him half of the ranch when he's ready. Junior will own the other half, but I want Boone to run all of it. He already does everything else. Will you help me convince him?"

I just blinked at him. Convince him? I wouldn't know where to begin.

"I know it would be a lot of responsibility. Especially for a new daddy, but he deserves it. Besides, I can't take it with me and I can't do it forever. It should stay in the family."

He deserves everything, I wanted to say. It was an uncomfortable feeling, wondering what Alden's life would look like if that happened. I didn't know what the difference was between running the ranch and owning it in terms of responsibility, but I couldn't imagine it would be any easier with a baby to take care of.

I didn't agree. Didn't say anything as we made our way up and down the aisles of the grocery store. Guilt and worry about the man I shared a home with warred in my mind until my gaze snagged on a familiar face as we passed the newsstand near the exit. A national tabloid paper. The headline was in bold white font over a blue background.

Alleged Chicago Crime Boss Bruno Serpa Killed.

Fifty-Seven
Sierra

Dead. He was dead. Bruno Serpa was dead. I stopped abruptly. A woman behind me grunted in annoyance. Snatching the newspaper from the stand to read the article.

"Sorry," I muttered, flipping the paper open.

Bruno Serpa, Chicago construction magnate, was killed along with several other suspected members of his organization after two affiliates resisted arrest. Police exchanged gunfire with the suspects after the conflict escalated. Serpa was declared dead on the site by first responders.

My eyes bounced over the rest of the details.

All other known associates were collected for questioning. Antoni's whereabouts were unknown. Unknown? Maybe he'd bolted like I had. According to this article, they had nothing left. Just like I did. A small flame of righteous anger fluttered to life in me. Now that horrible waste of life would find out what it was like to be on the run. I laughed bitterly, stuffing the paper back on the shelf.

Mr. Weaver looked over his shoulder at me, pausing by the grocery store exit.

"Good news?"

"Yeah," I smiled. "Good news."

The ride home felt like it went by in a blink, my mind so occupied with racing thoughts that I didn't say a word to Mr. Weaver. After asking me what the news was, I simply stated that Chicago's baseball team was having a good season. Who knows if that was even true? There were two teams. I had a chance at being right, at least.

My feet tapped on the weatherproof floor mats, anxiety coursing through me. It was over. I had resources now. I wished I had brought my wallet. I could have gotten money for Alden. To thank him. That gnawing guilt I'd felt about foisting so much responsibility on Alden burned away like mist in sunlight. I didn't have to rely on him anymore. I could do things for myself. I had options. So many options.

The world was wide open.

I couldn't sit still. Upon our return, I thanked Mr. Weaver for taking me out. I could talk to him about taking on the responsibility Mr. Weaver wanted to give him. Owning half of the ranch. Running it. Because I could move on. I could give him a chance at a life he chose. Just like I had the chance to now. My choice. Everything could be my choice now. I didn't have to burden anyone. Sitting on the sofa, I talked excitedly to myself as if the child inside could hear me.

"You can do whatever you want with your life. I promise. I'll get a job somewhere and find you a good school. I'll come to all of your parent teacher meetings and I'll never send the nanny in my place. Or the housekeeper. You'll have a home with someone who loves you."

The roaring of Alden's truck alerted me to his arrival. He was here. My fingers tingled with anticipation at telling him the news. It had only been an hour since I got home. I'd spent all of it wondering what I should do now that I could do, well, anything.

Freedom. I had freedom.

My feet padded on the hardwood floor as I rushed outside to meet him. Alden looked up at me in amused confusion, smiling as he watched me bounce on my feet.

"This is quite a greeting," he said as he removed his hat, bringing it to his chest as he climbed the steps. "Everything alright?"

"I can go home," I beamed.

Alden's smile faded, eyebrows narrowing as he came to stand in front of me. His head angled to one side, like he hadn't quite heard me. I repeated myself. Then I told him about Mr. Weaver taking me into town and going grocery shopping with him. Then the newspaper.

"Bruno Serpa is dead. His son, Antoni, is missing. I can go home now. I can go anywhere. I don't have to hide anymore."

Disappointment bloomed in my gut. I'd thought he'd be happy for me, but the look on his face. It wasn't that.

"That's great."

The words huffed out of him as he strode past me into the house, pausing in the middle of the room. He tossed his hat onto the sofa, scrubbing his hands over his face. I inched up behind him. Alden turned on me, the smile returning to his face. It felt wrong, somehow. Not like him, but like a mask. I'd worn enough fake smiles to know when I was looking at one.

"Let's celebrate."

"Celebrate?"

Alden took my face in his hands and kissed me hard enough to steal my breath. I'd known he would be a little upset about my leaving, but we never talked about the future. Nothing was set in stone. There was no conversation about feelings or commitment. We played husband and wife, but in reality, we had been strangers to each other only a few months ago. I hadn't had anywhere to go. I wasn't sure if how I felt about him was genuine or because I had no other choice. Staying here, raising a baby together.

It felt too big.

"I'm going to get cleaned up and we're going out. If you don't have to hide anymore, then I'm taking you on a real date."

Alden stuffed his hands into his pockets and strange look crossed his face.

I almost asked him about it. Almost asked what was wrong when his eyes snagged on the door to the den. Or more accurately, the doorknob of the den because I'd tied a ribbon around it.

"Oh, I," I paused, uncertain about the room I'd spent so much time working on. So much time making it beautiful, just like he'd asked me to. Now it felt like a waste of time. Because I was leaving. "I finished in there today."

He crossed the room, removing his hands from his pockets to take my hand in his as he approached the door. The ribbon. I'd wanted it to be a surprise. A new type of guilt sunk in my center like a hot stone as he turned the knob and beheld what was inside.

Fifty-Eight
Alden

She could go home.

The phrase was still ringing in my ears as Sierra watched me take in her work. Everything was tidy. The crib was sitting in front of a wall she'd painted with little sponge prints of half moons in different shades of green. Various sizes of embroidery hoops had thread wrapped around them in rainbow colors, hanging against the wall over the dresser. And over the crib...

Pinecones dangled on some fishing line from what I had to assume was another embroidery hoop, only this one was wrapped only in green thread. Each of the pinecones was half-dipped in green paint. She'd done it. Made it beautiful.

I hated her for it.

She was going home. She was going home and I'd be left to look at this thing she'd created. Without her. Without the things I'd been stupid enough to let myself want. My throat tightened. My hand fisted at my side. My chest felt like it was collapsing under a pile of bricks.

After I felt her give my hand a gentle squeeze, I looked at her. Sierra wouldn't meet my eye.

"I'm going to get freshened up," she practically whispered as she stepped out of the room.

I shut the door behind her. Let my back rest against the painted wood as I slid down the length of it, unable to stand holding up my own weight for another second. Shoving my hand back into my pocket, I removed the lump that dug into my side. An uncomfortable reminder of my foolish hope. Tears flooded my eyes as I threw the little velvet box across the small room and buried my face in my hands. I choked on a breath.

She was going home.

The night I'd cleaned out this space, I thought about all of the memories we'd create in here. Together. I'd wanted to spend my life making memories with her. With the baby, too. I'd fallen in love with this woman. Sure, I'd been too much of a coward to say it, but that was what I felt. It was love because what other explanation could there be for this kind of pain?

But she had her freedom now. She wasn't really my wife and I was never her husband. She had her life back. I shouldn't have expected her to want to spend it with me.

Sierra looked beautiful. She always looked beautiful. Hair tied up in a loose braid, a little bit of makeup on. Lips painted a slightly darker shade of pink. Wearing that scent that drove me crazy. I had to live with the idea that this beautiful creature, the one who felt like she was made for me, was leaving. It was all I thought about for the entire drive to Buckley's, a bar in town that had music and dancing. Sure, she couldn't drink and I didn't like to, but if my days with Sierra were numbered, then I wanted to have a dance with her. I'd dance all night if we could.

Coming to a bar when you don't drink is a lot like coming to a deer hunt with no gun. It doesn't make a lot of sense. The band made it worth it, though. The place was dark and moody, lit with stage lights for the band and neon beer signs behind the bar. Little lights dangled over the tables lined up against the wall. People were sitting at some of them, eating their fried chicken from the little window in the back. Younger couples danced to the lively music pumping out of the band's amplifiers. The electric guitar twanged with notes to a song I had to dance to because if I sat here having to listen to it, I wouldn't make it through the night.

"Come on," I extended a hand to her. "Let me have one dance."

She stood slowly, following me the few steps from our table to the dance floor as the song began. The singer warbled out the first few notes as Sierra lifted her ear to take it in, recognition crossing her face.

"You're a Whitney Houston fan?"

"This was a Dolly Parton song first, gorgeous."

She laughed gently as I spun her a little, bringing her into me for the dance. Sierra rested a hand on my shoulder and gave me a soft smile. I tried to smile at her, but I couldn't shake the feeling that something else was coming. Especially when she was looking at me like that.

"I'm going back to Chicago," Sierra declared quietly.

"Why?" The question just fell out of my mouth. I didn't have a chance to think better of my sharp tone.

"I need to wrap up my family's estate. I might stay there. Or move somewhere else. You told me the world was wide open. I want to see what it's like to stand on my own."

Music filled the space between us as I tried to patch the hole opening in my chest. Jesus, she was already planning everything. I thought I'd have more time, at least. I didn't know why I'd assumed that. After a few beats, I swallowed down the lump in my throat and nodded.

"We never," she paused, seeming to think better of whatever it was she was going to say.

"You told me yourself. You couldn't do this forever."

She looked away from me for a moment, but I could see the tears welling in her eyes. Sierra blinked a few times and they were gone.

"I don't even know who I am now," she explained. "I've never had the chance to live my life without someone telling me exactly what I should do. Who I should be. I need to find out if I can do things on my own. I don't want to stay here just because it's the safe thing to do, Alden."

I reeled back at her statement. It felt like a slap in the face. Safe. She'd stayed here because it was safe. Of course she had. She didn't have a choice. I'd thought we were building something together. A life. That small part of me that thought this was forever crumbled under her words. The nights we spent together. Her smile. Her laugh. Even if my head knew better, my heart had leapt into loving Sierra without any sense of self-preservation.

"When are you leaving?"

"A couple days, maybe. I want to get started on figuring things out before, well," she trailed off, glancing down at her little bump.

That bump. It was almost nothing right now. A lump lodged itself in my throat as I realized I may not get to see how big she would get. I wouldn't be there to rub her feet or melt cheese onto tortilla chips for her. That little velvet box I'd picked up off of the nursery floor to hide away in my sock drawer. It didn't mean anything now. Not when I might not even be there to see the look on her face when she became a mother.

Fuck it.

"Then I need to, uh," I insisted, clearing the tightness from my throat. "Since I may not get another chance, I need to say something to you."

"Alden," she warned, worried green eyes snapping to my face.

"Let me say it. I'm not trying to make you stay. I know I can't do that, but I need to say it because I can't let you leave here without knowing how I feel about you."

"Ok," she rasped.

"I used to work myself to death on the ranch. Every day I would come home tired as a dog, shower, sleep, and do it all the next day. I did that for years. I hated going home. Then you came into my life. And the end of the day couldn't come fast enough."

Sierra's eyes softened as she let my confession go on.

"What I'm trying to say is... well, before you every day blended together. But you. You make me feel like I want to live every moment. I appreciate everything because I want to rush home and tell you about it. I feel it all. See it all. Before you, I was sleepwalking. You woke me up."

A tear rolled over her soft cheek as she sucked in a shaky breath. I reached up and brushed it away. An instinct I'd had from the moment we met.

"Whether you're here or in Chicago or on the other side of the world, it doesn't matter. This has been real for me. What I feel is real. I love you, Sierra. I will. Always."

"Alden, I," she stammered, biting down on a quivering lip.

"Don't," I interrupted, squeezing my eyes shut just to keep from letting emotion get the best of me. Clearing my throat, I collected myself and looked at her. "Please don't say anything. I don't think I could take it either way."

Emotion swelled in my chest, causing that unbearable ache to burn there. It stole my ability to breathe. Or think. Or dance. So I stopped doing all three and kissed her. She was leaving. I wanted as many kisses as I could get. I wanted to taste her on my lips until the day I died. I wanted so many things all at once as her mouth moved against mine. As those little noises came out of her like tasting me was satisfying to her soul.

I knew the feeling.

Finally Sierra pulled away. Though she smiled at me, her eyes had gone sad. It should have been a comfort, knowing that it wasn't easy for her to walk away. That she felt something for me, too.

"You're a good man," she said, her voice hoarse with unshed tears.

The song was almost over, as it seemed my time was with this woman. I'd known it. I'd known it from the beginning and still jumped in with both feet, like a damn fool. Sierra rested her head on my chest, closing her eyes as we swayed together on the dance floor. I let my hand go to her side, enjoying the feeling of the new small swell of her belly pressing into me.

"Let's go home."

I'd begun thinking of this as our bed. Our room. Our home. Every day coming home to her had rooted itself in me a little more. Laying beside Sierra felt like sleeping in quicksand. She sighed, staring up at me with those eyes that I'd probably see every day until I died.

"Alden," she whispered, propping herself up to look down at me. "I'll always love this. Being here with you."

I was glad she wasn't listening to my heart. From the way it ached, there was no way it didn't make some awful sound to give me away. Words were impossible now, so I nodded and waited for her to go on. Only she didn't. Sierra leaned down and kissed me, soft and filled with tenderness.

Threading my arm beneath the crook in her leg, I rolled until she was on top of me. Her legs fell to my sides and she pushed herself up. I loved looking at her like this. There was a confidence in her that shone like a light in the dark. A confidence that hadn't been there before but grew as we let ourselves enjoy this time together. As I had let my heart attach itself to this. To her. I sat up and took her into my arms. Kissing her was second nature to me now. Sierra's hands threaded into my hair as she moved against me, hungry for more.

I sat up and tugged her top off, kissing the softest skin I'd ever felt in my life, savoring the feel of it against my lips. Her collarbone, her breasts, her neck. The way she smelled. All of it was familiar and sweet. Like a favorite dessert I'd never tire of.

Sierra shifted, pulling off her bottoms. I followed. Then she was astride me again, lowering herself onto me. For all of the pain I was feeling, I could never say no to this. Could never say no to her.

Especially because this felt like it was the last time.

Her hands laced together at my neck as she made those little moans I'd never forget, that long hair brushing me as she threw her head back. My mind flashed with memories of sunflowers. The front porch. The sofa that first night. Then her mouth was on mine.

Before tonight, her kisses ignited something in me. A flavor I knew so well. But even as I felt the thrill of being inside her, relishing every roll of her hips as she squeezed me, her kisses lacked that sweetness I needed. As I fisted her hair and kissed her through our mutual release, I couldn't ignore the way it tasted now.

I'd known from the very beginning that when Sierra left, she'd take my heart with her. It had been inevitable. For a minute, I'd let myself believe we would be forever. That this was the happy ending I'd stumbled into by sheer dumb luck.

After tonight, I'd let that dream go. Because I couldn't help but notice that even if she said it wasn't forever, every one of her kisses tasted like goodbye.

Fifty-Nine

Sierra

The silence that had grown between Alden and I was an uncomfortable, heavy thing. Before, when he got home from work, he'd tell me about his day. Ask me about mine and listen intently, even though most of my days were the same. Now he just went about his business. Asked me about my day, but the small smiles he'd give me as he listened were gone. The amused light in his eyes was gone, too. It hadn't taken long for it to fade. It was only two nights ago that I told him I was leaving. Two nights since he'd told me how he felt about me.

He loved me.

I'd been unable to tell him how I felt. Unable to speak the words. So, I showed him. With every kiss and caress, I'd hoped he would feel how grateful I was for him. The next day, he got up and went to work. No note. No text messages asking me how my day was going. Only one message.

> I'll be by at lunch so we can pick up your car.

It had been a long, silent ride into town. The car still needed gas, something I purchased with my long unused debit card. Alden and I left the lot separately. I followed him back to the house and he went off to work again without saying a word. There was only the tip of his hat and that empty look in his eyes.

Ungrateful.

That was when I'd decided not to delay my departure. The sooner I left, the better off he would be. In time, he would get used to not having me around. A pitiful, selfish part of me couldn't stand to see that look on his face anymore. The empty one. Not when I knew how much light there's been before. Those sunshine smiles he had for me were gone. Just gone. When I'd told him my choice last night at dinner, he didn't say a word. He only nodded.

We got ready to go to sleep. Watched each other brush our teeth. Dressed for bed. I sat on my side of the bed, braiding my hair when he took something out of his wallet and placed it on the dresser. A cashier's check. He pressed his index finger to the piece of paper, not meeting my eye as he spoke.

"This is what I got for your earrings. About twenty thousand. Take it and use it for the uh," he stopped, his throat bobbing with a swallow as he glanced to the small swell of my belly. "Use it."

I blinked, surprised he'd sold them for so much.

"Alden," I croaked, trying to get him to look at me. Hoping he would just lift his eyes to mine. "I wanted to pay you back for what you've done for me. Please keep it."

He loosed a laugh, baring his teeth in a bitter smile as he stared down at that little green piece of paper.

"Just take the fucking money, Sierra."

The snarl had barely left his lips, the angry command still resonated in my ears, when he went into the bathroom. I tried to come up with something, anything to say, as he shut the door behind him. He'd never talked to me like that. Angry. I crawled under the covers and laid my head down on the pillow as one word repeated in my traitorous mind.

Ungrateful.

I'd fallen asleep by the time he came to bed. I didn't crawl to his side as I'd grown accustomed to. Didn't fall asleep with his fingers combing through my hair. I curled up on my side and stared at the door. Though Alden had lain in bed beside me, he made no move to touch me. As I fell asleep, I felt only the breeze from the open window dance across my skin.

"Alright," I said to no one as I examined everything in front of me.

With an empty bed and only a day away from departure, I'd decided to focus on the future instead of dwelling on what I was leaving behind.

They looked like they belonged here as they stared up at me. Everything was organized neatly on the bed. If I was leaving, I needed to pack. I examined my things. There weren't many. Jeans. Dresses. Underwear. Compared to the closet that was hopefully still waiting for me in Chicago, it was practically nothing. And all of it together was probably worth far less than the evening dress I'd arrived in. Never mind the shoes and handbag.

Having come here with nothing, I put the designer heels in one of the paper grocery bags I'd rustled out of the storage room. A smirk tugged at my lips as I imagined the look of horror my mother would wear upon seeing the array of color I was going to add to the sea of neutrals.

The dresses. The jeans. He'd gotten it all for me. Even though I didn't know him, I felt more like myself in these clothes than I ever did in anything of my own. Still, I'd crashed into Alden's life. Derailed it as I scrambled to find a life of my own to live. A life without my parents planning every step forward for me. Now I had the freedom to do that. I was going to build a life that was mine.

Alden.

He deserved to see his life through without a complication like me. The baby was my choice. They were going to live a good life. I would make sure of that. I realized how much I'd come to rely on him. This was the right thing to do. He didn't need to take care of a baby and me.

My boots clomped on the wooden steps as I approached my father's car. It was the first time in months that I'd driven anywhere. The renewed independence felt good. I couldn't wait to drive my car again. As I backed the

Bentley out onto the little dirt road, I wondered if my little 8 Series BMW was still sitting in my parent's garage.

Then I realized I'd have to get something more child friendly because that expensive little coupe didn't even have a backseat. But since the car was worth so much, I could trade it in for a more appropriate car. A mom car. Maybe something with all wheel drive so I could make it up the dirt road to the house.

For a visit. It wasn't that far. I could come back and visit Alden with the baby. So they could meet their father. Because they should meet him. He was a man worth knowing.

Smoothing my skirt over my legs, I sighed. Leafed through the magazine I'd grabbed from the coffee table for the tenth time since I'd arrived. Without Alden here, I hadn't realized how incredibly awkward I would feel as Natalie eyed me in the small lobby.

Finally, I tossed the magazine back onto the little side table with a loud flop and spoke.

"I understand it, you know."

"What?" Natalie snipped.

"Wanting him back."

The door to the exam rooms opened, the other nurse silently beckoned me back. I stood up and crossed the reception room to follow the nurse.

"There aren't a lot of guys like him around here," she muttered only loud enough for me to hear, pretending to busy herself with her computer.

"No," I said, pausing in front of the desk. I waited for her to look at me. "There isn't anyone like him anywhere."

Natalie blinked. I gave her a polite smile and followed the other nurse through the door leading to the exam rooms. Alden had told me he didn't love her. Maybe that could change.

The thought of him alone in that house made my chest ache. He'd always taken care of other people. Even if I'd tried to be the one to take care of him, he needed more than that. He needed someone to lean on. Someone to be there for the hard days. To make him laugh. Someone who wouldn't rely on him the way I'd had to. I ignored the way the thought of him with someone else burned like salt in a wound.

The spiral of my thoughts had hypnotized me so thoroughly that I didn't realize what room I'd been brought to. There weren't very many rooms in here. Maybe four. But they brought me back to the same one. The same room as last time. The first time.

"We crashed into each other like shooting stars."

On a loud creak, the door swung open. Dr. Riggs hustled in and rolled the ultrasound machine over to the exam table I was now sitting on. With a pleasant smile on her face, she plopped down into the rolling chair.

"So! We're going to check and see how everything is going in there. We might also be able to find out the sex today, if you want."

"Yeah, I do. I want to know."

Alden wanted to know. He'd wanted to get pink bedding for the crib. Bright pink. I'd told him that was a terrible idea, even if it was a girl. We agreed to disagree.

"Great," Dr. Riggs chirped as she flipped on the machine. It whirred to life.

My hands squeezed and flexed, aching for Alden's callused fingers to wrap around my own. I pushed him away. I told him I was leaving. I'd thought it would be better to put distance between us now. Though I'd thought it was for the best, I couldn't help feeling the weight of his absence now.

"Daddy didn't want to be here?"

"No."

The lie sounded empty even as I spoke it. Of course he wanted to be here. He wanted me. Not the version of me created to draw men in. He saw a girl with cracks and flaws. A lost girl with nothing to her name. That girl was the one he fell in love with.

"I love you, Sierra. I will. Always."

Because he did love me. I stared at the screen, remembering the last time I'd been here. Alden's hand in mine. His reassuring touch. His kiss. The one who would have walked with me down any road I chose.

My mother would tell me I was being reckless with my life. That they had provided me with a wealth of opportunity and I was squandering it the first chance I got. But opportunity was a funny thing. Just because I was free to make a choice didn't mean I had to leave. It meant I had a choice. I could choose to leave. Take my money and choose to raise this child on my own. The one whose heartbeat I was hearing now.

"Listen to that! That's good and strong, mama."

Gentle thudding filled the room as I watched. The doctor held the wand thing into my stomach, gliding along with a small amount of pressure. Tears welled as my throat tightened. I could picture that big warm grin of Alden's, holding my hand as we watched this together. For everything he'd given me without asking, it was his kindness that had sheltered me most. His love had helped me believe I was more than someone's prize.

There would never be a final showdown between me and my mother. I would never have the opportunity to tell her the things I needed to say. That I wished she'd gotten to know me as a person instead of being treated like an extension of her. I'd never get to tell my father that I was more than a bargaining chip. I was someone worth knowing. Worth loving because I'd been shown how to love someone by someone who loved me. Not because I had anything to give. Not because of my name, his name. That he could hurt me but I'd found something better. That regret might stay with me forever.

Instead of a table in a doctor's office, I could feel myself standing in front of that wall of photos at the Weaver house. Family. Loving smiles. Kind faces. A cowboy seated against a wall, holding a young filly in his lap as he fed her from a bottle. That big smile on his face. The one that I'd seen every day for months. Because that smile wasn't for everyone. Just the ones he loved.

I was a cowardly idiot.

As I listened to the sound of our child's beating heart, I realized it was mine that was speaking to me now. Alden had opened himself to me, told me what was in his heart, and done so knowing I was leaving. Raising this child on my own was not the thing I was afraid of most. I was educated and had a lot of money in the bank. I could get a job and do what I had to do. Women with far less than I did it every single day. I wasn't afraid of it.

I was afraid of the man who'd seen me without the curated image. Without the money or the power that came with my last name. He saw me as just Sierra. Imperfect and his. And that was the truth.

Laying there on the table, a different fear took root. A fear that if I left, I'd walk through the rest of my life putting pressure on this child to compensate for the fact that I had no family. That they would feel like they needed to fill the cowboy shaped hole in my heart.

"We should be able to get a good look now."

He should have been here. Hearing this. Seeing this.

"Yes. Alright, there we go," Dr. Riggs said as she hit some buttons on the keypad to make the image on the screen freeze. I looked over at the screen. She must have seen something I didn't, because the image yielded no answers to me.

Something printed out of the machine. The doctor wrote on it, then stuffed it into a little envelope and handed it to me with a sympathetic smile.

"You can open it later. Find out when you're ready."

"Dr. Riggs?" the pleasant-looking nurse tapped on the door, poking her head through a narrow opening. "The father is here."

My heart sparked in my chest. He'd known I'd be here. I'd told him where I would be. He knew and he came. Shoes clicked on the linoleum outside. But that didn't sound like his stride. It wasn't long enough. Or heavy enough.

"Hey wait. He can't go in there," someone said from outside.

The door swung open and my heart stopped as it slammed closed. Because it was not the father of my baby standing there.

It was Antoni Serpa.

Sixty

Alden

Hoofbeats thumped on the dirt path in a soft and steady beat. The sun was high in the sky. Warm wind whipped through the trees as we headed to the house. Normally, I enjoyed this kind of silence. It was peaceful. When my mind wasn't a blitz of noise and regret. I'd been an idiot. I let myself fall in love with her when I knew it wouldn't last. I knew from the beginning that this was temporary. I knew it all the way through falling in love with her. I knew that she was going to break my heart and I still reached for her like a red hot iron, knowing I was going to get burned.

Such an idiot.

If it were up to me, we'd work all day. Anything to keep me from finding her at home packing. Or worse. Gone. I picked up every odd job. Every menial task. Breaking for lunch was out of the question. The bitter taste of my thoughts had filled my gut enough to destroy what was left of my appetite.

On the other side of town, she was alone. At a doctor's appointment. After we picked up her father's car from the impound lot yesterday, she told me she wanted to go by herself. To start distancing herself from me, I guess. It was a taste of what life would be like without her in it. Without knowing what was going on with her or with our child. The whole idea of those two moving through the world so far away from me filled my veins with acid.

"Boone."

I blinked.

"Are you even listening to me, boy?" Mr. Weaver squinted at me from under his straw Stetson.

"Sorry, sir."

Almost back to the house, we had been checking on the irrigation system in a nearby pasture. Making our way back to the house had been such a routine that I'd become lost in thought. Thoughts of the girl I'd be giving up and the child I may never get to meet. I tried to imagine what my life would look like without the future I'd foolishly imagined for myself. The one with a family.

She was going to live a big, beautiful life. I wanted that for her. After everything she'd told me, she deserved to create the life she wanted. Loving someone the way I loved her meant wanting the best for her. Even if that meant shattering my own damn heart in the process.

I knew I had to let her go.

Tall oak trees lined the trail, filtering bright sunlight through their canopy of leaves. We were getting close to the house now. A gust of wind rushed through the branches, quieting the snapping edges of my frayed nerves for just a moment as I looked over at the old man.

"That girl is on your mind."

My shoulders tensed. That girl. Not my wife. I gave a shallow nod, scratching my beard just to give my body something to do.

"Eddie told me she's moving on. Going to be raising that baby on her own. Is that what you want?"

There was nothing like my best friend telling everyone my business to make me immediately regret spilling my guts to him in some desperate, middle-of-the-night text messages I'd sent from the bathroom.

"She and I weren't married," I muttered, looking at him from the corner of my eye for any sign of surprise. When his expression didn't change, I went on. "It doesn't matter what I want, sir."

With a cough, I'd hoped he'd just ignore the crack in my voice. The sentiment felt empty, but that didn't mean it wasn't true. Mr. Weaver halted, his horse coming to a complete stop at his command. I stopped, turning in my saddle to see a face that was twisted with pity and disgust.

"Son, I love you more than you'll ever know, but you are a prize fucking idiot if you think I'm going to buy that horseshit."

"Sir," I started.

"No, Boone. You listen to me now. People raise kids separately. It happens every day. But this ain't about that baby. This is about the woman you love. I know you love her. I also know I lost the woman I love. I'll never get her back." He urged Mae forward to come eye to eye with me, the Quarter Horse mare snorting at the command. Even at well over sixty years old, I knew he could kick my ass if he really wanted to. From the look on his sun-weathered face, I knew he wanted to. "I would give everything I have in the world for one more minute with my wife. You love her. I know you do."

"You don't know what you're talking about."

The old man let out a joyless laugh and looked to the sky. Fighting for patience with me. I didn't care. All the energy I had to be agreeable disappeared on every night of sleep I'd lost in the last few days.

"So what? You think you're done fighting? You're laying down your cards and that's it? She loves you. You should hear her talk about you. I'm not in the business of raising cowards, so don't you dare give up and let that girl walk out of your life."

Coward? The cobwebs of my patience burned away.

"You think I'm letting her go because I'm too scared to fight for her? She's never had a chance to make a life for herself. I'm letting her go because she deserves to live the life that she chooses. I'm letting her go because she deserves to find joy, even if it means she's taking mine with her. That's what love is. It's a fucking choice, Sam. Love means I choose her happiness! Even if it means I lose."

Mr. Weaver blinked at me. I'd never raised my voice to him. Not once. But having to deny everything. To deny how I felt about Sierra. My spine felt like it was made of iron. My shoulders were wound tight enough to hurt. I could feel rage pumping in my blood as I forced myself to breathe. The big blue house came into view as I tried to summon the will to apologize. My phone began ringing. I pulled it from my holster and looked at the caller ID. Natalie.

"Fuck off," I muttered, shoving the phone back into the leather pouch.

"I'm sorry, son. I know I overstepped."

"No, not you," I held up my phone.

Then I saw the alerts ping in. Missed call. Missed call. Missed call. Natalie. Again. Text alerts came buzzing through as we got closer to the house and my phone connected to a signal. All from Natalie.

> Emergency.

> Pick up the phone, you jackass.

> 911. Your wife is in trouble.

> Call me now!

"Shit."

"What's wrong?" Mr. Weaver asked at my hissed curse.

Metallic ringing pelted my ear, drowning out the sound of my heartbeat. I kicked Annabel, urging her to speed up and make for the barn. Waiting for Natalie to pick up, I imagined all of the possibilities. Was she hurt? Was she losing the baby? If Sierra was going to the hospital, I wouldn't be able to get there for almost an hour. My gut twisted at the thought of her sitting there, scared and alone with no one to hold her hand.

"Alden?" Natalie answered, voice sharp and irritated.

"What's wrong?" I snapped. "Where is Sierra?"

"I'm at the hospital with Dr. Riggs. This guy came and took Sierra away. He had a gun. He shot the doctor. I don't know where they went, but she needs help."

I could hear an announcement through a PA system sounding in the background. She must be in the waiting room.

"Who took her, Natalie?"

"He was about six feet. Our age. Lean. Dark hair and eyes. Black suit. She didn't want to go with him, but she definitely knew the guy."

Antoni.

"Where did they go?"

"I don't know. They got in her car and left."

All I could think about was the fact that I wasn't there. I wasn't there to keep her safe. To protect her. To make sure this didn't happen. I should have insisted. I should have been there. For so many fucking reasons, I should have been there. The picture of her kidnapper was clear in my mind as I imagined all of the ways I could have prevented this. Almost all of them ended with the man six feet under.

I gruffly thanked Natalie for her call and hung up. Eddie took Annabel by the reins as I hopped off of her, making for my truck in big strides. He rushed out behind me, trying to catch up.

"Boone, wait!"

"They found her, Eddie. She needs help."

All I could do was move. My mind raced as I imagined the possibilities. We'd been foolish to think she was safe. To think the danger to her life had ebbed with the head of the Serpa family gone, but his son remained. Antoni. She had assumed he had left the country to avoid criminal charges. That he'd hunted her down instead of sheltering himself had me imagining horrible scenarios. Eddie grabbed my arm, turning me away from my open door.

"Hold on, Boone."

"Take care of the horses."

His boots slid on dirt and gravel as he tugged on me. For a scrawny guy, I always forgot how strong he was.

"Weaver's taking care of it. Just hold on for a goddamn minute!"

"There's only one way out of this town," I growled. "There's still time. I can get to her."

I had to try. I had to get there first. Unsheathing my rifle from the saddle, I opened the saddlebag and started loading it up. Stuffed extra cartridges into my pockets. She might be leaving me, but that guy sure as hell wasn't going to take her away.

Eddie's eyes flared with urgency. A fierce and defiant expression I'd never seen before crossed his features. He took a breath, holding me in place as he yanked out his keys.

"Wait, man. I've got an idea."

Sixty-One
Sierra

"**G**et up."

"She's not done here," Dr. Riggs interjected, giving me a worried glance. This was not okay. She knew it. I knew it. For all she knew, this was a possessive ex-boyfriend and she needed to protect her patient. I hoped for her sake I could stop shaking long enough to stand.

Antoni smiled at her. I'd never seen him smile. From the way it made my skin crawl and bones turn to ice, I knew I never wanted to see it again. He withdrew a pistol from beneath his jacket.

"I wasn't asking."

It was quick and quiet. Dr. Riggs grunted as the bullet pierced her side. The silencer muffled the sound of his fired shot. I didn't scream, knowing it would only make things worse. Pounding started on the door.

"I'm fine," I lied. "My husband deserves to know what's happening here."

The pounding on the door ceased. Antoni looked satisfied, throwing my dress at me from the chair.

"Get dressed."

I glanced at Dr. Riggs, who was holding her hand to her wound but watched us carefully. Antoni watched me button my dress. His eyes trailed over my breasts, down to the little bump. He scoffed.

"Looks like you really are good for only one thing."

After I stuffed my feet into my boots and took the canvas tote I'd been using for a bag, he grabbed my hand. It felt so cold and bony compared to the warm, large hand I'd grown used to holding. Antoni dragged me through down the hall, poking the pistol into my ribs to make sure I didn't get any ideas about going anywhere. No one was at the front desk. At least Natalie and that other nurse had gotten away unscathed.

"How did you find me?"

My question was almost lost in the sound of our hurried footsteps on the asphalt of the parking lot. We were heading toward the Bentley. How did he get here?

"You really thought we wouldn't track the car? I thought you'd ditched it by the side of the road and moved on. It was at the impound lot for months."

A small sense of victory washed over me. I'd done the right thing in leaving the car alone. It was quickly snuffed out by the regret of picking the car up in the first place. There was no accounting for my good sense in that regard. Antoni continued, clearly enjoying the sound of his own voice.

"Then it started moving around again yesterday. It didn't go to auction, so that meant the owner or next of kin picked it up. You. After your bank account confirmed you'd paid for it, I stole a car and headed to this shithole town immediately. I got myself a room down the street only two hours ago."

Antoni shoved the gun into my ribs, prompting me to give him the car keys with his other hand. I dropped the set into his awaiting palm and went to the passenger side of the vehicle. I debated running away, but there would be no sense in that. Not with his gun already trained on me.

As he peeled out of the parking lot, I tried to think of a way out. Something, anything, to get me out of this. I had my phone but I couldn't call Alden. There was no location tracker on a burner. Maybe that was for the best. If he'd shot the doctor for speaking up, there was no telling what he'd do to Alden for trying to help me. My eyes slid to the man in the driver's seat. His black suit and shirt were expensive but wrinkled. The sharp jaw was covered in patchy black stubble. Thanks to my annoyingly heightened sense of smell, I could tell he hadn't showered.

Buildings became less frequent as the small town disappeared around us. We were leaving. If he came here with nothing, I wondered what that meant for him. His father was almost as wealthy as mine. If he was dead, Antoni would have inherited everything. He didn't seem like he was living that way. His desperation was immediately apparent. And utterly terrifying.

"I was about to head to that valley you were parked in when you showed up here. A block away from the motel. Lucky me."

Snake-like fingers clutched the steering wheel, causing the leather wrapping to squeak under Antoni's firm grasp. My skin pricked at the number on the speedometer. Fast. We were going too fast.

"Why are you doing this?" I warbled.

"My father is dead. Everything he had was supposed to go to me, but it all got tied up. All his assets were frozen while they investigated his connection to your family's murder. They seized everything. But you. You have plenty now, don't you princess?"

He couldn't be serious.

"I don't have anything," I bit out.

"You have everything! The company," he seethed. "The family is gone. It's all yours. Billions of dollars in cash, real estate, and investments. And when we're married, you'll sign it all over to me."

I scoffed, casually reaching forward to turn the air conditioning up. Pushing the car as hard as he was, maybe I'd get lucky, and the engine would overheat. We were hurtling back to Chicago like a speeding bullet. If he was right, everything I'd ever known was waiting for me. Except it would all be his. He would lock me in a cage and let my sanity wither away with every little freedom he'd likely strip from me. It would eat at me. Chip away at me. If it didn't kill me first.

"I'm not going to marry you, Antoni."

Flopping back in my seat, I folded my arms around myself. Cows and fenceposts whipped past us. The road to Alden's house wouldn't be far. At least I could set eyes on it one last time and say goodbye. Even if the idea of never seeing him again made my heart ache.

"I've already had the paperwork drawn up. All you have to do is sign, little wife."

It sounded foul. Wife. Not sweet. Wrong. Wrong. Wrong. No. I would never be his wife.

"I won't sign a thing," I spat.

"You act like you have a choice. And you do. Sign the paperwork and I'll let you keep the brat in your belly. Something for you to play with in your little cage. Don't sign it and the only time you'll see it is the day I have it cut out of you to sell to the highest bidder."

Antoni grinned at me, enjoying the horrified expression I wore. Neither of us saw the truck. He hit the brakes, tires squealing and smoking as they stopped. My hands grappled for anything to brace myself. A familiar red Toyota blocked the road with a horse trailer attached to it. The old white trailer doors faced us, closed but empty of horses.

"Stay here."

Antoni got out of the car, striding angrily toward the truck. A blonde mullet popped out. Eddie. He hopped out of his truck, hands up, as he apologized loudly for the temporary blockage. He glanced at the car, at me, eyes widening as he spotted me in the passenger seat. His voice carried on the wind when I opened the door and stepped out, quietly shutting it behind me.

"Is this your woman? She's way too pretty for you, man."

My dress fluttered in the strong gusts, causing Antoni's response to get lost in the sound. But Antoni seemed to note Eddie's shift in attention, striding back to the car. Before I could move, his hand grabbed me by the throat and squeezed.

"I told you to stay in the fucking car!"

Those awful fingers clamped down as I struggled in his grasp. Tears flooded my eyes at the force of it. The loss of breath. I lost track of Eddie as my toes left the ground. My captor lifted me, snarling in my face.

"Antoni," I wheezed. "Please."

He pulled the gun from his belt, pointing its cruel steel end not at me. At Eddie.

"Get back in the car, Sierra, or I kill the hillbilly."

A crack rattled the wide-open blue sky as I heard something pop behind me. Then the sound of a rifle being racked. The trailer door swung open on a kick. The black barrel of the rifle winked into the sunlight, held by a large callused hand whose touch I'd come to know as well as my own.

Teeth bared and eyes wild, as Alden aimed the gun at Antoni. All our time tangled up in each other had made me forget how large he was as his long legs ate up the distance between us. Next to the tall wiry man holding me hostage, Alden was a raging beast. His voice was a merciless growl as he trained that big black rifle on Antoni.

"Get your fucking hands off my wife."

Sixty-Two
Sierra

He was here.

Swift feet had Antoni standing behind me as Alden approached us, fingers digging into my neck as he lowered me to the ground again. His pistol dug into my cheek as he pulled my body close to shield himself from the approaching cowboy. Like he knew the man I loved would never hurt me. Hazel eyes flashed with ire as he lowered the shotgun.

"I'm assuming this the daddy," Antoni laughed into my ear. "She was my fiancé before she was your whore."

Alden didn't move at Antoni's taunt. Didn't even blink. My captor gave a cruel laugh and went back to hissing cruelty into my ear.

"Did the Lincoln Park princess like spreading her legs for the big, dumb cowboy?"

"Stop it," I snarled, throat aching.

"Say goodbye to Daddy," Antoni sneered as he moved his gun from me to Alden.

I looked at him, the man who'd come to protect me in so many ways. The man who, even at gunpoint, still kept his eyes trained on me. Taking me in. Looking for injuries he couldn't see. I took a breath. I'd changed my mind.

Leaving wasn't the plan anymore. I wanted to choose him. Choose us.

That choice didn't matter anymore. Not if saying goodbye now could save his life. Even if it meant giving mine up. As if knowing exactly what I was going to say next, Alden shook his head slightly.

"Let him go," I begged my throat tight from where it'd been abused. "Antoni, let him go and I'll go with you. I'll go. Please don't hurt him. I'll give you everything if you just let him go. Please."

The man I loved looked at me in shock. Pleading eyes locked on mine. His mouth formed a silent syllable. *No.* We could have had a life together. At least this way he could still have his. Because this was always the way my story was supposed to end. Antoni laughed, the gun lowering a little as he held it between Alden and me.

"Fine. Maybe I'll let him have your pretty little corpse when I'm done with you."

Another shot snapped the air in two.

Eddie. Now standing behind us, gun aimed at us. I'd forgotten about him as Antoni gasped in pain, his gun clattering to the ground from his now mangled hand. Falling to his knees, he held his gnarled flesh in his other hand as breath sawed through his teeth. Alden moved, shoving me behind him with one arm as he kicked Antoni's gun away.

"I suppose the police are on their way," Antoni snarled, spit flying out through his bared teeth as he glanced at Eddie.

The blonde cowboy kept his gun aimed at Antoni, who cradled his destroyed hand against his chest. Alden racked his rifle, shouldering the weapon to aim.

"No. I'm the law today."

Up close, a rifle can do a lot of damage. One minute, Antoni's near-black irises were raging at me. The next, they were gone. His whole face was practically disintegrated with the shot Alden fired at point-blank range. My cowboy shoved the man over with a boot, kicking him once to make sure he was dead, then turned to hold me against him as he set his gun on the ground.

"Don't ever do that again," he panted, voice breaking as he took my face in his hands. "You scared the shit out of me, darlin'."

Alden pulled me against him, hands roaming over me as if he needed to feel that everything was fine because his eyes couldn't believe it.

"Hey, Boone?" Eddie chimed in from behind us.

Alden released me to look at his friend. Eddie had unrolled a black tarp next to Antoni's body. They had come prepared. They had come up with a plan.

"We need to get this guy off the street before someone comes by."

"How did you know I would be here?"

The men hefted the body onto the tarp, wrapping it up quickly and hauling it into the back of the trailer as Alden answered my question.

"Natalie told me."

I let that sink in. She'd helped me. The girl who I'd pointed a gun at helped me. I wouldn't make the mistake of thinking she was my friend, but at least she'd done what was right. I wondered about the doctor as Eddie pulled the truck off of the road and waited. Alden ushered me toward the Bentley, which I now realized had a flat tire.

"You weren't going anywhere. He was dead the moment he touched you," he remarked, nodding toward the tire. "Let's get the tire changed. We can get you a new one before you head back to Chicago."

Warmth flooded my body. I'd gone cold with fear. Fear that melted away in his presence. Alden moved to the driver's side door and hopped into the seat, adjusting it for his size as I sat down in the passenger seat beside him. My foot connected with the tote bag to reveal the little manilla envelope I'd forgotten about as he rolled the car to the shoulder. That conversation would have to wait.

"Can I use your phone?" I asked.

Without a word, he slid it out of his pocket and handed it to me. He made quick work of changing the tire as I realized where we were. Only a few feet away from where he'd wandered up to this same car to find a weeping, spoiled princess. With almost nothing to his name, he'd given me everything.

I emailed my father's lawyer, grateful we were close enough to a tower to have reception and then logged into my bank account. All of my money was still there. It wasn't much compared to my father's wealth, but it was a small fortune on its own. The life that Alden had given me was a simple one. Beautiful. It was beautiful without expensive things. Without designer clothes or elegant parties. It was more than I had ever wanted for myself because I was allowed to exist without consequence. No leash. No golden collar.

My finger tapped the screen, refreshing the web page over and over. A new email came through. The lawyer responded quickly, relieved to find me alive. After a quick phone call to confirm it was me and not some clever grifter, he sent documents for me to E-Sign and I did. Everything seemed so simple now. A life that was mine. My hand drifted over the small swell of my belly as I used the other to set the phone on the driver's seat.

"All set," Alden said as he pulled the door open.

I tugged the envelope free from my bag as Alden sat in the car again. He glanced at the item, pushing his hat up a bit as he turned to me.

"What's that?"

"The sonogram," I smiled weakly, still shaken by the events of the day but also from what I had just done. "Dr. Riggs gave it to me to open later. I haven't had a chance to look at it."

Pain entered Alden's eyes. He hadn't been there to see it. To hear his child's heartbeat for the first time. That was a regret I would bear the weight of for the rest of my life.

"That says what it is? Boy or girl?"

I nodded, slipping my finger beneath the flap to lift it open. But I left the slip of paper inside and handed it to Alden.

"You do it. Tell me what it is."

He hesitated before he took it from me, slipping the paper from the envelope. Then his mouth parted in a wide grin. He blinked back tears as he let out a breathless laugh.

Antoni's phone had been a temporary problem. One I'd solved with an envelope and postage. My father's lawyer, now my lawyer, would take care of it along with the story of what happened to him. I'd handed the cash in Antoni's wallet to Alden and split it with Eddie. Thousands of dollars. Enough to cover everything Alden had spent on me. As if remembering our conversation about the check the night before, Alden shook his head.

"It wasn't a debt."

"I don't need it and neither does he," I said, gesturing to the black tarp bundle they hauled out of the horse trailer. I decided not to tell him I was now hundreds of millions richer. That could wait. Eddie snorted.

"Let's get some food in us before we start this dig," Alden grunted, leading us toward the house.

I took his hand, tugging it gently as Eddie went in ahead of us. He cocked an eyebrow at me. My gut tightened, nerves whispering my fears back to me. I wanted the door to shut before I said what I needed to. No flowery words. Only the truth.

"I love you, Alden Boone."

With a small step forward, I circled my arms around his waist. I felt his breath go shallow as large arms took me in.

"Sierra," he hesitated.

"No, I need to say it," I said, looking up at him. Needing for him to see I meant all of it. "I love you and I need to tell you that because if I'm going to ask you to spend the rest of our lives together, you should know how I feel."

A large hand cupped my jaw as I looked into his eyes. Eyes that were now glistening with unshed tears. Our kiss was soft and warm. Slow and gentle.

Then Alden pulled back, grinning down at me.

"You're staying?"

I thought I was staying here because it was easy. Because I knew I could rely on him to take care of me, and I had nowhere to go. Now that the Serpas were gone, I didn't need to hide. The world was wide open for me. I could choose where to go. Who to be with. So I did.

"You're the only thing I've ever wanted."

Alden huffed a shaky breath, kissing me quickly before clutching me to his broad chest. Large fingers fed themselves through my hair. Lips brushed over my temple as he spoke.

"Letting you go once was hard enough. I'm never doing it again."

After a dinner of burgers prepared by Eddie, they went outside and began their work to rid us of the last of my problems. I let myself into the bedroom. My clothes were still laid out on the bed. Still waiting to be packed. I put them back in the closet and the dresser, item by item.

Eventually, I'd have to go back to Chicago. There were loose ends that needed tying and my family's remains to deal with. I wondered if I could steal Alden away for a few days now that the foaling season was over. A laugh burst from me at the thought of what I was choosing. With all the money I'd just inherited, I would probably always be a pampered princess. I had been raised to stand beside a powerful man. Someone with influence. But I'd found someone who wanted to stand beside me. Someone who let me choose for myself.

Eddie and Alden buried Antoni's remains on the property. It took them most of the night. They didn't tell me where they'd done it. It wasn't until I'd woken up with Alden's half-naked body surrounding my own that I'd even realized he'd come to bed. A flutter and tugging feeling pulsed in my belly. I jerked at the sensation.

"What the fuck was that?"

Alden stirred, lifting his head to see what I was talking about. Noting the attention on my belly, he moved the arm draped over my waist. The strange pressure and flutter happened again with his hand splayed across my bare belly.

"He's moving, darlin'," he muttered, half awake. "It's natural."

Epilogue
ALDEN

S o small. He was so damned small.

Our son squirmed in my arms as he stirred from sleep. It had been several months since he was born, but it still felt like it was yesterday. Watching him come into this world was more than a miracle.

It was poetry.

Of course, it wasn't just the birth of this little guy that had made this year an insane series of events. She'd told me she loved me. Beat me to the punch with her proposal. But she had business in Chicago to attend to first.

As the last living Volpe, Sierra told me she had some things she'd needed to wrap up. With Antoni Serpa being dead and buried behind the barn, there was nothing left for her to fear.

The Bentley made it to Chicago far easier than my truck would have. Sierra insisted on driving instead of flying. That she'd needed the fresh air and freedom of the road. I'd insisted on going with her. The old man was kind enough to give us some time to ourselves, insisting that I'd more than earned a vacation after years without one.

If I hadn't known the woman holding my hand loved me, I would have felt small in the grand marble foyer of her family home. Instead of inadequacy,

I'd only felt worried for her. She released my hand to walk through the large brick manor and examine it. The furniture that was upholstered in creamy fabric was so fine, I was afraid to touch it. Rugs that appeared to be handwoven in colors varying in shades of pale blue. Fine art in fine frames hung on walls painted in elegant dove gray.

The whole place felt cold, like a fucking museum.

Until we got to Sierra's room. It was furnished and upholstered like the rest. Except there were small things that hinted at the girl I'd come to know. A painting of a castle sitting on a hill, surrounded by trees. A small musical figurine of a carousel horse. I picked it up and cranked the knob. Metallic pinging filled the room to the tune of Somewhere Over the Rainbow. My hand met with a silk scarf covered in sunflowers tied on the doorknob of her closet. Colorful and out of place. That's what she was. A flower that grew from stone. When I first met this woman, I thought she'd never feel at home with me. That it wouldn't be enough for her. Now that I knew the real Sierra, I understood.

She never belonged here.

Seeing Sierra in the context of where she came from filled me with wonder. Wonder at having met her. At seeing how different our lives had been before they became one. She could have come back here and lived like a queen. Instead, she decided to give it up. Not for me. Not for the baby who would be born the following February. She told me she'd given it up for her freedom.

"I finally get to choose what my life looks like now. I choose you."

And I chose her. The very next day in a courthouse.

We said our vows to each other. She wore a white dress from her closet and I wore jeans. I put the ring I bought for her on her finger and she slid one that had belonged to her brother onto mine. To celebrate, we ate pizza in her bed and laughed together. The day after that, she sat at the large marble island in her family home as she signed everything over to some woman from Los Angeles who was giving her top dollar for all of her family's investments and properties. She even sold the cars. Then Sierra took that big check from

Caccia Holdings and opened a bunch of accounts for us.

Then we went home. Sierra got herself a new phone and spent the entire drive in the passenger seat of her brand-new electric SUV making calls. Sending emails. Working on something. It was hard to keep my eyes on the road because watching her work was something else. When I asked her what she was working on, she just smiled at me.

"You'll see."

I married a woman who never dreamed for herself. Before I met her, she'd been resigned to her fate of living in the margins of someone else's story. Seeing her like this, painting the picture for her life, was more than I could ask for. When she was given the freedom to create a life for herself, she dreamed big. She dreamed up an expansion for Evergreen Springs. Another hundred acres were added to the ranch. Bought half of the property. A guest ranch. And an addition to the house that would make our home as big as the old man's.

"Mr. Weaver asked me to talk to you about taking over half the ranch. I figured since what's mine is yours now, I'd make that mine. And, well, yours."

It took a little while to get over the shock. To go from only getting food from my school lunches as a child to never needing to worry about money again was a hell of a thing. Then things went back to normal. I went to work every day and Sierra painted, worked on her projects, and we got ready for the baby when I got home.

The addition was under construction. Everything was built up and on schedule to be finished before the baby was born. Until we made the mistake of getting busy on the couch, leading to early labor. Don't ask me how that works, but Dr. Riggs didn't seem all that surprised. After about twelve hours, Sierra gave birth to our son in a tub at the women's center. I did everything I could to help, but I was blown away by the strength of my woman.

"All good in here?"

Sierra smiled, looking over the small bundle I had on my bare chest. Her hair was still wet from the shower, dripping onto the shoulders of her clean lounge set. The soft rose-colored material made her olive skin glow.

"Oh yeah," I grinned. "He was just telling me he's going to be a rancher when he grows up. Also, he told me he's hungry."

The bundle, Samuel Russell Boone, looked up at me with large green eyes. I kissed the top of his little head. The boy whimpered as Sierra took him from my arms. I stood, giving my wife the rocker, and picked up the pillow she needed to support the little one. Sierra positioned the baby at her breast and began nursing.

"I don't think I'll ever get used to that," she laughed with a wince.

I squatted, placing a hand on her knee.

"Oh, you better. I plan on having six more."

Her dark eyebrows shot up in surprise. But I didn't miss the way her lips curved in a small smile.

"Don't act like you haven't thought about it, Mrs. Boone. The house will certainly be big enough for a whole herd of Boones."

Sierra snorted but blushed a little. With a sigh, she started rocking the chair gently.

"As tempting as that may be, having another one right now sounds like literal hell to me."

"Are you telling me no?" I smiled.

"I'm not saying no. I'm saying let's negotiate. You're asking me to birth a hockey team. I'm asking you to give my body a break."

My wife smoothed the brown wisps of hair on our son's head as she looked at me. To think this time last year, this room was still filled with old junk. I'd only just started falling for this gorgeous creature.

"You and I make beautiful babies."

She looked down at our son and smiled.

"He is beautiful."

"Of course he is," I smiled, standing to bring my mouth to hers. "Look at his mother."

Sierra gazed up at me with a dreamy look in those beautiful eyes. I stared down at them, remembering the day those eyes helplessly looked up at me through a car window. She'd looked so sad and lost then. Nowhere near the woman she was now. I nudged her nose with mine, kissing her again.

"Fine," she sighed. "You know I can't resist you in those grey sweatpants. One more."

"One more," I agreed.

Growing up, I used to think good luck was a lie. That I'd never see one bit of it. Then a year ago, this woman came into my life like a star falling from the sky. Lucky. Then she became pregnant with our son. Lucky again. And we fell in love.

So fucking lucky.

The way she made me feel was something you couldn't buy. She took care of me. I took care of her. We were all we needed. This woman promised to spend her life with me. Had let me create a beautiful life by her side. As I watched her feed our son, I remembered promising to give her the universe.

She was the one who gave it to me.

Epilogue
SIERRA – FIVE YEARS LATER

Wind rushing through the tall grasses always sounded like crashing waves to me. Strands of hair pulled away from my braid as a chill cut through my sweater and jeans. I leaned into the gust, taking in a deep whiff of all the scents that came hurtling toward me on the air.

Spring was here.

Sunlight flickered off of the creek down below. From up here, I could see the rest of the ranch. The Blue Side, we'd come to call it. Evergreen Springs had grown by a few hundred acres. When I'd invested in the ranch, I'd also purchased the property next to it.

Sable let out a huff as if she could see her baby running around the paddock down below. Kohl was a streak of black across a field of green. Faster than anything I'd ever seen. In the next paddock, a cowboy was riding a bucking horse. It raged and kicked. It reared up and tried to shake him off of her. With no luck.

There was no shaking that cowboy off.

I smiled a little. He'd come home stinking of sweat and grass. Dirt and faint remnants of his soap. And he'd pick up the kids as they charged him at the front door. Sam would laugh, smiling just like his father as he plowed into his legs. Stella would wait for him to notice her and pick her up.

My sweet, shy girl.

They wouldn't rush me the same way. No, the nanny would have put them down for an afternoon nap by now. Which meant I was in no hurry to get back. Riding was the easiest way to get home from the newest part of the property. A large, simple lodge with several studio spaces. Gigantic windows for a lot of natural light. A big porch overlooking the luscious scenery.

Enough space to accommodate ten people at a time. A retreat nestled in the Rocky Mountains. Perfect for artists. Outfitted with everything they could possibly need. And lots of oak trees.

"Good girl," I crooned, reaching down to rub Sable's neck.

The top of this hill was my favorite place to rest. For me and her. From here, I could almost see it all. Once upon a time, I was a princess whose kingdom burned to the ground. I'd used the ashes to build this place. A place to land. With no leash. No cage.

Just wild fresh air.

Mountains.

And a man who loved me.

We'd gotten married at the courthouse in Chicago in September. Had our honeymoon camping out at some glamping site near Yellowstone Park. I'd never forget what he'd whispered to me under the stars.

"That first night. The night we met. A star fell over us and I made a wish. For you. You were the only thing I ever wanted."

Walking down the hill toward our little holler, I remembered my first night here. Almost five years to the day. My mother. My father. My sweet brother. Everything I knew was wiped away like a hand sweeping over a chessboard to knock off all the pieces.

Gone.

After the dust settled on what happened. When no one came looking for the man buried under the sagebrush behind the barn. I started to wonder why I'd come here. If I just got lucky or if there was something bigger looking out for me as I drove for my life. I could have gone north. Or south. Or east.

I could have gotten on a plane and run to the other side of the world. They would have found me.

End of story.

But I'd gotten in my father's car and driven here. Ran out of gas right here. And lost all hope. Alden Boone walked into the middle of the worst moment of my life. He offered me sanctuary. Somewhere safe to hide. I was grateful for it. But more than that, he offered me a place to deconstruct the person I'd been molded into and become the person I wanted to be.

Bit by bit, albeit sometimes painfully, I peeled away the parts of me that I'd created to satisfy people for whom I'd never be good enough. Alden loved me through all of it because he didn't meet me when I was supposed to be perfect. He met me at the bottom and gave me space to find my way out.

Now I could pick up each moment and examine them. Study them like works of art. Moments with my parents. Understanding that they were flawed people. They paid the ultimate price for their mistakes. It didn't seem fair not to forgive them. My brother. Thinking about him still made me cry sometimes, but I could see him in Sam's curly hair and the way my son laughed with his whole body.

Still, the moments with Alden, even the hardest ones, meant everything to me. I couldn't count the fears I'd dumped at his feet about becoming a mother. He was there for the hours I spent weeping for what I had lost. There to hold my hand as I struggled.

I wouldn't give any of it back. Because if I had only the good moments, they wouldn't shine like shooting stars cascading through so much darkness.

The End